PETER ALBANO

ZEBRA BOOKS
KENSINGTON PUBLISHING CORP.

ZEBRA BOOKS

are published by

Kensington Publishing Corp.
475 Park Avenue South
New York, NY 10016

First Printing: March, 1993

Printed in the United States of America

DEDICATION

For Hugh Nolen Gilliland, Charles Tyszkiewicz, Ronald R. Kurz, John Jurovic, Michael R. Philbin, John J. Kuhn and Charles G. King who have endured my geriatric tennis with infinite patience.

ACKNOWLEDGMENTS

The author gratefully acknowledges:

Otto and Eileen Schnepp and William Byer who so generously contributed their expertise on the Middle East;

Master Mariner Donald Brandmeyer for his advice concerning nautical problems;

Dale O. Swanson for lending his experience with World War II aircraft;

Patricia Johnston, RN, and Susan A. Johnston, RN, who helped solve medical problems;

Mary Annis, my wife, for her careful reading of the manuscript;

Bebe Jean Earl for her careful, thoughtful editing and suggestions for plot and character development.

One

Commander Brent Ross raised his glasses and rested them on the rough concrete sill of the gun port. From the Israeli bunker called *Bren-ah-Hahd* (Fireball One), the Sinai Desert appeared desolate and forbidding. To Brent Ross, who was a creature of the vast wastelands of the world's oceans, the Sinai and the seas had much in common. Both were hostile and would destroy the unwary man who would challenge them, and both could kill by thirst, starvation, exposure to the elements. You could actually drown in the desert, lungs choked with super heated sand driven by the hurricane-force winds of the *khamsin*.

Brent had seen one such storm just north of El Kuntilla. He would never forget that black cloud that blotted out the entire southern horizon like an approaching typhoon. But no typhoon had ever been like this. As the wind roared out of Egypt, it swept up sand and sent grains billowing across hundreds of miles. The temperature shot upward by 35 degrees and visibility dropped to zero. Trucks were overturned, telephone poles and radio antennas were ripped from the ground. Tanks, half-tracks and armored personnel carriers were buried. Whirling sand created electrical disturbances and compasses went crazy. It was said that Bedouin tribal law permitted a man to kill his wife after five days of *khamsin*. After four days of huddling in a bunker, Brent began to appreciate tribal law.

Commander Brent Ross was searching for another type of tempest. Arab tanks and APCs (armored personnel carriers) were reported on the move and a small cloud of dust anywhere on the southern horizon could warn of the approach of a different kind of *khamsin* — an armored storm bent on testing this key link in the Ben-Gurion Line. A reconnaissance North American AT-6 Texan had reported sixty to seventy T-62 MBTs (Main Battle Tanks) accompanied by at least a brigade of motorized infantry moving parallel to the front in two columns. The force had been at least ten kilometers behind the lines when sighted. They could turn north and attack anywhere. However, the Texan's transmissions ended abruptly when it was attacked by fighters. Brent saw nothing, heard nothing. The desert was quiet. Perhaps the enemy column was a reserve unit and had gone into bivouac.

Dug into solid limestone, *Bren-ah-Hahd* was cleverly sited on the military crest of a small ridge — near the top and on the front slope. Its four-foot-thick, reinforced-concrete sides and rounded top were covered with earth and sand and camouflaged with artificial desert growth, rocks and boulders. Virtually invisible, it gave an unobstructed 180-degree view to the south. It was the most forward of all observation posts.

Brent moved his personal MIV/IT Carl Zeiss 7 x 50 range-finding binoculars over the terrain with the short jerky movements of a man who had spent most of his adult life at sea. He was looking for scouting patrols of infantry, perhaps a daring scout vehicle or APC. He found nothing except baked earth and sand studded with boulders like bared teeth. Flora was scarce—meager growths of stunted jujube, ground-hugging burnet, the tiny narrow leaves and minute flowers of tamarisk, marjoram with its faint aroma of mint, and a scattering of prickly camel's thorn bushes. Only poisonous scorpions and snakes lived here, along with the usual clouds of flies which had been gorging themselves on the dead.

This was a hellish place to fight a war. Even Dante Alighieri's inventive imagination would have been challenged to conceive of such a place. It was a wasteland devoid of almost all life; even the few Bedouin nomads had long since fled. Water could be obtained only from widely scattered cisterns or by drilling deep into the ground, and then it was usually brackish. Every item a soldier needed or wanted had to be brought up by truck or on a man's back. Brent chuckled to himself, thinking of an Israeli officer's description of the Sinai: "The last rung on the ladder to hell!" So true. So true.

Its torments were unending. Temperature fluctuated by as much as 70 degrees in a single day. Sand as fine as talcum powder clogged rifles, machine guns, and inflamed eyes. When the wind gusted, men wore goggles constantly. On clear days mirages played tricks with vision; concealment in so bleak and featureless land became a magician's art. Yet the open spaces and lack of natural obstacles made it ideal tank country. So did the absence of permanent human settlements. When Brent first came to the desert he had immediately seen the similarity between desert warfare and battles he had fought on the high seas.

Again and again when studying tactics of desert fighting, Brent had encountered the name of Irwin Rommel, the brilliant German general who had exploited this unique fluid quality a half-century earlier. Throwing out the textbooks of warfare, he favored daring wide sweeping flanking movements that left his own flanks uncovered but confounded and demoralized his enemy. So cunning and devastating were these tactics, his admiring British opponents grudgingly complemented him with the sobriquet, "The Desert Fox." The Arab and Israeli armies still studied his tactics and copied them whenever possible.

Brent Ross moved his search down into a small wadi where two Arabs lay dead. Both had been killed five days before, when their patrol had stupidly blundered down the wadi without detailing flanking scouts on the ridges. A single burst from a Browning 50-caliber M-2 heavy machine gun jutting from a port immediately to Brent's left had killed the two lead men — a burly sergeant and the private immediately behind him. The other eight Arabs had gone to ground and wormed their way out of range under a hail of mortar fire.

Brent brought the sergeant into focus. Flat on his back, his arms were outflung like a sleeping child, his Kalashnikov AK-47 close to his right hand. He had only been dead for a short time, yet the desert heat had brought the cadaver to an advanced state of decomposition. His chest had been ripped by at least four of the great slugs. His hands, arms, neck, and bulging cheeks were yellowish green with scattered purple splotches. Flies hung over the corpse like a black cloud, dropping into the midst of their progeny to claim their share of the feast. Brent had seen death at sea in its most violent forms, but nothing had prepared him for this horror. Despite his ironclad self-control, the inescapable stench brought bile to his throat and he thought he would retch. But he controlled himself. It would not be fitting for the other six men in the bunker to see weakness in "the American samurai."

"You're enjoying your vacation in our desert paradise?" a deep, resonant voice laced with irony and subtle humor chided in his right ear. Accented with a Teutonic-flavored Hebrew slant, the diction was guttural yet clear, vocabulary ample like all of the IDF (Israeli Defense Force) personnel Brent had met. But there was a sing-song counterpoint in the voice, too. An inflection of one who had spoken Yiddish once as his native tongue. This differed from the five other soldiers in the room who were sabras—native born Israelis. Accented too, their English was smooth with Aramaic intonations. Because of the American's presence, all spoke basic, school-taught English with a sprinkling of Hebrew and an occasional Yiddish word used as slang or expletive. Sometimes, Brent was surprised by the use of German.

Turning, Brent faced Colonel David Moskowitz. Wearing the ornate sword and wreath shoulder badge of the Infantry Corps, Colonel Moskowitz was Brent's guide on his tour of the Ben-Gurion Line. Over sixty years old, Moskowitz was as lean and tough as the thorn bushes just outside the bunker. Weathered by years of exposure to the pitiless desert sun, his face had its own assortment of wadis—creases and furrows crossing and crisscrossing the tanned skin. His goggles were pushed up over his helmet, and his glasses hung at his waist. As Brent stared at the colonel the realization that all desert fighters looked alike came home; gaunt with sun-cured skin of leather and the infectious aura of irony and inevitability of men who battled year in and year out to stay alive in an environment that could be deadlier than an artillery shell.

Six blue numbers tattooed on Moskowitz's left forearm gave indelible evidence of the horrors of Nazi Germany. Since arriving in the Middle East three

11

weeks earlier, Brent had had several lengthy discussions with the colonel. Sharing a bottle of scotch, the pair had talked late into the night on two of those occasions. Throughout both evenings the colonel adroitly avoided discussing his early years and the blue numbers. Instead, Brent found himself maneuvered into describing the great carrier *Yonaga* and its fabled captain Admiral Hiroshi Fujita, his ten years of service on the carrier, the many bloody battles against Arab battle groups and land-based aircraft, his four years at Annapolis where he had been an all-American fullback, and details of the life of his late father, Ted "Trigger" Ross. "And your family?" Brent had asked once, tiring of speaking of himself.

The colonel had brightened. "My wife, Miriam lives in Haifa and my daughter, Ruth, serves with Mossad — Israeli Intelligence."

"That's it? That's your family?"

Unconsciously, Moskowitz ran a thumb over the numbers. "Parents, aunts, uncles, cousins — gone." He shrugged and turned his hands up in a typical Yiddish gesture of hopelessness and used a German word, *"Kaputt!"*

"Kaputt?"

The Jew had tossed off his drink and turned away as he spoke. Brent would never forget the timbre of that voice. Hoarse, it was low and rustled in the room like the breath of death through dry leaves. "Please don't ask, Commander. This is not the time or . . ."

David Moskowitz never completed the sentence. Instead, he poured himself a double and downed it in two gulps. At that moment, Brent had decided to change the subject.

Now he was smiling back at Moskowitz's friendly, composed face. "You have a thoroughly relaxing resort here, Colonel," Brent said, catching the colonel's spirited mood. He moved a finger in an inclusive circle, "Luxurious appointments," stabbed a finger at a pile of field rations in a corner, "gourmet cuisine," the finger moved to a slop bucket on the other side of the bunker, "private baths . . ."

He was interrupted by the colonel's guffaws and the laughter of the other men. The laughter was high-pitched, the quick, skittering sound of frightened men in mortal danger. It was almost as if each man was releasing the high-pressure steam through his own personal relief valve. Brent had heard the same sound many times before when he had met the enemy at sea. It was universal, and he sensed the colonel knew it and had injected a playful mood for precisely that purpose.

Preserving the humor, the colonel continued, "Better than the Waldorf Astoria?"

"Indeed, Colonel." And then waving airily at the gun port, the young American continued, "A romantic, unobstructed view." He tugged on his chin and frowned wistfully. "But, Colonel Moskowitz, there is one thing I would like to discuss with the concierge."

"And what is that?"

Brent drew his 220-pound bulk up into as much mock indignation as the low ceiling would allow. "Where is the ambrosia, the dancing girls?" The other men in the room burst into laughter.

Moskowitz pursed his lips wistfully and tapped his temple. "Ah, yes, he answered gravely. Then, glancing at his watch, "The girls are late. I'll fire the entire chorus." He held up his canteen with a courtly gesture, "But the libation is here."

"Chateau Lafite Rothschild?"

"Right, commander. 1953." He tapped the canteen. Sixty-three degrees Fahrenheit."

Brent shook his head. "Sorry, Colonel, sixty-two

13

point five or pour it out. A half a degree makes a harlot of a lady. Ask James Bond." More laughter.

"Harlot or lady, I'll take either, Commander," the young gunner, Corporal Julian Feinbaum, said in halting English. Slouched on a small stool behind the Browning, the young man smiled up at the American commander, blue eyes sparkling through strands of blond hair that refused to be tamed back up beneath his helmet. Brent wondered about Feinbaum: blond, blue-eyed instead of the usual dark Semitic looks shown by most of the Israelis. Actually, the gunner was as blond and fair as Brent, and his eyes were just as blue. *Jews come in all sizes, shapes, and colors,* he said to himself. And the young lad was a cool, implacable killer. He had casually shot down the two Arabs slinking to their front and then lit a cigarette and sank back completely relaxed, like a man who had just sated himself on a night of frantic sex.

"Hear! Hear!" Feinbaum's teenage loader, Private Saul Blumberg, agreed. Two communications men and an artillery captain named Avraham Herzl added their laughter and stared at the American. Brent continued sternly, "You know friends, I sometimes feel the *Zahal* is far more interested in sex than in fighting the Arabs."

More laughter. "How did you ever get that impression of the Army, Commander?" Captain Herzl asked.

"Let's just say I'm uncannily perceptive."

Herzl rubbed the hard bone behind his ear thoughtfully. "You're in the Middle East to negotiate prisoner exchange, Commander Ross," he said, breaking the frivolous mood. All eyes moved to the American. There was no more laughter.

Brent was all business. "Correct, Captain. Kadafi holds twenty-five of our pilots and air crews."

"Survivors of your B-25 raid on Rabta?"

Brent winced at the cruel memory of the costly raid on the gas works the previous year. "Twelve of them are. The others were picked up by the enemy after we fought their battle group off Gibraltar. We hold forty-two Arab prisoners in Japan."

"With your permission, Commander"—Herzl waved toward the enemy—"then what in the world are you doing in this godforsaken place?"

Brent grinned. "Trying to find out if you know how to fight a war, Captain."

Herzl would not be put off. "Seriously, Commander. Why?"

Moskowitz began to speak, but Brent waved him off. Rubbing the stiff bristles of his two-day growth of beard, he said, "Because I was sent to Israel with another negotiator, Colonel Irving Bernstein, to be briefed by Mossad. You know the Arabs hold almost three hundred Israeli prisoners." Everyone nodded. "We intend to negotiate for the lot." He stared into Herzl's brown eyes. "We have been authorized to use the three thousand Arabs you hold as a bargaining chip."

Herzl shook his head. "We've been trying to arrange an exchange for years, Commander Ross." He shook his head. "It's no good. You can't deal with Arabs. Honesty and integrity are unknown to them."

"There is truth in what you say, Captain. But I met with Sheik Iman Younis in Taipei."

"I've heard of him. He's a real power—maybe, second to Kadafi."

"I think I can deal with him." Brent turned his palms up. "It's worth a try."

"Then you should be in Geneva with the Americans and Russians negotiating."

"Wrong, Captain Herzl."

"Wrong?"

"Yes. The Arabs insist we come to Libya."

The men looked at each other in surprise. "That would be foolish, Commander," Herzl said. "Typically Arab—put you in a position of weakness, and, incidentally, you'd be easy to kill."

"I know. We don't like it and I don't want to do it. The UN is arguing the point with the Arabs now." He tapped his helmet with his massive knuckles. "So you see, I'm on hold with time to burn." He waved a hand in an encompassing gesture. "Thought I'd see how you lads amuse yourselves in your spare time." He glanced at Colonel Moskowitz, "In your desert paradise." Good humor returned to the room.

The light mood was interrupted by one of the communications men, a husky Sergeant named Nisson Wolpin, who sat before an old American SCR-300 field radio and telephone. "Captain Herzl," he said, scribbling on a pad, "the Arab force has been sighted again. They're turning toward our front."

There was a silence of someone sprinkling cold water, a palpable force of expectancy and apprehension wiping all humor from the bunker. "Where? Where?" Captain Herzl asked, hunching over a chart. "Coordinates?"

"Coordinates *Dah-let sh'loh-shett,* (D-3), course due south."

Hunching down to clear the overhead, Brent followed Colonel Moskowitz to the map table, where they both stood behind Captain Herzl. There were two maps on the table. All the lettering was in Hebrew. The first was a map of the entire Ben-Gurion Line and the other was a detailed grid map of their sector. Staring at their sector, Brent read the lettering from right to left: *Ah-foo-reem bah-hoh-reff* (Gray Winter). Ten years of working closely with Colonel

16

Irving Bernstein of Mossad and hours of study had given him a high level of proficiency in reading Hebrew, but catching the fast speech patterns, idioms, and occasional Yiddish of the spoken language could leave him feeling like a man caught in an avalanche.

With a blue pencil, Moskowitz marked the plastic overlay with an arrow pointed directly at the bunker. Everyone stared silently.

"B'roo-heem hah-bah-eem l'Yis-rah-ehl (Welcome to Israel),"* Brent managed in Hebrew, stabbing at the arrow.

The American's cool demeanor and fractured Hebrew brought chuckles to every man's lips and for a moment broomed the tension out. Moskowitz pounced on the mood. Stabbing at the blue arrow, he said with a grin, *"Ah-nee m'kah-veh-kee hem-yeh-hah-noo mee-bee-koor-rum."*

To Brent, the words had come in a torrent. He groped, managing only a defensive "Ah." Then the meaning came through. "Colonel, you said, 'I hope they will enjoy their visit,' right?"

"Very good, Commander Ross," Moskowitz acknowledged. And then with a sly grin, "I mean, cool, man—off the wall."

There were chuckles and shouts of, "Hear! Hear!" However, the funereal silence returned when Corporal Feinbaum reported, "Dust—dust on the far horizon."

Instead of returning to the port, Brent stared down at the maps. The map of the Ben-Gurion Line showed the four-deep line of fortifications in great detail. With its southern anchor at Gaza, the line stretched east to Sedom on the Jordanian border and then turned north to Al Khalil, passing east of Jerusalem, through Nabulus along the Golan Heights to Al Khushniyah, where it veered west and ran to its northern anchor on the Mediterranean Coast at Gesher Haziv. It was a defense that would have daunted Irwin Rommel. Hundreds of bunkers with interlocking fields of fire had thrown back dozens of attacks. When the Arabs had threatened with a breakthrough, armored units held in reserve along with mobile infantry had plugged the holes and driven the enemy back. But there were only 4,000,000 Israelis trying to cope with nearly 200,000,000 Arabs.

Attrition was in the enemy's favor and he had his *jihad* (holy war), which gave his soldiers suicidal fury. Moammar Kadafi was their *Mahdi* (Muslim messiah), and he wore the mantle of holy power with arrogance and blustering pomp that would have embarrassed Benito Mussolini.

Brent often reflected on the irony behind the Arabs' power. It was laughable to think the Chinese with their incredibly inefficient star-wars system were responsible for it all. But they were. He had been a young ensign when the ten laser-armed weapons platforms went into orbit and promptly malfunctioned. Immediately, not one jet or rocket could be fired without drawing instant destruction from a lightning bolt from space. Then, Kadafi's ascent began.

The maps brought other grating thoughts to mind. Traditionally, the sheiks, kings, emirs, and military-backed rulers of the Arab world had ruled with bloody iron fists, guarding their domains like Chicago gangsters marking their own territory to loot. The only force capable of competing with the rulers had been that of religion. With the teeth of Russian and American militarism pulled by the Chinese laser system, Islam gained momentum and Kadafi managed to grab the reins of the *Mahdi* and turn the entire Arab movement into a *jihad*. Even the Iranians, who loudly proclaimed their Persian roots to anyone who

18

would listen, had joined with the Libyans, Algerians, Lebanese, Egyptians, Jordanians, Saudis, and Syrians. Megalomaniacs all, Hosni Mubarak, Hafez Assad, King Hussein, Hashemi Rafsanjani, King Fahd, Saddam Hussein, Walid Jumblatt, Yasser Arafat, and Abu Nidal grudgingly curbed their egos and pledged to follow the lead of the *Mahdi*. A tenuous alliance at best, it would seem, but the entire world had been stunned by its durability. Brent was convinced that only hatred for the Jews and Japanese held the Arabs together. Mountains of oil money sold at extortive prices also helped. The *jihad* was awash in money.

Brent's thoughts were interrupted when Captain Herzl turned to the other communications man, a young reservist on his first assignment at the front. "Corporal Goldstein, stand by to transmit!" he ordered.

Corporal Yosif Goldstein sat before one of the most complex communications systems in the world, the Elbit mini-SACU (Stand Alone Digital Communications Unit). His equipment was as modern as Sergeant Wolpin's radio and field telephone were antiquated. Nervously, Goldstein threw a switch and there was the sound of a hard disk coming up to speed. The processor beeped and he struck a key on the touch-panel. Drumming the table top with a typist's closely trimmed nails, he watched his monitor flash, "Please wait." Small beads of perspiration began to form on his forehead like tiny rain drops. Finally, every man in the bunker shared Goldstein's relief when the screen flashed, "Ready to transmit." He said in a high girlish voice, "Ready, sir. Mode, sir?"

"High-speed burst and use the twin line. No AM or FM."

Goldstein pressed a function key and typed in a

command. "Mode and means ready, Captain. Code?"

"Not necessary, Corporal. We programmed *Ah-doo-meem Sheh-leg*" — Red Snow — "into the micro-processor before you reported." He glared at Sergeant Wolpin. "You should have been briefed — known it."

"Yes, sir," Goldstein said sheepishly. Nisson Wolpin looked away. Brent shifted his weight uneasily. They were wasting time.

"Send the message," Herzl barked. " 'Addressee Division, Originator *Bren-ah-Hahd*. Enemy column approaching our front." He raised his glasses and peered through a port. "Estimate coordinates D-4, range approximately eight kilometers. No visual contact. Strength unknown'."

Goldstein ran his fingers over the keyboard, scanned his monitor, punched a key and said, "Sent, Captain."

Herzl nodded and grumbled acknowledgment. He was very unhappy with his new man.

Despite the clumsiness of the young technician, Brent was awed by this Israeli technological achievement. He had read a manual on SACU when he first arrived. The system was capable of transmitting by wire, AM, FM accessing VHF, UHF, or HF bands. It acknowledged messages automatically and its special-purpose computations included ballistic or navigation calculations. It even detected and corrected errors. This was fortunate, considering the inexperience of Corporal Goldstein. The machine was actually designed to forgive him.

Brent shook his head, mind filled with the accomplishments of these talented, brilliant people. Their achievements with armaments and sophisticated electronics devices had been nearly miraculous, especially in light of their limited resources. During his short stay he had seen Israeli radar and fire control devices that could outperform his own state-of-the-art equipment back in carrier *Yonaga*'s CIC. But the Israelis were driven by an evil force that would exterminate them. "Desperation plus IQ points," he had said to himself many times. "There's nothing like it."

"Receipted for, Captain," Goldstein said suddenly, staring at his display.

"Store it."

Goldstein struck a key. "Stored, sir."

"Sir," Sergeant Nisson Wolpin said suddenly, pounding his radio. "My SCR is *Kaputt!*"

"*Dreck!*" Herzl spat. "That *pisher* is older than I am." He pounded his fists together in frustration. "We need it for backup."

Brent returned to his port and raised his glasses. It was maddening. Nothing moved. But there was a faint haze of dust on the far horizon. He said almost to himself, "If they're going to attack, where's the artillery?"

"They don't always bombard us before an attack," Moskowitz said.

"Surprise?"

"That's right, Commander. With or without artillery preparation. Human wave attacks supported by armor."

"Old tactics."

Moskowitz chuckled. "World War One."

Brent shook his head. "Civil War without the tanks, Colonel. Gettysburg, Fredericksberg, Antietam, and a dozen more. It's a good way to pile up casualties."

"Iran and Iraq did it for years."

"They never learn."

Moskowitz shrugged his shoulders. "They're Arabs, commander."

Brent ran his fingers up under his helmet and

21

rubbed his temple. Thoughtfully, he said, "Sun Tzu, the great Chinese strategist said, 'Those who know the enemy as well as they know themselves will never suffer defeat'."

Arching an eyebrow, Moskowitz eyed the American. "True, we are well acquainted." The Jew smiled slyly. "And remember, American samurai, that here in the desert, the *Sun* also rises."

Brent smiled politely at the pun. Before he could continue, a flash on the far horizon and a familiar rustle turned Brent's attention to the port. The wings of death were parting the air above. The shell passed over, its sound Dopplering down, terminating in a sharp explosion a hundred meters past the bunker. Then the report of the gun drifted over the desert. More flashes in the distance. Hisses, warbles and two shells exploded on the ridges of the wadi that held the decomposing Arabs. Thunder rumbled over the horizon. "A hundred meters short," Moskowitz muttered.

"The first one was long, Colonel. They've got us bracketed," Brent noted.

Captain Herzl shouted at Corporal Goldstein, "To Division, receiving artillery fire." He turned to Colonel Moskowitz, "Colonel, caliber?"

"Heavies. One-hundred-fifty-two-millimeter at least." Herzl spoke to Goldstein. Goldstein typed.

Two more big shells landed much closer. The bunker shook. "Jesus Christ," Brent said.

Moskowitz leaned close, "Jesus Christ can't help you here, Commander. You're in Israel. Try *Adoshem* or *Bore Olam*."

"Who?" Brent asked, impressed at the colonel's aplomb.

"Our God. We have a lot of names for him. You'll have better luck with the Jewish god." He stabbed a

22

finger at two large craters, "Those are forty-nine-kilo-gram shells."

"A little over a hundred pounds," Brent converted quickly. He waved at the overhead. "Can't penetrate this stuff." He raised an eyebrow slyly and showed his own composure under fire, "And I'll stick with Jesus, thank you."

Moskowitz smiled at the retort. "You're wrong about Jesus but right about the shells. They won't penetrate, but they can give you one giant headache." He pulled down his goggles. Brent did the same, wiping the dust from the glass with his sleeve.

More shells landed, blasted closer. Dust and the smell of cordite drifted through the ports. Brent had been under artillery and bomb attack many times on carrier *Yonaga*. He was accustomed to seeing towers of water leaping from the sea, hanging for a split second, and dropping back down in a welter of spreading rings, showering drops and blowing clouds of mist. Here, the bursts flashed red-yellow, flinging humming shrapnel, dirt, dust, and boulders from the hard pan of the desert, leaving large smoking craters. Each explosion was marked by a hanging cloud of dust that drifted slowly on the face of the breeze.

Brent felt a familiar cold parasite come to life, boring through his guts. His old companion fear was beginning to make its presence felt, mind-numbing and nauseating. He clenched his jaw, choked back the sour taste of bile searing his craw. Impulsively, he gripped his holstered Beretta M-951, Brigadier, for reassurance. But the old nemesis remained, cold and visceral.

Suddenly, a freight train rumbled over. It was a big one. Real heavy stuff. Instinctively, Brent pulled his head down and tried to make himself smaller, as did all men under shell fire. Long ago he had heard Admiral Fujita call it "the turtle reflex." All the other men huddled low except Goldstein, who sat frozen in his chair. While the men cowered, the horror ripped the sky overhead like a piece of heavy canvas rent by a giant. It moved much slower than the smaller shells. Finally, it hit. The convulsive explosion reminded Brent of the power of a Semtex-tipped torpedo. There was an ear-splitting blast followed by a concussion that quaked the earth with seismic shocks. The block house jerked and creaked, concussion caps in the sides tinkling merrily. Wolpin's radio was knocked from its desk and the map table sagged. Dust rose from the floor, and chips of cement and fine white particles resembling talcum powder drifted down.

Now Brent knew why infantrymen hate artillery more than anything else on earth. Faceless men miles away, safe from his fury, could kill him casually, with impunity, like spraying an orchard to kill pests.

"What was that?" young Goldstein cried, half rising.

"Shut up and sit down," Captain Herzl shouted, pushing the young reservist back into his chair. Corporal Feinbaum and his loader, Private Saul Blumberg, had ducked under the Browning. Quickly, they returned to their posts.

Calmly like a man opening the bidding at a bridge table, Colonel Moskowitz speculated, "I would guess that was their three-hundred-five-millimeter howitzer — three-hundred-thirty-kilogram shell. Russian from breech to muzzle."

Brent waved at the ceiling. "That shell was over seven hundred pounds."

"Right. And it can make gefilte fish of all of us." No one laughed.

The bombardment became more intense. Shells rained down on the ridge and up and down the line.

About four times a minute—Brent found himself counting them—a great howitzer shell would plunge down and explode with frightening power. But the big shells were directed to the rear echelons, probably searching for dug-in tanks and reserves. Dust blotted out the sun, and the burned-solvent stench of high explosives was bitter on Brent's tongue and in his throat. It was hard to swallow. Everyone was coughing and holding his ears. Suddenly, a thunder clap struck the bunker and a bass drum reverberated inside Brent's skull. Men screamed. Concussion caps clattered. Chips of concrete rained down.

Brent heard Moskowitz's voice in the far distance, "Hundred-fifty-two-millimeter. Just a scratch. That stuff can't hurt us. Stand by the ports! They're rolling the barrage to the rear. The infantry should be coming!" He reached into a bag and handed Brent an American-made M-16. "Keep it clean! They jam."

"I know," Brent said, accepting the automatic rifle and a sack filled with thirty-round box magazines. Brent had trained with the A-2 model while an underclassman at the academy. It was fast—up to 750 rounds a minute—and was accurate up to 437 yards. But he did not trust it. Firing a high-velocity 5.56-millimeter round (.223-caliber) and weighing less then seven pounds, it was much like plastic toy guns he had played with as a boy. Though driven by gas, there was no piston, the gas being fed through a tube straight into the bolt carrier. This sometimes lead to fouling of the bolt carrier and cam; especially when dirt or dust seeped into the mechanism. And the bunker was filled with both. He found himself wishing he had been handed the old reliable Garand M-1, .30-caliber rifle with its tremendous killing power.

Shielding the M-16 with his body, Brent palmed a magazine up into the weapon until he heard the spring-loaded lock snap into place. Then he pulled the cocking handle and heard the first round slide into the firing chamber. After snapping the selector lever to "auto," he draped a handkerchief over the bolt and rested the weapon on the sill. The bombardment had definitely rolled to the rear and the dust had almost been cleared by the breeze. Then he heard the shouts.

At first Brent saw nothing. Just swirls of dust and streaming smoke. But a man fights by sound, too, and his ears told him a chilling story. Men howling for blood were closing on them. Even more ominous, he could hear the rumble of diesel engines.

"They're yelling *Allahu Akbar!*" Moskowitz said.

" 'Allah is most great,' " Brent said.

"You know?"

"Yes, I know."

"Mazel," the Jew said.

Brent nodded understanding. "And luck to you, too, colonel.

The unleashed fury of shrieking men reminded Brent of the deafening pandemonium at the Army-Navy games. But the football fans screamed for victory. These fanatics thirsted for blood. Suddenly, dread-driven thoughts clashed in Brent's mind like the fluctuant seas in the eye of a hurricane. He was caught in a nightmare, a convulsion of insanity. This could not be happening. He, an officer in the United States Navy on liaison with a Japanese admiral caught in an Arab attack on an Israeli blockhouse in the middle of the Sinai Desert. It was ludicrous. Unreal. A fantasy written by a drunken Hollywood scriptwriter.

Squaring his massive jaw, he took several deep breaths, hunched down, eyes riveted on the desert, butt of the M-16 pressed to his shoulder. He knew how to fight — how to fight in streets, gutters, and alleys. How to kill with guns, knives, even his fists. He had dispatched four with his sword alone. Perhaps he would learn how to die this day. "There is a time to live and a time to die," Bushido taught. How true, but he found no comfort in the old adage. He glanced to the right. Moskowitz was crouched behind his rifle. Strange, an inscrutable grin twisted the Colonel's lips. Was he hiding his own personal demons, too?

Moskowitz was the senior officer present, but it was Herzl's bunker, his command. "Feinbaum," Herzl said to the machine gunner, "in the name of Moses, don't fire until you see a target." Then to the rest of the men at the ports, including Nisson Wolpin who stood at the fourth port clutching an M-16, "Don't waste your ammunition on tanks. Kill the infantry." He nodded at Corporal Goldstein who sat wide-eyed, staring at his monitor, "I've called for artillery."

"They're close!" Moskowitz shouted.

"Our guns are already registered, have computerized control, and I'll spot. That's what I'm here for, Colonel."

"No need to tell me your job, Captain," Moskowitz retorted sharply.

Herzl sighed. Pounded his helmet with a clenched fist. "Sorry, Colonel," he muttered. Although it was a mild day for the Sinai, Herzl's flushed face was streaked with perspiration.

The rumbles grew louder. Brent could actually hear the squeak of bogies. The Arabs never maintained their tanks properly. Still, remaining wisps of dust and smoke obscured the enemy who Brent guessed was staging in the hollows and wadis.

Moskowitz said to Herzl, "I saw Ben-Gurions on the ridge behind us. How many?"

Brent remembered seeing the row of converted British-made Centurion tanks only fifty yards behind them. With their usual ingenuity, the Israelis had replaced the Centurion's gasoline engine with a diesel, installed new transmissions, new machine guns, new range finders, new cupolas, and new electrical systems. Well dug-in fifty yards behind *Bren-ah-Hahd,* only their turrets, with their vicious 105-millimeter guns pointed to the south, were visible.

"Twenty Ben-Gurions, a reinforced company," Herzl said. He glanced at Corporal Goldstein. "A battalion of self-propelled guns and a company of Merkava MBTs are moving up." The captain glared at Goldstein and vented some of the anger he felt for the Moskowitz on the enlisted man. "Right, Corporal?"

Goldstein's jaw was trembling. "Yes, sir," he said in a low voice.

"By Muhammed's balls, speak up, *shlemiel"* Herzl snarled.

The young man jerked his head around, "Yes, sir." He gestured at the clattering printer and pointed at his screen, "Straight from Division." Herzl tore the sheet from the printer and stared at it. "Thank God, infantry . . ."

A shout from Wolpin stopped Herzl in midsentence. "Here they come."

Then Brent saw them, tiny figures in desert camouflage, racing toward them. *"Allahu Akbar!"* they screamed. Then the squat chassis and rounded turrets of T-62s rose from the low ground behind the infantry. Like a swarm of huge deadly beetles they crawled toward Brent in a ragged line, dust billowing behind them.

The Russian-built tank was unmistakable. Brent had seen many captured and rebuilt T-62s in Israeli armored units. Also, he had studied Arab versions in secret IDF manuals: squat at less than eight feet to its highest point, two infrared searchlights mounted on the turret with an air identification stripe painted on its top between the two hatches, a 12.7-millimeter machine gun mounted next to the loader's hatch, three large white unit designation numbers on both sides of the turret, a 7.62-millimeter coaxial machine gun protruding next to the vicious 115-millimeter smoothbore with its fume extractor and muzzle brake. Most of the cannons seemed to be pointed directly at him.

The young American could see infantry riding some of the tanks, clinging to handgrips welded to the turrets. In the distance more infantry was leaping from about a dozen APCs. The second wave. Never in Brent Ross's thirty years had he ever felt the sharp blade of fear dig so deep, so cruelly. At sea he had fought surface actions from *Yonaga* and destroyer *Haida,* and been under bomber attack a dozen times. As attack officer of the submarine *Blackfin,* he had torpedoed the carrier *Gefara* and killed nearly 2,000 men. But never had it been this personal. In fact, outside of a few glimpses of enemy pilots, in battle he had *never* seen the men he killed and who were trying to hill him. He fought machines, impersonal mechanical devices devoid of humanity. Staring at the advancing infantry and armor, he felt tiny creatures run up and down his spine with frozen feet, and the hair on his arms and on the back of his neck seemed to rise. Clenching his teeth, he sighed out several deep breaths and tried to control his heart, which had become a hammer trying to drive itself through his ribs. Then he remembered an ancient maxim from the *Hagakure (Under the Leaves,* the Bible of the samurai), which Admiral Fujita had quoted many times: "If you die, Brent-san, die facing the enemy." Just the thought of the admiral had a calming effect. The breathing eased, the trip-hammer slowed.

Herzl's voice, high, tense and with a slight quiver, "Goldstein! To Division. Enemy attacking with at least a company of tanks and a battalion of infantry on my front. Nearest enemy elements one-five-zero-zero-meters off my front."

Overhead the air parted with shredding rustles and warbles, but traveling in the opposite direction. A four-shell salvo burst between the bunker and the Arabs.

"Two hundred short," Herzl shouted at Goldstein. The communications man pounded his keyboard.

"One-oh-fives," Moskowitz said.

"Those shell came from a battery to the rear," Brent noted. "Not the Centurions—ah, I mean the Ben-Gurions."

"Right, Commander. The Ben-Gurions will hold fire until they can engage the tanks—they prefer to fire at a hundred meters."

"The best weapon against a tank is another tank," Brent observed, looking over his sights at an enemy who was still far out of range.

"Right again," Moskowitz agreed. "In the Yom Kippur War we had TOW missiles, but it was gun power from tanks that stopped the Egyptians."

Brent was disturbed by a sudden realization. Scratching his chin he said, "You said the Ben-Gurions would fire at a hundred meters."

"Yes. The best killing range. Punch a hole in a T-62 and it will burn like a torch."

"They'll be coming through our ports."

The Israeli colonel looked at Brent, an eyebrow raised, a laconic grin twisting his lips. "As the French would say, Commander Ross, *C'est la guerre.*"

"*C'est la guerre,*" Brent repeated under his breath. Moskowitz returned to his port.

More Israeli shells ripped overhead. This time the

shells burst in the midst of the enemy. Brent actually saw two Arabs flung high into the air by one burst. "Fire for effect!" Herzl shouted.

Dozens of sharp barks behind them blended into a staccato rumble that brought shouts of relief from the men. A hail of shells screeched over, exploding with terrible execution. Whole squads vanished in flaming eruptions that flung men, heads, arms, stringy red detritus in gory circles. Tanks were hit and began to burn. Brent was awed by the violence, violence seldom seen on this earth, violence that only men could inflict on their own species. More shouts of joy.

"One-oh-fives and one-fifty-fives," Moskowitz said.

"Jesus, that was fast," Brent said.

"Jesus has nothing to do with our fire control," Moskowitz said with a unbelievable aplomb. And then like a docent explaining an art exhibit to a tourist, "We're using the new David Artillery Battery Computer. No tables, no charts, Commander. Herzl's observations are transmitted to a computer in the battery fire direction center and then the center transmits firing data to each gun, not just the battery command post."

Brent found the colonel's detached mood infectious. "The T-62s aren't firing," the American shouted over the din.

"Right, Commander," Moskowitz shouted back. "They only carry about forty rounds. They must be saving them for our tanks."

"They must carry HE."

"Right, high explosives. We will probably benefit from their attention very soon. But they're looking for our armor. The Arabs have a new APFSDS round."

Brent nodded. "Armor-Piercing Fin Discarding Sa-

31

bot with depleted uranium penetrators. That's why their barrels are smooth-bore, so that the sabot will fit and have a smooth run."

"Very good for a sailor."

"Your tanks use them?"

"Yes. And more—HEAT, APDS, HESH, hollow charge . . ."

Moskowitz was interrupted by cheers. The entire mass of men and machines had stopped. Four tanks were burning. The infantry went to ground, the surviving tanks backed into draws and wadis and idled. Brent felt sudden exhilaration. Maybe the Arabs were calling the whole show off. That was it. They had seen the pillboxes, the armor dug in to the rear, felt the lash of incredibly accurate artillery, and lost heart. Maybe he would never be forced to fire his M-16. But the Arabs had other cards to play.

There was a hum of an angry hornet, and an Arab light artillery spotter aircraft appeared to leapfrog over a small rise and flashed over the Israeli line like giant dragon fly.

Moskowitz said, "Storch, the old Fieseler FI-156."

"I'll be damned," Brent said. "Never saw one before."

"He's getting an eyeful."

And Moskowitz was right. A salvo of 305-millimeter shells rumbled over. More shrieks and warbles followed as at least a hundred guns counterfired. Brent could hear the reports, see flashes and rising smoke from the enemy batteries far to the rear. Strangely, the big shells arrived before the sound of the guns.

"My God," Moskowitz exclaimed. "They've moved up a lot of heavy stuff. That's counterbattery fire. They're zeroing in on our artillery."

Immediately, the Israeli fire slackened. And then, within a minute, it was almost silent. Brent said,

"Either our guns are destroyed, or they're being re-spotted, Colonel. You said they were self-propelled."

"Correct. Most are self-propelled." His voice was low and grim.

At that moment, the Arabs played their second card. "Dive bombers!" someone screamed. It was Herzl, yelling at Corporal Goldstein. "We need fighters! Fighters and where is our artillery!" Goldstein pounded his keyboard.

Craning his neck, Brent brought up his glasses and looked up at the southwestern horizon. He saw a frightening sight — at least twelve aircraft flying wingtip to wing-tip and echeloned up like stairs. With the elimination of jets and rockets, he was accustomed to dive bombing attacks by resurrected Arab Junkers JU-87, Stukas. Seven of the approaching aircraft had the Stuka's familiar gull wings, fixed slatted landing gear, bomb slung beneath the fuselage on a hinged belly crutch, and tapered nose of its in-line Jumo engine. But his lenses brought other unexpected aircraft into focus. Five had big radial engines, huge wings, retractable landing gear, long canopies that extended from the hood to the vertical stabilizer, thick stubby fuselages and fixed tail wheels. "JU-87s, but what the hell — those others . . . ?" Brent muttered.

"Curtis SB-Two-C Helldivers," Moskowitz said bitterly. He punched the concrete and reverted to German for his expletive, *"Scheisse!"*

"Where in hell did they find them?"

Moskowitz shrugged. "Who knows in this crazy world. But they have unlimited money." He looked at Brent with hard eyes. "Some international arms broker — Swedish, Swiss, British, Arab, American — even an Israeli *schmuck*."

Brent's mind sorted back through the old histories he had studied at the Academy. "It can carry a helluva load—the best dive bomber of WW-Two."

"Right," Moskowitz responded. "A ton under its wings and another ton in its bomb bay." Calmly, he stabbed a finger upwards through the port. "They're getting ready!"

The formation had spread with the seven Stukas leading. All of the bombers had their dive brakes down, and Brent could hear the sound of the engines drop to a throaty roar as the propellers were rotated to coarse pitch and the pilots throttled back. Hell would be raining down within minutes.

The leading Junkers dropped off on its port wing and began its dive. Feinbaum, Blumberg, and Wolpin huddled against the concrete walls. Goldstein, too, had curled up against a wall. The three officers remained standing. Herzl stared through a port to one side of his equipment, shaking like a coatless man in a blizzard. Brent and Moskowitz directing their eyes upward through the limited visibility of their ports.

Brent could not see the descending bombers. However, their sounds penetrated the shelling. Roar of the engines, howl of their sirens was like opening the door to hell and listening to the shrieks of demented souls. Brent had heard that sound many times in the past, and he felt the same terror again. No man could ever become accustomed to it. It was the howl of death, clear and unmistakable.

There was a change in sound as the first bomber pulled out—propeller to fine pitch, the big Jumo pushed to full throttle, followed by the shriek of the plunging bomb. Now the three officers dropped instinctively to the floor.

The blockhouse fairly leaped as a 500-kilogram bomb exploded just to the left and behind the bunker. Brent heard several of the men cry out. More engines. More sirens. Bomb after bomb exploded. Chips of concrete rained down and the bunker filled with dust and smoke. Now coughs were added to the cries of fear.

Following Moskowitz's example, Brent dampened a handkerchief from his canteen and quickly tied it around his head, covering his mouth and nose. Now the engines were fading and the men began to rise. Brent dropped his handkerchief to his neck.

Herzl was nearly out of his mind. *"Schmuckim! Schmuckim!* To your posts! To your posts, cowards."

"Control yourself, Captain," Moskowitz commanded in an unprecedented rebuke of an officer in front of his own men.

Eyes wide and blank like cue balls, Herzl stared at the Colonel, mouth working, breath cut off in short gasps like a man struck in the solar plexus. Gripping his holstered pistol, he screeched, "I'll not take . . ."

"Here they come," Brent said, picking up a squad emerging from a slight depression. Led by a sergeant, they were charging the pill box. Hunched over like all charging infantry, they wore baggy desert camouflage with grenades flopping from their webbing, extra magazines attached to their woven ammunition belts. Most clutched Kalashnikovs in both hands at low port. But one man carried a flame thrower, two others were burdened with satchel charges. They were almost in range.

Fear of antitank guns was so strong the Arabs would throw away infantry to silence Israeli bunkers before committing their precious tanks. The barrage had lifted and moved to the Israeli rear. This was a serious offensive. No feint. No test. Probably in corps strength or greater, this appeared to be an all-out attempt to break through and destroy the Jews. And the front was wide, smoke and dust rising far to the right and left. All of Sector Gray Winter appeared involved.

"More dive bombers!" Sergeant Wolpin shouted. Brent saw them, a swarm of specks closing in the far distance. But his whole world was the enemy infantry racing toward him. These were the men who would shoot him, roast him, blow him to pieces. Four hundred yards. They were in range. He tightened his finger on the trigger.

He thought the M-16 had gone off with impossibly loud explosions. Then he saw the first four men of the squad hurled backwards as if a giant's fist were punching them. He had not fired a shot. It was the 50-caliber. The sergeant's helmet flew off with most of his head. The man behind him spun around as great slugs smashed into his stomach and eviscerated him. The two leaders were hurled back into two more Arabs. All four fell in a heap. The remaining six continued their charge, screaming, *"Itbakh al Yahud!"* — Death to the Jews! — *"Allahu Akbar!"* But, Allah did not help them. Corporal Feinbaum shot them down like bloody garbage. "Welcome to paradise, *schmuckim,"* he screamed, excitement raising his voice to a high shrill timbre.

But Feinbaum's traverse was only about 60 degrees. Brent and Colonel Moskowitz had the remaining 60 degrees of their right flank. Seeing the slaughter of the first rush, Arab infantry quickly worked to the flanks where the big machine gun could not reach them. They burst from wadis, gullies, from the very ground itself. Swarms of them. Not the aligned solid wave Brent had expected, but compact groups forced by the terrain to zigzag around boulders, depressions and camel's thorn.

Brent's fear had come full circle back to courage. He would kill them before they killed him. There was ice water in his veins again, but this time it was from

36

anger and determination to stay alive, not fear.

Every man in the bunker seemed to open fire simultaneously. The torrents of bullets spewed by the M-16s was devastating. Brent cut down a group of five enemy with one long burst. Struck by the small, high-velocity slugs, the five whirled and flung their assault rifles in the air in a last macabre dance of death. Then dozens of others bowled over as if scythed. There were screams of horror, agony. Above it all, the Browning pounded away, heavy, relentless, deadly. Shouts of fear were replaced by the exultation of finally shooting down their tormentors. And Brent felt it. Deep down, warm, blood lust, the frenzy of the kill. It was like having a beautiful woman spread before him, dewy and wet, hungry to receive him.

Now there were new sounds. The whiplike crack and sibilant hissing of streams of sleeting small-arms fire. The iron ring of ricochets off concrete, the steady belch of heavy automatic fire. Arab machine gun squads had set up their weapons in outcroppings of rocks and were searching for the ports. Brent wondered about the other bunkers. Where was their supporting fire? Maybe they were all fighting for their own lives. Or, as many men in battle believe, perhaps *Bren-ah-Hahd* was the only surviving bunker and only he and his few companions remained alive. And where was the Israeli Air Force?

There were no more easy targets. The surviving infantry had taken shelter and were firing from behind rocks and desert growth. The fire from the M-16s slackened, but the rumble in the sky increased. Bombers were approaching. Maybe the enemy would wait. Let the dive bombers do it. Or maybe they were gathering for another charge.

Bullets were hailing against the bunker. About a dozen of the enemy's T-62 turrets were exposed above

37

the hollows and wadis. Black-clad crewmen clambered up, manned the big 12.7-millimeter machine guns, and added their fire to the infantry's. They were very brave men.

"Machine gun. The gunners on the tanks! The tanks!" Moskowitz shouted.

"Tanks!" Feinbaum repeated, shifting the Browning. Three short bursts killed three of the exposed machine gunners firing from the turrets. The others dropped back down through their hatches.

Brent was about to cheer when there was a slapping, pinging sound and chunks of concrete splattered against his helmet and clattered off his goggles. Other bits ripped into his face, stinging like thrown needles as something big and horrible like a great insect hummed past his ear and splattered itself against the back wall.

Crying out involuntarily, Brent whirled from the port, clutching his cheek. Blood seeped from a half-dozen wounds.

"Brent!" Moskowitz shouted, using the American's first name for the first time.

"I'm okay. Okay," Brent managed, pulling his handkerchief from his pocket and dabbing at his cheek. "Just a few scratches."

"You sure?"

"I'm sure! A ricochet." Brent returned to the M-16.

"You're lucky."

"Yes. I know."

But Sergeant Nisson Wolpin was not as lucky. There was a solid thud like a butcher's cleaver striking a solid shank. Hit full in the face by a 12.7-millimeter machine gun bullet, the communications man was hurled back from his port, his helmet, bits of bone, upper jaw and the contents of his skull splattering the back wall. Arms outflung, the sergeant lay twitching,

38

the last autonomic spasms of the freshly killed.

Herzl stood mutely, looking at the corpse with disbelief. The machine gunners, Feinbaum and Blumberg, sat stonily, staring wide-eyed. Corporal Goldstein sat in his chair in front of the mini-SACU, sobbing and wiping brains and bits of bone off his face and shirt. Retching, he added his vomit to the mess on his uniform and equipment. Moskowitz sighed, face a book of sadness and resignation.

Kicking the horror at his feet to the rear, Brent shook his head. Another dead man; young, intelligent. There had been so many—the good, the bright, the witty. Would it ever end?

Moskowitz shouted at Corporal Feinbaum, "To your right! A hundred twenty meters behind those boulders. A machine gun. See the flashes?"

"Yes, sir. Seven-point-two-millimeter. He's out of my traverse."

"*Dreck!* Do you see him, Commander?" Moskowitz asked Brent.

Brent saw flame leaping from some boulders. Squeezed off a burst at the exact moment Moskowitz opened fire. Chips of rocks and dust flew. Both men emptied their magazines. Reloaded. The firing stopped. Then began again. "No, dammit, no." Brent muttered.

Moskowitz turned to Herzl. "Captain. Mortars! Smoke! Call for . . ."

Before the colonel could complete his sentence, there was a flash, dull boom, and puff of smoke in the Arab positions. Then dozens more in quick succession. "Our mortars!" Feinbaum exulted.

"Eighty-one-millimeter *Soltamim!*" Moskowitz declared.

As Brent watched, two mortar rounds landed directly on the enemy machine gun. Two Arabs were blown out of the pit, and the gun was hurled over the rocks. A hail of mortar shells landed. The enemy fire slackened. Cheers.

But the cheers were silenced by a rumble overhead. Over twenty dive bombers were queuing up to deliver their loads. The cold hand of dread gripped the heart of every man in the bunker.

"They can't dive-bomb us," Brent said. "Their armor and infantry are too close. They'll kill their own."

"You don't know the Arab Army, Commander," Moskowitz said.

"Our fighters!" someone screamed.

Ducking down low, Brent looked up in time to see squadrons of needle-nosed North American P-51 Mustangs and Supermarine Spitfires rip into the slow clumsy dive bombers. The JU-87s were just target practice, the Curtis Helldivers little better. Then Brent saw some familiar frightening black shapes racing in from high to the south. "Messerschmitts!" he shouted. "Enemy fighters." Within seconds, the sky was filled with diving, twisting, rolling fighters, vapor trails and a latticework of tracers. Planes tumbled, burned, disintegrated, spun. A few white parachutes descended.

There was a sharp, whiplike crack of a high-velocity cannon and almost immediately the bunker was shocked by a sharp explosion. More chips of concrete and dust. "The tanks!" Feinbaum screamed. "They're firing and coming."

Herzl stood numbly, staring out of Wolpin's blood-spattered port. He had removed his helmet and placed a linen yarmulke on his head. Using Hebrew, he was shouting the most common Judaic prayer, *Shoh-meh-ah Yis-rah-ehl* (Hear, Israel), which Brent had heard his old friend Colonel Bernstein use many times before. He knew it as well as the Jews. "Hear, O Israel, the Lord our God, the Lord is one. And thou shalt love the Lord . . ." Brent shook his head. He had seen men break down in combat before. One of the worst had been Lieutenant Sinclair Ingilly, who had temporarily lost control on destroyer *Haida*. But unlike Ingilly, Herzl's mind was bereft of reason, completely out of touch with reality. In fact, he appeared to be stark, raving mad.

Luckily, Moskowitz's brain was working like Corporal Goldstein's computer. He took command. "Watch for their infantry. They'll try to work their way up on their bellies—throw in grenades, satchel charges, use flame throwers." He turned to Corporal Goldstein. "Take an M-16 and man Wolpin's port."

"The mini-SACU, sir?"

"*Dreck* on the SACU. Man that port, on the double, Corporal!"

Quickly, Goldstein grabbed a rifle and moved to the port. Still chanting, Herzl stepped back and raised his eyes to the roof.

The T-62s had spread across the front. But at least twelve were visible from *Bren-ah-Hahd*. They had come out of their holes and were moving through their infantry, firing.

The blockhouse rang with hits and stank with the rancid stench of explosives and the burned gunpowder of the M-16s. For Brent the strain had been so long, so hard, so draining that the separate events of the battle seemed to merge into single slow-motion kaleidoscope. Senses overwhelmed, he became an insensate machine like the SACU; emotionless, capable only of reacting on the primal level of self-preservation.

"Flame thrower!" Moskowitz screamed while he reloaded.

Brent saw two men rise from the ground and run

41

toward him. One had tanks strapped to his back and carried the fearsome nozzle. There was a wooshing sound and a tongue of flame shot toward the blockhouse at exactly the moment Brent squeezed the trigger. Caught in the chest by the burst, the Arab whirled, nozzle spraying in a wide circle. The rifleman next to him caught the full blast. Turned into a living torch, he raced screaming into the desert like a devil back to the infernal pits. With the dead man's finger locked on the release, the flame thrower whirled with its own force, spraying the earth, the sky, other Arabs. Finally, it stopped, a greasy black cloud of smoke drifting low across the desert.

Brent ignored the burning horror. Men were squirming along the ground like reptiles. Grenades aimed at the ports began to bounce off the bunker and explode. The tanks had raised their fire and were engaging targets to *Bren-ah-Hahd*'s rear. Probably searching for antitank guns.

There was the unmistakable sound of bullets slapping flesh. It was young Goldstein. Half his neck had been ripped away but he remained standing, blood spouting from a torn jugular. Unable to make a sound because his larynx had been shot out, he stood mouth agape, eyes glazed with pain and disbelief. Then, after a long moment, he sank slowly to the ground, gracefully, like a dancer making his final bow.

Clutching both hands prayerfully and rubbing his forehead from the bridge of his nose to his widow's peak, Herzl sank to his knees over the dying boy. In a high keening wail, he quoted the prophet Isaiah: " 'Wail, for the day of the Lord is near; as destruction from the Almighty will come.' " And then, punishing his forehead with repeated blows from his knuckles, he screamed, "Is come! Is come!"

"Man the port!" Moskowitz yelled at Herzl. The

42

captain ignored him as if his hearing had gone the way of his mind. Moskowitz said to Brent, "Take it, Commander. We're dead men if that flank isn't covered."

Brent grabbed his bag of ammunition and quickly moved to the port. His boots squished in blood-soaked earth. In the desert heat, some of Wolpin's blood had coagulated into sheets like liver. Goldstein's was still fresh and he was still alive, air whining through his severed trachea with a shrill whistle. Brent could not believe the human body contained so much blood. The sweet, sickening stench of death was already beginning to fill the bunker.

The enemy tanks were only about fifty yards away. Then the lead T-62 exploded with such violence, its turret shot high into the sky like a Fourth of July pyrotechnic. More tanks exploded. APFSDS, HEAT, and HESH rounds from the Ben-Gurions or self-propelled artillery. Depleted Uranium, Hollow Charge, and Tungsten Carbide penetrators were punching through the Arab armor. In less than a minute, six of the enemy tanks had been destroyed. Hastily, the survivors began backing into the desert, firing as they retreated. Arab infantry streamed back with their tanks. Everyone began to cheer. Brent missed Herzl's voice. He had disappeared. The low steel hatch at the right rear was open. He had deserted. Coward! Brent felt an amalgam of anger and contempt.

But Brent was wrong. Herzl was no coward. He was actually running after the retreating Arabs. "Come back, Captain!" Brent yelled.

"No! No, Avraham!" Moskowitz screamed.

Avraham Herzl ignored them. Waving a leather-bound holy book over his head, he shrieked, *"Sha-lohm!"* — Peace! — *"Sha-lohm!"*

Feinbaum and Blumberg both crowded close to

43

their port. Brent and Moskowitz continued to shout. Herzl never paused in his pursuit of the enemy. Suddenly, an Arab infantryman popped up from concealment, pointed his AK-47 and unloaded half a magazine into the crazed captain.

Herzl stopped in midstride as if he had run into a wall, twisted and fell on his side, face buried in the sand. The holy book was still clutched in his hand, yarmulke on his head. The Arab vanished.

"No, no, Avraham," Moskowitz cried out in agony.

At that moment the first Israeli Ben-Gurions, Merkavas and T-62s began streaming past *Bren-ah-Hahd*. They were the first of scores that charged across the entire front. The gunfire began to fade in the distance. The rout was on.

Suddenly, like a miracle, silence a thing of weight and substance filled the bunker. When the guns stilled, this always happened. Brent had known this phenomenon time and again. And the languor crept in with the stillness, the commander experiencing the same lethargy he invariably felt after every battle. Emotions had been so high for so long his life force seemed to have been drained away when it was finally over. Then the same words that had always run through his mind after a battle drummed through his consciousness: *It's over and I'm still alive,* he told himself over and over.

A slight groan turned his head. It was David Moskowitz. He was clutching his left arm. Spurting blood stained his sleeve and dripped off his fingers. Corporal Feinbaum and Saul Blumberg began to rise. "No!" Moskowitz growled. "Keep that gun manned."

Brent left his port and started toward the colonel. "Stay at your post, Commander." Moskowitz sank to the ground, back to the wall.

"By your leave, Colonel. Bullshit! That's arterial

bleeding."

"You're insubordinate."

"And you're bleeding to death."

Brent tore off his shirt, ripped off a strip and used it to tourniquet the wounded arm. The bleeding stopped.

"Brent," Moskowitz said in a voice weakened by the loss of blood. "Captain Avraham Herzl died the death of a hero."

The machine gunners looked at each other. Brent raised an eyebrow and then nodded understanding. "Of course, Colonel." His eyes shifted to Feinbaum and Blumberg. "We all saw it. Without regard for his own safety, Captain Avraham Herzl charged the enemy. This brave act led to his death."

"Hear! Hear!" the machine gunners chorused. Feinbaum said, "That's what we saw." Blumberg nodded agreement.

"Ruth, dear Ruth," Moskowitz said. "I'm sorry, so sorry."

Puzzled, Brent stared at the wounded man. He must be experiencing delirium. As Brent checked the tightness of the tourniquet, the hard line of the colonel's jaw softened and then his eyes closed and his head slumped forward.

Two

The drab military cut of the young woman's khaki shirt and trousers failed to hide her beauty. Tall and angular, at first glance she appeared somewhat slight in build. But her shoulders were wide for one so slender, tapering to a gazelle neck with a tilt of dainty head. Obviously unrestrained by a brassiere, her large rounded breasts peaked sharply to pointed nipples that challenged her shirt with full roundels. A snug belt circled a small waist that flared gracefully to full womanly hips and buttocks so perfect they appeared to have been shaped by a renaissance sculptor's chisel.

Her hair was dark brown, shot through with tones of russet and chestnut. Long and lustrous, like raw silk, it was brushed into a fine cascade that flowed over her shoulders. Long hours in the sun had deepened her skin to burnished golden hues, her delicate features exquisite with high-boned cheeks and long sensitive planes. Luminous eyes reminded one of black diamonds worked hard by a jeweler's cloth. They were enormous, seeming to fill half her face. There was mystery there. Sometimes they reflected the freshness of little-girl innocence, and at other times they flashed as implacable as the eyes of a cat with the fire of a fine intellect in their depths. Her mouth was large and ripe, like everything about her, unconscious provocation giving them an acquisitive quality.

She was one of the most desirable and exciting women Commander Brent Ross had ever seen. She was Corporal Ruth Moskowitz. Ruth Moskowitz was twenty-three years old. She wore the Intelligence shoulder badge.

Standing next to her father's bed, eyes riveted on his face, she turned her head only slightly when Brent Ross entered the hospital room. Colonel David Moskowitz had lost almost three pints of blood despite the tourniquet Brent had applied in *Bren-ah-Hahd*. Only the timely arrival of medics and quick transfusions had saved his life. Now in the Mordecai Military Hospital in Tel Aviv, he had revived quickly. His left arm and shoulder were heavily bandaged, and an IV tube was dripping dextrose and antibiotics into his right arm. But the sight of his daughter, combined with the best medical attention in the world, had had a miraculous effect upon the colonel. He seemed to be in high spirits.

With both arms immobilized, Moskowitz nodded at the newcomer. "This is Commander Brent Ross. He saved my life, Ruth." Turning, he shifted his eyes to Brent. "I told you about Ruth. She's of the Mossad."

She faced the American, her features brightened by a dazzling smile revealing perfect white teeth. Her large, black eyes were suddenly sharp and impertinent, as if to say there was nothing they would not dare to look at.

Fixed by her gaze, Brent felt a somatic jolt, jarred by something eerie; an arcane haunting quality about her. Suddenly, a strange feeling of *déjà vu* infected him, as if he had stared into those same eyes before.

47

She reminded him of someone; another woman, another member of Mossad. Captain Sarah Aranson. That was it. Same classic dark Semitic beauty. Sarah, who had exhausted him one night in a frantic twelve-hour sexual marathon in the Basel Hotel, interrupted only by short respites to regenerate strength and replenish drinks. They had both slept a drugged sleep after the last gasps and spasms; he too fatigued to leave the bed, she too tired and sore. "I think we just made the *Guinness Book of Records,*" Sarah had whispered with a happy, dreamy smile. That had been back in 1984, on his first short two-day trip to Tel Aviv. There would be no encore this trip. Sarah was on assignment in Washington, D.C.

Sarah fled when Ruth offered her hand. It was soft and very small, yet the grasp was firm. Brent held the hand too long. Dropping it, he cursed himself as an embarrassing warmth reddened his cheeks and the skin of his throat. He felt like a randy teenager.

"Oh, the American samurai — thank you," she said. Her voice was soft and deep, her English perfect as if it had been learned somewhere in the northeast part of America, perhaps New York, Boston, or Philadelphia. "I owe you a great debt. I don't know how I will ever be able to repay you."

Despite the hospital room, despite the presence of her wounded father, Brent sensed a double entendre in the statement — something Freud would have relished. And then he noticed, the burnished gold had a slight reddish tint of its own.

"Ah, Ruth," he managed without stammering, "your father is a strong man and he's in marvelous condition."

She smiled and he was suddenly trapped in the dark depths of her eyes. "True, Brent," she agreed. "But, my father told me he was a dead man without you."

48

Brent pinched his nose self-consciously, not sure of what to say. Then smiling broadly and glancing at Colonel Moskowitz, "Your father has *chutzpah*."

Both Israelis laughed uproariously at Brent's use of the Yiddish word for guts. Brent continued, "Good for a *goy?*"

"Yes," Ruth said. "Very good—I mean off the wall, right on." They all laughed. She gestured at Brent's bandaged cheek, "You were wounded."

"Nothing, Ruth. Just a few scratches. Nothing a Band-Aid or two can't fix."

"Not true," David countered. "His face was bleeding. It must have been very painful and he kept on fighting. He's as tough as last week's *chala*."

Brent looked at the floor. "I had no choice, Colonel."

"I've seen men drop out of battle for less." Brent felt relieved when Moskowitz shifted his attention to his daughter, "Ruth, the battle. How great was the Arab defeat?

"They took heavy losses, father. We counted sixty-two destroyed tanks."

"I thought they were in at least corps strength?"

The girl nodded. "According to Mossad, they attacked with the Fourth Armored Division and the Twenty-first and Thirty-second Infantry Divisions."

"They left a lot of their armor and infantry in front of *Bren-ah-Hahd*," Brent offered.

Ruth said, "We lost twenty-seven tanks and one hundred eight men." The colonel groaned. The girl turned to Brent. "Those are light casualties to you, but for a nation of only four-million they're huge— equivalent to more than six thousand dead Americans."

"There is no such thing as 'light casualties,' " Brent insisted. "The loss of one man is too much."

Ruth stared at Brent curiously as if she had uncovered a hidden secret. She shocked him with her insightful mind. "You die with them."

Brent glanced at David Moskowitz who nodded knowingly. Brent inexplicably exposed his soul to this lovely girl, "Each and every one," he conceded softly.

"True, true," the colonel agreed. "Good boys, Goldstein, Wolpin and Herzl."

"Captain Avraham Herzl died bravely," she said, voice as soft as a blessing. "Mossad has the report of Corporal Julian Feinbaum." She gestured to the bed. "And my father gave his report this morning."

"He charged the enemy—exposed himself to enemy fire," Brent said honestly.

The girl turned her lips under and Brent could see her teeth working her lower lip. "It was actually useless, wasn't it?" There was undisguised bitterness in her voice.

Brent exchanged an uncomfortable look with David Moskowitz. "No, Ruth," the colonel said in a hard flat voice. "Herzl thought it was a necessary tactic and gave his life." And then prayerfully, *"Alav hasholem."* Eyes moist, he turned away. Brent wondered at this softness in the iron-ribbed colonel, the emotion. The currents were strong, palpable.

Brent said to Ruth, "You knew Avraham Herzl?"

She sighed and nodded at her father. "We dated. We were," she paused, chose her word carefully, "close."

Brent's eyes narrowed. So that was it. He wondered how close. He remembered Moskowitz's last words in the bunker before he lost consciousness. They both had known Herzl well, perhaps . . . the girl had known him intimately. Somehow, he found the thought repugnant.

Brent's musings were interrupted by the colonel. "You weren't engaged, daughter?" he asked. She shook her head negatively.

"I'm very sorry," Brent said.

"He was a fine, gentle person," she murmured. "And devout."

David Moskowitz explained to Brent, "His father was ultra orthodox. In fact, he was a Hasidic rabbi."

The girl's voice was bitter, "Yes, and until this *jihad*, Avraham was determined to follow in his father's footsteps. He had *imu-nah*."

Brent felt confusion. "I thought the orthodox refuse to fight — are exempt from military service?"

Ruth nodded. "True. It was a terrible struggle for Avraham. "

"He never really gave it up, did he?" Brent said to the colonel.

"What do you mean?" Ruth asked before her father could respond.

Brent felt the clutch of uncertainty. He was out of his element. Thus far, the true circumstances of Herzl's death had been concealed. Had he opened the door a crack?

The wounded man came to the rescue. "He studied the Torah, Talmud, Mishna and Midrash, remembered to pray, carried his yarmulke, phylacteries, holy books, and tallith with him."

"He was holding the Penteteuch when he died," Brent added.

"You know about the Penteteuch?"

"All good Christians do, Colonel. The first five books of Moses, your ceremonial Torah. It's part of my Bible, too, you know."

"But Avraham never forgot his duty to the *Zahal*, father," Ruth said in a slow, husky voice.

"Yes, Ruth, he was a career soldier to the end."

She caught her breath and turned away, moisture deepening her eyes to the blackness of the grave. An

51

ethereal silence filled the room. Unable to look the colonel in the eye, Brent toed the carpet and stared at the floor. Although he had not lied about Herzl, he felt like a hypocrite. He was very uncomfortable.

David broke the hush, addressing Brent, "You must think Avraham was a mass of contradictions — an ultra orthodox yet an artilleryman who called down his fire and brimstone on the Arabs."

Brent shook his head. "We all live our contradictions."

"Hypocrisy?"

"No. On the contrary, strength."

Father and daughter looked at each other with surprise. Brent continued, "The Japanese believe the more the contradictions a man can live with, the stronger the man."

"He was a man of great strength," David said. The American remained silent.

Ruth said to Brent, "You admire the Japanese."

"They're a great and wise people."

David Moskowitz nodded and then changed the subject. He said to his daughter, "Your mother was here this morning."

"Oh, I missed her."

"She had to return to Haifa. She's involved in Civil Defense and the relocation of children to Italy and Greece, you know."

"I know, father."

"She'll return in a few days. We tried to phone you at Mossad, but those *golemim* never know anything."

"I was hand-delivering dispatches all morning, father. They didn't know where I was and they will only use radio for extreme emergencies — you know that." She turned to Brent, "I understand you're waiting for a conference — a prisoner exchange. Right?"

Brent chuckled. "It's no secret. It's been in the me-

52

dia for weeks."

"When?"

Brent explained the difficulty the negotiators were having on agreeing on even a site for the discussions. "So," he concluded, "I'm marking time just waiting for some progress at Geneva and at the UN."

"Your colleague, or fellow negotiator, is Colonel Irving Bernstein."

"That's correct, Ruth. He's been on liaison with me on *Yonaga* for over seven years. He's great in communications — ciphers, codes. We're very close friends."

"He's taught you a lot about the Jews?"

"True. We've spent many long hours at sea talking about everything. Sailors do that."

"And reading."

Brent grinned at the girl. "It's a very lonely life."

"You must do without a lot . . ." Freud was back and so was the sunset tint. "I mean you must miss civilization."

Brent sighed and looked away and said simply, "That's true. It can be very lonely and we all read incessantly."

The girl overcame her discomfort quickly, "Colonel Bernstein's a fine person. We've known him for years and miss him."

"Your father's told me." He rubbed his chin and found the usual afternoon stubble like fine iron filings. "Irving's in Israel." He waved a hand in a sweeping gesture. "No insult meant, but this is a small country and he is Mossad. I'm surprised you haven't seen him."

"No, Brent. He's not in the country. I hear he was sent to Geneva."

"That's why he didn't answer my calls," Brent growled. "No one tells me anything." He glanced at

Moskowitz, who was staring at the ceiling with half-closed eyes. He appeared fatigued and seemed to be dozing off.

Ruth glanced at her father and said to Brent, "You're an American, a member of Naval Intelligence Command with no official function in Mossad. But I promise to keep you informed as much as my superiors will permit." She brushed an unruly tendril of hair back from her forehead and lowered her voice, "Where are you staying?" Her eyes caught his and held.

"The Hilton on Hayarkon Street."

"I know where it is. Do you have a car?"

"No. I took a cab."

"They're scarce, Brent."

"I know."

"I'll drive you if you wish."

"I don't want to take you out of your way. Gas is scarce."

"No problem. It's government issue and you're government business." She continued to look up at him unwaveringly.

Staring into her eyes, he was suddenly acutely aware of her sexuality. They were both uncomfortable, like two resigned insects trapped in the same web. It was almost as if they had just agreed upon an unspoken tryst. He wondered about her grief for Herzl. If he had been her lover, the attachment must have been tenuous. Or she was a woman who could shed a man and quickly shop around for a replacement. He had seen it before. After all, Israel had been at war for the young woman's entire lifetime. Inevitably, she had felt the force that shaped them all: the urge of life itself, as abstract, as ruthless, as unsentimental, as inexorable as death, their constant companion.

Brent had learned much about men, women, and

love in wartime. With death so eager to reap his bountiful harvest, life was greedy, too. He had many times said his farewells to courtships and convention. Done away with ritual. Frightened young people under the shadow of the black angel snatch wildly at the flimsiest promise of life. He had found that men and women tend not to "love" in war. Instead, ruthlessly pragmatic, they desire, they demand, they take; conventions, morals, obligations be damned. He wanted Ruth Moskowitz very, very much, and he thought he saw his own desires reflected in her eyes.

The sound of the door opening broke the electricity and they both turned. A slender young nurse in a tight-fitting uniform stepped into the room. Eyeing the big American up and down like a woman in a meat market surveying the choicest cuts, she announced in a husky voice, "Sorry, Commander Ross and ah, ah . . ."

"I'm Ruth Moskowitz," Ruth announced brusquely. And then with a sarcastic twist to her lips, "I wouldn't expect you to remember."

"Oh, yes, yes, of course," the nurse said awkwardly. And then in an attempt to regain her composure, she said firmly, "It's time for you to leave. Colonel Moskowitz must rest."

Brent and Ruth offered their good-byes to the patient and Ruth kissed her father's cheek. Her lips seemed to revitalize him. Eyes flashing with new energy, he raised his head from the pillow and before the pair could leave, his taut voice stopped them, "Remember, Brent, when dealing with the Arabs ask yourself this old Jewish question, 'How can you tell an insane man to reason, a blind man to see?' "

"I know it will be difficult. We've discussed it before, Colonel." Brent smiled. "I'll keep in mind a great

American who said, " 'With reasonable men, I will reason; with humane men I will plead; but to tyrants I will give no quarter.' "

"Why that's William Loyd Garrison," Ruth said, surprising Brent. And then with a hard line altering her delicate jaw, "Prepare to give no quarter, Brent. I'm afraid you'll find reason and humanity in short supply."

"I know. I know," Brent admitted with resignation.

David nodded knowingly and said, "Before you leave, my friend, *mazel tov.*"

Brent smiled and responded in his best Hebrew, *"Shah-lohm-oo-leh-heet-rah-oht."*

"Very good. Very good," David said. Ruth and the nurse chuckled.

As Brent followed Ruth out of the room, the nurse stepped too close. Brent felt a round, firm breast brush against his arm. "You can return tomorrow morning," she said softly.

"Am I invited, too?" Ruth shot at the young woman.

The flustered nurse turned into a room marked Staff and slammed the door behind her.

Corporal Ruth Moskowitz drove an old 1977 Datsun 280Z. Slipping the gear selector into drive, she roared from the curb with so much acceleration Brent was pushed back into the seat. He said, "Have you ever flown off a carrier, Ruth?"

"A carrier?"

"Yes. You'd be good at it."

She laughed. "I can't fly."

"You fooled me."

Slowing for a three truck military convoy which was crossing at the first intersection, she asked, "You in a hurry?"

"What do you have in mind?"

Her giggle was much like a teenage girl who had just heard an off-color joke. "Not that."

"Not what?"

"What you've had on your mind from the first minute you saw me."

"I'm clairvoyant. I was reading your thoughts."

"Touché!" And then laughing, she pushed down hard on the accelerator as the last truck passed and whipped the sports car into a sharp left turn. Glancing at him slyly from the corner of her eye, she said, "You are attractive, Brent."

"You aren't exactly repulsive, Ruth."

"But you must understand, I just don't hop into bed with the first available man."

"Who asked you to?"

"Protecting your maidenhead?"

"Make up your mind. That's supposed to be my line."

She laughed and concentrated on her driving. Although civilian traffic was light, military vehicles were abundant. Shifting down, she changed lanes and whizzed past three trucks and a command car that reminded Brent of a modified Humvee. The trucks were all American-built ten-wheelers.

He looked around. Tel Aviv was the center of the country's commercial and artistic life and in peacetime held over a million people. He did not like it. Despite its Mediterranean flavor, the mundanity of its hodgepodge of ugly square buildings impressed one as the archetypal concrete jungle. In particular its boldness and garishness repulsed Brent, bringing to mind a poor imitation of the Ginza. And the crowds were there, uniformed or in Western dress. He chuckled to himself with a new thought. Maybe, no city could ever please a sailor.

Brent tore his eyes from the city and focused on the girl. "Why aren't you driving a utility car or a Jeep? I've seen a lot of them, even some of the old American Willys Jeeps that are older than I am."

"I can draw one from the motor pool, but I prefer my own Z, and my superiors don't object. After all, there's a terrible shortage of vehicles of all types. I even have military plates."

He noticed the street signs. They were headed south on Petach Tikva Road. The taxi had brought him to the hospital on Shaul Hamelech Boulevard and to return to the Hilton they should be driving west toward the sea. He said, "You're not taking me back to my hotel."

"Right."

"Where are we going?"

"I've changed my mind. Woman's prerogative."

"Changed your mind?"

"Yes, Brent, I'm taking you to some secluded place where I can ravish your body. After all, I've known you for almost an hour."

"You're a sex maniac." He covered his mouth in mock horror.

"That's the best kind. What kind of maniac do you prefer?"

"Can't argue with that."

Her demeanor veered to the serious. "Thought I'd show you some of the sights of our fair city." And then almost as an afterthought, "Do you have the time?"

"Plenty. I've got to wait for Colonel Bernstein, and I hear he's bringing a new aide. We've got to prepare for the conference."

She pounded the steering wheel with open palms and pleaded with near desperation, "Let's not talk about the war, Brent, please."

Taken off guard by the mercurial mood swing, he said hastily, "Lord, I'm with you."

She took his hand and her voice softened, "Just the two of us sight-seeing—right? A boy and a girl on their first date. No killing, no bombs, no shells—just a boy and a girl, maybe falling in love." Eyes wide, she looked straight ahead.

He was sure her eyes were misting. And then an eerie realization struck with the force of his alarm on *Yonaga* awakening him for a midwatch. The girl was playing out a fantasy, a golden dream, a refuge from a lifetime of war, death, and hate. At the moment he was her sanctuary, a haven where she could hide from the horror of reality. Of course her mind—her abrupt changes in temperament were not quite normal. But who was in wartime?

He played to her, "Right. I'm with you. We're on our first date and I'm a stranger in town."

The gay, sprightly girl returned, bright and chirpy like a little silver sparrow. "Oh, wonderful. But you're the handsome stranger."

"If you insist."

"No, your looks insist."

"Thanks. There's no shortage of beauty on your end of the seat."

"You like my butt?"

"I wasn't talking about that."

"I know, but do you like it?"

"Nothing better this side of the Louvre."

She giggled, too long and too hard. But, she was under control and seemed to be enjoying herself. "Thanks. There's some of the poet in you." And then in her little girl's naive voice, "Why do men like big butts?"

"Not big, well shaped."

"Like mine."

"Right."

"Someplace to get a good grip, Brent?"

"And to sink your teeth."

"Ah, that was the poet." They both laughed. She continued in a candid mien, "You know Brent, you have a great sense of humor. You can be a lot of fun."

"You don't know how much."

"Back in bed?"

"Why not?"

She laughed. "Do you realize we've talked about nothing but sex?"

"I understand that subject occupies the human psyche on rare occasions."

She let the challenge slip by and stabbed a finger straight ahead. "We're headed for Old Jaffa. Know anything about it? We'll be there in a few minutes."

"A little. Like the average tourist."

Brent and Colonel Bernstein had flown low over Jaffa and Tel Aviv when their Douglas DC-6 had landed at Ben-Gurion Airport. "Jaffa is the oldest port in the world, founded by Japhet, the son of Noah," Bernstein had said solemnly like a tour guide. He had gestured dramatically at the domes and minarets, "That's where it all started, Brent. But the founders of modern Israel decided to move the center of their culture to the scrubby sand dunes to the north. Those sand dunes are now called Tel Aviv."

With traffic light, Ruth raced south on Old Jaffa Road. She asked Brent about his boyhood. Seemed fascinated when he told her of his peripatetic life, following his father who was a military attaché all over the world. He avoided *Yonaga* and the war.

"You must speak many languages, Brent?"

"Yes. I was lucky. My parents insisted I attend local schools whenever possible. I have a handshaking acquaintance with French, German, Italian, Greek, and

60

Japanese."

"And, ah." A mischievous smile twisted the full lips, *"Hah-m'dah-Eev-reet?"*

He pondered a moment. "You asked me something about Hebrew. Probably if I can speak it, too."

"Very good. You have a good mind, Brent. I heard you say your 'good-byes' to my father in Hebrew."

He laughed. "Thanks. I'm glad you were impressed. But I've only learned a few words and phrases. Only what Colonel Bernstein and Mr. Berlitz have taught me. You have a tough language." He gazed at her perfect profile for a long moment while she nodded understanding. From the side her resemblance to Sarah Aranson was striking. He shook the ghost from his head and said, "Speaking of language, your English is too good—too colloquial—to have been learned in Israeli schools."

"Mossad sent me to Washington when I first joined. I divided my time between the Israeli Embassy, the Pentagon, and CIA Headquarters, and I spent two summers at Columbia taking English Lit."

The street narrowed and she slowed. "This is old Jaffa." Gesturing to the right she continued, "The clock tower." Then circling the small heart of the old town she pointed out the Great Mosque, the museum, and the ancient Armenian convent.

All the buildings were jammed together, old and in disrepair. Most were built of masonry, weathered an ugly, gray-streaked black by time and the incessant attacks of salt air. Not even a scattering of smart shops and restaurants could dispel the atmosphere of decay. Some of the pedestrians were in Western dress, others in Arab garb: men in loose fitting caftans and burnooses; women all in black, only hands and face visible to the world.

"You're not impressed," she said, completing the

circle and heading north along the coast.

"It's an important part of history," he said noncommittally. "There are a lot of Arabs here."

"Yes."

"You can trust them?"

"We have good Arab citizens. These are *madanis*."

"Townspeople?" Brent hazarded.

"Very good. Most of them are Druze. Some even serve in the IDF and have fought alongside us since 1948."

"Against the Sunni and Shi'ite. Those Shi'ites are the fanatics—the most dangerous."

"Right! And our Druze hate them."

"The PLO will kill them."

"It's a real problem even with the protection of the Army." Gesturing to the vast blue expanse of the Mediterranean that stretched to the western horizon, she returned to the oasis of her other world. "Beautiful, isn't it?"

He took the cue. "Yes. Yes," he said softly. "There's nothing like it."

"You must love the sea," she said ruefully. "You're so free out there—have so much room and it's clean."

"Love the sea?" he said as if he were asking himself. "At times, true. All sailors must or they give it up." He tugged on his ear, "But she can be a violent mistress."

"Isn't that the best kind?"

"I wasn't talking about that."

Laughing and talking they roared north up Hayarkon Street to the huge tower of the Hilton. It was less than a ten-minute drive.

"Care to come up," he asked as Ruth whipped the little sports car into a parking space.

"You want to lay me."

"Better than watching 'Brady Bunch' reruns."

"Can't argue with that."

Side by side they walked through the entrance, crossed the lobby, and entered an elevator.

On the seventh floor, his apartment had a magnificent view of the Mediterranean. Actually a suite, it had a living room with two enormous windows giving on the sea, a small kitchenette, bedroom, and bath. The furnishings were of the usual cold plastic and chrome of most of the world's hotels. However, a plump sofa was placed near the windows. Fronting the sofa was a low table with a simulated marble top and Formica legs that were supposed to fool one into believing they were made of walnut.

Sighing, Ruth sank onto the sofa and dropped her head back onto the soft cushion. "Drink?" Brent asked, heading for the kitchen which was separated from the living room by only a short two-stool bar.

"Love one."

"Scotch?"

"You have scotch?"

"Chivas Regal."

"It's a miracle."

"How would you like it?"

"Neat on ice, please. No sense in spoiling it."

"Your American background shows," he said, placing a bottle, two glasses and a bowl of ice on an artificial silver tray.

He crossed the room in a half-dozen long strides, placed the tray on the table and sank down on the sofa next to her. He free-poured two identical drinks, both doubles. They picked up their drinks.

He raised his and she countered, barely touching rims. Her glass trembled slightly. The tense soldier was back. She gestured to the sea, brilliant under the flat Mediterranean sunshine, warm rays playfully caressing tiny wavelets with crowns of diamonds. It looked like a deep blue carpet scattered with precious stones. Brent loved the sea in the late afternoon. This was when it was most beautiful.

Struck by the beauty, she said softly and with unexpected seriousness, "To peace, as deep and eternal as the sea."

He remembered a traditional toast Bernstein had used for years, *L'chayim.*"

She grinned and repeated, *L'chayim.*"

He drank half of his drink, she emptied her glass as if she had inhaled it. He recharged it. Looking deep into his eyes, she raised her glass. "This will sound corny, Brent, but, to us."

"To us, a long and enduring, ah — friendship."

"Friendship."

They both emptied their glasses. He replenished them and eyed her through the corner of his eye. She had drunk over four ounces of hard liquor within a minute. It should take effect quickly. And it did. Sighing, she sank down into the embrace of the couch much like a balloon with a puncture. Her tensions seemed to be escaping. Maybe the soldier would leave and the vivacious young girl return.

"I feel better," she said. This time she only sipped her drink and then swirled the amber fluid around the glass until it peaked and the ice cubes clinked. Then she stopped, holding the glass before her, watching the fine scotch drift down the sides of the glass. "You're delightful and I like you, Brent."

"I like you."

"Can we ever be the boy and the girl?" she asked wistfully.

"Of course."

"Falling in love?"

"Why not? It wouldn't be hard to do."

"You're sweet. It has happened that way, some-where on this earth, hasn't it?" She waved. "I mean, there haven't always been wars to separate people, to kill people. I know. I've read history books." She drank and took his hand, ran her fingers up his wrist and rubbed the hair on his muscular forearm. "Lord, you're a sexy bastard."

"You do all right, yourself."

"You want to know if Avraham Herzl was my lover." It was a statement, not a question.

"That's not necessary."

She shook her head. "He was."

"Did you love him?"

There was resignation in her shrug. "What's that?"

It was one of mankind's oldest and toughest ques-tion, but he tried, "When a man and a woman want each other more than anything else on earth and com-mit to a lifetime together."

Her laugh was bitter. "Here? In this place? Do you know how many Avraham Herzls I've had?" She emp-tied her glass. Silently, he refilled only half of it. She continued, the words rolling off her tongue with a slight slur, "There were three others, all young, all bright, and now all dead." She looked at him, eyes narrow, darkened by shadows. "Don't fall for me, Brent. I'm dangerous. I'm a curse—a hex."

"Nonsense," he said, raising her hand and kissing the soft flesh. And then smiling, "You're the best thing that's happened to me since I came to Israel."

She looked down at the table and slowly circled her glass on the slick top, imprinting rings of interlocking moisture. There was a new hard line to her mouth and a frown to the set of her eyes. "You noticed those blue numbers on my father's arm?"

"Yes. Colonel Bernstein has his. German concen-tration camps."

"My father spent two years in Dachau." Her voice broke and her eyes filled, making them huge and glistening, a single tear spilled over the lid and clung to the thick dark lashes like a drop of morning dew. She returned to her drink like one seeking strength.

"Please, don't Ruth," he pleaded. "Why relive it?"

"Every Jew will relive it for all time." A big gulp almost emptied her glass. "You know, Hitler really won."

"I don't understand."

"He killed six million of us, didn't he? Murdered us, cremated us, turned us into lampshades."

He wanted to say something, anything to break her mood. But he knew it was useless. Better to let her pour it out. Maybe, the words would be a catharsis, a temporary cleansing, if nothing else.

"Then he won, Brent. He won. Don't you understand?"

He sipped his drink, stared at the distraught girl. "I understand this, you're giving him another victory."

She looked up. "Why?"

"Because he's claiming you, too. The poison of hatred, bitterness can kill you as dead as Zyklon B."

"All Jews are bitter."

"Of course." He took her hand. "But once Colonel Bernstein put the Holocaust into a different perspective — a perspective that, I'm sure, has helped him live with it."

"How? What?"

"I saw him kill a German, a Nazi named Werner Schlieben, in a knife fight. I'll never forget what he said as he stood over Schlieben's body." She looked at him expectantly. "He said, 'It can't be avenged. It's only a lesson. That's what it will always be. A lesson taught six million times over.' " Kissing her forehead, he found a patina of moisture. "Does that make sense?"

"Yes. I think so, Brent."

He was pleased, her mood was swinging back. "Can you think that way?"

She ran her fingers lightly over his cheek. "I'll try, dear Brent, because it does seem wise and sensible." Then sighing, she said, "You have one helluva big mind to go with that great body."

He laughed and kissed her hair, the hard spot behind her ear.

"Oooh, that gives me goose bumps." Twisting away, she smiled up at him, tracing fingers over his corded neck. The shadows vanished from her eyes and the little girl began to break through, "Did I tell you you're a sexy bastard?"

"Yes. But I don't mind repetition."

"Play it again Sam?" She giggled.

"Why not." He glanced at his watch with exaggerated seriousness. "After all, memories of our relationship stretch back almost two hours now." He poured a small amount of scotch into her glass and added two fresh ice cubes.

She laughed and drank. Her words seemed oiled and slippery again, "You must think I'm suffering from MPS."

"MPS?" He scratched his head. He knew what she meant, but decided to feign ignorance and reach for humor. "Does that have something to do with the female cycle?" he asked seriously.

It worked. Her laughter was deep and she rocked forward and backward unsteadily, spilling some of her drink on the table. He braced her with a hand to the shoulder. "No, dear Brent," she gasped. "You're thinking of PMS. Same letters, different order. MPS is Multiple Personality Syndrome."

He weighed her words for a moment. She was obviously becoming very drunk, but her mind still seemed sharp. He said, "We all, in a way, have our MPS, different faces for different people and situations."

Slumping back as if her bones were wilting, she said, "You're very kind, Brent, and sometime, when I haven't been drinking, explain it to me." She held up her glass. "You're trying to get me drunk, aren't you?"

"Not really."

"Oh, yes you are." Still looking at him she tried to table her drink. He caught her hand before she could spill it and did it for her. "You'll make me drunk and then lay me. Right?"

"Wrong."

"Wrong?" She was a hurt little girl. "I don't understand. That's all you had on your mind."

"You're very desirable."

"Then why haven't you kissed me—I mean on the mouth, really come on to me?" She raised her lips and circled his neck with her arms.

He brushed her lips with his, but she pushed hard against him, pulling him down on top of her. Her tongue slipped between his lips and his responded, touching, twisting, searching. Electricity prickled on the back of his neck, and he felt heat at the base of his spine.

Moaning, she pulled away slightly. Lips still touching his, she whispered, "I'm not wearing a brassiere."

"That's the first thing I noticed."

They giggled into each other's mouths and the hard, searching kisses returned. She took his hand and guided it to her breast. It was hard, round and pulsed up and down with her rapid breathing. Her other hand drifted downward, found his turgid manhood and grasped it. He winced, felt the jump in his chest and the heat mount up his spine. She gasped with delight.

Then Brent did something he would never completely understand. The girl was near a breakdown or was actually in the midst of one, had drunk too much, had just lost her lover, and her father was seriously wounded. She had little family and, apparently, few friends. She was more than vulnerable, she was helpless. What was happening was very wrong, nearly obscene. Was he moral? Ethical? He thought all those things had gone by the board years ago. But something ineffable pulled him away. Maybe he was having his own breakdown. He sat up and then pulled Ruth up into a sitting position.

"What's wrong, Brent?" she asked, palming tendrils of hair back from her forehead. "I thought you wanted sex. I certainly know you're ready."

He shook his head. "I want you so much it hurts."

She grabbed his big biceps with both hands and pushed a breast against him and spoke with her lips brushing his ear, "Then, why? Why?"

He gestured at the glass. "You've drunk too much, lost Herzl, your father's wounded—had too damned many shocks for one person."

A look of astonishment crossed her face. "You have honor? Chivalry? Incredible! I thought they were casualties of war."

"I don't know what I have, but I know if we go to bed now, it would degrade both of us, maybe end whatever we have between us. Couldn't it?"

She shook her head. "I don't know. I don't know, dear Brent. I've never met anyone like you." She kissed his cheek. "But I don't want it to end. You're too precious." And then plaintively, "When can I see you again?"

"Anytime. You know I'm waiting for Bernstein."

She ran her hands through his hair and kissed him

69

full on the lips. Her breath was very sour. "I can't see you tomorrow, but two nights from now. Friday night, at my apartment. I'll fix you a special dinner. 1800 hours."

"It's a date."

She came to her feet, weaving, a reed in a strong wind. She clasped her forehead, "Whew! I can really feel that scotch." And then with a panicky look, "Where's the bathroom?"

Instead of pointing, he took her by the arm and pulled her to the hall. She almost fell, staggering through the doorway to the bathroom. Within seconds, he was holding her forehead as she leaned over the toilet and vomited. The room was filled with the sour smell of half-digested lunch and raw scotch. Now he knew he had made the right decision.

Finally, she straightened, moved to the sink, rinsed out her mouth and washed her face. While she dried her face, he flushed the toilet. Brushing back her hair, she said, "Romantic as hell, wasn't I?"

Holding her, he laughed into her ear, "I'm not objecting." He kissed her neck.

"You were right, Brent. This would've been the wrong time." And then waving at the toilet with disgust, "Still want to see me after that?"

"Someday you may do the same for me."

She looked into his eyes reflected in the mirror. "You always say the right thing. You'd be easy to love, Brent."

"You, too."

Long hair brushed neatly back, she turned to him. "But not in the bathroom. Too damned uncomfortable. Knobs, faucets and stuff." She managed a weak giggle.

"Can't argue with that."

She kissed him and walked to the doorway. She was

70

still very unsteady.

"I'll drive you home."

"No. Not necessary." From behind, he clasped both of her shoulders and shook her. "Sorry, I'll take a cab. After all, I must outweigh you by over a hundred pounds, so don't try to argue."

"You're right." Then, she mimicked him, "Can't argue with that."

"A wise decision and I like your choice of words," he said.

She traced a line across his cheek with a single finger and followed the line with gentle, soft kisses. "Have you ever been to Jerusalem, Brent?"

"No. Why?"

"It's beautiful."

"I didn't know a city could be beautiful."

"You have the heart of a sailor."

"Certainly possible."

"Maybe, Friday we could go. It's a beautiful drive and then we could have dinner here."

"I have work to do. The meeting in Tripoli, you know."

"You must've studied your briefing papers a hundred times by now. You need a break."

The girl was right. He was weary of the same material. "I'll phone you," he said.

"Early."

"Yes, early."

Her smile was brilliant, warm as a summer's day. She was feeling much better. "I'll stay sober and I'll be good."

He smiled, a slow tender expression. "I might argue with that."

He kissed her through her giggles and left.

71

Three

Colonel Irving Bernstein had changed little during the seven years Brent had known him. True, new lines had crept onto his craggy face and his hair, which had been gray-white when Brent first met him, was now a brilliant white, as if a fine layer of snow had powdered his head. He still wore the desert fatigues and combat boots he always favored.

When Brent had answered his knock he grabbed the colonel around the shoulders and hugged him, crying out the traditional greeting, *"Sholem aleichem."*

The Israeli hugged Brent and pounded his back, answering with his own, *"Aleichem sholem!"*

That was when Brent had noticed the stranger standing to one side in the hall. He was a tall, angular young man with a grin as wide as sunrise and friendly sparkling blue eyes. In dress blues, his sleeves flashed one-and-one-half gold stripes of a lieutenant junior grade, and there were aviator's wings on his tunic. The Department of Parks badge worn by all members of Fujita's forces on their dress uniforms was visible on his left shoulder, and the gold chrysanthemum indicating *Yonaga's* ship's company fronted the peaked cap he held under his arm. He looked familiar, and

Brent felt he should know this man, but he could not place him.

Standing back from his friend, Bernstein grasped the stranger by the arm and said, "Commander Brent Ross, this is Lieutenant Elroy Rubin."

Brent shook Rubin's hand and said, "Glad to meet you, Lieutenant."

"Likewise, Commander," the young man drawled in low leisurely tones that spoke of a lifetime spent south of the Mason-Dixon line. "Came a far piece to meet you, sir."

Brent ushered the two men in. Pulling up a chair, he sat opposite the newcomers who seated themselves on the couch. Bernstein placed an attaché case on the table, unsnapped its two locks with loud metallic sounds, and lifted the lid. "Lieutenant Rubin's our new aide, Brent. Did a good job at Geneva with me. Made my job easier. Took a ton of detail off my shoulders." Bernstein began sorting through stacks of documents.

"Welcome aboard, Lieutenant," Brent said to Rubin.

"Thank you, Commander. Them Arabs are sure ornery critters to deal with, nothin' but flannel-mouth talk."

"Rubin. Rubin," Brent said to himself, meditatively. "We've met, should've met in Japan, or are you new to our forces?" Brent avoided the word *recruit* which all new men loathed.

"No, sir. I'm no greenhorn an' I spec't you're thinkin' of my brother, Marv."

It came back with a rush. Ensign Marvin Rubin from the vast cattle lands of southwestern Texas. One of Air Group Commander Yoshi Matsuhara's bright young pilots, *Oberleutnant* Rudolph "Tiger Shark" Stoltz had blown his head off with a squirt of 20-mil-

73

limeter in the great air battle south of Iwo Jima six months earlier. He recalled how his most valued, closest friend, Commander Yoshi Matsuhara, had praised the young Rubin: "Great talent. Smart. Someday, he'll be one of our best pilots." Then, in his first battle, Rubin had been decapitated, and his corpse lay fathoms deep in the cold, black Pacific with legions of other fine young men.

Now a new Rubin, bright, friendly and, Brent guessed, as intelligent as his dead brother despite their legacy of ruptured idiom and outrageous syntax. Brent knew Marvin Rubin had used his colorful cattleman's lexicon to cloak a sharp, trenchant intelligence. In a way, he had reminded Brent of the great Chuck Yeager, one of the world's most talented pilots and aeronautical geniuses who seemed to enjoy hiding behind the facade of the simple country boy from West Virginia. Brent suspected Elroy Rubin was cut from the same cloth. After all, the wings he wore showed he had accomplished much with his life.

"I knew your brother," Brent said simply. "He was a good man and a fine pilot."

"Right kind of you, sir. Marv had gumption." The warm eyes turned as cold as a tomb. "There's a yeller skunk out yonder name of Stoltz whose hankerin' to 'ave his hide staked out."

"Yes," Brent agreed. "There are some debts to be paid." Then hunching forward, "How long have you been serving with us?"

"Nigh on a year, sir."

"Strange we haven't met." He gestured at Rubin's cap, which was laying on the table. "You're ship's company."

"Don't pay it no mind, Commander. After trainin' at Tsuchiura I was detached and assigned to Fighter Eight at Makurazaki. We sport the flower, too."

74

"The southern tip of Kyushu?"

"Keerect, sir. I never bunked on *Yonaga*."

Now Brent understood. Of course. The man had been one of over 200 pilots assigned to home defense, patrolling between the home islands and the Marianas. Others protected Tokyo Bay and other key areas and installations. With the Self Defense Force virtually wiped out by a savage carrier strike in 1986 and the surviving units shot through with *Rengo Sekigun* (Japanese Red Army) agents, only men like the Rubin brothers and hosts of others who flocked from all over the world to Admiral Fujita's standards stood between freedom and slavery.

And there had been little help from the politicians. Brent, Fujita, and the other officers had been outraged by the Diet. Hating politicians even more than reporters, Fujita had declared repeatedly: "All politicians should be beheaded!"

"Just after the lawyers," Brent had added.

Old Admiral Fujita had nodded, old parchmentlike skin rearranging its wrinkles into what passed for a grin, "And don't forget the reporters, Brent-san." Then the entire staff laughed uproariously at the admiral's rare quip.

Actually, there had been little humor to be found in the government. Fujita and his officers had been incensed by the bombastic speeches inevitably followed by the inability to act, to show leadership, or even a spark of courage. With ultraconservatives clashing with antiwar isolationists, and socialists and communist adding to the stew, the Diet had been in virtual grid-lock for years. The fact that after nine years of bloody warfare a declaration of war had not been made, defied reason-sanity. But the pacifists, goaded by communists and terrorists, always blocked the way, waving Article Nine of the constitution, screaming

"War is unconstitutional!" Admiral Fujita and his officers would throw up their hands and groan in rage and frustration.

However, Brent had been delighted with Emperor Akihito and his late father, Emperor Hirohito, who had backed Admiral Fujita with the full power and prestige of the Chrysanthemum Throne. Through their efforts the convenient though ludicrous designation of *Yonaga* as a national monument had funneled money through the Department of Parks, and troops and supplies had been made available as long as their use complied with the Diet's definition of "defensive uses." Of course, Admiral Fujita had stretched this interpretation to suit his own strategic and tactical needs, politicians be damned.

Brent glanced at Bernstein. Jaw tight with frustration, the Israeli was still riffling through his papers. Something was troubling the man, big and ominous. Brent knew him too well to miss a hint in the rigid body language, the shadowy things that moved in the depths of his dark gaze when bad news upset him. His preoccupation with the contents of his attaché case was typical. Yet, as usual, Brent expected him to skirt around it at first, discussing other things before he finally trudged into the swamp.

Brent turned to the young American flyer. "Your training, Elroy. Where did you learn to fly?"

"My father ran a big cattle spread, sir—almost a whole county. He had two Cessnas—we needed 'em. I started flyin' when I was knee-high to a ground hog." He described his early experiences in the air. His enrollment in the Confederate Air Force's new flying school in Corpus Christi which had been established after the orbiting of the Chinese laser system. He was eighteen at the time. Here he flew almost every piston-engined aircraft in the world. He specialized in fighters. Brent could tell from the timbre of the man's voice, the slight flush of excitement that colored his cheeks, that Rubin loved flying. Also, it was obvious, he liked to fight. Brent wondered about the man's combat experience.

Bernstein answered the unvoiced thought without looking up from his documents. "Lieutenant Rubin has four kills—two Messerschmitt 109s, a Heinkel 111, and a Cessna."

"I'm obliged, sir. With your permission, Colonel, I only cold-cocked three."

"Three?"

"Yes, sir. The Cessna don't count. Like shootin' a hog in its wallo'."

Brent laughed. Irving continued his search. Then the Israeli sighed a long "Aah," followed by, "Here it is."

"What?" Brent wondered if this was the bad news he suspected Bernstein was preparing to break.

"Your copy of the minutes of our last meeting, Brent. We had a tough time at Geneva." He handed Brent a thick sheaf of papers.

"How tough?" Brent glanced at the documents.

"The Arabs were inflexible. They still insist that you and I come to Tripoli or," he turned his palms upward in a hopeless gesture, "or no talks."

Brent let air escape through his teeth with a slight whistling sound. "Real tough."

"I declare, them Arabs could shuck the hair off'n a man's balls, sir," Rubin offered in a soft matter-of-fact voice.

Despite the grim news, Brent almost laughed at the young man's colorful vernacular. "What about Sheik Iman Younis?" Brent asked. "He seemed reasonable—ah, for an Arab."

Bernstein nodded. "He guarantees our safety."

"What is Admiral Fujita's opinion?"

"He leaves it up to us."

"Our decision." Brent pounded the table, forehead etched by the force of his thoughts. "Do you think we should do it, Irving?"

"There are a lot of lives at stake."

"Ours, too."

"I know, Brent."

Brent stopped the drumming and rubbed his jaw, pulling his mouth to the side like a man in pain. "I say go."

"Trust them?"

"Of course not. But we've got to try."

"I agree." Bernstein glanced at Rubin "And you, Lieutenant, you're a player, too. You're not compelled to go."

"We sure 'nuff could get dry-gulched by them no account, sheep-killin' dogs."

"True."

"But y'all are fixin' to ante up?"

"Right."

"Then, deal me in, Colonel."

Brent rose, went to the kitchen and returned with a carafe of coffee, cups, sugar, and canned milk. Each man poured his own and sipped. "Needed this," Bernstein said.

Brent said to Rubin, "Admiral Fujita personally selected you."

"Yes, sir."

"But Commander Matsuhara needs you. He's training new pilots."

"Shoot, I know, sir. I near begged myself to death like a hound dog at the supper table to get this here assignment — tol' 'em I could spot planes better'n a starvin' hawk huntin' a rat's ass. Sharp eyeballs an' the like, sir."

Brent laughed. "Can't believe that convinced Fujita, but I'm glad you're here Lieutenant."

"I'm obliged, sir."

Brent turned to Bernstein. "Our occupation of the Canary Islands?"

"It's working, Brent. We've landed a full division on the two main islands, Tenerife and Gran Canaria."

"A division? That's not enough."

"You know the Diet. We're lucky we got them. They would've sent two troops of Boy Scouts and Mother Teresa."

Brent let the weak attempt at humor slip past. He shook his head, "We're holding a million people hostage."

"But, Brent, the Arabs hold Saipan and Tinian."

"I know. I know. But now we're no better than our enemies."

Sighing, Bernstein rubbed his wrinkled forehead. "In war you seldom are, my friend. Killing is the great homogenizer."

"I can't buy that."

"I'm glad you can't, Brent." Bernstein gripped the sleeve of his shirt. Brent knew six blue tattooed numbers were under the hand. "This world needs its idealists." He smiled sadly. "My altruism went up the stack at Auschwitz years ago."

Shifting his weight uncomfortably, Brent brought the exchange back to strategic matters. "Realistically, then, Colonel, we've got to put our invasion of the Marianas on hold."

Bernstein was the calculating officer again. "True. But strategic imperatives have forced our hand."

The Israeli sipped his hot coffee with a soft slurping sound, and Brent felt disquieted by the shadows that still lurked in the dark gaze. Was it memories of the concentration camps? Brent thought not. Something

79

else was gnawing at the Israeli. The deep trouble he first suspected still seethed there, unvoiced.

Bernstein continued, "We have excellent fields on the islands of Tenerife and Gran Canaria and our long-range bombers can reach Libya."

"But they don't have the range to return."

"I know, Brent, but we can range Gibraltar, force Kadafi's battle groups to exit the Med through the Red Sea, track them easily with American nuclear-powered submarines patrolling the Gulf of Aden." Bernstein glanced at a document. "We have six fighter squadrons and three bomber squadrons operational in the Canary Islands. And fuel is no problem. The islands are oil rich."

"But supplies?"

"How long were you in the Ben-Gurion Line?"

"Two weeks."

"Our second convoy made Las Palmas last week." The Israeli explained how Britain was sending supplies and Spanish merchant ships were also allowed to dock at the principal port of Las Palmas. "Anyway," Bernstein concluded, "the islands produce most of their own food—no one is starving. You know we wouldn't allow that."

Brent was not yet convinced. During staff meetings, he had repeatedly spoken out against the occupation of the Canary Islands, pointing out the difficulty of supply and the necessity to strip home defense forces of aircraft. And the invasions of Saipan and Tinian must be postponed. But Fujita argued that the Spanish, who were busy licking Kadafi's boots to insure their supply of oil, would be no problem and the Marianas invasion could wait.

Bernstein remembered the heated debates. "Three weeks ago our fighters based on Kyushu turned back four converted Arab DC-6s and two Constellations—

shot down two and damaged the others."

"I know."

"So Fujita's right."

"Thus far."

"And Brent, the Spanish won't attack our forces in the Canary Islands. They only have one small helicopter carrier left—an old converted American escort carrier. Don't forget, they sold their one large fleet carrier, the *Reina de Ibérico,* to the Arabs last year. They'd be massacred."

Brent stared at his drink and shook his head, doubt and reservation edging his voice. "And I know Fujita said we'd withdraw if the Arabs pull out of the Marianas."

"Right. He's put the proposal in writing and sent it to the UN."

"Fat chance, Colonel. The Arabs won't do it."

The Israeli shrugged. "Could tie prisoner exchange to the whole deal. Fifty, sixty Arabs or more for one of ours. After all, we hold forty-two Arabs, the Israelis have three thousand and we are bargaining for only twenty-five of our aircrews and three hundred Israelis."

Brent shook his head. He had known the Arabs too long, met with them, negotiated with them. Such a disproportionate exchange would be a loss of "face" and "face" was as important to Arabs as it was to the Japanese. He felt trapped, like a man pursued by hoodlums and blocked by a brick wall at the end of an alley. "Won't work. They'll hold out for other concessions—the Canaries."

"We must try."

"I know."

"And you know Brent the Spanish government has taken it to the UN?"

"Months ago."

81

"Well, last week there was another vote in the Security Council."

"I heard, Colonel. The US and Britain blocked it."

"Right. And you know this will happen every time the Arabs and their lackeys bring up a resolution." A sardonic twist to his lips removed all humor from his chuckle, "After all, Saipan and Tinian were once Spanish."

Rubin broke his silence. "No one hunkers down to the UN, no-how."

"True," Brent agreed. "But don't forget those million people on the Canary Islands." Brent felt a sharp stab of pain in the back of his neck like a muscle cramping after too much exercise. Slowly and deliberately he rubbed the knobs of hard vertebrae and bunched muscles until he felt the skin heat from the friction. The pain eased. "Now, more than ever, we must go to Tripoli—meet with them, make progress or there's going to be another bloody showdown and this time it may involve the Spanish."

"I know. We leave the day after tomorrow."

"Saturday?

"Yes. I arranged for the flight yesterday."

Brent's eyes narrowed and then a slight smile turned up the corners of his mouth. The pain vanished. "Then, you knew, you sly old con man." He slapped the table so hard the coffee cups rattled, "You knew I'd go."

The Israeli laughed. "Of course I knew. After all, I've known you for a lot of years."

"But you maneuvered me."

"Why not, you've done the same to me."

Brent sipped his coffee thoughtfully. "NIC reports Kadafi's got *Reina de Ibérico* and *Magid* ready for sea."

"Right. Confirmed by Mossad and they've renamed

the *Reina de Ibérico, Al Marj.*" A troubled look pulled down the corners of Bernstein's mouth and his eyes became slits. Brent knew bad news was coming. "There's a nasty rumor, Brent."

"What?"

"The Russian Republic has sold the carrier *Baku,* and cruisers *Dzerzhinsky* and *Zhdanov* to the Alexandria Scrap Iron and Metals Company."

"Oh, no. That's just a cover."

"I know."

"And I thought the Ukraine claimed ownership of the Black Sea Fleet."

"These ships were based at Murmansk and, anyway, both of the cruisers date back to the early fifties."

Brent nodded. "I know — about sixteen thousand tons, twelve six-inch guns. Fast. Very formidable." Brent pounded both armrests with his big fists. "Damn! What happened to *glasnost* and *detente?*"

Rubin came to life, "Tits on a boar, sir."

Brent rolled his knuckles together nervously. *"Baku's* of the same class as *Magid.* Almost forty thousand tons, can operate sixty to seventy aircraft — modern, got the latest radar." He slapped the table. "They'll have three modern fleet carriers and with *Babur,* three cruisers against *Yonaga* and *Bennington.*" He punished the table some more. "Ah shit, won't those bastards ever stop?"

A heavy silence filled the room. All three men drank, reflecting gravely. Then Bernstein managed to shock his companions out of their doldrums. "The U.S. Navy has stricken the *New Jersey* from the lists and it looks like we have her."

Both Brent and Elroy straightened. Brent found the enormity of the good news coming on the heels of so much depressing information all but overwhelming.

With near reverence he whispered as if he were alone in a sacred place, "Nine sixteen-inch guns, fifty-seven thousand tons, thirty-three knots." Then, eyes flashing with new energy he almost accosted the Mossad agent, "We'd have a real heavyweight punch. But how do you know? How can you be sure? I've heard nothing from NIC."

"According to my reports, the deal's almost complete. She's been bought by our cover, the East Asia Scrap Iron Works."

Brent sagged and the timbre of his voice dropped. "It'll take months to tow her from Puget Sound all the way across the Pacific."

"Negative. Her engines are in perfect shape. According to my reports, they were never really mothballed. In fact, the entire ship is in nearly perfect fighting trim."

"The crew?"

"So far, all American. Even some of the original plank owners are volunteering."

Brent sighed. "Lord we can use her. She'd make a big difference." And then hunching forward: "You're sure?"

The Israeli shrugged. "My sources are unimpeachable. It looks very good. In fact, she may be underway already."

"Great! Great!" Then Brent laughed, hard and almost out of control as if the roller coaster of emotions had overwhelmed him.

"What's funny?"

He stabbed a finger at Elroy and then Bernstein. "Can't you see." He rocked back and forth, *"Yonaga* sank *New Jersey* at Pearl Harbor. Took over a year to raise her and repair her." He slapped his head. "What irony. Now she's on our side."

"Shoot, Commander," Elroy said. "This here is

the craziest world there ever was."

Brent nodded, drank, and brought himself back under control. He wiped his cheek with the back of his hand.

"Put succinctly," Bernstein said, chuckling. He eyed Brent who now sat with a quiet smile on his face and then a new thought wiped the grin from the Israeli's face. The gray-green eyes darkened as if black shades had been drawn in their depths. Very bad news was coming, far worse than the cruisers and carrier. Brent could read it in his friend's slumping shoulders, sagging visage, downcast eyes. Bernstein spoke with a grimness that sent the humor flying, "There's another rumor that is very disturbing." He pulled a single document from his attaché case. "Two of our Druze operatives working out of Chad report some more mysterious activity near Rabta."

"I thought our B-25 strike wrecked most of their gas works — at least that's what we've been hearing lately. The reports have been so damned mixed — confusing," Brent said.

"Possibly, but as you say, the reports have been mixed." He tugged on the tip of the spade of whiskers hanging from his chin, "But, that isn't it. It's something else. Something horrible. Atomic bombs."

Silence filled the room like an polar wind. Brent felt the chill penetrate all the way to the marrow of his bones. He thought he would shiver like a man with malaria in his blood. "Can't believe it," he blurted. "I thought every nuclear power agreed to the Non-Proliferation Treaty. Israel, India, Pakistan, South Africa, China, England, France — all of them surrendered their nuclear weapons to the UN's special commission."

"They did, but we have unconfirmed reports the Libyans are developing their own bombs at Rabta."

And then bitterly, "We even demolished our nuclear reactor and weapons center at Dimona a year before the *jihad* began, all because of pressure from that damned UN and the United States."

Brent slapped his head, Rubin pounded his knee. Brent said, "The Arabs are in violation of the treaty?"

"Of course, they're Arabs. What do you expect?'

"They don't have the technology," Brent persisted.

Bernstein looked at the documents. "They have the help of thirteen companies, most of them German, but one is American."

"But they still couldn't get the state-of-the-art technology from the U.S. that they need to produce U-235 weapons-grade uranium. Not even the Russians would help them with that, I'm sure."

"That's right, Brent. According to my reports they've gone back to the very first process that ever worked, electromagnetic separation."

Elroy Rubin entered, showing his keen mind. "You mean they're fixin' to use calutrons to separate isotopes from uranium, Colonel?"

"Right."

"Calutrons!" Brent exclaimed. "Why they're offshoots of the first cyclotrons used by the University of California. Jesus, that was a long time ago."

"Correct. You don't need gaseous centrifuges, supercomputers, and other exotic equipment if you use calutrons. They're slow, but they're easier to build than any other enrichment process known. Why they're basically nothing but twelve-foot discs with forty-ton magnets."

"That stuff is near fifty years old and, leastwise, you still gotta have vacuum pumps, iron cores and copper wires for the magnets," Rubin said, the droll Texan vanishing, replaced by the sharp intellect of the well-informed man.

"And you need highly skilled machinists," Brent added.

Bernstein tugged on his lower lip. "I know. Remember, this isn't 1945. All those things are available on the world market, if you have the money, and the Arabs are drowning in dollars." He punched his open palm for emphasis, "There are a lot of unemployed Russian scientists and technicians shopping around for work."

Brent said, "It takes about thirty pounds of enriched uranium to build one bomb and to get that much you need hundreds — maybe thousands of tons of pitchblende."

"That's right. Some is mined in southern Libya and we know there are huge deposits in the Sudan. Pitchblende isn't hard to find, its's a question of building the industrial capacity to refine it. Mossad figures they have about ten pounds of U-235 and should have enough for their first bomb in maybe six months, a year — we're not sure when. We figure their target will be either Tel Aviv or Tokyo."

Brent's hand returned to his neck which had started to pain again. "But you're not sure they're even building bombs."

"We have no aerial reconnaissance, and our two agents have vanished."

"Then, they could be developing other weapons — artillery, tanks and even more deadly gas."

"True. But any way you look at it the center must be taken out."

Brent said, "It's one of the most heavily defended installations on earth — everyone knows that — AA, fighters, elite troops."

"We know," Bernstein said in a heavy voice. "We suffered heavy casualties to our bombers in two raids without inflicting any damage."

"Too far."

"Of course. We refueled them over the Med. But it was no good. We lost twenty-four—two whole squadrons. No chance for fighter cover. There's a limit to what even courage can do." He sank back, face long with fatigue and frustration.

Brent gathered up the cups, walked to the kitchen and returned with scotch, bourbon, ice, and glasses. "Here," he said, placing the tray on the table, "we need this more than coffee."

"I cotton to that, sir, won't give you no lip over that one, least-wise," Rubin said, the Texas cowboy again. He picked up the bourbon, "Panther's breath, put iron in a man's twang."

"Feel free to pour your own," Brent said.

"I'm obliged." The Texan poured himself a generous shot of bourbon.

Bernstein and Brent did the same with the scotch. The three men held up their glasses. *"Mazel tov,"* Bernstein said.

"Mazel tov," Brent repeated.

"I could scarcely ken that," Rubin said, holding his glass high. "But I'm a thinkin' y'all said somthin' about luck." Bernstein nodded and smiled. "Then to my thinkin', we sure 'nuff we'll need it, too—luck!"

They all drank. Bernstein emptied his glass and Brent poured another. The Mossad agent sank back as if his quintessence was a tightly wound spring that had suddenly released its tension. For a moment, Ruth came back to Brent's mind. She had done the same; a big drink followed by spreading relaxation. Without a doubt, constant warfare and the threat of extermination had taken a terrible toll on all Israelis. He wondered about their rate of alcoholism. And then, he wondered about his own attachment to drink.

Bernstein gulped down more of his scotch and turned to Brent. His voice was suddenly lower, softer and his thin jowls sagged as his visage eased. "You met Colonel Moskowitz?" he asked casually.

"Met him? We fought side by side at *Bren-ah-Hahd.*"

"I know. He was badly wounded." Again, he rubbed the sleeve that concealed the blue numbers on his forearm. "We were in the same fraternity, different campuses, during Schicklgruber's late unpleasantness."

"Don't ken that," Rubin said.

Bernstein smiled and drank. "We were both in concentration camps during World War Two."

"You never said nothin' about that," Rubin said.

"I know."

Brent sipped his drink and then leaned forward. He had to know more of Moskowitz and the terrible things he had left unsaid. Somehow, he felt the virus of those years had spread to Ruth. He guessed Irving was ready to talk, perhaps, even eager to talk. In all the years he had known Colonel Irving Bernstein, he had never heard the Israeli explain the horror behind the six blue numbers. "Were you in the same camp?"

"For about a year—Auschwitz. We were both Ashkenazim," he glanced at Rubin, "Jews from eastern Europe, especially Poland. Jews from Spain and Portugal are Sephardim."

"I ken that."

Bernstein moved on into the horror. "My father and mother were given their whiffs of Zyklon B and baked, my brother Isaac was in the Polish army, the Third Cavalry Division. I heard he was captured by the Russians and murdered in the Katyn Forest massacre. My sister, Rachel, was used to pleasure German officers. They called them 'field whores.' They used young Jewish boys, too. A lot of those proud Prussians were homosexual, you know." He emptied his glass and recharged it. Unable to look at each other, Brent and Elroy stared stonily at their drinks. "My sister vanished. I hear she went mad and they shot her — threw her in the pits with the rest of the garbage."

"And Moskowitz," Brent asked softly.

"I met him and his family in the Warsaw Ghetto. Actually, he was from a small village near Lwow, but the Germans herded over a half million Jews into the ghetto."

"Crowded."

"But not for long, Elroy. No indeed. The Germans were clever about relieving congestion. They did it at places like Treblinka and Auschwitz." He chuckled, a chilling, harsh sound that seemed to come from the haunt of the damned. "Very efficient people, those Germans. Why, do you know they could 'process' twenty-thousand people a day at Auschwitz? The sun would be blotted out by the smoke." He drank. "But they needed me — yes indeed. I had been a medical student and I cut hair, pulled gold fillings from corpses, even Doctor Mengele found me of great help in his experiments — especially with twins. I did the autopsies. That's how I stayed alive." His voice broke and he gulped his drink. Guilt was scrawled there, across his face in harsh lines.

"Irving," Brent said softly. "No more. That's enough."

"No, my friend, you wanted to know about David Moskowitz."

"It can wait."

Bernstein forced a smile and poured a small portion of whiskey. His voice steadied. "David and I fought together in the Warsaw uprising. I met him in the sewers where we hid with our families. When it was over we were all sent to Auschwitz together."

"But I heard he was at Dachau."

"True, Brent. He was an expert engraver and printer and they sent him to Dachau to forge documents for their agents and even to counterfeit American dollars. That's why he remained alive."

"His family?"

"His father, mother, two sisters, and two brothers were all gassed and incinerated for the glory of the Third Reich."

There was a moment's silence and then Elroy showed his knowledge again, "He was cut loose by Japanese."

"That's right, Elroy, Japanese-American troops liberated Dachau." A welcome smile creased the Israeli's face. "He loves the Japanese." He tapped his glass, making a tiny ringing sound. "We both arrived in Israel in 1946, joined up with Menachem Begin and the Palmach." He glanced at the two young men. "We had nothing to do with the Stern Gang and the bombing of the King David Hotel. The Jews who did that were terrorists killers." He stared hard at Brent Ross, "No better than their enemies." A slow smile spread across Brent's face and he nodded.

"We fought against the Arabs, stopped Glub Pasha's Arab Legion in its tracks." There was pride in his voice. "And, from then on, we've been fighting them." He gulped down half his drink. "It'll never end."

Brent eyed the Israeli over his glass. "Maybe, you're wrong this time, Colonel."

"What do you mean?"

"The Arabs understand power."

"That's all they understand, Brent."

"Then if we can mass enough strength, punish them enough, it could come to an end."

Bernstein released his breath with more of a groaning sound than a sigh. "There are so many of them, they have so much money, oil . . ."

"I know. But we must do it, will do it."

"God knows, Brent, we were finished back in '84 when *Yonaga* stormed into the Mediterranean and smashed them, sank their fleet. And again and again . . ." He seemed to choke, coughed, drank. Collecting himself, he continued. "Men like you, Lieutenant Rubin, Admiral Fujita, Yoshi Matsuhara . . ."

"Commander Matsuhara is the dangdest pilot I've ever know'd," Elroy said, quickly grabbing the new topic.

Brent turned to the young man, continuing the fresh tack, "He's quite old for a fighter pilot, you know. The oldest in the world."

"Sure 'nuff don't bother him none. Best pilot I ever done laid eyes on. Can fly wildern' a hawk with a burr up his ass an' shoot the eyes outta field mouse at five hundred yards." Rubin looked at Bernstein. "His kind's meaner'n a polecat sniffin' pussy in heat, got gumption, never cut an' run."

Brent said, "He's a hard worker, does a great job with the new men."

"Smarter'n a whip an' tougher'n last year's beef jerky." Elroy stabbed a finger at his companions. "Shoot, right now, I'd bet the skin off my balls he's workin' his tail off, teachin' jackasses like me."

Brent and Irving laughed. "I don't know if I'd agree with all of that," Brent said. "But, I know he's working. That's all that man knows."

"Right," Bernstein agreed, glancing at his watch. And then reflecting almost to himself, "Seven hours ahead of us. In Tokyo it's 0100 hours tomorrow morning." He looked up grinning, "He's working, all right. Won't be asleep for hours. No doubt about that."

The three men raised their glasses and touched rims. "To Yoshi Matsuhara," Brent said.

"The hardest-working man on earth," Bernstein said.

"I cotton to that," Rubin said.

"Agreed," Brent added.

The three men drank.

Four

Rapture twisted the woman's face, glazing her half-open eyes and pulling her lips back into a rictus of ecstasy. She cried out unintelligibly, arching her back, head pushed back into the black halo of hair that spread across the futon. Moving her hips in rhythmic elliptical movements, her breath was short and labored, like a long distance runner nearing the finish line. A fine patina of perspiration covered her voluptuous nude body. She felt liberated, free, meeting his thrusts, the maddening relentless strokes grinding him deep into her. From the depths of their union, she could feel the devastating release she hungered for welling up relentlessly like mounting flames in a furnace.

"Work, Yoshi, work!" she cried. "Don't stop! Yes! Yes! Work!"

It had never been this good, not with Yoshi Matsuhara or anyone else. The blissful waves bore her beyond reality, a euphoric realm of the gods that too soon would became unbearable and be annihilated by her own burning explosion of sensation. She tightened her arms around his broad back, pulled down hard, desperate to be crushed under him, to feel his hot skin everywhere on her body. He made sounds

"Perhaps."

"And you seek revenge for your dead comrades, for Kimio, for every affront."

The point was apt and painful. His voice deepened, "Revenge is sacred to the samurai."

"An eye for an eye makes the whole world blind, Yoshi-san."

"Then the Arabs are sightless, too. It is all equal."

Her gaze seemed to sear his soul and she said bitterly, "You and the Arabs are the same. You have become one with your enemies."

He ran a hand over her smooth cheek and gazed deep into her eyes. A thin mist of moisture had darkened them to the blackness of an open grave. He wanted to ameliorate her distress but could only say, "You are very wise, Tomoko-san."

"Then who is right?"

He cupped her face in his big palms, kissed her tiny nose and smiled. "The winner!"

"That is how it has always been."

"True."

She shook her head and let air escape from her lungs in a primal mourning sound. She seemed defeated. "You will return, soon, my darling. Remember, I return to work Monday."

"Not even Susano"—the storm god—"could keep me away."

"When?"

"Sunday night."

"That is too long, my love—an eternity."

He sighed. "I know, but I have the duty."

Looking away, she rubbed her chin thoughtfully. "Then, if I cannot see you, I will see the other man in my life."

"Your son, Ryo?"

"Yes. He is in Ashikaga. He has a woman there and

99

he wants me to meet her. It is less than a hour by train. I will spend the weekend with him."

"Do not become a burden, Tomoko-san."

She smiled craftily. "It is not necessary to serve on *Yonaga* to know when to make a strategic withdrawal, Yoshi-san." They both chuckled.

"And return by Sunday night. I have plans for you, Tomoko-san." He kissed her. She kissed him back fiercely. He tried to pull away, but she held him tight, her hands like the claws of a frightened kitten.

"Please, my darling," he said, grasping both of her hands and pulling them free. "I must leave."

"Someday I will kill Admiral Fujita."

He laughed. "Many have tried for nearly a century, Tomoko-san."

"But never a woman."

Rubbing his chin, he cocked his head and smiled slowly. There was something in what she said that disturbed him.

Her face was solemn and her chin was trembling as she watched him walk to his staff car.

Five

Carrier *Yonaga* dwarfed Dock B-2 and the yards the way Fuji-san could blot out the heavens when you draw close. Over 1,000 feet long, with a superstructure that soared into the sky higher than many of the garish steel and glass towers in the Ginza, the great warship displaced 84,000 tons. Although she had been commissioned in 1940, loving maintenance by her tireless crew still gave her a youthful, lethal appearance.

Because of the "dragon's teeth" of concrete barriers, it was impossible to drive to the accommodation ladder of the carrier. Instead, visitors and crew were forced to park outside the gates and walk. Admiral Fujita had designed this defense after the beautiful, vicious terrorist, Kathryn Suzuki, had tried to crash a truck loaded with twelve tons of high explosives into the graving dock where *Yonaga* was under repair for torpedo damage. Coldly, Brent Ross had shot her between the eyes while she lay on the ground, injured and helpless. This had been ironic because Yoshi knew the pair had had a fiery love affair. But true to the sobriquet, "The American Samurai," and honoring the traditions of Bushido, Brent did not hesitate to pull the trigger. It was just, right, and very Japanese.

Passing through the gate in the 10-foot high chainlink fence crowned with barbed wire, Commander Yoshi Matsuhara returned the salute of the young burly duty chief, Chief Watertender Eiji Nakahashi. Then the zigzag walk through the barriers. He could see at least twelve Nambu machine guns in sandbagged emplacements, helmeted crews in Number 2 green battle fatigues, lounging, talking and smoking. Other guns were placed on warehouses and machine shops and still others pointed down from the ship, covering the entire area. There would never be a repetition of the Suzuki incident, which had nearly succeeded.

Although *Yonaga* had been Yoshi's home for over fifty years, he never grew inured to her awesome size. As one neared the ship, her battleship genesis became apparent. The *Yamato* hull on which she was built was squat and heavily armored. The fourth hull of the most powerful class of battleships ever designed, Admiral Fujita had personally taken over her design when the conversion began. He had lengthened her and installed more powerful engines than her sisters, *Yamato, Musashi, Shinano.* Still, basically, *Yonaga* was a converted battleship with seven decks, a triple bottom, torpedo blisters, over a thousand watertight compartments, and a sixteen-inch armor belt. An enormous eight-inch armored box Admiral Fujita called "The Citadel" enclosed her vitals: boilers, engine rooms, steering engines, high-octane aircraft petrol tanks and magazines.

Rear Admiral Byron Whitehead had once pointed out the similarity between *Yonaga* and the powerful old American carriers, *Lexington* and *Saratoga,* which had been built on converted battle cruiser hulls in the early twenties. Fujita conceded nothing. He only grunted and busied himself with other matters.

Fujita had tried to bomb-proof *Yonaga* by building a 33-inch-thick cushion beneath her 1,000-foot armored flight deck. He filled the space with boxed steel beams, latex, cement, sawdust, and recently, new plastic sheeting. Not even a 500-pound bomb could penetrate to her hangar deck, which was actually a battleship's splinter deck, armored to a thickness of up to 7.5 inches. Only new 1,000 pounders with tungsten and depleted uranium tips had managed to pierce the flight deck. But with courage and luck, damage control parties had managed to contain the fires and repair the damage. During the Arab wars, she had withstood bomb and torpedo hits that would have sunk lesser ships many times over. Yoshi never wondered that her crew loved her like a wife, mother, mistress.

There were a few of her old "plank owners" still serving her. These were the men who had burst upon the world in 1983 when *Yonaga* broke free from her forty two-year entrapment in a remote anchorage on Siberia's Chukchi Peninsula. Although Yoshi had seen most of the senior officers die during the four-decade imprisonment, the remainder of the crew seemed to have challenged time, almost preserved by the frigid austere isolation. "Of course we are young," Fujita had answered the curious on numerous occasions. "No liquor, no tobacco, and no women for over forty years. What did you expect?" Then he usually hacked out his rare laugh.

This phenomenon of enduring youthful vigor was not reserved for *Yonaga*'s crew, but was characteristic of Japanese soldiers who had held out for decades on Pacific islands, too. Yoshi had met two: Sochi Yokoi who had eluded capture on Guam for twenty-seven years, and Lieutenant Hiroo Onoda who waged his war on Lubang for thirty years. Curious about the ultimate hold-out, the pair had come aboard the carrier immediately after she entered Tokyo Bay in 1983. Remarkable men, both in their sixth decade when Yoshi met them, they both looked at least twenty years younger.

Yoshi laughed to himself, thinking of Onoda's reaction when the lieutenant first saw him. The surprise had been mutual. He remembered how the wiry army officer had looked him up and down from his black hair, unlined face, thick neck, broad shoulders, narrow waist to his straight, strong legs. "Why, Commander," Onoda had said with awe in his voice, "you do not look over forty years old and you must be nearly sixty." He smiled. "Or did you fly in China at the age of five?"

Yoshi had laughed. "No, Lieutenant, but I did join the Imperial Navy at the minimum age of fifteen."

What *Yonaga*'s crew discovered in Japan when they returned was not a source of amusement. Some of the crew found their families dead, victims of American B-29s. Others could not fit into the new Japan, a strange, incomprehensible world as remote as the prison of ice they had just left. Like many newly released prisoners after long captivity, they could find comfort only in their comrades and, strangely, their place of incarceration. Yoshi Matsuhara was one of these men. His decision to remain had been easy to make. His entire family had been burned to death in Curtis Le May's great Tokyo fire raid of March 9, 1945.

Mounting the accommodation ladder, the commander stepped onto the quarter deck. Here he saluted the colors first and then returned the salute of the duty officer, young Lieutenant Junior Grade

Tokuma Shoten, and two enlisted men wearing duty belts and side arms. Shoten said, "The admiral wishes to see you immediately, Commander Matsuhara, in his cabin."

"Very well." He glanced at his watch. It was 0845 hours. Quickly, the commander walked forward to the ship's lone elevator.

Admiral Hiroshi Fujita's cabin was the largest on the ship, at least four times larger than Yoshi's, which by flag country standards was considered quite spacious. The desk was of polished oak, decks carpeted. Low bookcases lined the bulkheads, and above them were charts, a large portrait of Emperor Akihito, and, next to the emperor, a small wooden shrine which looked like a tiny log cabin with a wall removed to expose the interior. An exquisite golden Buddha and a black ivory tiger were visible, along with two deities, Ebisu and Daikoku, who brought good fortune to sailors. Overhead, four caged bulbs glared in a jumble of pipes and conduits.

When Yoshi entered the cabin, Admiral Fujita was seated behind his desk. A diminutive, shriveled old man, he sat with astonishing erectness. His white hair was sparse, a few errant strands glittering in the glare like powdered glass on a pate as flat as *Yonaga's* flight deck. Although he had been thinned by the years, the folds of wrinkles hung from his cheeks like layered jowls. His neck was a withered reed, shoulders narrow as a young boy's. Dating back to the early forties, his old-fashioned, single-breasted tunic with its uncomfortable stand collar hung from him like a shroud.

But the eyes challenged it all. Looking into those black and piercing depths, a man knew he was in the

105

presence of a living allegory on the passing of cultures, lives, and time. And they asserted innate authority, impressive arcane knowledge, and at times seemed to possess quasi-magical powers that looked into a world lying outside the realm of ordinary experience. This was Fujita's power, the protean force that filled the room and made a man feel as if he were standing on Mount Usuzan's hot slopes, knowing that at any instant the volcano could boil over into cataclysmic eruption.

There were four other men in the room. Seated next to the admiral's desk was the tottery old scribe, Commander Hakuseki Katsube. The arthritic old man was so aged and dried up that he reminded Yoshi of an exhumed corpse. With a permanent bend to his rheumatoid spine, he hunched over his pad, brush in his one good hand; his other twisted by arthritis into a grotesque claw. Disdaining modern recorders, Admiral Fujita still preferred ancient *kanji* characters. Or perhaps the admiral could not bring himself to dismiss his old companion of over sixty years. Yoshi suspected some vestiges of sentimentality were still buried deep in the old "iron admiral."

Seated in one of the five chairs facing the admiral was the executive officer, Captain Mitake Arai. A destroyer captain during World War II, Arai still carried himself with rigid, youthful, military bearing. He was intelligent, highly efficient, and the best navigator on the ship.

Next to Arai sat the American rear admiral, Byron Whitehead. Whitehead, on permanent liaison from NIC, had seen extensive carrier duty during the war. The portly, white-haired rear admiral had been in fourteen battles and been sunk six times. To the superstitious Japanese, who saw *kamis* (spirits) in practically everything and everyone, this record did not

106

augur good fortune. In fact, near the end of World War II, his reputation was so notorious that captains of American carriers were flooded with requests for transfers whenever Whitehead reported aboard. Whitehead and Mitake Arai, whose destroyer was escorting battleship *Yamato* when she was sunk south of Kyushu in 1945, had actually fought against each other. Sometimes, Yoshi believed, they had never stopped.

The fourth man was the new CIA agent, Elliot "Ellie" Amberg, who had reported aboard only an hour earlier. Yoshi recognized him from a picture he had seen in a dossier given to all members of the staff a week earlier. Slight of build and short in stature, he was a plain young man with skin as white as a bleached sheet. Dominating his face were wide green eyes that skipped around the room nervously like a man startled by everything he saw. His full head of hair was the color of blooming mustard, appearing electrified like Albert Einstein's. With his sparse build and a mop of unkempt hair, he challenged every aspect of the stereotypical secret agent. In fact, he looked as if he belonged behind a clerk's desk in some huge corporate office, not in the inner sanctum of planning that could change the world forever.

Yoshi chuckled to himself. Young Amberg's visage seemed frozen in a chary mask of apprehension and he shifted in his chair uneasily. Was it fear? This would not be hard to understand. Certainly, the fate of his predecessors could not raise the spirits of the most inflexible optimist. In the great battle in the South China Sea in 1988, *Yonaga's* first CIA liaison, Frank Dempster, had had most of his head neatly severed by a piece of shrapnel the size of a discus. His successor, the loose-tongued Horace Mayfield, had been hanged from the yardarm by an infuriated Admiral Fujita. Then, the last, Alfred Gibney, had been injured in a drunken barroom brawl over a Ginza harlot. He had been sent home in disgrace. Only desperate pleadings by Rear Admiral Whitehead and Commander Brent Ross had saved Gibney from chains and imprisonment in *Yonaga's* brig. Yes, indeed, the history of Amberg's predecessors was not a chronicle that could stimulate enthusiasm.

Although two of the three men facing Admiral Fujita outranked Yoshi Matsuhara, Arai and Whitehead rose with Amberg when he walked to a chair indicated by Admiral Fujita. Matsuhara bowed toward the admiral and then exchanged bows with Arai. No salutes were made. In the British tradition, no one saluted below decks on *Yonaga,* and the bridge was considered below decks on all Japanese warships. Fujita introduced Elliot Amberg and Yoshi shook his hand. It felt like a speared carp.

Katsube did not even attempt to struggle from his chair. Instead, he tilted his head like Charles Laughton playing the hunchback, Quasimodo, ogling the luscious Maureen O'Hara. He smiled, crossed his eyes, not sure of what he saw. Then, hearing the other men greet Yoshi, he shouted for no apparent reason, *"Banzai!"* Everyone ignored him.

Fujita opened the meeting by addressing the CIA man, Elliot Amberg. He spoke in precise English, the language of the old Imperial Navy and still the language of *Yonaga.* "The latest reports on Kadafi's atomic bombs, Mr. Amberg," the old mariner asked, in a deep timbre that belied his wizened appearance. The men shifted uneasily. Atomic weapons held a special horror for the Japanese and everyone knew Fujita's wife, Akiko, and two sons, Kazuo and Makoto, had been reduced to radioactive dust at Hiroshima.

Rising, Amberg pulled a document from his attaché case which was on the deck before him and said in a low, self-conscious voice, "Nothing new, Admiral. We have reports that the Arabs are enriching uranium with calutrons."

"I was under the impression these were rumors."

"They still are, sir," Amberg said, appearing to gain confidence with each word. "But they are very persistent and from a variety of sources."

"At Rabta?"

"Yes. That is still their research center."

"Where they manufacture pharmaceuticals, not mustard and nerve gas," Fujita added sarcastically. Everyone acknowledged the admiral's wit with appropriate chuckles. His next question silenced the humor, "The Russian carrier and the two cruisers?"

Amberg confirmed what everyone knew. "The three ships, carrier *Baku* and cruisers *Dzerzhinsky* and *Zhdanov,* are underway for the Mediterranean."

Fujita pinched his tiny nose and spoke almost to himself, "With carrier *Magid* and cruiser *Babur,* that will give them three carriers, three cruisers and escorts."

"Yes, sir. We estimate conversion and training will take from four to six months. You wiped out their carrier-trained air groups in the battles off Gibraltar and south of Iwo Jima."

The old man rubbed his shining pate for a moment and muttered to himself while everyone stared, "Four to six months." Finally, he said to the CIA man, "You may be seated, Mr. Amberg." Obviously relieved, the CIA man sank into his chair.

Yoshi looked at the CIA man from the corner of his eye. Young Amberg seemed somewhat disconcerted, but conducted himself well enough in his new assignment. There could be a strong, capable man buried under that shy, unimpressive exterior. The news about the Russian ships was disquieting. A lot of power was gathering in the Mediterranean.

Fujita eyed Rear Admiral Whitehead. "The prisoner negotiations, Admiral?"

Whitehead rubbed his ample thighs and hunched forward. "Commander Ross and Colonel Bernstein will fly to Tripoli, Saturday, their time zone, sir."

Yoshi came half out of his chair. "They'll be murdered."

"It was their choice," Fujita countered.

"They will be murdered and the hostages will be executed."

"That is the chance we take and if it happens, we will kill ten for one, Commander."

"We will run out, Admiral."

"Then we will borrow Arabs from the Israelis and kill them."

Grimacing, Yoshi sank back. He could not believe the admiral could be so cavalier about sacrificing his two trusted aides. He knew the loss of Brent Ross would be particularly grievous to Hiroshi Fujita. No one was indispensable, including the Admiral himself. Nevertheless, Brent Ross was someone special to Fujita. Yoshi was convinced the old man saw some of his immolated son, Kazuo, in the big American. Yoshi had met Kazuo once in 1941. Kazuo had been his father's favorite. A big, strapping, intelligent young man with a brilliant mind and a gift for athletics, he was very much like Brent Ross. Many times the commander had sensed unease in the admiral when Brent Ross's life was at risk; especially in the early years when the young American flew several missions as a gunner on bombers. Fujita's casualness was a calculated facade; the usual hard exterior of the commanding officer with the cast-iron backbone. Yoshi knew that, deep down, the old man agonized at the prospect of losing Brent Ross.

Fujita continued, "All of you know we have *New Jersey?*" An excited rumble ran through the room. "She will help balance the scales against those new Russian ships."

"Sir," Whitehead said. "The whole world will know when she stands in Tokyo Bay."

Fujita gestured to Elliot Amberg, who said with new confidence, "She won't do that, Admiral Whitehead. The CIA has arranged for her to put into Tarawa. We will circulate the rumor that she sank while under tow."

"Fat chance," Whitehead said.

Fujita showed his uncanny knowledge of World War Two trivia. "Why not, Admiral Whitehead. It is not unprecedented. Battleship *Oklahoma* sank while under tow to the United States after she was damaged in the attack on Pearl Harbor."

"Respectfully, I think that she was sunk deliberately," Whitehead offered. "She was a horror to see and an embarrassment to the navy."

There was a short awkward silence while the aging warriors relived those bloody years. Fujita broke it, "Deliberate or not, *Oklahoma* sank while under tow. That's what the history books show," the old man countered. He turned to Amberg, *"New Jersey's* AA guns. I understand she had her secondary battery brought up to full strength, ten gun houses, twenty-five-inch, thirty-eights. She has been stripped of those useless Tomahawk and Harpoon cruise missiles."

"True, sir," Amberg said. "And we already have sixty twenty-millimeter and eighty forty-millimeter guns waiting at Tarawa with ammunition, plus a full load of five-inch and sixteen-inch shells!"

"Banzai!" Katsube shouted, half-falling from his chair with the effort. Quickly, Yoshi rose and

111

straightened the old man, who snapped, *"Bakana!"* at him, angrily waving his claw and spraying him with spittle.

"Gun crews. It will take hundreds of gunners, radar operators," Whitehead said.

"We are flying men from the states and others from Japan. She will be fully manned and ready for the operation within six weeks or less," Amberg countered.

The officers looked at each other and then at Admiral Fujita. Whitehead asked, "What operation?"

Fujita said, "This is top secret. What you hear here, remains here." He looked around at the expectant faces. "We will move against Rabta."

"Banzai!" Katsube shouted. This time his head thumped down on the desk like a rubber mallet and he drooled onto his pad. The officers looked at each other and there were excited whispers.

"Our last B-25 raid against Rabta was costly. We lost them all," Yoshi said.

Amberg said, "They bought us time — inflicted more damage than we were led to believe. The Arabs are past masters at deception. Their cover-up was masterful. Our Chadian agents reported heavy damage to most of the facilities."

Captain Mitake Arai entered the discussion. "But we did not take out Rabta."

"True, Captain Arai. But we know we disrupted the production of poison gas — both nerve and mustard," the CIA man said.

Fujita halted the exchange with a wave. "Enough!" He stood and walked stiffly to a chart of the Mediterranean Sea mounted on the wall behind him. Picking up a pointer, he stabbed the rubber tip at a point about 250 miles off the coast of Libya. *"Yonaga* and *Bennington* accompanied by *New Jersey* will steam into the Mediterranean and launch air strikes here —

against all of the Libyan bases." He tapped the chart with in five different places. "Fighter and bomber bases at Al Kararim, Mistatah, Zuwarah, and Tripoli and destroy Rabta, their poison gas works and the nuclear facilities which I believe exist. The Israelis have promised to launch extensive land and air offensives to coincide with our attacks." Apparently tiring, he returned to his chair.

Arai said, "The Israeli Mossad agent Ephraim Schneerson is not here, Admiral. We need his report."

"He is at the Israeli embassy. He should be here at any moment."

Whitehead came erect. He was bursting with arguments and facts to back them. "Sir, the enemy can throw three carriers and three cruisers at us plus his land-based aircraft. And with all due respect, the Mediterranean is no place for a capital ship — especially one the size of *Yonaga*. Remember what happened to carriers *Illustrious, Ark Royal,* and *Hermes* when Margaret Thatcher sent them into the Med in 1986 to teach the Arabs a lesson. Arab aircraft sank them all. The British have never recovered. In World War Two the Royal Navy lost battleship *Barham* and carrier *Ark Royal* there just to submarines. And aircraft took a terrible toll of cruisers and destroyers." He gestured at the chart. "You would violate all the basic tenets of carrier warfare by bringing our carriers within easy range of enemy land-based aircraft while challenging a powerful battle group. And remember carrier *Franklin* when Task Force Fifty-Eight steamed too close to Japan in 1945. Only one plane dropping two bombs. Set her off like a firecracker — terrible losses." He clutched his head with both hands in a gesture of futility.

"Yonaga is no *Franklin."*

"But *Bennington* is."

"I know, but I have never heard of a risk-free war, Admiral Whitehead." Fujita thumped his tiny fist on the oak. "I am no Margaret Thatcher! We did it before—in 1984—and we shall do it again."

Whitehead was undaunted, "And took heavy casualties—you were lucky to escape. We'll be spotted the moment we enter the straits of Gibraltar."

Fujita caressed the leather-hound copy of the *Hagakure* (the handbook of Bushido) which was always at his right hand. "The book teaches us 'The warrior who refuses to retreat gains the strength of two men and if he attacks quickly he can pass through a wall of iron.' "

Katsube raised his head, shouted *"Banzai!"* and dropped it back on the desk with a thump. No one turned a head.

Fujita's wrinkles took on new creases as a smile broke through the scabrous parchment. "The English have informed me that they will cooperate. The airfields at Gibraltar are ours."

This time, Yoshi Matsuhara and Mitake Arai joined Katsube in his *"Banzai!"*

Fujita continued, "Admiral Whitehead, you know two squadrons of the new American Grumman FX-1000 fighters have been made available to us." He turned to the other officers, "Thirty of our men are training with the new fighter in California at this moment. By the time we enter the Straits of Gibraltar, those twenty-four aircraft will provide us with cover from the fields at Gibraltar."

Whitehead's skepticism was still alive. "But we'll still be spotted. It's inevitable. If not by aircraft or subs, there'll be a lot of curious eyes focused our way from Morocco and Spain, sir, when we stand in. Her neutrality is a sham, Admiral, and the forces opposing us are powerful."

114

"You make a good point, Admiral," Fujita acknowledged. "But we will enter with *Yonaga*, *Bennington* and *New Jersey* and an escort of at least twelve destroyers. We may take casualties, but I am convinced we have the power to complete the operation."

Arai said, "But the prisoner exchange, sir?"

"It will probably fail."

"Then, we can lose Commander Ross and Colonel Bernstein—the whole negotiating team."

Looking upward, Fujita pulled his pencil-line thin lips back from his teeth. They looked like the worn keys of an old piano. "That is a strong possibility."

A clammy silence filled the room, broken only by the faint sound of auxiliary engines and the whir of blowers. Whitehead pressed on, "Then, they will buy time—is that it?"

The admiral tugged on a single white hair hanging from his chin. His rheumy eyes were narrow, voice low but firm with resolve, "Yes, that is true."

"We need more help from the Americans," Arai said, staring at Amberg and Whitehead. The decades-old hostility was breaking through.

Whitehead sighed with the resignation of a man who had faced this same complaint many times. Amberg stared at his shoes and said, "You know we're doing all that we can." He waved over his head. "The Chinese laser system paralyzed our entire defense establishment."

"And the Russians are just as paralyzed. And do not forget, the Soviet Union has collapsed," Arai retorted hotly.

Yoshi saw Admiral Fujita sink back. He would give his subordinates free rein in their quarrel, allow them to air their conflicts—short of violence. He had seen the admiral in similar circumstances many times.

115

Yoshi felt it was a legacy from the long entrapment in Sano Wan, where inevitably nerves had become frayed, feuds had exploded. In fact, at least a dozen disputes were settled in the Shrine of Infinite Salvation with *wakizashis* (nine-inch knives, pointed and sharpened on both edges). It was not only a catharsis Fujita used in the hope of precluding uncontrolled violence, but Yoshi always felt the old man found secret pleasure in the bitter exchanges. And there was natural resentment in *Yonaga*'s samurai who had not only carried the brunt of the fighting, but had been forced to fight some of their own people as well. As Yoshi had heard Admiral Fujita say many times, "They will tolerate us as long as we provide petrol for their Toyotas."

Amberg looked up. A small fire had been fanned. It glowed in his eyes. He had backbone, spoke with the surprising strength of a man who could be a formidable adversary, "There are still thirty thousand nuclear warheads in the Russian republics. The Russians need hard currency. Those warheads could be sold to the Arabs. We can't afford to antagonize them too openly. Don't ever forget that."

Arai pressed on, "You could still do more for us. We are fighting your battle, doing your dying."

Whitehead entered the fray, "That was low — unconscionable!" he spat, face flushed. "Hundreds of our best have died fighting this war and you are receiving our entire Alaskan oil production."

"Ha! Your old ships, a few volunteers!" Coming to his feet, Arai stabbed a finger at the chart of the Mediterranean. "And now we must once again enter that trap and slide between the loins of the foul old woman of death."

Whitehead leaped to his feet. "Then, if you're afraid of your old woman, don't go. God damn it! I

116

was a line officer for most of my career. I'll take your place! Find yourself a hot geisha and wallow in a whorehouse while we fight your damned war."

The crimson flooding Arai's face showed the vitriol burning in his guts. His voice cut like a whiplash, "No one talks to me like that! I will see you in the Shrine . . ."

"Enough!" Fujita roared before the challenge could be completed.

"My honor, sir!" Arai declared, rage breaking through decades of discipline. "A samurai cannot allow anyone the liberty of insult." Such a declaration was menacing, it had the sound of breaking bones in it and the stench of fresh-spilled blood.

Fujita's voice rolled like a cannonade. "You do not teach me Bushido or of the *Hagakure*." He waved the book at the executive officer and quoted it, " 'Wrap your angers in needles of pine, and seek Kannon, the goddess of mercy.' That is an order. Now sit down, both of you." Slowly, the two officers sank into their chairs.

"Respectfully, sir," Arai said with a quivering voice that defied control, "when we finish this mission, I claim my right as a samurai," he gestured at Rear Admiral Whitehead, "to settle this matter with the admiral on a personal basis."

"In the Shrine of Infinite Salvation, if you wish," Fujita allowed.

Whitehead leaned toward Arai and growled, "Enough of this Bushido bullshit. If you have a problem, let's settle it here and now." He rose. Yoshi Matsuhara grabbed him.

"Find your seat, Admiral," Fujita bellowed, Mount Usuzan finally erupting. "Find your seat or you are transferred!"

Muttering oaths, Whitehead sank into his chair. He

117

glared at Arai, who shot a venomous look back.

Yoshi expected the admiral to dismiss both officers summarily. But instead, showing one of his vagrant unpredictable mood changes, he sank back and spoke with great calm and authority, "Commander Matsuhara, I want your report." He would let Whitehead and Arai cool while Yoshi gave his report. He wanted more input from one or both of them. In any event, he would not allow them to leave in such a state of anger.

Yoshi pulled a document from his inside pocket and glanced at it as he rose. Looking up, he said, "The training of our new air groups is progressing at Tokyo International and Tsuchuira on schedule. In addition to our own Japanese volunteers, we have had the pick of the finest pilots from all over the world. We have received enough new Nakajima Sakae Fifty Arashi, two thousand, five hundred horsepower engines for seventy-six of our Mitsubishi A-6M2, Zero-sens."

"Our bombers, the Aichi D-3As and Nakajima B-5Ns and the other Zeros?"

"Sorry, Admiral Fujita, the Nakajima factory still does not have the capacity to equip our bombers and all of our fighters. We have enough engines and spare parts for our thirty-six shipboard fighters and forty more for our land-based aircraft. All of our remaining Aichis, Nakajimas, and Zero-sens will keep the two thousand-two-hundred-horsepower Sakae 42."

Elliot Amberg glanced quizzically at Admiral Fujita. The admiral nodded assent, and the CIA man entered the conversation. "If I may, I understand you fly a very unusual Zero, Commander Matsuhara. The American media call it 'The Rocket.' " Yoshi sensed the agent was spreading his own oil on the troubled waters by adding a distraction. He was gaining respect for young Amberg.

Yoshi noticed Fujita's slight nod of approval. He chuckled, "It is completely rebuilt, is powered by the Nakajima Sakae 43, which is a modified Wright Cyclone R-3350—the engine that powered the B-29."

Amberg showed his knowledge, "That's a lot of muscle for a Zero. I understand the original Mitsubishi A-6M2 was designed for a very small power plant."

"Nine hundred fifty horsepower."

"Good Lord! The R-3350 is a monster."

"True. Three thousand, two hundred horsepower, and, as I said, we completely rebuilt my A-6M2—new longerons, stringers, formers, engine mounts; even a new main wing spar, arresting hook and arresting hook cable." He shrugged and turned his palms up. "It works, I'm still here."

For the first time, Amberg laughed. Arai and Whitehead bared their teeth in hints of grins, Katsube shook his head as if an insect had found a home in his ear. Things were cooling.

"Why not use it in the other Zeros?"

Yoshi shook his head. "It is highly compressed and compact. Hard to cool and too much magnesium was used in its construction. I'm still testing it—it runs too hot."

Amberg showed his keen mind again, "Magnesium is one third the weight of aluminum."

"True, Mr. Amberg. But it's flammable. I've overheated twice in combat. We've modified the engine and replaced most of the magnesium in the crankcase with aluminum and titanium, and we've added cooling fins and fans." He looked around. Whitehead and Arai looked back. They both had calmed and seemed interested although Yoshi was well aware they both had knowledge about the subject. He shifted his eyes back to Amberg, "Don't forget, my engine is a Nakajima version of the R-3350, needs a lot of work, and is still strictly experimental. You might be interested, it is only ninety kilograms—ah, two hundred pounds heavier than the old Sakae 42."

Yoshi fidgeted uncomfortably. Although he had been born in America, he was not at home with English units and would slide in and out of metric before he was aware of his own words. It was hard to think in two different disciplines. The large number of foreigners, especially British and American, had even forced a change in the ship's phonetic alphabet to the NATO system. The English language was easy for him, but Yoshi disliked the other changes—especially, the clumsy English system of measurements. All of the old hands did.

Turning to Admiral Fujita, the air group commander moved on to another subject, "Commander Steve Elkins's Squadron of Grumman F-6F Hellcats is up to a full complement of twelve fighters, sir. Also, we have six Supermarine F-47 Seafires, bringing our fighter air group up to full strength at a total of fifty-four fighters."

"And the bombers, Commander Matsuhara?"

He had been over this ground with the admiral many times. Either the old man was becoming forgetful, or he wished to reassure himself the training procedures were progressing at a satisfactory rate. Or, perhaps, he felt the discussion would continue to dissipate the heat generated between Arai and Whitehead—if that was really possible. Yoshi said, "I have one hundred thirty dive bomber and the same number of torpedo bomber aircrews training. As per your instructions, Admiral, I will select the sixty best Aichi pilots and the same number of Nakajima pilots to man *Yonaga*'s bomber groups. The rest will be as-

120

signed to home guard squadrons."

Amberg whistled. "With the fighters, that's one hundred seventy-four planes."

"True," Yoshi said. "*Yonaga* operates one hundred fifty. We need reserves, of course."

"Of course."

Fujita began to show impatience. "When will your groups be ready for operations, Commander?"

Yoshi pondered for a moment. "Now, Admiral. Today, if necessary."

"Very good. Said like a samurai."

"But the more training time I have, the better, sir."

Nodding, Fujita tucked his thin lips under, dampened them with the tip of a tongue like a tiny silver fish. "All commanding officers believe that, Commander Matsuhara, including myself. But military imperatives do not always allow us that luxury."

"I understand." The other men nodded.

There was a knock. Usually a seaman guard would have been stationed at the door. However, because of the secret nature of the meeting only the five officers and the CIA man were in the room. Yoshi, who was junior to Captain Mitake Arai, obeyed a signal from the admiral and opened the door. A small, dark officer in desert fatigues, wearing the ornate shoulder badge of Mossad, was standing in the passageway. He was flanked by two burly seaman guards. A large box was under his arm. It was chained to his wrist. "Lieutenant Ephraim Schneerson, here," he said in perfect English. Fujita waved him in and the guards shut the door.

Schneerson was very young and very tired. He wore fatigue like a heavy garment; uniform wrinkled, face crumpled like an unmade bed. Pulling his credentials from his pocket, he approached Admiral Fujita and said, "I am a member of Colonel Irving Bernstein's

121

staff and I'm replacing Lieutenant Arnold Greenberg, sir."

All the men stiffened, the clammy hand of horror gripping their hearts. Greenberg had been murdered by Sabbah, the Arab terrorist organization named after the ancient assassin, Hasan ibn-al-Sabbah, "The Old Man of the Mountains." They preferred the knife as did their ancient predecessors, but murdered enthusiastically with every weapon from the AK-47 to their fingernails and teeth. Efficient and fanatical, they were Kadafi's deadliest killers. It was said they still became high on hashish before undertaking an assassination. Yoshi had killed five, three with his pistol and two with his bare hands. They were the fiercest fighters he had ever met.

Yoshi and two seaman guards had found Greenberg's corpse. Kidnapped on his way to Narita to catch a flight to Manila, Greenberg's body had been tied to a roadside Shinto Shrine on the outskirts of town. The torture had been exquisite. He had been blinded with a hot poker, teeth and fingernails pulled, tongue cut off and skin peeled in long strips. In typical Sabbah fashion, his penis had been hacked from his body and stuffed into his mouth. A crudely lettered sign scrawled in the Israeli's blood proclaimed an ancient quote from the Egyptian Pharaoh Merenptah: "Canaan has been plundered into every sort of woe. Israel is laid waste and his seed is not." And then the expected, "No god but Allah! Death to the Jews!" The sign had been lettered on butcher's paper and driven into his crotch with nails while he was still alive. One of the seaman guards had vomited.

After examining Ephraim Schneerson's credentials, Fujita introduced him to the other men and waved him to a chair. The young Israeli dropped more than sat. Placing the box on the deck, he groped in his

122

pocket and found a key. Quickly, he unlocked the chain and pocketed it.

"You are late," Fujita reminded him.

Rubbing his wrist, Ephraim said, "Sorry, sir, but I was up all night hard-wiring this new encryption box to access code Green Eight." He gestured at the box. "The ambassador had just received the hardware and software yesterday evening by special courier from Tel Aviv." He pulled a small package from a belt which he wore under his shirt. "This is the software, sir. Green Eight is polyalphabetic. These disks give priming keys, nulls, sequences of time, and frequency hops."

"The encryption box usually does that."

"Yes, sir. Back-up, sir, in case we lose a hard disk."

Fujita nodded at Whitehead, "Admiral Whitehead is NIC and coordinates communications with NIC and Mossad. After this meeting see him and he will take you to CIC and show you our computers and introduce you to our cryptographers and electronic technicians." He drummed his desk. "I want your report . . ." Schneerson began to reach into an inside pocket. Fujita halted him with a raised palm, "However, you interrupted my air group commander."

"Sorry, sir."

"That is not necessary. I will hear from you after commander Matsuhara and Captain Arai have given their reports."

"I understand." Schneerson sank back like a mattress with broken springs, both arms hanging loosely at his sides.

There was a pause as Fujita placed his elbows on his desk and rubbed his bony palms together. He stared at Yoshi, who was still on his feet. Schneerson had been blotted from his mind. The old man could be so single-minded, he sometimes seemed to exist in a tunnel. "Your new bomber commanders, Lieutenant Sahei Tsuda and Lieutenant Taneo Nogi, they are skilled pilots with strong leadership qualities and they are both from fine, old samurai families."

Yoshi's smile did not reveal the turmoil he felt. Lieutenant Tsuda, who commanded the Aichi D-3A dive bombers, was a veteran of the Self Defense Force. Eager, intelligent and a natural leader he had fit easily into *Yonaga's* air groups. But Nogi, the Nakajima B-5N torpedo bomber group commander, was the antithesis of Tsuda. Also a veteran of the Self Defense Force, he was arrogant and abusive to his men and surly when he disagreed with Yoshi's orders. His conceit and quixotic flamboyance would have embarrassed the author of the *Hagakure*, Tsunetomo Yamamoto. Yoshi traced most of the man's abrasive attitude to his antecedents.

Lieutenant Taneo Nogi was a great grandson of the fabled General Nogi who with his wife had celebrated the supreme act of *seppuku* by disemboweling himself as Emperor Meiji's funeral entourage passed their home in 1912. Taneo Nogi never let anyone forget about his great grandfather's supreme gesture of Bushido and considered himself the quintessential samurai. To make things more difficult, Admiral Fujita had been a personal friend of General Nogi and had actually discovered the white-clad bodies. In fact, at moments of crisis, the old admiral would often recite the general's death poem. It was an impossible situation. Yoshi saw nothing but problems ahead with Lieutenant Taneo Nogi.

Fujita's next question was typical of his samurai mentality, "Can they die as well as their predecessors—enter the gates of the Yasakuni Shrine as gloriously as Commander Takuya Iwata and Lieutenant Shinji Hamasaki?"

Schneerson suddenly came erect. Caught Amberg's

eye. Both men exchanged a startled look. Neither had ever heard words like these.

Yoshi's mind's eye brought back all the horror of the great battle south of Iwo Jima. Hamasaki leading his torpedo bombers in a wave-high suicidal attack on carrier *Al Kufra;* Iwata ramming a Stuka as it dove on *Yonaga.* Both men had died splendidly, in the best tradition of Bushido.

Yoshi's response was discreet, "All of my pilots and crews are ready to die for our cause, sir, regardless of nationality. In all briefings our foreign airmen are constantly reminded of *giri,*" he glanced at the two Americans and the Israeli, "moral obligation, and *chugi* which means loyalty—the two pillars on which the whole structure of Bushido rests, the two caveats that define our fighting spirit." And then as an afterthought, "Don't forget, 'Bushido' means 'way of the warrior.' "

Rear Admiral Whitehead broke his silence, "Well enough, Commander, but you can't make samurai of our Americans, Poles, Englishmen, Germans, Russians . . ." He threw up his hands in a gesture of frustration.

Fujita responded, "That is true. A samurai is born, not made. But we can imbue all of our volunteers with the spirit of Bushido—*chi, jin,* and *yu.*" Whitehead signaled understanding, but Schneerson and Amberg appeared confused. Fujita explained, "Wisdom, benevolence and valor." The pair nodded. Fujita continued, "And this approach has been effective, because each of our has warriors fought fiercely and shown his word—'the single word of the warrior' *bushi-no ichi gon,* is sacred, and lying, deception or the disobeying of orders, *ni-gon,* means death." He glanced at Yoshi. "Six *seppukus* in the Shrine of Infinite Salvation have honored this sacred doctrine."

Amberg turned his palms up and stared at them as though he were looking for a hidden message. Schneerson rubbed his forehead and stared like a man dreaming while wide awake. Fujita placed his hand on the *Hagakure* and continued with one of his favorite passages, " 'True courage is to live when it is right to live, and to die only when it is right to die.' " He looked at Amberg and then Schneerson, "You understand?"

The CIA man made claws of his hands and tapped the rigid fingers together in front of his chest as if he were trying to trap a fleeting thought in a cage of fingers. Finally, he said, "Yes, sir. A powerful code and way of life and death, Admiral."

Schneerson managed a muted, "Yes, sir."

Chuckling, Fujita gestured to Arai and Yoshi found his chair. "Captain Arai, your report. Extent of repairs, gunnery, engineering?" And then hunching over his desk, "When will *Yonaga* be ready for sea?"

Breathing evenly but with his face still slightly flushed, the executive officer pulled a dossier from a valise at his feet and stood. He spoke in a well-modulated monotone. He seemed almost completely composed. "We have nearly completed repairs on the bomb damage we took between frames eighty-one and one hundred seven. Our best estimates are that the bomb was a four hundred fifty-five kilo . . ." He shook his head, flushed slightly, "I mean a one thousand pounder with a tungsten-uranium tip. The hangar deck was not penetrated, but heat did cause some warping of plates and bulkheads on deck three. Transverse stiffeners between frames ninety-one and one hundred one were broken or seriously deformed on the hangar deck and deck three. They have been replaced. The pump and dynamo rooms were damaged by water and foam pouring through one of the vents which had been blown open, but they have been completely repaired and are in operation. One-hundred-twenty-seven-millimeter magazine Number Four has been rebuilt and is fully loaded. All electrical systems and the hoists were replaced because of water damage when you ordered it flooded, Admiral. The flight deck substructure is not yet complete, but we should have it ready within a week." He looked up. "As you know, Admiral, the hydraulic piston of the aft elevator was slightly warped. It has been replaced and just this morning the elevator functioned perfectly. We could launch and receive aircraft now, if necessary."

"Well done, Captain Arai. Engineering? Gunnery?"

"Chief Engineer, Lieutenant Tatsuya Yoshida, reports boilers four and nine still down for descaling. They should be on line by the end of the week. The rest of his department is ready for sea."

"Very good." The men nodded. "And Commander Atsumi's report."

Arai pulled another document from his valise. Then, rapidly, he continued, commenting on Gunnery Officer Nobomitsu Atsumi's report, indicating all 32 of the ship's 127-millimeter dual-purpose cannons and 186 25-millimeter, triple-mount machine guns ready. "All magazines are fully loaded," he concluded.

"Fuel?"

"All tanks should be topped off by tomorrow, Admiral."

Fujita surprised everyone. "Then we could put to sea tomorrow?"

"Yes, sir. But with two boilers down, we could only make twenty-seven knots and we are still making repairs . . ."

"I am well aware of that, Captain," Fujita cut in curtly.

"Yes, sir," Arai said, his eyes seeking refuge in his papers. Whitehead smiled.

Fujita turned to Lieutenant Ephraim Schneerson, "Your report, Lieutenant."

Grasping a clutch of documents, Schneerson struggled to his feet. The timbre of his voice was low, hollow like a man speaking in a mausoleum. "A Russian carrier and two cruisers have been bought by Kadafi and are underway for the 'Med.' "

"We have been briefed on them. I am particularly interested in any intelligence you have on Rabta."

The Mossad agent continued, "It appears that Kadafi is enriching uranium at Rabta."

"And we have heard those rumors."

The young man shook his head. "No, sorry, Admiral, more than rumors. Just yesterday one of our operatives confirmed the presence of a nuclear reactor—a fast breeder—at Rabta, and the Arabs are definitely on their way to building a bomb with a yield of about twenty kilotons."

The men looked at each other and groaned.

"About the size of the Hiroshima bomb," Amberg said, before thinking. He reddened as his gaffe caused a stir amongst the Japanese. Fujita shifted his weight, Yoshi caught his breath, Arai glared, even Katsube looked up and breathed a spray of spittle in the direction of the American agent.

Sensing the poisonous static in the air, Schneerson hurried on, "We estimate they may have it in a minimum of three months, maximum of six."

Arai shouted, "We must strike. The enemy carriers, the bomb . . ."

Fujita silenced his executive officer with a wave. "Prisoner exchange?"

"Colonel Irving Bernstein, Commander Brent Ross, Lieutenant Elroy Rubin are to fly to Tripoli,

Saturday, their time zone."

"We know."

"The IDF has put all three thousand of our Arab prisoners at their disposal as bargaining chips, and, incidentally, the Arabs are holding your twenty-five airmen and three hundred of our men at a place called Al Aziziyab, which is a small town about fifty kilometers south of Tripoli." He glanced at the Americans, "About thirty-one miles."

Fujita said, "Now, we have no choice. We must sortie into the Mediterranean as quickly as possible." Every man in the room nodded.

Schneerson shocked everyone, "You have the *New Jersey.*"

"How did you know that?" Amberg blurted.

The sagging, tired countenance showed an ironic twist. "I'm afraid that is the worst-kept secret on earth. The terrorists have agents everywhere. They may even have informants on the battleship, itself."

Cheeks glowing, Amberg glared at Schneerson. The old invidious antagonism between the CIA and Mossad was becoming evident even in these two newcomers. Time and again Yoshi had seen heated arguments break out between members of the two organizations. CIA men were particularly galled by Mossad's consistent ability to outperform their agency while working on a budget that would not support the janitorial services at CIA headquarters. *Some things never change,* Yoshi said to himself, resignedly.

"Do they know her condition of readiness?" Fujita asked Schneerson.

"Not with great accuracy, Admiral, but they expect her to rendezvous with *Yonaga* and *Bennington* somewhere in the Pacific."

"They are preparing for us."

129

"We should make that assumption, sir."

"And the Canary Islands?"

"We don't expect an attack on them in the near future. The Arabs are hard put to maintain their bases in the Marianas and Tomonuto Atoll. We expect the Arab negotiators to try to trade off the Canary islands for prisoners and to stall for time to prepare their battle group."

The men snickered and looked at each other.

Whitehead said, "Have you heard of Sheik Iman Younis? I met him at Taipei."

"Yes."

"He seemed reasonable."

The Israeli nodded. "I met him in Geneva."

"He's still an Arab, Admiral," Amberg said, suddenly. However, Fujita never diverted his attention from Schneerson and Amberg's impromptu burst floated off like a bubble, weightless and unnoticed. Gritting his teeth, the young American glared at his shoes.

"Could you negotiate with him, Lieutenant Schneerson?" Fujita asked.

The Israeli looked at Amberg and smiled mockingly. "Let's say he's not as mad as Kadafi."

Amberg tried again, "Who is?" This time he managed to elicit a small titter.

Fujita said to Schneerson, "Your forces will attack when we enter the Mediterranean?"

"Yes, sir. We will attack by land, sea and air. A maximum effort, sir."

"Good." Fujita nodded at Arai and Whitehead. "We will begin our planning this afternoon at 1500 hours. I want both of you here and leave your personal quarrels elsewhere."

"Aye, aye, sir," both officers chorused.

Schneerson pinched his pursed lips. More trouble

130

was brewing in his eyes. "We are almost certain Harry Goodenough is in Japan."

"High Wire Harry," Amberg blurted incredulously.

"An assassin," Fujita said. "I have heard of him."

"Not just an assassin, sir," Schneerson said. "He's Kadafi's most talented, inventive, and efficient killer, Admiral. He makes amateurs of the best, or worst, of them." He took a deep breath like a diver on a high board, and then to make his point he ran through a frightening list of international killers and thugs, "Goodenough outdoes Carlos the Jackal, Mohammed Jamal, Abu Nidal, George Habash, Bassam Abu Sharif, Mario Moretti, Ahmed Jibril, Petra Krause, von Arb, Ulrike Meinhof, Gudrun Ensslin, Jan-Carl Raspe, Armando Carrillo . . ."

Fujita cut in, showing all he, too, was well informed, "But we have our own killer-rabble—Taketomo Takahashi, Jun Nishikawa, and dozens more of *Rengo Sekigun*. They are not amateurs, Mister Schneerson. On the contrary, they have proved themselves to be fanatical, ruthless murderers." He glanced at Yoshi. Yoshi and Arai looked back and nodded concurrence.

"True, Admiral," Schneerson agreed. "But Goodenough is in a class of his own. He's not a common terrorist who plants bombs in airports, airliners, or other crude attacks. No indeed, such mass, mundane killings are beneath him. Instead, he's a murderer who thrives on contract killings, usually of prominent politicians. Incidentally, his fee is a million dollars a hit. He always stalks an individual or individuals until the most propitious moment for the kill and then strikes with ruthless savagery. He has never failed an assignment."

"Then he could be after Prime Minister Kiichi

131

Miyazawa, cabinet ministers, ambassadors," Captain Mitake Arai exclaimed.

"True, Captain Arai. He could be stalking someone famous, but, on the other hand, his target could be one of small stature nationally and internationally but of key importance to our effort."

The old admiral clamped his remaining teeth together and tugged on the white whisker, "You have a description."

"All eyewitnesses are dead, but, we have reliable reports that he is a big blond Englishman with very white skin. Interpol has helped us with this."

Elliot Amberg said, "He's also known as 'Garlic Mouth.' "

" 'Garlic Mouth'!" The ludicrous sobriquet filled the room with laughter.

"True," Schneerson said over the noise. "AKA 'Garlic Mouth.' He believes garlic gives him strength. Eats raw cloves of it."

"Tall, blond Englishman. Easy to identify in Japan," Captain Arai noted.

"And easy to smell," Rear Admiral Whitehead quipped. "Just don't get to leeward of him or his breath will do the killing for him." More laughter.

Schneerson was not amused. He fixed his attention on the executive officer. "Perhaps you're right, Captain Arai. But he is a master of disguise. He could look like an Italian, a Greek, Frenchman, a bent old man, Buddhist monk." The Mossad agent threw up his hands in a nugatory gesture and then looked around at the skeptical faces.

Captain Arai said seriously, "That is hard to believe."

Schneerson moved his eyes from Arai and held his gaze on Fujita. "That is the complete truth of the matter, sir."

"The truth is not enough," Fujita said, Zen breaking through.

"Not enough?"

"Not here." Fujita waved at the Japanese, "A samurai cannot fear the 'truth' of his enemy's killing prowess. The samurai, himself, is the most efficient killing machine on earth — and that is the truth."

"Banzai!" resounded in the cabin.

The admiral waved the shouting off. "We cannot allow ourselves to be distracted or intimidated by the supposed presence of this one man. We have thousands to fight and kill."

"But, sir," Ephraim Schneerson persisted. "You could post more guards, send escorts with your staff members when they go ashore . . ."

"We are short of seaman guards now." His hand made an encompassing sweep. "We must guard all of this facility — *Yonaga, Bennington,* twelve *Fletchers, Haida,* the shops, warehouses, graving dock. We are stretched too thin now, Mr. Schneerson." He pounded the desk with both fists. "To us this 'High Wire Harry' is just another killer and we know how to deal with him."

Yoshi sensed a false note in the admiral's voice, his demeanor, the rigidness of his body. He had known the old man for over a half-century and could read him better than anyone. Was he putting on his usual iron front for his subordinates? If he were apprehensive about Goodenough, he was not allowing it to show. Indeed, he seemed almost disinterested in the killer's presence in Japan. Something was amiss.

Tucking his lips under, Schneerson's face became a masterpiece of frustration. "Mark me, sir. He will strike — quick, fast, like a cobra."

The old man hunched over his clenched fists, still the unimpressed iron admiral. "Remember, Mr.

Schneerson, the cobra must poke his head out of his hole before you can chop it off." More cheers.

Schneerson waited for the cheers to die, the frustration fading from his face. He knew the Goodenough matter was ended. He spoke to a far more pleasant topic, "You know the Arabs made a major effort to break through our lines last week."

"We have had the reports. It failed."

Schneerson smiled and his fatigue seemed to slake off. "Your 'American samurai,' Commander Brent Ross, distinguished himself at our most forward observation post, *Bren ah Hahd*. In fact, the battle has taken that name." He looked around at the eager faces. "He fought like a tiger and saved the life of Colonel David Moskowitz. According to reports he personally killed at least ten of the enemy."

"Banzai!" Katsube, Arai and Matsuhara shouted. Then Whitehead said, "By God, I'll add my own *'Banzai!'* to that."

The men laughed and nodded at each other.

Fujita raised his hand. "He is a samurai. We could not expect less."

"Hear! Hear!" Whitehead shouted.

Schneerson demolished the high spirits. "You may lose Commander Ross in Tripoli—lose them all."

"We know," Fujita said. He tapped his bony knuckles on the oak and stared at a spot high on the opposite bulkhead. "The great Emperor Meiji said in his rescript to the famous Sendai Division, 'Death is as light as a feather, duty is as heavy as the mountain.' "

"They know their duty, Admiral," Rear Admiral Whitehead said. "But death is no feather, sir."

Fujita smiled, inscrutable cracks in the old parchment. "It depends on your viewpoint, Admiral Whitehead."

"True, sir."

"Tenno heika banzai!" Katsube shouted abruptly, head lolling from side to side, saliva running off his chin. Yoshi braced him again. And again the old scribe brushed off the fighter pilot with an angry swipe of his claw, spewing, *"Mamushi!"*

Fujita rose slowly and every man followed. Even Katsube managed to struggle to his feet by bracing himself on the desk. Facing the small shrine, Fujita clapped twice to attract the gods. He believed odd numbers were unlucky. The other Japanese also clapped twice. Speaking in reverential tones, the old admiral invoked the usual powers of both Shintoism and Buddhism, "Oh great sun goddess Amaterasu-O-Mi-Kami and our god of war, Hachiman-san, combine to smile on our efforts. Guide us in our struggle to save our sacred islands from these monsters who would enslave the world. Free us from the illusory chains of ego and reality and guide us to the Eightfold Path of Gautama Buddha—right views, right resolve, right speech, right action, right living, right effort, right mindfulness, and right concentration." Pausing, he gazed around the room at the intent faces and then found the shrine again, "And if we die, let us die nobly, facing our enemies." There was a long hush. Fujita broke it, "Gentlemen, you may return to your duties."

Silently, the men began to file from the room. Arai helped old Katsube find his way. This time the bent old scribe did not resist. Admiral Fujita's voice stopped one, "Commander Matsuhara, please remain."

"Aye, aye, sir." The aviator returned to his chair.

After the door closed the old man sagged down in his chair, eyes unfocused as though his mind had just received a phone call. Idly, bent tendril-like fingers toyed with the white hair that hung from his chin like

135

a thread overlooked by a careless seamstress. Maybe his mind had opened the door on the past, where he often dwelled with amazing vividness. Or, perhaps, he was mulling the coming attack in the Mediterranean, developing strategy, designing tactics. Was he concerned about Harry "High Wire" Goodenough? One thing was certain, no man could fathom the complex workings of that Gordian mind.

The old sailor refocused on Yoshi and opened innocuously enough, "Yoshi-san, we have served together for over five decades."

"I could not have served the Emperor better, Admiral."

The deep chiseled lines crumpled into a pattern Yoshi recognized as a smile. "You are the best air group commander in the world, Yoshi-san."

A rare compliment. The old man had something unpleasant on his mind. Alerted, the pilot said, "You are kind, Admiral."

"No, Yoshi-san. I follow the sacred Buddha's noble Eightfold Path. Speak the truth."

"Of course, sir."

"*Yonaga* faces her greatest challenge. A powerful battle group is assembling and uranium prepared for an atomic bomb." The admiral sighed. "We must act before we are prepared to act."

"An axiom for men of our profession," Yoshi said, trying to appear confident. However, he knew the odds against the admiral's plan were long—perhaps, too long. He sensed disaster was almost inevitable. But the samurai always attacked, regardless of odds. Everyone knew that.

The old man made a circle with a finger on the desktop, raised his hand and struck a single point in the center as if he were pointing at an important object. And indeed he was. "Sicily!"

"Sicily, sir?"

"Yes. It is the key." He waved at the chart behind him. "Easy range to Tripoli."

"But it's Italian, and they will not fight. They are lovers, not fighters. Everyone knows that. Why, it has been said, 'If Italy is neutral you must send a division to watch her. If she wars against you, you must send two divisions to fight her and if she is your ally, you must send four divisions to save her.' " Yoshi waited while the old man chuckled and then added, "And the Italians need OPEC's oil."

Fujita said, "England's Prime Minister Major and the President of the United States are pressuring the Italians. As you know, the British have rebuilt their North Sea platforms and production is rising daily. This time they have installed antitorpedo nets and barriers around all twelve platforms. They can supply the Italians with all the oil they need, and the Americans will extend twenty billion in credits through the world bank. And the Vatican, too, is pressuring the Italian government. The Pope is deeply concerned about the *jihad*—the spread of militant Islam."

"Then you've been negotiating?"

"Secretly with the Italian ambassador. And our two top special negotiators, Nishio Kanji and Mori Tokumitsu, are in Rome. It appears we will get our base in Sicily. And, of course, Yoshi-san, this is top secret. I am discussing this with you because you cannot attend the meeting this afternoon. You are the only staff member who knows. Not even Ephraim Schneerson and Elliot Amberg are privy to this information."

"It is secure with me, sir." Yoshi rose and walked to the chart. "How will we ferry aircraft to Sicily?"

"We will not."

"I don't understand."

137

"The Israeli Air Force can fly squadrons there, and when we attack, they can support us with strikes on Tripoli and the Arab battle group."

Joyfully, Yoshi punched the chart three short jabs. "Sacred Amaterasu! Then, we can do it!"

The disturbed look returned. "We face a great bloody struggle, Yoshi-san."

The pilot felt a cold visceral spring tighten as he returned to his chair. The trouble he had sensed was about to surface. Seating himself, he said, "True, sir. But we've defeated the enemy every time we have met on the field of battle. Defeat is a stranger to *Yonaga*."

"At a cost."

"True, Admiral. But we all know a samurai's karma is enhanced by the tenacity and skill of his enemy." The aviator gesticulated at the *Hagakure*, "It is written: 'Meditation on inevitable death should be performed daily and one should consider oneself as dead before battle—fight as one already dead.' "

Obviously pleased, the old man nodded and quoted some lines from an ancient poem: " 'As everything in the world is but a sham, Death is the only sincerity.' "

"The only sincerity, sir," the pilot mused. Then he remembered another ancient verse: " 'If in one's heart, He follows the path of sincerity, Though he does not pray, The gods will protect him.' "

"Yes. Yes," the old man agreed, patting the book. "There is the wisdom of the ages, here, Yoshi-san." Then Fujita crossed his hands across his chest and rubbed the knuckles of one hand with the palm of the other. "You have a personal feud with that renegade American, *Oberst* Kenneth Rosencrance."

"And with his fellow butcher, *Oberleutnant* Rudolph Stoltz, Admiral. You know Rosencrance murdered my wingman, Colin Willard-Smith, in his parachute." He pinched his furrowed forehead and stared at the overhead. "Revenge is sacred and I seek it, Admiral."

"Of course. None of us can forget the lesson of *The Forty-Seven Ronin*. Revenge is more precious than life itself." The old man straightened and gripped Yoshi's eyes with his. Yoshi knew the disturbing subject he had sensed earlier was coming. Fujita picked up the book and balanced it on his palm. "You know the book well, Yoshi-san."

"I have studied it for over a half-century, sir."

"Then you know the Buddhist priest Laion said: 'It is a difficult thing to truly know one's own limits and weak points.' " He dropped the volume on the desk. It struck with a sharp slapping sound of finality.

Yoshi felt alarm tinged with fear deep down on the very periphery of his awareness. The spring coiled tighter painfully. "My weak points, sir?"

The old man sighed. "These men you fight are young."

Now, Yoshi knew the old man's mind. "Yes," he agreed, candidly. "Very young."

"And you are the oldest fighter pilot on earth."

"I can fight with the best of them."

"True, but time ignores none of us. No man can avoid the inroads of the years."

Yoshi tasted the sour bile of panic. "You would ground me, sir?"

Fujita fingered his pate. "As air group commander you could command from *Yonaga* just as well. Most air group commanders do not fly."

"Send my men out to die while I sit behind armor plate and wait to count them when they return?"

"It comes to all of us, Yoshi-san. I have spent years counting—searching for your Zero-sen up there."

"Respectfully, sir. I would prefer to commit *sep-puku*."

Fujita pointed at the overhead. "You would do the same up there."

"What better place to die, sir? In the realm of the gods."

The response had been perfect. The old man rubbed his tiny chin and turned his thin lips under in a thoughtful grimace. "You are a samurai through and through, Yoshi-san."

"Yes, sir. Thank you, sir." He stared expectantly.

Fingers began to war with the oak. Finally, Fujita clasped his hands, sighed deeply, conceding, "I will not deny you, Yoshi-san."

"Thank you, sir," Yoshi said, the tight, cold spring uncoiling.

"But promise me this, if you feel you cannot perform without endangering your own men, you will ground yourself."

"My word pledged before Izanami and Izanagi, who gave birth to our sacred islands. I owe that to my men."

"Very well. I ask for no more."

Yoshi felt the conversation was over. But he was wrong. "You have a woman," the admiral said, bluntly. "Her name is Tomoko Ozumori and she is a secretary in the supply office of the Maritime Self Defense Force. She is a widow and lives in a remote outskirt of the Itabashi District."

Yoshi was not surprised at the admiral's knowledge. Everyone knew he had informants; his personal intelligence network. But it was more than that. Sometimes, it seemed he controlled unseen waves that penetrated a man's psyche, read his innermost secrets.

"Yes," Yoshi answered. "That is true."

"You have deep feelings for her."

"She enriches me."

"Women can, and they can also distract."

"No man is complete without his woman, Admiral."

"I know, Yoshi-san. I was not always an old man."

"Sorry, sir. I spoke without thinking."

The old sailor sighed sorrowfully, and Zen crept in. "Youth is truly the moment of greatest power in a man's life and he does not see it until he looks back from old age." Shaking the musty webs from his mind, be asked crisply, "You would marry her?"

"No, sir. She has lost her husband to the Arabs. I would not make her a widow twice over."

"You must love her very deeply, Yoshi-san."

"True, sir."

"Her safety is a concern."

"I have offered to ask you for seaman guards, but she refuses, sir. She knows from her work that most of our guards are detailed to guarding our ships and the yards. The Tokyo police have promised to maintain a watch."

"Hah! They are women. Less than useless."

"I know, sir."

"An alley cat with broken claws could break into any of our houses — tissue paper and bamboo."

"Not her house, sir. She has moved into a two-story, Western-style home with solid doors and strong walls. It is much like the house I lived in when I was a youth in Los Angeles."

"But it is not a fortress and you still worry, Yoshi-san."

"Of course, sir. But her doors are double-bolted, windows secure, and she has her telephone. If Sabbah or *Rengo Sekigun* assassins move against her, it would be in attempt to ambush me." He patted his seven-millimeter Otsu "Baby Nambu" automatic pistol bulging in its shoulder holster under his tunic. "And

141

you know I'm very careful and a seaman guard is my driver."

"I understand. However, I believe we should provide her with some security. A new company of seaman guards will report from Kyushu Monday. We will have adequate manpower and I will assign guards to her if she approves or not."

"My gratitude, sir. I will see her Sunday night and inform her, Admiral."

The old man fell silent, fingers of one hand beating a tattoo on the oak. Then he admitted to a depth of concern not evident during the staff meeting, but suspected by Yoshi. "This Harry 'High Wire' Goodenough deeply disturbs Ephraim Schneerson."

"His infamy has spread worldwide, sir."

"I know. It is well-earned."

"Yes."

"I will personally inform the Emperor, alert the palace guard and order Schneerson and Amberg to apprise all government Offices." He pounded the desk for emphasis, "But I do not want the crew to feel we are overly concerned by this one thug. It would be contrary to the code of Bushido and bad for morale. We cannot have this."

Now Yoshi understood the admiral's ambivalence and recalcitrance in the presence of the other officers. One man could not be allowed to upset the supreme commander of the forces of freedom. "Of course, sir. Good idea, sir."

"It is the big men, the leaders he stalks."

"That is his reputation, Admiral."

"But sometimes he kills little-known people if significant in their influence."

"Yes, sir." Yoshi shifted his weight uneasily. "My woman, Admiral, you are thinking of her."

"It is a possibility."

142

"He doesn't know Tomoko exists."

"Good, Yoshi-san. Good. The less our enemies know of our personal lives the better." He pressed the fingertips of both hands together to form a temple. "I am happy you have found her and may the gods bless both of you," he intoned like a priest in a temple.

"Thank you, sir."

"You are dismissed."

The commander stood, bowed, and left.

Stepping into the passageway, he passed two guards and turned aft toward his own cabin. He was reaching for the doorknob, when his old friend and fellow plank owner, Gunnery officer Lieutenant Commander Nobomitsu Atsumi, entered the far end of the passageway. Atsumi was much like Yoshi, resisting the years, black hair showing only a few inroads of gray, clear skin traced by a scattering of lines trailing down from the corners of his eyes and mouth. He had a wry sense of humor and loved to kid. Nothing was sacred.

Atsumi grasped Yoshi's hand with a powerful grip and pounded his shoulder. "Back aboard, Yoshi-san. Good to see you. It has been weeks."

"Good to see you, Nobomitsu-san. Your department is ready?" Yoshi said.

"Affirmative. And yours?"

"Always," Yoshi said. They both laughed at the obvious exaggeration. Yoshi tilted his head toward the door. "Come in. We have much to discuss." He glanced at his watch. "I have a few minutes before I return to Tokyo International."

"Sorry, old friend. I must report to the admiral. I have requisitioned some new proximity fuses and they have not arrived." He smiled. "Through the secretary at the supply office of the Maritime Self Defense Force."

Yoshi knew Atsumi was toying with him. "Lack of efficiency," Yoshi said with a blank face.

"You are still seeing the secretary, Tomoko Ozumori? She is a beautiful woman."

"Yes," Yoshi said guardedly. "I saw her last night."

The gunnery officer looked the pilot up and down and he said slyly, "You look tired, Yoshi-san."

The pilot shifted uneasily. "I left — ah, early. It's a long drive."

Atsumi knew he had breached a sensitive area, and he pushed the needle in further, "Then she has a chance to rest — get some sleep."

"Yes," Yoshi said, keeping his aplomb. "She lives in a remote area. It is very quiet. I am sure she slept well." And then sarcastically, "I'll tell her of your concern." The gunnery officer laughed.

Quickly, Yoshi opened the door but before he could enter, Atsumi halted him. "Oh, Yoshi-san." There was warmth in his voice.

"Yes."

"I am happy for you. You are a very fortunate man."

The pilot smiled. "Thank you, Nobomitsu-san." He stepped into the cabin and closed the door behind him.

Six

Minutes after Yoshi left, Tomoko had dropped on the futon on her back, arms and legs outflung, in the deep sleep of the sexually sated. It seemed only minutes later that something had tried to intrude, disturb her sleep. Perhaps it was the chirruping of crickets in the fields, or the unseasonable heat that still rose from the earth long after the sun had vanished. She was not sure. Certainly, the heat from the fierce lovemaking had left her skin warm and rosy as if she had rubbed too vigorously with a Turkish towel. In any event the usual sea breeze had failed and it was hot—so hot she did not even cover her nude body with a sheet.

But something disturbed her again, this time jarring her from the enveloping mesh of the web of darkness. Then she saw him. Standing just inside the door in a shaft of early dawn's weak light streaming through the room's single window. Young. Tall. Was he an apparition, part of a dream torn from her subconscious? No. She could hear his heavy breathing. Her nerves jerked tight like a line struck by a marlin, and a hollow nauseatina sickness gripped her stomach. She drew her legs up like a fetus, lips trembling, unable to speak, staring.

His hair was long and so blond it glistened like strands of silver, face rough and white like boiled rice.

145

And he remained standing in the light as if he enjoyed the terror his appearance struck in the woman. His pants were tight denim, his jacket leather, and he was big. Very big, not like a sumo wrestler, but like a body builder. Even his wrists were thick and sinewy, and his tree-trunk legs filled his denims. Strangely, a coil of wire was hanging from his belt.

"Been fuckin' *Yonaga*'s bloody butcher," he said casually, in a soft high voice that rustled in the room like the wings of death. His inflection told her she was dealing with an Englishman.

Grabbing the phone, she lunged to her feet. He laughed. Stepped toward her. "I cut the bloody wires, 'ore." He threw his head back and laughed. "If you think your Nip gave you a good jig-a-jig, wait'll I 'ave a go at you."

He threw a switch and the room filled with light. He looked her up and down. "Smashing body for a Jap baggage — got the whole lot. Nice, round titties, good 'ips, nice arse an'," he smiled, looking at her mound of black pubic hair, "a nice warm pussy. I always 'eard Jap pussies was cut at a bias, now I'm going to find out for me-self." He giggled. "Your Matsuhara left somethin' there tonight, but even sloppy seconds is a bit of all right."

Fear made her legs rubbery, and her insides turned to ice water. "Stay away from me," she screamed hysterically, raising the phone.

"Quit playing silly buggers and put your arse on that ruddy thing you call a bed," he said like a scolding schoolteacher. He waved at the futon. "I'm going to give you the bullocking of your life." He stepped toward her.

She wanted to flee, but there was nowhere to go. Rape. And be intended to kill her afterwards. She was certain of that. He was wearing gloves. Would leave

146

no prints. He stepped closer. Slowly. Relentlessly. Heavy steps that creaked on the wooden floor. She screamed. He laughed. "Who's to 'ear you, 'ore. We're out in the boonies."

A part of her wondered if she were losing her mind. Surely, she was dreaming it all. But he was real, his blue eyes chips of ice shining with frigid passion. She screamed again. He laughed. Reached for her.

At that instant the fear was supplanted by a more powerful emotion: hate, anger, fury. Hers was not the calculated anger of a woman facing an arrogant man's usurpation of her dignity, her rights. It was more primal than that. He had broken into her private space, her sanctum sanctorum, threatened the very sanctity of her body. Her nudity added to the violation. An atavistic rage blurred her vision and sent her heart racing, blood pounding in her neck, her temples. She skinned her lips back, growled deep in her throat, reduced to an unconscious animal response.

She threw the phone. With the force of pumping adrenaline behind it, it bounced off of his forehead with a gay ringing sound, opening an ugly gash.

He faltered. Then staggered back. Reached up and found blood and she was around him, running through the doorway into the main room. He was no longer in a perversely playful mood. Hard on her heels, his voice was filled with anger, "Bloody bitch! Bloody bitch!"

He cut her off so that she had no chance for the door. Instead, she turned to the corner of the room which held the *tokonoma* behind a large diagonally placed couch. The *tokonoma* consisted of a table, two vases, flowers, a Heian scroll. She grabbed a vase by the neck, moved behind the couch, and waved it menacingly.

147

He stopped on the other side of the couch, hands on hips, arms akimbo. The playful mood was back. He laughed heartily. "Buggeration, you're a dotty little cunt." He reached up and wiped blood from his wound with the back of his glove. "I say, if you fuck the way you fight, you'll be better'n any 'ore I've 'ad at Soho."

She hurled the vase. He ducked with quick, instinctual quickness. The porcelain struck the heavy front door and exploded like a bomb, fragments raining down on the wooden floor and tatami mats.

"Blimey, good show, old girl," he said mockingly. " 'ave another go." He pointed at the other vase.

She grasped its neck. Weighed the vase in her hand, this time testing its balance. Most of its weight was in its base. She faked a throw.

Deceived by the feint, he dropped low and to one side to avoid the missile.

With a cry of triumph, she threw the vase.

Off balance, it caught him squarely on the ear and bounced off, crashing to the floor in a rain of bits and pieces. This time he cried out and grabbed the side of his head. He did not go down. No new blood. He was not even seriously injured. But she had hurt him again and the pain and frustration transformed him. The pasty white rice flesh turned to baked salmon, mouth a line drawn by a straight edge, lips tightly compressed. Fury had wound him up like the spring of an old clock; the muscles of his neck bulging, taut, hard. He dropped into a crouch, ready to charge.

She expected him to come around the couch and she intended to circle away from him, using the couch as a barrier between them until she could find another weapon. She eyed a large gold Buddha resting in its small shrine on the opposite wall. She envisioned smashing it into his hateful face.

Snarling, he came after her. But there was no stalking, no subtle feints. Instead, he charged straight at her without finesse, like a corrida bull goaded by picadores into a blind rage. He leaped on the couch, tilting it with his weight, and crashing down. He kept his balance perfectly and reached out with one massive arm to trap her.

Screaming, she ducked under the arm and raced around the couch, anger giving way to fear again. The front door was no good. Double bolted, she would never throw off both locks in time to escape.

He had crashed into the *tokonoma,* splintering the table and, apparently, bruising his hip. Running toward the stairs, she grabbed the solid brass Buddha from its shrine. He jumped over the couch and was close behind her, footfalls thunderous, cursing, "Bloody 'ore. I'll sort your hash good, now."

The upstairs were a trap and she knew it. But she had no choice. Maybe the attic. Anything to prolong her life. Breathing hard, she took the stairs two at a time. But he bounded after her like a hungry predator closing on its quarry.

He caught her in the second-floor hallway. Panting, sweating, he yanked her around like a toy and pulled her against him. She drove the Buddha into his ribs and she heard the air explode from his lungs. He knocked the statuette away and pulled her tight against him, grabbing both of her wrists with one massive hand. He pulled her so tight she could feel his erection.

Apparently, he had never encountered a woman who fought back so fiercely. She had tricked him three times. Hurt him. He had expected timid prey, easily subdued. This one had turned and struck back with fangs and claws. But now he had her. He slapped her so hard across the face, comets soared across her retinas and a black curtain dropped. "Oh! Oh!"

Holding her up with one hand, he pushed her against the wall with her hands pinned behind her, wrists still grasped by his hand. The pain in her upper arms and shoulders was excruciating. Shocked her back to full consciousness. She cried out.

"I've got a bloody jugful of this lot," he growled. "Stop fightin' or I'll bust you again an' this time I'll break your jaw an' then bust up both your arms, tear 'em out o' their bloody sockets."

She knew he could do it. "All right. All right," she sobbed.

"What's in there?" he waved at a door.

"A spare bedroom."

He pushed her through the door and pointed at the futon. "Assume the position—on your arse and spread 'em."

"No. Please, I'll pay you anything."

"Shut up and do what I tell you!"

She walked to the futon on rubbery legs and dropped on it weakly. He turned on the light.

"Why the light?" she asked.

"I get my bags off better when I can see you." Now he was the smug, calculating, almost playful rapist she had first faced in her bedroom. But something had been triggered deep inside, switches thrown, programs changed, new circuits coming to life. There were wants and needs to be read on the pasty face and squinting blue eyes of hungers that were far more disgusting and perverted than anything Tomoko had first envisioned. There was no semblance of rationality anymore. His demeanor was that of a lunatic. The ice was gone from his eyes, replaced by a watery, steamy, unblinking stare. Sweat beaded on his forehead and streamed down his cheeks. Not only was rape there, but death, too.

150

He tore off his jacket, unzipped his pants and pulled them down with his underwear. He was huge. Tomoko had heard Western men were bigger than Japanese men, but she had never expected a man to bear such an enormous organ. She thought of kicking him in the crotch and escaping. But that would not work.

He loomed over her. "Spread 'em, I said!"

"No!"

He slapped her again; once, twice. The comets were joined by planets and small flashing suns. She felt her legs pulled apart and a great weight settled between them. He was like a great beast on her, rough, heavy, crushing her, leering down, his frightening glassy eyes deep and empty, breath foul and stinking of garlic. Roughly, a big hand reached down, fingered the lips of her sex, and plunged in. "Straight up an' down, no bias," he said, giggling. "Still wet an' 'ot from your lover-boy. But wait'll you get a bit o' this. No Nip ever humped you with a cock like mine."

When a young girl, Tomoko had fantasized about rape—even romanticized it a little in her teenage fancy. But now she discovered its horror, its violence. She cried out with pain as the turgid staff drove into her. She had had a child and had loved many men. But she was not prepared for this. With both hands, he pushed hard on the inside of her thighs, widening the gap between her legs.

"Please," she cried. "You're hurting me."

"It'll be tickety-boo, sweetie. You'll see."

She writhed in pain as he thrust deep, withdrew and thrust again and again. She was not ready for him and could never be. She felt as if she were being split apart, ripped, torn. The thought of the damage he could do to her softest tissues made her gag with horror. It was possible to even kill a woman this way. She whimpered, clawed at his back.

151

He misread her. "See! I tol' you. A fuckin' like you never 'ad."

Finally, he grabbed her buttocks and pulled her so hard against him, she cried out in agony.

He shuddered, slobbered on her neck, bit it, groaned, and went limp.

Thank the gods, she thought. *It is over.*

But she was wrong. He lay on top of her and stroked her hair. "Now that wasn't too bad," he cooed. "Got it off, too, didn't you sweetie."

"Yes, yes," she lied, trying her final ploy. "You were right. I have never felt anything like it. You will have to come back."

His laugh was frightening. "Yes. I'll come again." More laughter. Then she understood. There was a swelling inside of her. He was aroused again. She could not believe it. No man had ever done this. Again, the thrusts, the pain, the spurting inside of her. Thankfully, this time he rolled off of her. Maybe he would go to sleep. She would escape. But she was wrong. He rolled her over on her side and spooned against her back, arms around her, hands grasping her breasts, limp organ pressed against her buttocks.

"Nice titties. I like 'em." He fondled her breasts for a long time, rubbing his thumbs over the nipples. Tomoko felt nothing but pain and revulsion. His assault had left her sore and too wet. Maybe she was bleeding. Unbelievably, the organ began to swell again. He pushed it against her buttocks.

"No! Please! Not that!"

"Shut up!" He pushed her roughly onto her stomach. She felt his weight on her back push her into the hard mat of the futon. She turned her head aside, gasping for air.

It seemed the nightmare went on forever. He had

expended himself twice, so the third horror lasted longer. Finally, it was over, and he rolled off of her with a loud groan. Breathing hard and sweating, he rested.

Pain flamed deep down. She had been injured by the perversion. She was staining the sheet with blood. "Can I go to the bathroom," she whispered in a barely perceptible voice.

The question seemed to galvanize him. "No!" He rolled from the bed and dressed, never taking his eyes from the woman. "Get up!"

"I cannot."

"Get your arse outta there, you bloody twit!" He grabbed her by the arm and jerked her to her feet. She thought she would faint, reeled backwards, knees buckling. Cursing, he dragged her into the hallway and to the head of the stairs.

She watched him numbly as he pulled the wire from his belt, looped it around the top post of the banister and tightened it. She wondered why. How strange.

Then he turned to her and holding her with one hand, wrapped the wire around her neck twice, tied it, and secured it with a clamp.

Fear that went beyond fear into the realm of hysteria tore through her. Even in her weakened condition, she fought him with both hands, grabbing his hair, scratching his face.

He punched her, knocking her to the floor and breaking her jaw. She could only moan as he picked her up like a broken doll, walked to the bannister, and held her out over the main room for a moment. "Hate to do this, Missy," he said with mock regret. "You were one fine piece."

He dropped her.

Seven

The 1985 Cadillac left an ostrich plume of dust in its wake as it roared over Route One, the highway to Jerusalem. Corporal Ruth Moskowitz jerked the wheel hard to the left, passing a caravan of four buses so quickly the vehicles seemed rooted in the concrete.

Clinging to his armrest, Commander Brent Ross pleaded, "It's only thirty miles to Jerusalem. At this rate we'll be there in nineteen minutes or dead in nineteen milliseconds."

"Whoa, girl," came from Lieutenant Junior Grade Elroy Rubin. "It's right neighborly o' you to take strangers on this here hoe down, but, respectfully, this ain't no bronc you're a-bustin' an I ain't hankerin' for that great roundup in the sky, nohow."

There was a giggle from a young woman seated next to the Texan. "Oh, Elroy," she said in a squeaky voice that grated on Brent's nerves like fingernails across a chalkboard, "you say the cutest things."

Brent sighed and relaxed his grip on the armrest when Ruth passed the last bus, whipping the Cadillac back into its lane and decelerating.

"All right, boys," the driver said, grinning. "We'll rein the maverick in a bit."

"Whew! All the way down to Mach one," Brent said glancing at the speedometer while releasing pent-up breath like steam from a pressure cooker.

Ruth laughed. "Sorry. Hope no one lost sphincter control."

"I don't know nothin' 'bout that, but I pert near wet my pants."

The fingernails scratched the board, "Oh, Elroy, you're so naughty, you'll be the death of me."

"You ain't seen nothin' yet. Come here, you little filly. I'm hankerin' to show you a thang or two."

"Can't. Seat belt, you know."

"Don't pay it no never mind." There was a metallic snapping sound, a loud giggle, grunts, groans and, "Oh, Elroy. Stop, you naughty boy."

"Hey, back there," Ruth shouted with her usual bluntness, "no copulating in the back seat—against regulations."

"Don't bother your pretty little head none, Ruth. I reckon I can kiss Linda, cain't I?"

"No humping. No love juice on the upholstery," Ruth said. "This is the only Cad in the motor pool and I almost surrendered my maidenhead to get it."

"Maidenhead!" Linda exclaimed, shocked.

"Figuratively, not literally," Ruth explained.

"Figura-ah, figure what?" the perplexed Linda muttered.

Ruth chuckled politely. "Don't take me seriously, Linda." And then brusquely, "I didn't screw anyone for the car." A wicked little smile toyed with her lips and she caught Brent from the corner of her eye. "Flirted a little, let a guy or two cop a feel, but I kept my honor."

Knowing she was deliberately baiting him, Brent blanked his visage into a stoic mask, determined to deny the girl the satisfaction of seeing the slightest reaction. Notwithstanding, he liked her demeanor. From the moment she had picked him up, he had seen the change like an inner illumination; a blithe spirit that contrasted sharply with the dark, embittered cynicism of the girl he had left Thursday night. And she was animated, smiling and vivacious, treating Elroy and Linda like old friends although their acquaintance was less than two hours old. She was completely at ease; rank meant nothing to any of them. They were just four young people out on a double date together. Precisely what she wanted — war and gold stripes be damned.

To Brent she appeared even more beautiful, sensual, and sexy. It seemed she had as many moods and faces as the sea and was as unpredictable. When she laughed her eyes shone like coal freshly cut from the face. Carefully brushed and groomed, her long brown hair fell in folds to her shoulders, glossy as satin. Deliberately hiked higher than necessary, almost to midthigh, her short khaki skirt flaunted her slender yet muscular legs. He shifted uneasily, his emotions goaded by the pervasive force of her sexuality.

Elroy's jest distracted Brent, "I'm rightly proud 'o you, Ruth, gettin' this fine car. You drive a hard bargain — get it, *drive a hard bargain*."

"Oh, Elroy," Linda snickered.

Brent turned to stare at an Israeli modified Humvee as the Cadillac shot past it. In desert camouflage, it mounted a pair of American M-60 machine guns in a cramped, jury-rigged turret. Very unusual, very clever, very deadly.

"Funny-looking car, isn't it Brent?" Linda said, following his eyes.

Brent twisted around. Linda Crane had unbuckled and snuggled close to Elroy. Staring at Brent, her blue-green eyes were wide, waiting for something, needing something, but comprehending so little they seemed to open on a vacuum. Although she was slow-witted, had poorly frosted brown hair worn in that popular scraggly, disheveled style that Brent loathed, her face was attractive — much like a nubile adolescent without the zits. Her body was spectacular. Big, jiggly, swaying breasts that made Brent wonder about quarts of silicone, small waist, rounded high-riding buttocks and a nice accommodating spread to her hips; not too wide, just broad and curvaceous enough to provoke the passing male and give him thoughts of the slippery hot delights to be found there. "Right sexy filly. 'Nuff shaky puddin' for the whole bunk house," Elroy had confided when he first described Linda Crane. On that score the Texan was right.

"My, it's pretty out there," Linda murmured, waving at well tended farms and distant stands of pine, eucalyptus, and oak. "I thought it would be dry like a desert."

"Yup," Elroy agreed. "I fancied another panhandle, pure and simple."

Brent felt that Elroy was overworking the country bumpkin guise. The sharp intellect seemed buried under an avalanche of twisted verbiage. Brent suspected he was playing the part to the hilt for the dense Linda's sake.

Waving her left hand, Ruth said, "We have our desert. In fact, the Negev is the southern half of the country. But we're on the coastal plain — the Plain of Judea. It's like a different world here. The western mountains hold in the sea air and give us good climate here." Her hand left the wheel and made an encompassing sweep. "Believe it or not, once, centuries ago, this was all a great forest."

"Cain't ken that."

"It was," Ruth insisted. "But the Arabs cut down

157

the trees, overgrazed with their damned goats and turned it into a wasteland."

"It's no wasteland now," Linda countered.

Ruth nodded at the long hood stretching ahead of her. "We've had to reclaim it. Even replace topsoil." She stabbed a finger, "Over there, citrus groves. And there plums, apricots, peaches, and over there lettuce, tomatoes, cucumbers, carrots, and all kinds of vegetables.

"Like south Texas," said the Texan.

"More like Southern California," Brent declared.

"The Arabs planted nothin' hereabouts."

"That's right," Ruth said.

Brent insinuated himself in slyly, "According to the Book of Genesis, the sons of Adam and Eve started it."

"Started what?"

"Farming and domesticating animals, Elroy," Brent replied.

Smiling, Ruth quoted Genesis: "Now Abel was a keeper of sheep, and Cain a tiller of the ground."

"Our preacher told us Cain killed Abel," Linda said, eager to show her knowledge.

"That's another story."

"Oh."

They began to pass a village and Ruth slowed. A few of the buildings were built on a grand scale, an ageless permanence of stone and cement. Arches were prominent. Most of the other buildings were little more than shacks made of scrap lumber and sheets of galvanized iron. A few Arabs were visible.

"An Arab village?"

"Right, Linda," Ruth said.

"Are they friendly?"

Ruth shrugged. "Some are, some aren't. You never know."

Brent stared and pondered. Although he had spent over three weeks in Israel, he had seen very few Arabs. When he had first arrived and was on his way to *Bren-ah-Hahd* with Colonel David Moskowitz, they had driven their Jeep in low gear through the streets of a miserable Arab village. Chickens, goats, and children had squawked, squealed, and scattered before them while adults stared stonily from doorways and windows. Moskowitz had intoned soberly, "Take a good look at it, Brent. You're looking at a microcosm of the whole Middle East, the essence of Islam and what it can do to its followers. It can be alien, impenetrable, even frightening to outsiders." Brent would never forget the bitterness of Moskowitz's next statement as the convoy finally accelerated out of the squalor, "Their language is virtually inaccessible, history nothing but a blurred record of ancient feuds, war, corruption, and fanaticism, and they can hate—lord they can hate in any direction their religion points them."

"And the bow is strung and the arrow's pointed at us, Colonel."

A smile had purged the tension from the Colonel's face. "You put it succinctly, Commander."

Now Brent stared at the Arabs as Ruth slowed behind a battery of 105-millimeter guns, towed by American ten-wheelers. Thoughts clashed in his mind like waves in a hurricane. Who were these men watching so passively through the iron grates of their windows? Were they friendly or seething with hatred? What were the children shouting from the hot, dusty streets? Were their words invectives? Harmless? Friendly? What were those women thinking who were dressed all in black, only their hands and part of their face visible to the world? Brent shook his head. Moskowitz had been right. A stranger could not understand, had no way to see behind those walls. Those

159

eyes, those veils. Arabs were as inscrutable as Japanese temple icons.

Elroy's voice jarred Brent out of his reveries, "Farmin' in these parts sure 'nuff takes a passel of water, pure and simple."

"True," Ruth concurred, passing the battery's command car and increasing speed. The village was left behind. "We have a highly developed irrigation system and we have perfected drip irrigation to a science."

"You still need a reservoir."

"The Sea of Galilee, Elroy."

"Sea of Galilee. Fancy that. I'll be hornswoggled."

"Salt water?" Linda asked.

Ruth laughed. "No, Linda. It's not a sea at all. Actually, it's a large freshwater lake." She pointed to a walled settlement on the crest of a hill just visible ahead. "A *kibbutz*."

"Farms," Linda said proudly, again showing everyone she was informed.

"Right," Ruth said. Collective and cooperative farms. *Kibbutzim* or *moshavim* and the farmers are called *kibbutzniks*."

"Sumpin' like the 'Russki' system."

"At first very socialistic," Ruth said. "Actually an idealistic society that didn't revolve around money."

"Cain't ken that."

"Not a very good idea," Brent said. "Socialistic like the *ejido* in Mexico, the communes in China. They didn't work, either."

"True, Brent. They grew out of the Utopian socialist theories of Eastern Europe and Russia." The Israeli became very earnest, "When my father first arrived he spent over a year on the *Kibbutz Beit Oren* near Haifa. There were a lot of survivors of the Holocaust there." She brushed some wayward strands of hair from her brow and continued, "Vigorous. Ideal-

160

ists, building a nation. That's what they were — like the early American pioneers. Father said they had a selfless spirit of cooperation and sacrifice he had never seen anywhere. Wealth and poverty were shared equally. And in those days work was assigned by centralized committees and the children slept in communal centers, not at home with their parents. Everything from teacups to television sets were distributed on a need or communal basis."

"Helluva speech," Brent said, smiling affably. "But that's nothing but classical Marxism." Lowering his head he knuckled his forehead, riffling through the pages of his memories. Then, looking up he said, " 'From each according to his work, to each according to his needs.' " He turned to the driver, "Money be damned."

Ruth snickered. "You've been reading *Das Capital*."

"There are good lessons there on how not to run a country." Brent worked his tiring shoulders against the restraints of the seat belt and waved at the *kibbutz* which was now broad on the right side. "There had to be head-on collision between the *kibbutzniks* and the old, militant, conservative Jews. They didn't mix, did they?"

"Like oil and water."

Brent resumed thoughtfully, "Survivors of the death camps had to be cynical, skeptical of the laws — Judaism itself, the Torah, the Talmud, even God, who was AWOL at Auschwitz."

Ruth was impressed. "You're very insightful, Brent. True, to many survivors the old Judaism was a relic of the past. They believed work with one's hands on Jewish land would redeem Jewish history. Of course, they were considered heretical and un-Jewish by the conservative orthodox."

"But in their way, these *kibbutzniks* were very

161

idealistic, too," Brent added.

Her eyes met his for a fleeting instant. Then she stared ahead and spoke as if she were addressing the ornate hood ornament, "I'll never forget what an old rabbi told me years ago. He said, 'I've seen the Buddhist temples of Java, sat with sadhus on the Ghats of Benares, smoked hashish in Kabal, and worked on a *kibbutz*."

"Marvelous," Brent said.

Linda broke her silence. "Then they didn't eat kosher."

Tactfully, Ruth answered in a level voice, "You've made a good point, Linda. Rabbit and pork were eaten."

"Pork!" Brent exclaimed in mock horror.

"Yes, and holidays weren't observed properly or not at all." Ruth glanced into the back seat. "May sound trivial to you, but these things are critical to Jews."

Linda injected humor inadvertently, "Were the boys circumcised?" The men squirmed.

"Of course. Nothing could change that." Ruth swiveled her right eye to Brent and grinned maliciously.

He shifted away from the uncomfortable topic. Waving at the *kibbutz* which was now almost out of sight behind them, the military man returned, "That whole place is ideally sited for defense."

"Had to be. The natives were restless and the wagons were drawn up in a circle."

"Then the *kibbutzim* are coming back," Brent said.

"Yes," Ruth said. "The *Jihad* forced that. Nearly three hundred *kibbutzim* and *moshavim* are in operation now."

"But they've shifted away from socialism," Brent said. "Moved toward capitalism and the market economy—had their own *perestroika*."

"No choice," Ruth said. "They were going broke."

They flashed past a grove of broad-leafed trees. "I'll be danged," Elroy said. "Bananas."

"Right. With enough water we can grow almost anything here." Ruth waved at some foothills ahead. "David and Goliath fought there."

"Fancy that. But, why there?"

"Why not, Elroy?" Ruth said. "The Israelites lived in the hills and the Philistines on the plains."

Linda remarked, "They always fought. Seems like in Sunday School and church that's all you hear about in this place—war, war, war. The Bible's full of it."

"And fornication," Brent said. Laughter. Then his military mind asserted itself again. "Israel is the only land bridge between Africa and Asia to the east and Europe to the north and west. It was a natural funnel for armies of Egypt and Mesopotamia to attack each other."

"And we got trampled under their boots," Ruth said bitterly.

"Sandals and bare feet, too," Brent added. Then, looking at the countryside, he casually segued into another topic, "We're really in the Jerusalem Corridor. Right Ruth?"

"Why, yes, Brent. Haven't heard that used much lately."

"Corridor?" Linda asked.

Ruth said, "Yes. Until the Six Day War, Route One was the only link between Tel Aviv and Jerusalem. The Arabs held most of this area and the Old City until 1967. That's why the *kibbutzim* were fortresses."

"Then you settled their hash—kicked butt," Elroy said. Linda giggled.

"You could say that." Ruth gestured at a magnifi-

163

cent orange grove ahead. "Jaffa oranges. Best in the world."

The Cadillac passed through the enormous grove, redolent with the smell of blossoms like nectar. Then, on the right, loomed a solid wall of high shrubbery. "Kfar Habad," Ruth said.

"What?"

"Kfar Habad!" the driver repeated. "It's a village built by the ultra-Orthodox Hasidic sect, the Habad Massidim."

Brent said, "I've heard of them. Their leader is, ah . . ."

Ruth came to his aid, "He's called *Lubavitcher Rebbe,* which translates, 'the rabbi from Lubavitch.' "

"Right," Brent said. "He lives in the states."

"They hanker to be lonesome as pole cats."

Ruth laughed. "Actually, Elroy, the high hedge cuts out their view of the highway so they won't have to see their fellow Jews transgressing by driving on the Sabbath."

"I'll be hornswoggled. That's Saturday, ain't it."

"Yes, tomorrow. But it begins this evening at 'first star' and ends tomorrow evening at 'first star.' " The Israeli became the tour guide, indicating a sign pointing to Lod, the birthplace of Saint George the dragon slayer. Pointing at a low ridge of hills, she told them of the town of Ramle, which was the only town in the country established by Arabs. "Napoleon stayed in Ramle," she said. And then added, "There are ruins of Crusader fortresses scattered all around." Stabbing her finger at a cluster of trees, pain crept into her voice. "And over there is the Ramle War Cemetery, the largest in the country. Twenty-two nationalities are buried there."

A hush filled the car as it entered the foothills and began the climb to Jerusalem. Ruth shrugged off the depression and almost gaily continued in her tour-guide persona, glibly describing features most of which were not visible from Route 1. To the historian and theologian she added the botanist, picturing the vast botanical park where every plant mentioned in the Bible and Talmud are grown. "I'll take you to it some day when we have more time. It's only a few kilometers from here and it's stunning."

They passed Latrum, marking the exit to the Ayalon Valley. Ruth remarked on the strategic position of the valley and how it had been the scene of numberless battles throughout the ages. "Maccabees, Philistines, Romans, Crusaders, Arabs, Turks, and the British all fought here," she pointed out. "And, incidentally, it is here that Joshua commanded the sun to stand still."

"Shucks, you cain't really ken that."

Ruth turned her hands up from the wheel for an instant, making an abbreviated gesture of skepticism. "The orthodox believe every word, Elroy."

"You orthodox?"

"No."

"What are you?"

"I don't know, but I'm certain of one thing."

"What?"

"I'm a Jew."

"You cain't forget that."

"No, the world won't let me."

The subject was changed abruptly when Ruth waved at a huge monastery visible on a hill to the right near the jumbled ruins of an ancient fortress. The Israeli said, "The ruin is a twelfth-century Crusader fortress and the large building is the Latrum Monastery run by Trappist monks. Make great wine. Got drunk there once with Avraham Herzl."

Brent stared ahead silently.

They passed Emmaus where Christ supposedly revealed himself after the Resurrection. Although Brent knew Ruth did not believe this, she did not scoff or show the slightest cynicism while describing the sacred place. Elroy was impressed, Linda awed.

"Such a small place for so much history," Linda said. "It's all crammed together."

Ruth laughed. "True, and its been accumulating for thousands of years, Linda. Don't forget, the history of the whole New World began only five hundred years ago. That's only a few ticks off the clock of history."

"Guess so," Linda said vaguely. "But there's been so much fighting here, goes on and on. So many religions." She waved her hands helplessly as if the profoundness of the thoughts had exhausted her not only of energy, but of words, too.

"Yes, yes," Ruth agreed. She became uncharacteristically philosophical. "This small country's not just the center of history, for many it *is* history." Pausing, she turned the wheel and eased the heavy car around a sharp bend. "And, you're right Linda, unfortunately, history seems to be nothing but a chronicle of unending wars."

"Guess so," Linda muttered, somewhat beyond her depth. "But who was here first?"

"My people."

"Not the Arabs?"

"Hell no, Linda. They didn't show up until the seventh century. That was late."

"There are a lot of Palestinians."

"The Arab armies herded most of them here in 1948," Ruth said.

Linda showed new boldness, "You'd like to get rid of them."

"Not true," Ruth retorted, voice rising. "There are

166

good Arabs living in Israel. Some are citizens, guaranteed equality by the declaration of independence. They attend Israeli universities and are even eligible for welfare benefits. And most Israeli Arabs speak Hebrew. Actually, Arabic is their second language."

Brent said, "Yes, and a few Druze have even served in the army. But this is a minority, a very small minority."

"True," Ruth conceded. Her voice became thick, "But you must remember, the PLO has murdered hundreds of good Arabs for cooperating with us — just trying to get along and be good citizens."

Elroy came in, "I have no truck with Kadafi, Arafat, and the rest of them hombres. They could rightly gag maggots, in my mind. But they sure 'nuff have staked out a claim on this here territory — 'specialy Jerusalem as a holy place, right along with Christians and Jews. Ain't that the truth?"

"True, they've made their claims, but it's lies, hypocrisy!" Ruth said with new passion in her voice. "In fact, it's one of their biggest lies promoted by Kadafi, Arafat, Jumblatt, Assad, Hussein and the rest of those thugs." She rubbed her mouth with an open palm as if she were trying to wipe the distaste of the names from her lips. She continued, "Islam's great holy cities are Mecca, Baghdad, and Cairo. Even Cordova in Spain has a greater Muslim heritage than Jerusalem." She pounded the padded wheel so hard the power steering wobbled the front wheels. "And every Arab knows this," she spat.

Linda said, "I don't understand."

Calming, Ruth said, "It goes back to the Turks. They ruled most of the Middle East and Jerusalem for over four hundred years, up until 1917. Till then, Jerusalem was an unimportant backwater town."

"Then the Arabs freed it."

167

"No! No, Linda," Ruth countered, pounding the wheel again and pushing the accelerator to counter a steepening grade. "You're thinking of Peter O'Toole playing Lawrence in *Lawrence of Arabia*. Allenby and his British army liberated Jerusalem and all of Palestine from the Turks. Lawrence and his Arabs blew up a few trains, but generally got in the way. Anyway, he was a fag like most of the Arab men he led."

Brent glanced at the girl. Her jaw was hard set, eyes narrow and fixed on the road. A wellspring of deep-rooted angers and suppressions had been tapped and everyone in the car knew it. It was a new side of the Israeli. She looked even more attractive. Brent was fascinated and so was Elroy. The Texan bored into the topic. "I hear tell that Arafat and his boys claim Jerusalem as the capital of the Palestinian nation. I reckon it don't make no sense, does it?"

"Of course not," Ruth said, easing the throttle and her emotions at the same time. She slowed as they entered a small valley heavily planted with citrus. Stretching for several kilometers on both sides of the road, the trees were a magnificent verdant carpet. People could be seen weeding the furrows and pruning the trees. It was a beautiful, peaceful counterpoint to the conversation. Oblivious to the beauty around her, the Israeli pushed on, "The truth is there is no Palestinian state so there can't be a Palestinian capital. And true, that's Yasser Arafat's old line. The media has swallowed it along with the rest of his garbage."

"Oh, okay," Linda said, reentering the exchange. "Now I see."

Brent smiled. He was not sure the girl could see much of anything. But, at least, she was curious and not disinclined to put her nearly blank mind on display. *If she were as intelligent as she was sexy, she would be a genius,* he thought.

Leaving the valley, the road began to wind through the hills. They passed the twisted, burned-out wreckage of an old Model "A" Ford truck with pathetic sheets of thin armor bolted to its cab. The vehicle had been blasted by artillery, blown over the drainage ditch and onto a small escarpment. The wreck was encrusted with rust; dull, brown, and heavy.

"An accident," Linda cried out.

"No," Brent said. "Probably an ambush. This is an ideal place for a surprise." He pointed, "That Ford was hit by artillery, and look at the bullet holes."

Ruth said glumly, "You're so damned military and so damned right."

They passed two more blasted and burned vehicles, one almost concealed by growths of scrub brush. Ruth explained that in 1948 convoys of trucks with provisions for Jerusalem had to regularly fight their way through Arab forces. "Run the gauntlet," she said.

They drove by more wreckage; a late-model yellow school bus with an enormous hole blown in its side. Fresh flowers were piled against it.

"That's not 1948," Brent said.

"No," Ruth said, voice low and husky. "1982. Arab terrorists hit it with an antitank rocket. Killed about thirty children outright. They finished off the rest with AK-47s. It's a memorial now. It will never be moved or forgotten."

"Sheep-killin' dogs," Elroy said in a rare display of emotion. "Only chicken-livered cowards could do that."

"Oh, Jesus," Linda said. "How horrible."

"Jesus wasn't around," Ruth said.

"And neither was his father," Brent said in a rapid

169

voice. And then before Ruth could respond, he muttered, " 'For hate's sake, I spit my last breath at thee.' "

Ruth worked her fingers on the steering wheel like tappets in the engine and narrowed her eyes. Brent expected a retort involving the massacre. Instead she surprised him with one word, "Melville."

"Right," Brent said, happy to leave the murdered bus behind. "Ahab to Moby Dick."

"A fish," Linda offered, catching the change in mood.

"A whale," Brent said.

"Ahab's fate, his search for false gods," Ruth said.

"All that?" Linda said. "I thought he was just fishing — trying to make a living and kill that white whale he hated."

"Not quite," Brent said, managing to keep a straight face.

"Y'all know," Elroy said, eyeing another savaged truck, "them Arabs outnumbered you — shoulda been able to kick your butts."

With the grade steepening and the heavy car slowing, Ruth shifted down from "Drive" to "Third." Then, she said, "You're right. Nearly two hundred million of them and only four million of us."

"Leaders like sun-crazy hounds, an' stupid."

"True," Ruth acknowledged. "That's what helped save Israel."

Shifting in his seat to ease a cramped muscle in his back, Brent said, "Most Arab leaders are nothing but corrupt thugs — the sheiks, kings, emirs, and military-backed rulers. What's ironic is that they invariably claim authority by divine right."

Ruth nodded approval. "Descent from Mohammed, and also, the cause of Baathist ideals, don't forget the party."

170

"Like a bunch of rambunctious Indians on the war-path."

"Very accurate simile, Elroy," Ruth said. "Always the clans have actually been the dominant force. House of Saud in Arabia, the Sabahs in Kuwait, Hashemites in Jordan, Alawites in Syria, Takritis in Iraq."

"But they're all Muslims," Linda blurted, suddenly.

"True. But ideals and religion fade in their world and progress is a force from hell," Ruth said.

Brent said, "Hypocrisy isn't in short supply, either."

Ruth smiled. "How true."

"And the favorite pastime of Arabs is killing Arabs."

"Second to Jews, Brent."

"Of course."

Driving silently for a few moments, they breasted a small hill and suddenly Jerusalem lay before them. Brent's reaction took him completely by surprise. He caught his breath. The city was white, so pure it seemed to emit an eerie luminescence, gleaming in the sun like polished pearls. Cradled by a natural theater of hills, the sun seemed focused on it from a pristine blue sky marred only by a few long stringy clouds like angel's hair. The entire vista had such jewel-like clarity that it suggested a painting by Andrew Wyeth. But it was actually there! Not a painting. It existed! A glistening spectral relic for all time. This fabled city, the fountainhead of so many tales, stories and beliefs that had shaped his life with their power. It was Oz, and Route 1 the yellow brick road. But this was real, not phony props worked by Frank Morgan.

Abruptly, a lifetime drenched in Christian milieu and strict Catholicism in his youth, claimed his senses, dictated his reactions. This was not just a city, this was far more: The locus of history's desires and

171

counterdesires; the wilderness watering place where the different species came in perpetual common need and common estrangement. Yes, that was what it truly was. And he was like the rest. He suddenly realized he was there to slake his thirst, too, despite nearly ten years of saturation in Buddhism and Shintoism. Wide-eyed, he shook his head, feeling an atavistic rise of emotion that bordered on the metaphysical. His throat swelled upon itself and he knew he would have trouble speaking.

"Beautiful," Ruth said, softly, sensing her companion's emotion.

Sucking his lungs full of air, Brent sighed, "Yes. I didn't expect this."

"What?"

He waved while trying to find the words. "That it — ah, would be so impressive." He was almost embarrassed by his thought, but blurted it out anyway, "It's almost unearthly."

"Actually, they're very pragmatic."

"What do you mean?"

"There's a strong building code. The buildings must be consistent — light-colored masonry. And, of course, the setting is beautiful, the hills, the trees, and when we get closer you'll see the flowers in large beds and carefully tended."

Brent nodded, enjoying the sudden peace and near fulfillment in just seeing Jerusalem. Then, he suddenly realized Linda and Elroy were sharing a different kind of emotion. In fact, they had dropped out of the conversation and out of sight. Only the sounds of heavy breathing, the slurping, smacking sound of deep, wet kisses and an occasional, "Oh," from Linda could be heard. Brent heard Elroy whisper, "You're sweeter than honeysuckle." More giggles and, "Oh, oh." The near-spiritual ambiance vanished.

Glancing into her rearview mirror, Ruth said, "Elroy, if you get your tongue off Linda's tonsils and your hand out of her crotch, you can see Jerusalem dead ahead."

Giggles and snickers. Two heads reappeared. Then, catching his breath, Elroy said, "Sure 'nuff. Big city like Odessa."

Linda's voice, quavering slightly with sexual heat, "My, how pretty. Let's see where Jesus lived."

"Lived! I don't know about that." Turning into a street on the outskirts, Ruth paused. "But we should be able to see 'The Way of the Cross.'"

"Oh, good."

"But, remember, I told you when we first started that this was not exactly the height of the tourist season. Security is very tight. There's a war on, you know."

"But this is Good Friday," Brent said, "and we've passed a lot of buses. Must be a lot of visitors — pilgrims from all over and the hell with the war."

"True, true, Brent. But our uniforms may give us a problem."

"With the Arabs?"

"Possibly, and with the Army, too."

Squat houses and low commercial buildings began to crowd both sides of the street. Most were built of bleached stone and masonry. Pedestrians in Western and Arab garb were to be seen in small numbers. Occasionally, a bearded Hasidic wearing a squared black hat and black suit passed.

"Apartments," Linda said, waving at some tall buildings a few blocks distant.

"*Shikunim,* planned developments," Ruth said. "The government's been building them since 1967. They're for people who tend to be of the same background. Lots of refugees."

173

"Like what?"

"Oh, Polish Jews, Hungarian Jews, even people of the same political parties or professions. We Jews are very clannish, you know." She waved to the west, "Most government buildings — public agencies, ministries and parliamentary buildings are out there on the west side."

"The *Knesset*," Elroy Rubin said.

"Right."

Brent looked up at the aching blue sky. "It's so clear here. We're at a fairly high altitude."

"About seven hundred meters," Ruth said. And then to the back seat, "Over two thousand feet."

Linda asked, "What's the biggest industry?"

"Hellfire and damnation," Elroy injected, suddenly.

"That's right," Ruth said. "Religion."

"One God," Elroy persisted, shaking off a little of the hay seed.

"Why yes," Ruth said with surprise. "That's the city's single great resource." Her fingers played a tattoo on the steering wheel. "Jerusalem is holy to about one third of the world's population. In fact, in the Old City, there are separate Jewish, Christian, Armenian, and Muslim quarters." She stopped at a cross street to allow two buses and a car to pass and then continued across the intersection.

Linda pondered while the traffic cleared. She surprised Brent with a rare insight, "Then it's holy to the Arabs, too."

"Yes."

"Why?"

Elroy interrupted the women, "I reckon 'cause Mohammed climbed up from a rock there all the way to heaven — jus' like Jesus, keerect Ruth?"

"Right," the Israeli answered. "The Arabs call it the

174

Dome of the Rock. There's a mosque built on it." And then she added hurriedly, "But it came late—seventh century."

Linda said, "All these people with all their religions jammed into one city?"

"Yes," Ruth said. "And the Old City's a small place. You'll see."

Elroy said, "But everyone's a-knowin' they been fightin' like a covey o' wild cats in a privy since it all began."

Ruth chuckled. "Colorful and correct." She waved ahead, "There it is, the Old City."

"Walls," Linda said. "Big, like a fort."

"The Turks built them recently—the sixteenth century," Brent explained.

Ruth and Elroy chuckled. Linda missed the humor. Turning sharply to the left, Ruth said, "We'll take Sultan Suleiman Road around the city to Saint Stephen's Gate." She glanced over her shoulder. "That's the closest entrance to 'The Way of the Cross.' "

"That's where Jesus walked."

"Yes, Linda. It's supposedly the route Jesus followed carrying his cross from the place of his trial to where he was crucified. It starts at the temple esplanade and ends at the church of the Holy Sepulchre."

"Oh."

"I'll show you, Linda. I've been there many times."

"A very holy route," Linda mused.

"Depends on your religion."

They reached the northeast corner of the wall and turned sharply to the right onto Jericho Road. "Them walls look like they was built yesterday," Elroy noted.

"Yes. They're very well-maintained. All of it is."

"Like you said, ain't very big," Elroy said.

"About a square kilometer," Ruth said, turning

175

to the right toward a gate in the wall.

"Ah, how much is that?" Linda asked.

Brent intervened smoothly, "About two hundred twenty acres."

"Shoot. We've got vegetable gardens an' dog runs biggerin' that back in Texas."

Everyone was laughing as Ruth wheeled the Cadillac into a small parking area just outside the gate. A Jeep with an American 30-caliber Browning machine gun mounted on a pedestal was parked at the entrance. Two soldiers sat casually in the vehicle's seat. One was smoking. Both watched the newcomers pass. Despite the war, the lot was crowded, and Ruth was forced to drive to the far end to park. Most of the vehicles were buses.

"That's the gate?" Linda asked with surprise. "It's small."

"Not very impressive," Ruth said.

They exited the car, stretched and joined the crowd approaching the gate. Not even the war could interrupt the appeal of the city—especially on a holy day. Brent knew that zealous pilgrims would make the trek if they had to brave the nine rings of hell to do it.

Four Israeli soldiers, three enlisted men and a middle-aged captain, stood watching the visitors enter and exit. All four had automatic weapons slung over their shoulders and all wore bulletproof vests. Ammunition pouches and side arms were attached to their belts. The captain spotted them immediately and halted them with a raised hand. His men watched curiously. He exchanged salutes with Ruth, Brent and Elroy.

"Captain Yaron Ezrahi, here," he said in guttural English to Brent who was the senior officer.

"Commander Brent Ross of NIC," Brent responded. And then waving at the stream of people moving freely through the gate, "Why do you stop us, Captain Ezrahi?"

The captain did not answer immediately; instead he narrowed his eyes and dampened his lips with the tip of his tongue. Obviously, naval officers in dress blues were not a common sight. His eyes scanned the officers, examining the strange uniforms; the gold stripes, chrysanthemums on the peaked caps, the DOP shoulder patches. "Ah," Ezrahi finally responded, "you are Brent Ross, 'the American samurai.' " Staring curiously, the other soldiers stepped closer. A few civilians stopped, and Brent became uneasy as a small crowd began to gather.

"I'm called that," Brent snapped testily. "If you don't mind, we'd like to see 'The way of the Cross.' "

The captain puffed his cheeks and then compressed his lips, releasing his breath with a hiss. He was obviously disquieted. "Respectfully, sir," he said, "this is not the best time for a Christian pilgrimage—any pilgrimage, for that matter."

"I know that. But you obviously have a lot of visitors. Is it dangerous?"

"It is Good Friday," the captain said. "It is always a little risky, Commander Ross, and you are wearing uniforms of the forces of Admiral Fujita. Naturally, you will attract attention, and you will be entering the old Arab Quarter." He stabbed a finger at three different areas, "The Jewish Quarter is on the other side, Christian Quarter over there and the Armenian Quarter in the southeast corner. Perhaps you should consider visiting them."

Before Brent could respond, Ruth spoke up, "*Shalom,* Captain, I'm Corporal Ruth Moskowitz of Mossad. We will only walk part of 'The Way of the Cross', Captain. I've been here many times."

The captain stared long at Ruth and then said

177

slowly, "You are related to Colonel David Moskowitz?"

"Yes, I'm his daughter."

"I know your father well. He is a fine officer." And then with concern, "I heard he was wounded at *Bren-ah-Hahd.*"

"Thanks to Commander Ross, my father survived his wounds and is making a rapid recovery."

"Haruch ha-Shem," Ezrahi murmured, reciting that the Lord's name should be blessed.

Ruth thanked him in Hebrew: *"Toh-dah rah-bah l'hah ah-doh-nee.* May we proceed, Captain?"

"Very well, Corporal." Ezrahi turned to Brent and said somewhat reluctantly, "Be—ah, discreet, Commander." He gestured at Ruth. "You have an experienced guide, but, still, there could be an incident."

The crowd had grown larger, and people were whispering and pointing at Brent. He cursed his celebrity and only wished to enter the city. "Thank you, Captain," he said. And then brusquely, "Let's go." More salutes and the foursome joined the pedestrians streaming through the gate. He heard Captain Ezrahi shout, *Mazel tov!"*

The gate gave on a small open space where groups of Arabs and pilgrims were gathered. Almost every Arab seemed to be trying to sell something. In traditional dress, the men wore the *burnoose* that hung like a hooded gown or the *jalabiyah* which seemed like nothing more than a nightshirt to Brent. Most of the men had a *kuffyah,* or headcloth, wrapped around their heads, held in place with a rope. The women were in long black gowns, heads covered with scarves, faces veiled.

Ancient limestone and rock buildings crowded the area. Incongruously, television antennas ranged like a spindly forest above it all. Ruth led them to a crowded, narrow street like a cobblestoned path lined with stalls and more shouting, gesticulating Arabs hawking their wares: religious icons, pottery, fresh and dried fruit, dates, lamb, cheese, pita bread. Some actually hung out of their windows, dangling crosses and rosaries in the faces of the pilgrims and tourists. Brent waved them off like annoying flies.

"This is a holy place an' Good Friday to boot?" Elroy asked incredulously.

"This way. This way," Ruth shouted over the cacophony of hundreds of shrill voices speaking dozens of languages. "A few meters more—the Via Dolorosa!"

Finally, they stopped at a semicircle of cobblestones arranged around a plate marked with a "I." "This is Station One," Ruth said. She pointed to a school with a yellow metal door. "That is the Antonia Fortress and supposedly the location of Pontius Pilate's judgment hall." She waved across the street. "Station Two, the Monastery of the Flagellation, where Jesus was scourged and given the cross."

Carried by a current of humanity, they moved from station to station, enveloped by the sights, smells, and sounds of the Old City: pedestrians in suits, long dresses, baggy trousers, cutoffs, jeans, T-shirts; nuns in habits, dark-clad priests clutching rosaries and chanting with the nuns; Caucasians, Asians, Africans, Latins and mixed races that defied identification; flower shops, food stands, book and magazine kiosks, felt-lined boards covered with icons. And everywhere, shouting, crowding Arabs with their wares, most standing behind their stalls while others followed the visitors, peddling their goods. Brent felt he was at the headwaters of gutted creation, carried along by a river—the mainstream through Jerusalem fed by tributaries of zealots, the curious, the merce-

179

nary, the mendacious, gorging the stream, all redolent of piety, faith, dishonesty, and mutual abhorrence.

Captain Yaron Ezrahi had been right. An assassin would have an easy time of it. Brent could see concern on Elroy's face but Linda just stared with those big wide eyes that saw everything but comprehended little.

They passed under the *Ecce Homo* (Behold the man!) Arch. Brent was listening to Ruth, but he wasn't sure what Jesus or Pontius Pilate did there. They met a widening thoroughfare Ruth called El-Wad Road and then Station III. "He fell here," Ruth said over the tumult. Then Station IV, where the Virgin Mary came out of the crowd was followed quickly by Station V, where Simon of Cyrene was pulled out of the taunting throng to help carry the cross. A turn to the right and a short climb and they were at Station VI, where a woman stepped from the crowd and wiped Jesus' face with a cloth.

The mob and chattering Arabs clung like lint and Brent tried to listen to Ruth and keep a wary eye on them. The split was too severe even for his concentration and his sense of spirituality had early on been crushed under the boot of mundanity surrounding him. They moved to Station VII, where Jesus fell again and this is where Brent's patience fell as well. "Enough!" he said, staring around at the press of Arabs, tourists and pilgrims. He glanced at his watch. "I appreciate the tour, Ruth, but I think we'd better leave."

"Oh," Linda moaned. "I was enjoying it so."

Elroy's eyes darted around and he said, "The top brass done gave an order." He looked Linda up and down. Sacred thoughts were not on his mind. Linda cast her eyes down and giggled. "Time's a-wastin'," Elroy said.

180

Quickly, the foursome turned and retraced their steps. When they exited the gate, Captain Yaron Ezrahi stopped Brent with a raised hand. Elroy and a curious Linda flanked the commander. Ruth continued toward the Cadillac, rummaging in her purse for the keys and shouting over her shoulder, "I'll bring the car around — real valet service." The Jeep was gone.

"Enjoy your visit, Commander?" Ezrahi asked Brent.

"Disney World without the sanitation department," Brent said.

The captain laughed and his men chuckled as if they thoroughly understood. Suddenly, Linda cried out, "Ruth!" and pointed at the parking lot.

Ruth was near the far end of the lot, just behind the Cadillac. An Arab with something shiny in his hand was approaching her. She had dropped her purse and faced the advancing Arab, knees bent, hands flat like blades and at her side.

Pulling his Beretta from his holster, Brent broke into a run. Elroy was at his side, tugging at his shoulder holster. Brent barrelled through the crowd, knocking down a priest and sending people scurrying, the sight of the Beretta raising panic. Streaming from a bus, a group of pilgrims masked any chance Brent had for a shot. He cursed. Then yelled, "Ruth! Run! Run!"

Either the girl did not hear him, or she felt flight was futile. The Arab was too close. That was it.

Behind him, Brent could hear Captain Ezrahi shouting, "Stop! Stop! It's Mad Moh . . ." But the rest of his words were drowned out by the screams and cries of people in panic — especially the shrill shrieks of women.

The Arab was on Ruth. He was tall, rangy, heavily bearded, and slightly stooped. His long white *jala-*

181

biyah was filthy. Extending his hand, Brent saw a long glistening blade. A straight-on attack. Sabbah!

At last, the crowd was clear. He had a shot. Fifty feet. He and Elroy stopped simultaneously, raised their pistols, crouching in the shooter's stance.

It was over before they could pull a trigger. Instead of fleeing, Ruth sprang forward, left hand chopping down hard on the Arab's wrist. There was a spiraling glint as the knife was knocked from his hand and clattered across the asphalt. Twisted by pain, the man grabbed his wrist and turned away from the girl. With incredible speed and the grace of a ballerina, Ruth pivoted behind him, locked an arm around his throat, kicked her right foot into his knees to throw him off balance, bent almost double, and flung him over her hip. The Arab did a complete flip and crashed onto the pavement on his face. Groaning, he rolled onto his back, holding his wrist. It was broken.

At that moment, Brent and Elroy arrived. Elroy picked up the knife and extended it to Ruth. But it was not a knife, it was a cross, long, with a gold finish and encrusted with fake jewels. "I reckon he was just trying to peddle you a cross," he said. Ruth took the cross.

Captain Ezrahi and one of his men pushed through the crowd that had quickly gathered. He was highly agitated. "That is only 'Mad Mohammed.' He is retarded, cannot even talk. He is harmless." He bent over the squirming, groaning Arab. "You broke his wrist, Corporal, and you did not help his back."

Ruth held up the cross. "Look at the handle, the finial."

Brent took the cross, tested the finial with his palm. It dug into the flesh sharply. "Sharp as a knife," he said. And then to Captain Ezrahi, "Maybe your 'Mad Mohammed' wasn't as harmless as you thought, Captain."

"He's been selling these for years, Commander."

"And maybe he's been waiting for years, Captain. Sabbah prefer to kill with the knife, and they're very patient."

The captain snorted disdainfully.

Mad Mohammed, cried out in pain, and there were angry mutters from the Arabs in the crowd. A tearful Linda broke through and clung to Elroy's arm. "Please, let's leave," she pleaded.

"I'm not ready," Brent said, glaring first at Ezrahi and then at the Arabs in the crowd.

"Please," Ruth intervened. "It's late, Brent."

Grudgingly, Brent followed the women to the car. No salutes were exchanged.

Eight

Sunset was filling the western sky with furnace colors of hot orange and smoldering red when Brent and Ruth arrived at her apartment, a small one bedroom in the Maxim Hotel. Located on Hayarkon Street, it was only a few blocks from Brent's apartment at the Hilton. However, it was quite modest in comparison. When they entered the fifth floor apartment, Ruth had waved and said, "Not fancy like the Hilton, but it's warm, cozy and home."

"Where's the bar?"

Ruth had managed a chuckle and walked to the kitchen. "Coming right up," she said. "Scotch neat, right?"

"Right."

Elroy and Linda had been dropped at the Dizengoff Square Hotel where Elroy had a room. The place boasted an Indian restaurant, and Elroy had little trouble convincing Linda she should try the cuisine. "Great grub, an' then I have a fancy dessert for you, little lady," the Texan had promised.

"Oh, Elroy. You're being naughty again."

Laughing and giggling the couple had vanished through the entrance.

Then Brent and Ruth had made a short visit to the hospital where her sedated father continually nodded off. Finally, giving up and acceding to the nurse's advice to return in the morning, the couple had left. Ruth seemed buoyed by the news that her father was making a rapid recovery.

Now seated on a deep sofa, night had fallen suddenly like a black blanket. Gazing at the subdued lights of Tel Aviv through the large window, Brent and Ruth sipped their drinks. The mood was somber, memories of the encounter in the parking lot still too fresh to allow festive feelings to break through, even after the good news at the hospital.

"I was wrong back there in the parking lot."

"I don't think so, Ruth."

"I did a terrible thing."

"Not true."

"Could be arrested. Arabs have rights. Mad Mohammed has rights."

"That's crazy. He came at you with a weapon. You have witnesses."

"It *was* sharp, wasn't it?" She looked at him hopefully, the little girl searching for reassurance.

"Yes, a dagger."

She pursed her lips ruefully. "I wanted this to be our day, a happy day, you and I on a date. That boy and girl I told you about."

"It was a happy day, a wonderful date for that boy and girl."

She drank and then held up the glass, rotated it and smiled at Brent pensively. "Don't worry, Brent, I won't get drunk. You won't be pulling me out of the toilet again."

"I'm not worried." He took her hand and she pushed against him, thigh to thigh. "You're good at martial arts."

185

"All Mossad personnel take a special self-defense course—judo, karate."

He shook his head. "More than that. You're very good at it. You have a belt, don't you?" He tossed off his drink, she nursed hers.

"A black belt in karate." She recharged his glass and stabbed a finger at a spot high above the horizon. A moonless night, mountains of clouds had blotted out the starlight, leaving a patch of sky as black as death. "Speaking of black," she said with a troubled voice, "a black hole."

He felt like laughing, but the grim visage told him the girl was serious. Studying the strange phenomenon, he sipped his drink. "Ruth," he said, "a black hole wouldn't be visible to the naked eye. You know that."

"This one is, always has been but we've been blind."

He was fascinated by her mood, felt compelled to go along with her, explore that keen, enigmatic intellect. "A singularity? When stars use up all their nuclear fuel?" he proposed.

She nodded, drank. "They collapse on themselves, reach a point of infinite density."

"And"—he pointed at the sky—"that's the singularity."

"Right, Brent. Time stops and gravity is so strong not even light can escape."

"And a black hole is born."

"Yes."

"I don't get it, Ruth," he said, encouraging her. But he was beginning to suspect the drift of her thinking, the metaphor she was building. Such a remarkable mind.

She took another drink and looked at him from the corner of her eye. "You'll think I'm silly—the amateur philosopher."

"No, I won't."

Taking a deep breath, she looked away. "Sometimes, I think this whole world is falling apart around us, slipping into its own black pit. No ray of light, no hope can escape the force of our hatreds." Eyes fixed on the sky, she stared unwaveringly, unblinking. Moisture had made her brown eyes as shadowy as the sky.

Wondering at the complexity of her thinking, he pulled on his chin, felt the bristles, groping for a way to pull her out of the darkness that had shadowed her. "That's one helluva way to put it," he said thoughtfully. "And it makes sense. The black hole is there and we've spent thousands of years slipping into it." He brightened. He would make a game of her mood, perhaps that would pull her from her gloom. "Let me try one of my own."

She looked up at him expectantly, "Please, yes."

"Freshman Philosophy One A-B."

"Right," she smiled.

"Are you ready for the 'final'?"

"Crammed all night."

Smiling, he threw it out, "Then, you could say we're Estragon and Vladimir waiting in vain."

She chuckled and he was pleased with the change. She had no trouble with the challenge, "Beckett, *Waiting for Godot,*" she said quickly.

"Right. Waiting for something that will never come."

"That was their black hole," she said, becoming reflective again.

"Of course. With Ahab it was a white whale, Don Quixote a windmill, Ulysses his battle to return to Penelope."

"But he found her."

"Yes."

She showed her Russian side. There was eagerness

in her voice, "And there were Tolstoy, Dostoevski, Pasternak—their heroes always searching, finding, but not knowing what they had in their grasp."

She was in one of his favorite domains. He had studied the Russians for years and obviously Ruth knew them thoroughly. Savoring the subject, he said, "Yes, Doctor Zhivago searching in the hurricane of the revolution, Pierre caught in Napoleons's invasion, hunting for sanity where it did not exist, and poor Alyosha looking for meaning in a jungle of hate and lust."

"You love the Russians."

"They have lousy politicians but great writers."

"But Brent, did they show us a way out," she waved, a helpless little gesture, "a way out of this lunacy—the black hole? Do you see a way?"

He pinched the bridge of his nose with his thumb and forefinger and smiled. "My wisdom is not infinite and neither was theirs."

"Mutual annihilation?"

"Possible."

"Rapprochement?"

"Also possible, Ruth. We're going to try it in Tripoli tomorrow when we meet with Kadafi."

"You're optimistic? He could teach evil to the devil."

"I'm always optimistic, Ruth."

"Pull us out of the black hole?"

"Why not?"

"Damn, Brent, you have one big brain."

He smiled and kissed her forehead. "Thanks, but all jocks aren't illiterate, and I've had a lot of time to read at sea."

"I didn't mean that."

"I know."

Instead of answering, she fixed him with a steady

gaze, eyes hooded and piercing, lips pouting slightly as if she anticipated his passion and could no longer wait for it. He had seen that look on women's faces before, and it excited him. Taking both of his hands, she placed them in her lap. He could feel the hardness and firmness of her thighs. She kissed his cheek. Her lips were soft, cool. He wondered if it were really so, or if his own skin was hot. Maybe it was the liquor. He felt hot, felt a furnace come to life deep within him. Melville, Cervantes, the Russians fled from his mind like typhoon-driven sea birds. She seemed to radiate heat, and she wanted him. That was his whole universe.

Her lips moved to his ear, and he deliberately reached across, pulled buttons loose, caressed a breast. He felt the flesh and she thrust it out into his palm. Shuddering, her breath quickened with little hissing sounds in his ear. Then, her tongue circled his ear and darted in like a tiny, hungry serpent. Never had his arousal been so abrupt.

He had wanted her from the first moment he had seen her. Two nights before he had kissed her, felt the curves and planes of her hard body and had actually refused to bed her when she became staggering drunk. Like a malignant sprite, the memory of that night had danced across the edge of his mind incessantly. And now he had been with her the entire day, watching her, studying her, the flow of her magnificent body under her tight clothing, perfect rhythm and oscillation of her pert young buttocks when she walked. Even the fight in the parking lot in some strange way had heightened her sensualness.

Pulling her shirt aside with numb fingers, he kissed her throat, the rise of her breasts, cupped one high, kissed the roundness and then took the areola in his mouth and tongued the nipple which had swollen and reddened like a ripe raspberry. The rush of blood narrowed her eyes into bright arrowheads, the scattering of freckles on her nose and cheeks glowing like specks of gold leaf. Moaning, she clutched the back of his head and pulled him against her. His hand dropped lower and lower, curling under the skirt, finding the damp heat.

She pulled him down on the sofa on top of her, arms locked around his neck, near madness in her kisses. Arching her back, she thrust her hips against him. Her short skirt hiked up and he slid between her legs, pressed his hardness against the hot mound. He tugged on her panties with fingers that trembled like a man with malaria. She gasped into his kisses, "The bedroom. The bedroom."

He picked her up like a rag doll and carried her out of the room.

She was pressed against him, the soft plastic curves of her body conforming to his hardness. She was limp, gratified like a starved kitten who had eaten her fill and sought nothing but sleep. But she was not sleeping. Instead her hand wandered almost aimlessly over his body; the entwined ropes of his neck blending into his massive shoulders, the broad expanse of his chest. She found the bare grooves in the hair and the question came — a question he had heard from many women before and he answered it in the same way: "Tracers. It's the phosphorous. Kills the hair follicles."

"God, no. How? Where?"

"An air battle. I've flown as a gunner."

"And these?" she asked, caressing scars on his abdomen.

"Knives. *Sabbah,* in an alley in Tokyo, years ago."

"You've had your black hole."

the innocent little girl was back, sweet, undemanding in repose. And something else was back. Sarah Aranson. The hair spread on the pillow like a dark halo, the perfect nose, parted full lips, just like Sarah almost ten years ago. Ruth was very young, true, but the resemblance was there. Semitic. That was it. There was that resemblance. No doubt about that.

She stirred, moaned, rolled toward him, and wrapped an arm around his neck. He pulled her to him. "Oh," she said, "it wasn't a dream. You're here. I've wanted you for so long."

"I'm here." He kissed her ear. "But, it's time to get up."

"What time is it?'

"A little after 0400."

"It's early." She pushed her pelvis against him. The mound of her swollen sex was warm, damp. She kissed his neck, his chest, the grooves, and moved lower.

He felt his loins stir. "Please, darling, I'll be late." Gently, he pushed her away, sat up and dropped his feet to the floor.

"All right," she said, disappointedly. Turning away, she sat up. "Oh!"

"What's wrong?"

She giggled. "I'm a little sore. You must have enough testosterone in you to kill fifty healthy men."

He grinned. "Sorry."

"No need to apologize," she chided. "And you're a big man."

"I'll get circumcised."

"Don't you dare."

They were both chuckling as they dressed. Finally, fully clothed, they faced each other. He held her close. "I've never known anything like that," she whispered.

"The same. The same," he said, kissing her ear.

"It was great because we care for each other."

"Yes. True. I do care for you, Ruth."

"How much? Do you love me?"

"I thought you didn't believe in love."

"No. I said I didn't know what it was."

"Do you now?"

"I'm not sure. It's easy to feel great emotion for you after . . ." she waved at the bed, "after what you did for me there." She kissed his cheek and ran a hand over the back of his neck. Then a long, hard kiss. Pulling away slightly, she held his eyes. "You told me about love the other night. You said a man and a woman love each other when their attachment is so strong they commit to a lifetime together."

"Yes, I remember. A little corny, but yes."

"Do you feel that way about me, Brent?"

"After two days and one night?"

"War compresses everything."

"True. And it also separates people."

She sighed resignedly. "I know. I know, dear Brent. Forgive me, I'm becoming the nagging woman."

He chuckled. "Never. And yes, I told you before, you'd be easy to love."

"The boy and the girl."

"Yes. The boy and the girl. No war, no separation, together, loving."

"You're so sweet." She kissed him again. Then she stepped back, holding his biceps in her hands. Anxiety shaded her eyes. "I told you I'm a hex, Brent. Be very careful. You'll be entering a den of vipers."

He sighed. "You're no hex. Herzl, the others, it was chance, Russian roulette. That's the nature of war."

"I know. I know, but don't turn your back on them. I can't bear the thought of losing you, too."

"You won't lose me."

196

"Promise?"

"Yes. I promise."

She kissed him again, hard, demanding.

He glanced at his watch. "It's time."

"I was going to make you some coffee."

He shook his head. "I'll get some at the airport. Don't forget, we've got to stop at the Hilton."

She mumbled, "All right."

As they walked to the door, they passed the table. The candles had burned down to the holders and the flames had been extinguished by their own melted wax.

It was early afternoon before Ruth began to slowly mount the stairs of the Mordecai Military Hospital. She was depressed, spirits at low ebb after watching Brent Ross, Colonel Irving Bernstein, and Elroy Rubin board the DC-6 at the Ben Gurion Airport. She had stood by a huge window and watched the strange white aircraft with dozens of green crosses take off. Using a special IFF transponder sent from Libya, the negotiators had been promised safe passage. And the special paint job was suggested by the Arabs for easy identification and to help protect the aircraft. But these were Arab promises, untrustworthy and easily violated. She stared until the big plane vanished to the west and the glaring sun hurt her eyes, causing tears to streak her cheeks.

And Brent had held her, kissed her, pledged his return.

"I care for you Brent," she had said, voice trembling on the edge of tears.

"And I for you." They both avoided the word "love."

"And remember, you're no hex," he had added, tapping her nose playfully with his big knuckles.

Then they kissed for the last time—long, hard, deep.

She was distracted by a call behind her. "Ruth! Ruth!" A striking woman of about forty dressed in the uniform of Mossad was racing up the stairs behind her.

"Aunt Sarah!" Ruth cried joyfully. The women embraced.

"I'm on my way to see your father," Sarah said. "How is he? They tell you damned little on the phone."

"He's recovering fast. Just chafing to get out."

"Baruch ha-Shem," Sarah murmured.

And then Ruth stepped back and stared at Sarah at arm's length, studying the gold and dark green insignias on her aunt's shoulder boards and on her cap. "You've been promoted, Aunt Sarah."

"Yes," the officer smiled. "Just call me Lieutenant Colonel Sarah Aranson, now. I've been assigned to Mossad headquarters for at least three months."

"Stay with me, Aunt Sarah. I have a nice place at the Maxim."

"For three months?"

"Why not? I haven't seen you for so long. It would be fun. Better than BOQ."

Sarah shrugged. "All right—if you can stand me." Then she said with concern, "You've injured yourself, you're walking so—so carefully, and you have a slight limp, Ruth."

The girl felt heat on her face. "Just a pulled a groin muscle, Aunt Sarah."

"Try heat."

"I did. All night long."

The two women entered the hospital.

Nine

As the four Pratt and Whitney Double Wasp engines powered the Douglas DC-6 upward to 21,000 feet, the pressure built and Brent Ross felt stabs of pain on his eardrums. Pounding his ears, shaking his head and yawning, he heard small popping sounds, and the discomfort dwindled. Then, looking out of his window, he had a breathtaking view of sea and sky.

In less than an hour he had seen the unsullied blue above mottled by swirling clouds, buffeted mercilessly by the jet stream. Veins of cirrus marred the blue vault like torn sheets of soiled linen while far below scattered clouds, all puffs, spurs, spires, and ridges, passed in an endless parade. The brilliant Mediterranean sun played tricks with his eyes, the vaporous intruders casting their shadows on the dark sea as black and crisp as paper cut-outs while reflecting from their convoluted tops with an eye-aching white glare.

Most fascinating were the thunderheads that had climbed imperiously above the northern horizon, tossing their monstrous billowing heads to the sky. Their tops were white like cream whipped for a wedding cake, while below ominous gray and black where shadows darkened them. By the minute, they appeared to grow taller and more numerous, massing like a legion of giants preparing to march southward. Brent smiled to himself, amused by his own overactive imagination.

Blinking, Brent turned his head from the window. To his left, Colonel Irving Bernstein and Lieutenant Junior Grade Elroy Rubin were studying their briefing papers. Brent's unopened attaché case remained beneath his seat. He had studied his notes so long and so intensively that he knew every detail by heart. Anyway, Ruth was on his mind. That was inevitable.

Not only was he tired, his body actually ached from the night's frenzied, sometimes maddened, lovemaking. Did he love her? He had only seen her twice. It didn't make sense, war or no war. But attached to her? Yes, indeed. Not only was he mesmerized by her beauty and sexuality, but she personified the deep-rooted melancholy, the sense of tragedy that seemed endemic with the Israeli nation. And she had many sides. She was brilliant, witty, caustic, sarcastic, urbane, and at times the guileless, naive little girl, all wrapped in the same extraordinary package. But above it all, she exuded an abstruse aura of anguish that trapped him in his own desire to help, to comfort. And Ruth was all of them — all the oppressed, brutalized people of the world who by their very existence stirred his yearning to help. But he was fated to come away feeling helpless, frustrated in his own web of inadequacies.

He was trying. Lord, he was trying. That was why he was on this plane, perhaps flying to his death. And he had fought, killed, and nearly been killed for most of a decade fighting this war. But this same war had been waged for millennia. Untold millions of good men had died fighting this battle. "Would it ever end," Ruth had asked. He shook his head. *Not unless the nature of man changes,* he told himself. The insight wrenched his guts. Pounding a palm with a fist, he sighed.

"Hard night last night?" Rubin asked, slyly, misreading Brent's thoughts.

Brent grinned. "Missed a little sleep. And you?"

The Texan looked at Brent from the corner of his eye. "A mite tired, but not plum tuckered. We Texans grow up a-bustin' broncs, you know." Elroy returned to his papers.

Brent looked around. The big plane was almost empty. Bernstein had been offered secretarial help by Mossad. He had refused. Brent knew his thinking — if they were put to death, why sacrifice innocents? However, seven other seats were occupied. In an unprecedented show of magnanimity and good will, Kadafi had consented to allow pool reporters to accompany the negotiating team. There were reporters from France, England, Italy, Germany, Russia, China, and Canada on board. All were men, at risk and courageous.

Seated across the aisle from Elroy was the British journalist, Robert Kingsbury. Thin and fiftyish with a craggy face that could have fallen off Mount Rushmore, the man reminded Brent of the old actor John Carradine suffering from malnutrition. He had a peculiar way of speaking, his East Sussex inflection drawing out "a" and slurring out his other vowels while his protruding Adam's apple moved up and down like a metronome beating time to his syllables. He was the only man on board who had ever met Kadafi. He was interesting, witty, and very articulate. Brent was curious.

"I understand you met our host, Mr. Kingsbury," Brent said. Everyone looked up.

"Met the bloke years ago—had a five-hour exclusive," Kingsbury said, with a friendly smile. Heads turned, some looks were curious, others unmitigated envy. Several reporters stood and moved closer. Bernstein and Rubin looked up from their notes.

"Interesting," Colonel Bernstein said. "You're syndicated and I have read you for years, but I don't remember your column on Kadafi."

"Of course you bloody well don't. Those buggers at the Foreign Office suppressed it. 'Not in the best interests of the Commonwealth,' they said." He snorted. "A lot of rot."

Bernstein said, "Is it still off the record?"

"Not anymore. No indeed, not now when we know the creature for what he really is." Kingsbury looked around and seemed to speak to each man, "It was quite a while ago, 1980, just after the Camp David agreement and Anwar Sadat was chopped arse over tit. Of course, our friend Kadafi was gloating."

"Naturally."

The Englishman tilted his head back, reviving memories, words bitter and shocking. "Clinically speaking the man's a bloody fool with the intelligence of a chicken. His mind's nothing but an accumulation of septic rubbish. Actually, he's a mental case, completely blotto, a cretin who begged Chou En-lai for nuclear bombs." He looked across the isle. "Can you see that balmy imbecile with atomic bombs? He'd throw them like a bowler pitching at undefended wickets."

"We've heard," Brent Ross said. "And you know the object of this mission."

Discreetly, Kingsbury showed very little of what he really knew, "Prisoners and — ah, exotic weapons, is the rumble."

"Right."

The Englishman's laugh was sardonic. "Well, dash

202

it all, if you can reason with a mental case—try. But remember, his word's not worth a two-penny shit."

"We'll try, anyway."

Kingsbury stretched his lips as if they were elastic and he could wrap them around his teeth. "It was the strangest five hours of my life. First I got a long lecture on Islam—fancies himself a combination muezzin-ayatollah-theologian. A lot of balmy rot and I hear he inflicts his sermon on everyone within earshot. Do you know, when I was allowed to ask questions, I didn't extract a single reasonable sentence out of him? He answered with bursts of stupid laughter, quoted or misquoted the Koran or cited idiocies from a little green book."

"Green book?" several men chorused. They moved closer.

"Quite so. It's his favorite color. In fact, when he first noticed I was taking notes with a green pen, he started shouting as if he were completely crackers, 'green, green, green!' over and over. I never thought he'd stop, almost got his bloody bags off. Then he whipped out a green handkerchief and wiped his nose."

The Russian, Vladimir Rostovsky, suddenly asserted in Oxford-pure English, "Green and white were the colors of the revolution when he overthrew the monarchy and established his Arab *Jamahiriya* or state of the masses."

Kingsbury eyed Rostovsky like a fighter who had just entered the ring and was measuring his opponent. A former writer for *Izvestia,* it was well known that Rostovsky had strong Marxist leanings. Brent suspected Kingsbury was well acquainted with the Russian and loathed him. In fact, he could see it in the eyes of both men. There could be an explosion.

However, Kingsbury continued in a level, cordial

timbre, "Right you are, Vladimir, but I've only told you of the beginning of our soiree." He turned to the entire group, "When he explained to me he was the new Mohammed, the leader of the *jihad,* the needle stuck again, 'I am the gospel, I am the gospel, I'm the gospel,' for at least six minutes. Even his aides seemed terrified enough to spew—turned as green as his bloody handkerchief."

Brent had heard Kadafi was eccentric, a heartless killer. But this was shocking. "I can't believe this," he muttered.

The Canadian reporter, Sidney Grant, asked, "Then why has he lasted? He's ruled the country for twenty-four years."

"Hah! The very reason that all the other bloody and absolute dictators last. He rules through terror and ignorance which in turn feed on terror. Keep in mind, the illiteracy in Libya exceeds even that of Iran, where it reaches seventy percent. Libyans are humiliated and obedient, fit to be buggered, and he puts it to them. Just like Stalin bullocked the Russian people." Rostovsky winced but held his tongue.

"But some are literate, intellectuals who can think for themselves," the Canadian countered.

"True, but anyone literate enough to think of rebelling has long since been brought to book and eliminated. One must remember the students he has hanged and goes on hanging, the exiles he has assassinated and keeps assassinating with his manhunts—his Sabbah, Harry 'High Wire' Goodenoughs, the bloody lot. And now, he has his *jihad*. That unites Muslims like nothing else."

"There have been assassination plots, coups must have been planned, if not attempted," Horst Wasserman, the German reporter said in a guttural Bavarian accent.

204

"Quite so, Kingsbury said. "But remember, in a repressed society like Libya's only army officers can overthrow Kadafi. And there have been a few officers with courage and intelligence who have tried to hatch plots to sweep out the madman. But each time this has ended in failure and a bullet up the arse."

Vladimir Rostovsky reentered the exchange. His defensiveness surprised no one, "But we must remember, when he took over in 1969, he was the first man who ever succeeded in uniting Libya's murderous desert tribes. Why, for centuries they've feuded all across the Sahara and even to the coastal plains."

"How did he do it?" Sidney Grant asked.

Rostovsky continued, "By a blend of Islam, Marxism, feminism, and populism. And he drew prominent tribal leaders into key positions of responsibility in his new government." The Russian eyed Kingsbury, "And that green book contains his manifesto for the cultural revolution, Robert."

Now it was obvious the pair knew each other, very well.

"I'm quite aware of that, Vladimir," Kingsbury shot back. "And don't forget his ruddy killers. They issue his manifestoes most effectively through the barrels of AK-47s, at the point of a knife, or at the end of a wire." Laughter filled the compartment.

Staring at the Russian, Bernstein interrupted forcefully, "If you think he doesn't use terror, Vladimir, you're totally naive. He has seven secret-security services to keep the population whipped into line, and his mass executions are well known." He patted his attaché case. "We have detailed documentation. You can read them if you like."

The Russian's lips tightened, eyes narrowed, and his brow furrowed as if a rake had been pulled across his forehead. He grunted something in Russian that

Brent caught as, "Not needing your lies," and dropped down into his seat. Impatiently, he began to rummage through some papers. An embarrassed silence filled the compartment.

Sidney Grant filled the vacuum. "His security?"

Releasing his pent-up breath with a whooshing sound, the Englishman's chin sagged down almost to his bony chest. "If you're thinking an attempt can be made on him, it's hopeless."

"Hopeless?" the Canadian echoed. "I heard he lives in Tripoli in a tent — just like the common folks. Saw it on a Barbara Walters show. Why, he said he was against capital punishment."

The compartment resounded with laughter. Only the Russian remained placid and the Canadian red-faced.

"Rubbish, old boy," Kingsbury chuckled over the din. "Strictly for the media. When I saw him he lived in a barracks filled with his most trusted." He stroked his long, lank chin. "Actually, more than a barracks, it was an elegant, inaccessible bunker surrounded by a number of other bunkers like a game of Chinese boxes. Open one and find another. The corridors teemed with bloody brutes with Kalashnikovs at the ready. I had to pass through six checkpoints before entering the palace — and believe me, it could make Buckingham Palace look shabby. Then they searched me, my clothing, my shoes, my body, and they bloody well didn't miss a single orifice." The men squirmed.

Bernstein said, "You've heard of Sheik Iman Younis?"

"Yes. I met him in Geneva."

"What is your opinion?"

All eyes were on Kingsbury as he rummaged through his thin yellow hair with long fingers. "A different breed."

"Reasonable?"

"I didn't say that, Colonel."

"Then what?"

"He seems to be sane."

"Nothing more?"

"He's an Arab." Kingsbury shrugged and turned his palms up. "What else? If you can deal honestly with an Arab, Adolph Hitler was a humanitarian." He glanced at Vladimir, "And so was Stalin."

The Russian looked up and shot a glance of distilled hatred at the Englishman. He returned to his documents.

"Yes. Yes, of course, quite true," Bernstein said, grinning at Vladimir. He turned his eyes back to his notes.

Tiring of the subject, Kingsbury pulled a magazine from his briefcase and began reading. Silently, the reporters returned to their seats.

Robert Kingsbury had been right. Kadafi's headquarters were just as elegant and secure as the Englishman had pictured. Brent had expected blindfolds, some extraordinary measures of personal security, but none were imposed. Instead, the entire party, reporters included, was driven into the compound in three Mercedes limousines. Bernstein seemed to read Brent's thoughts, "The Libyans know we know precisely where this complex is. Anyway, you'd need nuclear weapons to put a dent in it. It's one of the most heavily defended spots on earth." He waved, "Fighter bases, radar, at least two armored divisions surround the place, security fences, laser surveillance." He stretched his neck and rubbed it as if he were easing a cramp. "We've given this problem considerable thought."

"But no solution?"

The Israeli grinned. "Not yet."

Brent had noticed a fighter strip as they put down and more fighters, numerous ME 109s, two Spitfires and a halfdozen Fock Wolf 190s were parked at the airstrip when they landed. Bernstein was so right; this would be a tough nut to crack.

Brent, Elroy, and Colonel Bernstein had been shown to private rooms where they were body searched; their personal handguns had been left in Israel. After the ordeal was finished, they showered, and dressed; Brent and Elroy in their Number One blues, Bernstein in his usual desert camouflage. Then, precisely as Kingsbury had described, they were escorted to the conference room by guards carrying automatic rifles.

Four men were seated side by side at the highly polished conference table. Two were strangers, Arabs dressed in Western-style suits. They appeared to be secretaries or recorders of some sort. Brent recognized the other pair: Sheik Iman Younis, heavyset, dark, wearing a gold-trimmed black burnoose, and Major Alai Said Otoba, short, slender with the long thin face and tiny black eyes of a weasel. Younis was rumored to be second in command to Kadafi. Otoba was from *Jihad* headquarters in Tripoli and represented the Arab League. Brent had met them both at the conference in the Hilton Hotel in Taipei the previous year.

Taipei, what a waste of time. Kenneth Rosencrance had attended and completely disrupted the meeting. Brent smiled to himself, thinking of his fight with Rosencrance. How he had beat the American renegade senseless. He almost regretted not seeing him now. He would love to do it again. Kill him with his bare hands. The dog had murdered Captain Colin Willard-

Smith in his parachute. There was a debt to repay.

The Arabs stood stiffly, and following Younis' gesture, Brent, Irving Bernstein, and Elroy seated themselves facing the Arabs. Polite if not effusive greetings were exchanged, but there were no handshakes. Brent heard voices and the seven reporters, escorted by the usual armed guards, entered. They were taken to a long table at one side of the room where word processors were arranged in a long row. Filled with excited expectation, the journalists seated themselves. Every man had a recorder.

Colonel Bernstein said to Sheik Younis, "Colonel Kadafi? Will he attend?"

"We expect him momentarily," the sheik answered in his precise English.

At that moment, six young women entered carrying trays loaded with hot beverages and cakes. They were all dark, beautiful, with Junoesque bodies showing under the scant covering of their traditional belly-dancer's costumes. Most of the men ogled the nearly naked girls with unabashed lust. No liquor was visible; not even beer. "Muslim hypocrites," Bernstein whispered in Brent's ear while he watched the girls. "They do their drinking in private."

"And everything else you can't imagine or even dream of," Brent said back. Both men snickered. Younis and Otaba shot hard glances across the table. Brent grinned in their faces.

"Coffee? Tea? A pastry?" a young woman asked in English with an inflection that indicated she had learned the language phonetically, probably from Libyan teachers. Turning his head, Brent saw the most beautiful girl of the performers.

Pulled back with gold clasps, her hair was so fine and silky it formed a silk sheet, flowing nearly to her waist. It was the color of roasted chestnuts, but it flickered with glowing ruby stars and highlights each time she moved her head. Her features appeared Egyptian, with a straight fine nose and huge dark eyes above high vaulted cheekbones.

Her body was voluptuous, skin shining with a golden cast, limbs long, hands and feet narrow and delicately shaped with tapered fingers. And she moved with such lyrical grace and syncopation Brent was reminded of the opening bars of his favorite symphony, Beethoven's Fifth. You would know she was a dancer even if she had been wearing a black, shapeless sack.

And her costume was the most spectacular of all. Held by tiny strings, her bra was made of gold lamé, decorated with pearls and dangling beads. Her hips were almost completely bare, covered only by a narrow hip band that was little more than a skimpy bikini sewn with jewels, beads, baubles, and bangles. A two-part skirt of filmy transparent chiffon dangled between her legs in front and clung to her buttocks in the rear, as substantial as a wind-blown cloud. The splits showed her long, perfectly shaped legs, adding to the power of her eroticism. Elaborate bracelets covered her wrists while a jeweled pendant hung almost into the cleavage of her high-riding breasts. Swaying from her brassiere was an elaborate brooch made of concentric ringlets of pearls and other gems, while another dangled from the front of her hip band, guarding her most private place. She was breathtaking and fiercely exciting. Brent felt the tempo of his heart speed, face radiate a new warmth.

"Coffee, please," Brent said with forced nonchalance.

The girl poured his coffee and hung low over his ear, again she labored out the peculiar English like a foreign student at an American university, "I am Nadia, Commander Ross. I am to take care of your every need. Give you whatever you wish."

Brent sat bolt upright. "Ah—thank you," he stuttered. "Ah, just coffee, please."

He heard the Arabs snickering and his face turned as hot as the coffee steaming in the cup in front of him. He cursed himself and sipped the dark liquid. Double-boiled, it was very thick and sweet, laced with cardamom. He disliked it, but he drank it anyway. It gave him something to do with his hands which were suddenly as big and unmanageable as chopped logs.

The girls left. Brent did not dare watch Nadia's exit. He knew the Arabs across the table were following his eyes. Instead, he toyed with his cup and sipped the coffee.

There was a stirring at the entrance. Eight armed guards entered and fanned out around the room, Kalashnikovs at the ready. Brent felt a hollow illness begin to build in his guts and wished he had his Beretta. He felt naked. He could see concern on Bernstein's and Elroy Rubin's faces. Either there was going to be a massacre, or the "great man" was about to make his grand entrance. And, indeed, the entrance was grand.

Kadafi did not walk in. Head high, he swept in like a desert *khamsin*. His dense sienna hair was darker than Nadia's—far too dark for his lined face, and very curly; it was obvious he had a permanent and his hair had been dyed. Vanity showed in his spectacular clothes, too: a white silk suit, green shirt without a collar, red sweater, white silk cape with gold braid, back alligator mules and no socks.

"No socks!" Brent said. "What the hell?"

"He has more clothes than Imelda Marcos," Bernstein said into Brent's ear.

"But no socks."

"His feet need the air."

211

Brent chuckled to himself.

The Arabs leaped to their feet, chanting, "Our leader! Our leader! *Allah Akbar!*"

Kadafi stopped at the head of the table where a fawning underling pulled a chair back and then seated himself. A short wave and the four Arabs dropped into their chairs as if they had been shot. Quietly, almost unnoticed, a small portly man in his middle years entered. Following Kadafi's gesture, he took the chair to the dictator's right. He did not appear Arabic. Another tall, thin young man, obviously an Arab, padded in softly and sat on Kadafi's left.

Kadafi looked at the three negotiators and said in a high-pitched voice, *"Essalamu alaykum."*

Brent looked at Bernstein whose face was tight with concentration.

Bernstein said, "Peace . . ."

"Peace be with you," the young man to the left of Kadafi said in English so mangled it was almost unintelligible. "I am Haj Walid Khaled, the Colonel's interpreter."

"What did he say? I didn't ken that," Elroy said.

"He's the interpreter," Bernstein said.

"But he cain't talk English."

"Makes sense," Brent said.

Silence charged the room, harsh, electric while Kadafi's eyes roamed over the occupants. He ignored Haj Walid Khaled and spoke to Brent in English that was better than his interpreter's. "You are Commander Brent Ross, the 'American samurai'?"

Brent eyed the dictator. This was the source, the head of the murderous octopus he had fought for nearly a decade. Here was the man who commanded the most ruthless band of cutthroats on earth. The man who, rolling in oil money, had hired killers like

212

Kenneth Rosencrance and Rudolph Stoltz and attacked freedom-loving peoples all over the earth. Trained terrorists at home, supported others abroad. Gloated over the mountains of corpses of his enemies, real and supposed, and raged at defeats, in fits of pique killing his own as readily as his enemy. Stalin, Hitler, and Kadafi all cut from the same cloth. He felt an insensate cauldron heat deeply, his heart begin to race and a familiar urge to obliterate was upon him. Coming erect, he clutched his fists into tight balls. Then, taking a deep breath, he forced it all back, remembering the object of his mission. He caught Bernstein's face from the corner of his eye and realized the Israeli was experiencing identical emotions — perhaps more intense, if possible.

Brent managed to respond in a controlled voice with a disciplined, "Yes, sir. I am called that."

Kadafi stared at the American for a long moment. There was a malignant spark in those inky eyes. His expression, solemn and enigmatic, was at odds with his welcoming words and manner. Brent expected something ominous. He was not disappointed. The dictator smiled suddenly, an expression completely devoid of humor and good will, and said, "You might be interested in knowing, I have made you quite a valuable young man."

The Arabs giggled.

Brent was on guard. He suspected a bounty. He spoke evenly: "I am in your debt; may I inquire as to the amount."

Kadafi was impressed. "You have a quick mind. Yes, you may inquire. A half million for your—ah, for your exit."

Bernstein gasped; Elroy gripped Brent's arm. Brent felt his temper stir, but maintained a calm exterior. The man was baiting him, but he would reverse it. He shocked every man in the room, "Respectfully, sir, I find that demeaning."

"Demeaning?"

"Yes, sir. You've placed a bounty of a million dollars on the head of Commander Yoshi Matsuhara." He looked around at the amazed faces. "I feel that I'm worth at least that much."

"You overestimate yourself, young man." Laughter from the Arabs.

"I think not, sir. I've personally killed at least a dozen of your best — beheaded three." Brent felt a nudge from Bernstein's knee, but he was on a roll, "A million dollars for my head would be a fair sum, indeed. It would certainly attract a lot of attention. Some might even try to collect it, if foolish enough."

The taunt widened every eye in the room. The dictator sat bolt upright, gimlet-eyed, his stare spiced with venom, "I would be delighted to pay it, young man."

"I'm at your disposal, sir."

Now Bernstein's knee was pounding and his fist knuckled Brent's arm. He used American idiom, "For Christ's sake, cool it," he whispered.

Seeking easier game, Kadafi's eyes moved, and he nodded at Bernstein, "You are Colonel Irving Bernstein of Mossad."

"Yes, Colonel Kadafi."

"A most efficient organization."

"Thank you."

A puerile smirk curled the dictator's lips. "Have you found a way to assassinate me yet?"

"No, sir, but we are working on it."

"May Allah be with you," was the sarcastic response.

"My God will do, thank you. He's been around a lot longer than yours."

"But he's a fraud," Kadafi shot back. And then in Arabic, *"La ilaha illa-l-Lah."*

"No God but Allah," Bernstein translated. "But it depends on your viewpoint." And then in Hebrew, *"Baruch ha-Shem."*

It was Brent's turn to nudge Bernstein, "For the Lord's sake, cool it man," he whispered into the Israeli's ear.

Either Kadafi had not understood the Hebrew, or he was tiring of the banter. He was already addressing Elroy Rubin. Obviously, the dictator had been thoroughly briefed, "And you must be the Texan, Lieutenant Junior Grade Elroy Rubin."

"Keerect, sir."

Kadafi looked at his interpreter. The man whispered into the dictator's ear. Brent suspected the dictator was acting, a charade to conceal the fact he could understand English much better than he affected. Kadafi nodded and returned to Elroy, "You meant I was correct, Lieutenant."

"Keerect, Colonel." Then the Texan showed his leathery pluck with his own daring taunt, "I declare Colonel, I busted four o' your boys an' you ain't put no green-stuff on my haid." Brent choked back a gasp and Bernstein occupied himself with his mint tea.

Again, Kadafi conferred with his interpreter and then turned back to Elroy. "You speak of money — a bounty. I can correct that situation."

Brent could not believe the ludicrous exchange. Kingsbury was right. Kadafi had the intelligence of a chicken. A head of state allowing himself to fall into a no-win exchange with representatives of enemy powers who were far beneath his station. Only a fool would allow himself to be baited and degraded like this.

"Least-wise I reckon my hide's worth half of Commander Ross's. A quarter million," Elroy goaded, obviously enjoying himself.

Kadafi looked the Texan up and down and scored his own points. "I do not pay for dogs with no teeth." The Arabs cheered.

Elroy, smiled, "Shoot, Colonel, remember, I done gummed a few 'o your boys to death."

Face reddening, Kadafi stared hard at the Texan. "Your mouth is bigger than your brain," he said dangerously. "I suggest you hold your tongue while you still have it."

Elroy began to rise, but Brent pulled him back down, whispering, "Enough! Enough!" The Texan relaxed.

Tiring of the exchange and feeling he had bested his opposition, Kadafi turned away from Rubin triumphantly and pulled some prayer beads from his pocket. Looking high over everyone, he found a change of topic in religion, "Infidels know very little of us, the Koran, Sunna, and Jinn."

"Oh, God," Brent heard Bernstein say. "A lecture. Not the ninety-nine names for Allah!"

They were spared the ninety-nine names, but Kadafi rumbled on, "Islam means 'the submission to God's will.' We Moslems submit." The black rodent-like eyes darted around the room. Brent could see Robert Kingsbury sink back in his chair, a look of hopeless resignation on his face. The sermon was coming. Kadafi spoke out with the missionary zeal of Jimmie Swaggart without the tears, "Mohammed was a poor camel driver from Mecca. One day he climbed Mount Arafat and stayed there for forty days. There, he received his instructions from Allah himself."

Kingsbury clasped both hands over his eyes and turned his head down. Bernstein yawned. The Arabs sat with rapt expressions.

"What is wrong, Colonel Bernstein," Kadafi said. "Am I boring you?"

"I've heard this before, Colonel."

The dictator waved. "Yes, yes, of course. A *Yahud*, a Jew to our Christian friends, would know. But not all of you know." He drew himself up, "The whole world will hear this message one day." His eyes turned upward and he continued, "Mohammed spent the rest of his life preaching and the Koran is a collection of his sermons." His eyes flashed to Brent and then to Bernstein. "And since he was the final prophet, all other religions are obsolete."

"Allah akbar!" the Arabs shouted.

"All?" Elroy burst through the yells. "You ain't funnin'?"

Brent clasped a hand over his mouth, Bernstein chuckled, even some of the reporters tittered. Kadafi consulted his interpreter.

Kadafi said, "No, I am not being humorous." His eyes turned heavenward. "One night while in Mecca, Mohammed was awakened by the angel Gabriel and was told he was about to take a journey to paradise. To prepare for this journey, the angel cut him open and removed his heart and washed it. Then, when it was replaced, it was filled with faith and wisdom."

"No shit," Brent heard Elroy whisper.

"Then Mohammed mounted his mighty horse, el-Buraq, an extraordinary animal with a woman's face, a mule's body and a peacock's tail. In a single stride, el-Buraq could travel as far as a man could see."

"Sure like to have a passel of them critters in my corral," Elroy whispered into Brent's ear.

The voice droned on, "When Mohammed reached Jerusalem, he tethered el-Buraq to the Western Wall of the Temple of Herod and ascended to the Temple Mount. Here he discovered the great rock of

Abraham's sacrifice"—he nodded at Bernstein—"which is also the altar of the Hebrew Temple."

"Right. Right," Bernstein acknowledged.

"Mohammed leaped from the rock onto a ladder of light that led to paradise. The rock rose after Mohammed, but the angel Gabriel ordered the rock to stay in place, and the rock obeyed." He looked at his audience triumphantly, "Later a great shrine was built over it. It is called the Dome of the Rock, and nearby the Al Aksa Mosque was built." He looked at the reporters, "Al Aksa means 'the fartherest place.' " He stared at Bernstein, "Our Jerusalem!"

More shouts of, *"Allah akbar!"*

"Respectfully, Colonel Kadafi," Brent said, pre-empting Bernstein. "I was under the impression we came here to negotiate."

"You will negotiate when I am finished, Commander," the dictator rebutted with a tone that scalded. He continued addressing heaven, "El-Buraq was waiting for Mohammed when he got to heaven. Once mounted, Mohammed rode through the seven paradises of heaven. He met the patriarchs and the prophets of the Book and saw all the angels at prayer." He looked around at his audience and smiled. He was enjoying himself immensely. "Actually, he met Moses who was a small reddish-faced man and Jesus who was quite average in appearance but had a lot of freckles and wore a filthy *jalabiyah*. Solomon, too, was quite ordinary, a little old man with a gray beard and bent back. He suffered from a severe case of arthritis, you know."

Aghast, Elroy looked at Brent, who tapped his temple while Bernstein grimaced and closed his eyes tightly. Brent could see Robert Kingsbury peek out between spread fingers. His shoulders were shaking. All the other reporters sat stonily, eyes fixed on the dictator.

Kadafi seemed oblivious of his audience, seemed to be reciting to himself, "Mohammed quickly gained all the knowledge and wisdom of the saints, angels and prophets and was allowed a private audience with Allah. He was the only man who ever saw Allah unmasked. They spoke at great length and defined the various aspects of Islam. Allah demanded that the people pray to him thirty-five times a day, but Mohammed argued for five times daily. Mohammed prevailed and returned to Mecca but not before being instructed on the Five Pillars of Wisdom."

Surveying the assembly, a haughty smirk twisted the dictator's face. Brent heard Bernstein spit under his breath, "Oh Lord, there's more to come."

Kadafi resumed with all the fervor of an American charismatic fundamentalist trying to swindle money out of naive viewers on television, *"Muwahhidun!* God is one," he translated. Most of the men nodded. "And *Muhammadun rasulu-l-Lah,* Mohammed is the messenger of God." Then he quoted the Koran: " 'He is God, the one; God the eternal. He begets not and is not begotten; nor is there like unto Him anyone.' "

"Allah akbar!" the Arabs shouted obediently.

"Verse one twelve," Bernstein muttered to himself.

"The second pillar, a Moslem must pray five times a day, kneeling, and bowing to Mecca and prostrating himself." He raised both hands upward in a supplicating gesture, *"Allah akbar!"*

"Allah akbar!" echoed back.

Dropping his hands dramatically, he described the remaining pillars in great detail. Almsgiving: "Observe prayer, pay the alms, and kneel with those who kneel." Next, fasting during the high holy day of Ramadan, the ninth month of the Islamic calendar when the gates of heaven are open and Gabriel asks grace for everyone. Finally, to Brent's relief, the dictator arrived at the Fifth Pillar, the pilgrimage to Mecca. " 'It is a duty toward God, incumbent on those who are able to visit this House,' " Kadafi quoted again.

The beady eyes surveyed the assemblage. They came to rest on Robert Kingsbury. His erratic mind changed direction the way a chameleon changes color. "We have met. You are British."

"Correct, Colonel. I interviewed you back in 1980."

The dictator nodded vaguely. "Yes. A long time ago." He smiled suddenly. "I remember. It was a long interview, but I never saw your article."

"It was never published."

"Complimentary, I presume."

"It was accurate, Colonel."

"Very good."

Bernstein snickered into his hand and Brent bit his lip. All the other reporters managed to keep a straight face. Fear was there, powerful and infectious.

Kadafi turned to the strange round man to his right. He waved casually, "This is Emil Bouchett, a special emissary from the United Nations, appointed by President Francois Mitterrand himself. He will act as an observer and mediator." He stared at the Israeli and the American, "I will see you gentlemen again. Affairs of state call." He stood quickly, and escorted by four soldiers, swept from the room. Everyone, including the Arabs, sighed with relief.

Bouchett smiled and nodded, looking around the room in short jerky movements. Thankfully, he spoke with studied, easily understood English, sprinkled with only a few French words. *"Monsieurs,"* he opened. We have an *extraordinaire* opportunity to further the cause of world peace." Everyone nodded, although none were convinced. "First, we must agree on an agenda." He looked around. "And you, Sheik Younis, can you begin?"

The reporters adjusted their recorders, readied pencils or hunched over word processors. Elroy threw a switch on his recorder and raised a pencil over a large yellow pad. Brent and Bernstein concentrated on Younis, who was already standing. Glancing at a pad, the Arab said, "We must first discuss the exchange of prisoners." The opposing delegation nodded as one. "Then there are a few other minor items to discuss. Just what the battleship *New Jersey* is doing steaming westward in the Pacific? Why are *Yonaga, Bennington* and at least twelve destroyers making frantic preparations to put to sea?" He stared hard at Brent and Bernstein, "And what is your occupation force doing in the Canary Islands? After all, this is not the tourist season."

The Arabs guffawed at Younis's wit.

Brent looked at Bernstein as the Israeli rose. The Arabs knew more than they had expected. But he was not surprised. Arab intelligence, trained and deployed by the Russians before the Soviet Union collapsed, was very efficient. And it was backed by a "Gulag Archipelago" that made the Russian system seem philanthropic in comparison.

Bernstein spoke without reference to notes, "Yes, Sheik Younis, I agree, we must give prisoner exchange the highest priority. But, we, too, have some minor items that give us concern—the poison gas works at Rabta, the calutrons enriching uranium, your fast breeder reactor, your purchase of the Russian carrier *Baku* and cruisers *Dzerzhinsky* and *Zhdanov* from the Russians. If they aren't in your yards, they'll be there soon. We know they're underway. Also, the Spanish carrier *Reina de Iberico,* which you call *Al Marj,* carrier *Magid,* cruiser *Babur* and more than a dozen escorts are ready for sea. That's a powerful force and they aren't preparing to celebrate the Ramadan." Brent and Elroy laughed.

"And Sheik Younis, you complain of our troops in the Canary Islands, what about your occupation of the Marianas. Your LRAs continuously prowl over Japan, all the way to Tokyo Bay."

"You shoot them down."

Bernstein's retort was rancorous, "What do you expect, a welcoming committee? An invitation to the *sanja-matswei* festival?"

"S'il vous plait, monsieurs," Bouchett said. "Control yourselves. We cannot make *progress* if we argue."

The antagonists nodded and Younis spoke. "Then, Colonel Bernstein," the tone was conciliatory, "can we agree. All issues will be set aside until we settle the prisoner exchange?"

"That would be a good start," the Israeli agreed, but his face was tight with frustration.

"Excellent," Younis said. "Then we will start those discussions first thing in the morning."

"Why not now?"

The Arab shook his head. "It is late and we are preparing a special welcoming meal for you and some other special guests." He smiled. "And entertainment." He looked at the reporters. "Sorry, gentlemen, only for the negotiators." There was a groan. He turned back to Bernstein and the Americans, "I trust your quarters are satisfactory?"

The men nodded. "Very good."

"Then, Colonel Bernstein, with your agreement, this meeting is closed." Bouchett nodded his approval which had not been requested.

Everyone stood and filed toward the door. Brent could hear the reporters complaining. Some were cursing, others slamming attaché cases and brief cases shut angrily.

Passing the reporters, he felt no sympathy. The fourth estate was never satisfied. They were lucky to be invited to the opening meeting. He left the room.

Ten

Before the dinner, Colonel Bernstein and Lieutenant J.G. Elroy Rubin visited Brent. Brent had a luxurious suite with a living room, bedroom, a king-sized bed, and a gleaming bath. Bernstein was upset by the meeting and felt depressed about chances of reaching any agreement. Brent tried to be optimistic and Elroy joined in the effort. All this was done over tea; everyone had drunk too much coffee, and liquor had been left home with their weapons.

Speaking from a plump easy chair, Elroy said to Bernstein, "Kadafi's not as stupid as Kingsbury said."

"He's mad," Bernstein rumbled.

Brent said, "Definitely unstable. That makes him very dangerous."

"Do y'all figger he'd cut off my tongue?" Elroy asked grimly.

Bernstein nodded. "As casually as chopping salami."

The Texan gulped. "I ain't hankering for none o' that. I don' like salami."

Beginning to shed his depression, Bernstein asserted himself as the elder statesman of the group. "I despise him, but we must control ourselves. We were all a little foolish."

"Agreed," Brent said, encouraged by Bernstein's improving mood. Elroy nodded.

Elroy rubbed his chin. "He's throwin' one fancy shindig tonight. Keerect?"

"Right."

"To him we're lower'n snakes' bellies an' he's a mind to skin us. He don't want no truck with us. So I don't put no store in this invite."

Bernstein said, "Remember, Younis said there would be some other special guests?" Brent and Elroy nodded. "I overheard two guards talking—there is a special ambassador from Turkey here and another from Morocco."

Brent said. "Oh, I get it. Morocco is still ostensibly neutral and he wants to strengthen his ties with Turkey, which is also neutral and a traditional enemy of the Arabs. Cover both flanks—cover all bets, if he can."

"Yes, a good analysis. Must be his thinking."

"Then this hoe-down is for them dudes."

Bernstein nodded at Elroy. "And to impress us with his power and support from Turkey and Morocco. A negotiating ploy. Don't forget, our B-25s flew over Morocco on their run to Rabta unmolested. As far as we know, they were not even reported on Moroccan radar."

"They flew on the deck," Brent reminded the Israeli.

"I know, but, still, Brent, chances were very good that they would've been spotted."

"Possibly."

Elroy rubbed his chin and spoke hesitantly. "Ah, Colonel, your gunna think I'm a stupid yahoo."

Bernstein chuckled. "No chance. What is it, Elroy."

"Well, Kadafi mentioned Sunna and jinn an' didn't tell us nothin' 'bout them. I'm still a-wonderin'." And

225

then self-consciously, "You don't think I have brain one."

"Of course not," Bernstein said. "You have a very strong intelligence.

"I wasn't anglin' for that."

"I know Elroy." Bernstein brushed a few stray hairs back from his forehead. "Very few Westerners know of these mysterious beliefs of the Muslims. As you saw, Kadafi's mind isn't very well-organized, and he skipped and hopped around from topic to topic, from man to man. He never told us how important the Sunna is to Muslims. Actually, it's an interpretation of the Koran by experience and tradition — something like the Hebrew Talmud. Those who believe in the Sunna are called Sunni. The Sunnis make up most of the Muslim world."

"But most of 'em cain't read it."

"True. Usually it's passed along orally, often mangled and distorted."

Brent offered, "Just like their whole damned world."

"Right."

"An' jinn?" Rubin asked.

"Evil spirits," Bernstein said. "Muslims believe these evil spirits can change form, can look like an animal or a person and have supernatural powers. The Sunna teaches them to fear jinn because they can get inside a person and cause every illness you can think of. Once afflicted, only the will of Allah can make you well again."

"I'll be hornswoggled. They actually put store in that voodoo?"

"They'll kill for it." The Israeli put his tea cup down on a highly polished walnut table. "Have either of you ever attended an Arab dinner?"

"I ate in a Moroccan restaurant once in Philly,"

226

Brent said. "No silverware. Had to eat with my hands. Never went back."

"You're funnin'."

"No, Elroy, that's true. We'll eat with our hands."

Bernstein smiled. He had shed his depression. "The Arabs say there are four ways of eating. One finger to show revulsion, two fingers to show pride, three fingers to show average or typical, and four fingers to show voracious enthusiasm." He licked his lips, "Take my word for it, this will be strictly a four finger affair."

There was knock on the door. "It's time," Brent said. "Polish your fingers, gentlemen. They'll be your silverware tonight."

Elroy whooped, "Yah-hoo, boys, here's hopin' the grub'll be finger-lickin' good!"

Chuckling, the men rose and walked to the door.

They were led by a pair of well-muscled guards dressed like old Turkish janissaries with bloomered pantaloons to the ankles, wide red sashes about the waist, and fez head coverings.

"Trying to impress the Turkish guest," Brent said into Bernstein's ear.

"This is only the beginning," Bernstein said. And then grinning at Elroy, "You ain't seen nothin' yet."

"Your a-learnin', Colonel," Elroy joked back. Infected by a growing festive mood, they all laughed.

The dining room was straight out of the *Arabian Nights*. Obviously designed for celebrations, a tent like ambiance was created by large embroidered cloths hanging from the walls and ceiling. Mirrors were strategically placed, some overhead so that the revelers could admire themselves from several angles simultaneously. Brent suspected the room was used for sex orgies as well as dining. Rich oriental rugs covered the floor. Thick pillows and low tables added to the sense of debauchery inspired by the mirrors.

Colonel Moammar Kadafi, Sheik Iman Younis, Emil Bouchett, Haj Walid Khaled, and three strange men were already seated. One of the strangers was in traditional Arab dress, while the other pair looked as if they had been outfitted by Brooks Brothers. The three strangers rose and faced the newcomers. From his pillow, Kadafi gestured and introduced them. The first was the Moroccan special envoy, Mana Zaki Alaqi, who wore a flowing rich burnoose made of silk and trimmed with gold and silver. Dark, he had an ominous glow in his black eyes that spoke more of hostility than neutrality. He nodded stiffly. The nod was returned.

Equally disconcerting was the Turk Hadja Khalfay Pasha, a short ruddy man with a noncommittal stare that left everyone speculating. He was neutral, and obviously he walked the line like a tightrope walker with no net. This would be especially difficult in Kadafi's tent.

The third man took Brent, Irving and Elroy by surprise. He was a Spaniard. Appearing to be over sixty, he was tall, patrician and natty. His name, Saavedra Miguel de Medina-Sidona, was as formidable as his appearance.

"All them names for one old critter," Elroy muttered.

The Spaniard glared with a laserlike stare and slowly creaked back onto his pillow. Obviously, the Canary Islands were on his mind. All of the other men seated themselves.

"The Canary Islands must be sticking in his craw," Brent whispered, adjusting his pillows.

"All their craws," Bernstein replied.

Brent wondered about the appearance of his delegation. Would the three special guests think the trio were there to beg, compromise, beseech the mighty Kadafi for some favors, perhaps a degrading peace? He knuckled his forehead. No chance. Everyone knew how determined the Israelis and Admiral Fujita's forces were to prosecute the war. There had been no hint of compromise, and there would be none now. If Medina-Sidona, Alaqi, and Pasha had any idea that a demeaning peace was in the offing, they would be stripped of that sentiment very soon. Brent hoped the trio would attend the negotiating sessions.

"We're supposed to be impressed, Brent," Bernstein whispered in his ear.

"I know. Just two thugs and a question mark."

Bernstein's chuckle was interrupted by a quintet of musicians that began whining out a repetitious melody on three guitars, an accordion and a clarinet.

"They're playing 'Dance Into Your Sultan's Heart,'" Bernstein said, ignoring the strangers and the purpose of their presence. The sounds of the orchestra had immediately struck a cheerful chord in his Middle Eastern heart. "That's usually played for belly dancers," he added, smiling in anticipation.

Brent felt his spirits rise, too, and accepted a cup of tea. Just as he brought the cup to his lips, Nadia slithered out from behind a curtain and began the familiar gyrations of the belly dancer. She was incredibly limber, bending, twisting, jiggling her large breasts and swaying her delicious hips seductively, hands clicking finger cymbals. She undulated toward Brent like a snake, with spins, bumps, grinds, explicitly parodying the sex act. The closer she came, the more tea the American drank. Every man stared, saw the object of her concentration, and then began to snicker. Brent was sure the girl's approach had been prearranged. Kadafi, Younis, Khaled, the special emissaries, must be far more important than he. But she came on, ignoring them.

Only a few feet from him, she bent her knees and dropped down backwards onto the floor, leaning on her arms. Then she performed one of the most erotic movements Brent had ever seen. Raising her hips high, she twisted her left hip toward him and then the right. Then the left and right again. Faster and faster. It seemed physically impossible but she continued the movements for several minutes while the musicians, too, seemed caught up in the eroticism of the moment, pounding out their melody with near sexual fury. The other men stared; perspiration began to appear even on the brow of the old Spaniard.

Then she was on her feet and slipping closer and closer to the American, finally pumping a firm hip within a few inches of Brent's face. She turned ever so slowly, so that her pelvis was almost in his face. Her hips moved in a frantic series of bumps and the huge brooch flew back and forth, coming within an inch of his nose. Brent gulped down his tea and Nadia turned away. He could hear laughter. Even Bernstein and Elroy were giggling. "She has a hankerin' for you, boy," Brent heard Elroy say with his usual lack of discipline.

Kadafi raised a hand and the orchestra stopped suddenly as if their hands had been chopped off. Nadia vanished. The dictator was in an effusive mood, "Gentlemen," he said, looking first at the negotiating trio and then at his other three guests, "tonight you are guests in my tent. Now you will see, will feel, the warmth of Arab hospitality. Tonight is not a night for politics, that will come in the days to follow. By the prophet's beard, I promise to make this a night you will remember with happiness."

"Sounds rational enough," Brent whispered into Bernstein's ear. The Israeli said nothing.

Kadafi clapped twice and the musicians resumed their music instantly. Accompanied by seven more dancers, Nadia reappeared and the girls swayed and slithered around the room.

Bowls of water and small towels were passed, and after the ritual hand-washing, food came in battalions, regiments and divisions. At least twenty women wound through the dancers ladened with two dozen salads. Brent watched the Arabs rip Pita bread asunder and swish the pieces around in the pasty salads or dip their fingers in and lick them clean.

As the plates and platters were stacked on the table, Kadafi fell silent and Younis spoke to the visitors as he gestured, "Hummus and tahini of cold mashed chick peas, sesame seeds, olive oil, and garlic." He dipped his fingers into a bowl and stuffed his mouth. He spoke while still eating, "Over there, steamed grape leaves with pine nuts and currants, deep-fried crushed wheat and chick peas, lamb livers, peppers, pickled cabbage, eggplant, lamb pie, fish balls."

He scooped up some lamb livers and munched loudly as he relished the delicacy. There was more: squash dishes, okra, leeks, and beans prepared in a variety of ways. Brent picked at first, then, seduced by the exotic flavors, dipped in like a native. Bernstein whispered astonishing news into his ear, "These are only the appetizers."

The women trooped, ladened with the main course. Some of the platters were so heavy they had trouble carrying them. Roasted chicken, rice sprinkled with lamb's eyes and testicles did not appeal to Brent. But the smell of racks of spring lamb sauted in dill, lemon, and herbs did. And there was more lamb: lamb with eggplant, lamb with onions, lamb with

231

prunes. There were loud chomping sounds and sighs from the diners as they tore chunks of meat free and stuffed their mouths. The musicians pounded away, the girls swayed and whirled like trees caught in a storm, and the men gorged.

After the main course, the women cleared empty platters and replaced them with trays of melons, fruit, and layered pastries of honey and nuts and other paper-thin sweet cakes.

Then came coffee and a fusillade of belches that reminded Brent of the artillery barrage at *Bren-ah-Hahd. Narghiles,* the water pipes, were passed from Arab to Arab. They inhaled deeply, adding huge sighing clouds of smoke to the barrage. Even Medina-Sidona took his drags. However, Brent, Elroy and Irving declined without apologizing.

Kadafi rose and every man stood. "I must bid you good evening, gentlemen. It is time I retire," he said. Everyone shouted praise for the food and entertainment and the great hospitality.

Nodding and smiling, the dictator turned. Saavedra Miguel de Medina-Sidona, Mana Zaki Alaqi and Hadja Khalfah Pasha stepped back from the table with him as if an unseen signal had been given. They were obviously expecting something more. The dictator pointed at three girls, all statuesque and spacious in the hips. Then he and the special envoys left with the girls and guards close behind. As the party exited, they passed a young turbanned page, a boy of about fifteen. The boy followed the group.

Nadia was not chosen. Brent was bewildered. She was the most attractive by far. Strangely, he felt thankful, as if something special had been preserved. Then he noticed that several of the dancers were throwing glances of unmitigated jealousy after the departing girls. He smiled to himself. Professional jealousy. Then, a growling stomach gave him a start and he squirmed in discomfort.

Feeling so bloated his thinking was confused, Brent said to Bernstein, "Would it be poor etiquette if I left, too. I ate too much."

"I'm of the same mind," Elroy said. "Ate more'n a hog ruttin' in a potato patch. Need some shut-eye."

Smiling, Bernstein addressed Sheik Younis with unusual cordiality, "We all enjoyed the meal immensely. We are tired. It's been a long day for us. We need to rest."

"Of course," Younis said. "You had a long flight and you must be tired."

After expressing their gratitude for the meal, the three men left.

Nadia watched Brent until he disappeared into the hall.

Too tired and lethargic to shower, Brent had just put on his robe and was preparing to read until his stomach settled when the shy knock came. Again, he missed his Beretta. He opened the door. Nadia was standing in the hallway. She was still in her dancer's costume, and a jeweled bag hung from her shoulder.

Brent was suspicious. Something was not quite right. She had come on to him from the moment she first saw him, and he was convinced Kadafi, or one of his underlings, had put her up to it. And why wasn't she chosen for an evening of pleasure for the dictator or his special envoys? Was she after information? Was she a killer? After all, his head was worth a half million.

"May I come in, Commander Ross?" she asked, wide brown eyes filled with innocence. She seemed nervous, even frightened.

Brent blocked the door. "Why?"

She looked up and down the hall. "Please, Effendi, I must see you."

"But why?"

"It is personal," she almost whispered.

Brent relented and Nadia entered. He waved her to a chair. "What is it, Nadia?" he asked impatiently.

"I—I have a duty to perform."

"A duty."

"Yes, Effendi. You do not understand Arabs."

"I agree."

"I am part of your host's hospitality."

Now Brent understood. *"I am to take care of your every need. Give you whatever you wish,"* she had said that afternoon. He rubbed his chin and shook his head negatively. He was not adverse to making love to beautiful women, but not on these terms. Not when a woman had been ordered to bed him. It would be like buying a prostitute. Unthinkable.

And there was something else, "Why weren't you picked—picked by the colonel to, ah, entertain his guests or even himself?" His eyes roamed over her fabulous body. "Frankly, you are the most attractive of the lot."

"Thank you, Commander Ross. But you do not understand Arab men."

"What do you mean?"

She ran a hand over her bare shoulder and rubbed her neck thoughtfully. "Many Arab men prefer to love men. Some, tonight, chose boys. This, you did not see."

"My God."

She shrugged. "That is how they are."

Again, he ran his eyes over her. "They all aren't that way. Many must want you."

"I am an Egyptian."

234

"So?"

"Colonel Kadafi hates Sadat."

"He's been dead for over a decade."

"It makes no difference. He hates his memory. He is an Arab. Arabs do not forget."

"Crazy. Not even the dead?" Brent scratched his temple. "And he's transferred it to you?"

"Not really. But Egyptians are not regarded well here. They did deal with the *Yahuds*."

"Then why are you here?"

She answered without hesitation, "Because I am the best dancer in the world and he likes to show off to his guests. And he pays me very well."

"And he hasn't expected anything else from you?"

The girl reddened. "Not yet, Commander, but I must obey the rules just like the other girls. I am an Arab, too."

"But he sent you here—part of the rules."

"No. Another, I cannot reveal his name, made this arrangement."

Brent felt his brimming stomach churn and begin to sour. "You owe me nothing. I will take nothing from you. You may leave, Nadia," he said curtly.

Fear crossed her face, "But Commander, you do not understand. I *must* provide you with a service."

"You *must*? A service?"

She looked at her feet. "You do not know Arab men. If I do not, they will punish me—they have that right."

"Punish you?"

"Something terrible—something that leaves you less than a woman."

Now Brent understood. He had heard the horror stories. Arab women were the worst-treated women on earth. Often, they were forced to have their clitorises—the Arabs called it "the pleasure button"—removed, sometimes as a punishment, at other times to deprive young girls of the ability to enjoy sex so that they would remain virgins until married. It was a barbarous, sadistic practice and typically Arab. Obviously, Nadia feared this disfigurement.

"But, how would they know?"

"There is an old woman, Hanan. I will be examined. Hanan knows what to look for."

"Good, God. I can't believe this."

"A massage." Brightening, she patted her bag. "For the first night, it will do. I brought my oils."

"How will they know about that?"

She smiled. "Hanan will measure the amount of oils I have left and you may even be asked. It is quite easy." She gestured toward the bedroom, "Please, Effendi, a massage and I will leave."

"And the next time?"

She sighed. "We will see. He who commanded this may change his mind. Arab men often do."

A new thought struck Brent. *Baksheesh,* it fueled the Arab world. "A bribe," he said. "Can you bribe Hanan?"

The girl tucked her lower lip under and looked the big American up and down. There was disappointment in her voice, "With enough money, perhaps, Effendi."

"All right. A massage tonight and a bribe the next time you have the duty." Brent walked into the bedroom. The girl was close on his heels. "Begin your massage, Nadia." He sat on the bed.

"Please. On your stomach and remove your robe."

"I'll be naked."

"Of course." Brent hesitated.

"Please, Commander."

Turning away from the girl, Brent removed his robe and lay face down on the bed. He felt the girl sit down beside him and heard her open her bag. Turning quickly, he grabbed the bag and searched it. "Only oils to massage you with, Effendi. No knives."

Grunting, Brent turned his face to the mattress. She began to rub his back. Lubricated by scented oils, her touch was soft, slippery, yet firm, seeking out the tired, taut muscles. "You must learn to allow yourself to be touched," she said.

"I'm trying."

The hands moved lower, pushing, kneading, always in motion, and the muscles began to loosen. "There, that is better," she said softly. "You have such a magnificent body. Relax it."

Slowly, Brent began to feel the eroticism of the moment. The girl was an artist. Her hands slipped down from his back over his buttocks and pushed down hard on his hamstrings. He felt like a clock with its mainspring running down. There was no way, absolutely no way he could feel nervous or worry about anything. She pushed on his hip.

"What—what now?"

"On your back, Effendi."

"No."

She laughed, apparently as relaxed as Brent. "I will not seduce you, Commander." She continued pushing and Brent rolled over. He watched her as she looked him up and down, finally fixing her eyes on his endowment. "Ah, you are a great man." She giggled. "Any maiden would be happy to be with you."

Brent smiled, but said nothing.

The hands went back to work, her head dropped and he could feel her hot breath on his cheek. She began to lick his neck, moved to his clavicle. It was like having a small hot wet snake roaming his body. His impulse was to object, but he found it impossible. Feeling almost helpless, he sagged back while her tongue moved across his chest. She did not mention his scars. He guessed she had seen many. She moved lower to his stomach, tongue always ahead of her hands. Toyed with his navel.

Yet, strangely, his arousal did not come on. No man alive should be able to withstand this. But he could and did. It was Ruth. She meant more to him than he had realized. Her pathetic search for the simple love of the boy and girl in a world free of war, of hate. And there had been love in her eyes when he left her at the airport. He was sure of that. He meant a lot to her. Too much.

"Stop, Nadia. Please." But his arms seemed paralyzed.

Nadia moved lower, stopped, looked up from the hair that began to thicken on his abdomen, "You have been with another woman. Last night?"

Brent was amazed. "You can tell?"

"She is still with you, Effendi."

He sat up. Now he felt Ruth's presence with a impact that was almost physical. Even Nadia knew of her now. Suddenly feeling cheapened and disgusted with himself, he said, gruffly, "That's enough, Nadia. You've discharged your duty. The massage is finished." He gripped her by the shoulders and pulled her up.

She looked at him in amazement. "This is all?"

"Yes. This is all. Please leave."

"The other woman—I have offended you." Her voice trembled. "I did not mean to. Most men would be complimented."

"No. You have not offended me," Brent lied.

"You will not complain?" she asked, face a dictionary of fear.

"Of course, not." He felt compassion temper his irritation. She was a pathetic girl, much like Ruth when she showed her little girl's face. He ran a hand through her hair and forced a smile.

"You like me, Effendi?"

"Very much."

She sighed and her shoulders slumped. "Thank Allah."

Quickly the girl gathered up her oils and left.

The next day the negotiating session began promptly at 0900. All parties met in the conference room and Emil Bouchett was in charge. Sheik Younis was there with his two secretaries, who had appeared almost as nonentities. One secretary, a slight, delicate young man named Merhdad Amini, sat close to Younis. Too close. Brent wondered about what Nadia had told him. Major Alai Said Otoba sat almost across from Brent, perpetually scowling. Despite Otoba's expression, Brent felt this would be a congenial morning. Coffee and tea had already been set out on the table and poured by serving girls.

Moammar Kadafi, the Spaniard Saavedra Miguel de Medina-Sidona, the Moroccan Mana Zaki Alaqi, and the Turk Hadja Khalfah Pasha were nowhere to be seen. The angry reporters were excluded. Confined to a large conference room of their own, they were not even allowed to monitor a closed-circuit television system. The entire apparatus had been installed and only required the throw of a switch. Instead, they were promised releases, not complete transcripts. They were left to their own designs. Robert Kingsbury was on the brink of apoplexy. Luckily, four of the journalists had brought playing cards.

Just as Brent, Irving, and Elroy seated themselves, Colonel Moammar Kadafi entered. He was closely followed by his interpreter, Haj Walid Khaled, Medina-Sidona, Zaki Alaqi, Khalfah Pasha, and eight guards. Everyone stood as the five newcomers seated themselves at the head of the table. The guards stationed themselves around the room where they could observe everyone. Kadafi nodded at Younis and the sheik stood.

Brent felt encouraged when Sheik Younis impressed everyone with his opening statement, "Patience dries up oceans and erodes mountains. Allah is with the patient. Patience is the key to salvation. We cannot be jackals tearing at a carcass. We must control our ambitions until we have solved the momentous problems before us." He stared directly at Bernstein and closed, "And remember, Arabs and Jews come from the same father. We are all sons of Abraham. There must be room in our father's house for all of us."

Kadafi's *"Allah Akbar!"* was followed by a roar of approval from the Arabs. Bernstein, Brent, and Elroy nodded and mumbled, "Hear! Hear!"

Bernstein stood and answered. Brent expected a prayer, but instead the Israeli showed the depth of his philosophical mind. "All of us have tasted the sweetness of victory and drunk the bitter draft of defeat. Between the two lies compromise, neither sweet nor bitter, but the most precious draft of all. We have all learned over the past decade that sorrow always follows war, as the gull follows the wind. Sadness has always been separated from joy by time, by men, by hate." He looked around at the intent faces. "And now the time has come to turn the page, open the door," he nodded at Younis, "and find our place in our father's house—the house of Abraham."

"Hear! Hear! *Allah Akbar! Allah Akbar!*"

Kadafi leaped to his feet and proved Robert Kingsbury's assessment of him eminently accurate. "I am

Abraham!" he screeched.

"Abraham!" the Arabs chorused back.

"I am Abraham! I am Abraham! . . ." the dictator repeated so fast he became breathless. It went on for minutes.

"My God," Brent said, "He's off his rocker."

"Plum loco."

"Mad. Mad," Bernstein said.

The Spaniard, Moroccan, Turk and Frenchman stared in befuddled awe. But the Arabs cheered and urged The Leader on as if they believed it all. "An asylum, insanity," Brent heard Bernstein mumble.

Finally, tiring, Kadafi fell silent. Sipping some coffee, he looked around, finding each man with his beady eyes. Silence, a dense weighty thing like a saturated blanket followed his eyes, weighing on everyone. Then he spoke softly, repeating an ancient prayer, "God is most great! I testify there is no god but Allah; I testify Mohammed is the messenger of Allah, Come to prayer, Come to salvation."

"Allah Akbar!" the Arabs roared.

Again the beady eyes surveyed the gathering. He seemed to be under control. "May your efforts bear the fruits of success," he said in a surprisingly calm voice. He gestured to Medina-Sidona, Zaki Alaqi, and Khalfah Pasha. Followed by the guards and interpreter Haj Walid Khaled, who scooted behind like a trained dog, Kadafi's party left. The guards followed.

Everyone sighed with relief. Now the negotiations could begin in earnest. The mood of conciliation had blown out the door with Kadafi. Younis spoke out with impossible demands. "We will return your prisoners but you must evacuate the Canary Islands," he demanded.

"Impossible!" Bernstein shot back.

Pounding the table, the almost forgotten Emil Bouchett leaped to his feet. *"Messieurs,"* he shouted, catching everyone's attention. There was more strength in the man than anyone had guessed. "We cannot make progress this way."

"What would you suggest," Bernstein asked.

"The exchange of *prisoniers* is first, no?"

"Yes. True."

"Then *listes*. Let us exchange lists."

Everyone motioned agreement. Younis turned to Merhdad Amini and the young man handed the sheik a sheaf of papers. Bernstein pulled a much thicker stack of documents from his attaché case. Brent noticed all names were in Hebrew.

Although there was a huge difference in dialects, depending on the capturing units, the identification of prisoners held by the Arabs should not have been difficult. There were only about three hundred Israelis and about thirty airmen—mostly Americans shot down during the B-25 raid on Rabta—to account for. And service numbers were worn by all members of the Israeli and Japanese armed forces, either on "dog tags" worn around the neck or on tags attached to collars.

But the Arabs had been very careless with their own fighting men. Most of their men did not even carry identification tags with service numbers. Some units were made up of irregular volunteers who would fight for a battle or two and then return home to their goats. Now, the identification of these men became a formidable task, indeed. And the Israelis alone held over 3,000 of them.

The arguments began in a tangle of crossed languages. Neither side seemed capable of understanding the lists of the other despite similarities in language. Arabic has twenty-eight letters, Hebrew twenty-three. Both languages are Semitic and both alphabets are primarily consonants, written from right to left with vowels being indicated by dots and strokes. There the resemblance ends, Arabic having a much larger vocabulary than Hebrew and an enormous variety of forms. The Libyans used the *naskhi* form, which was nothing more than ordinary cursive writing. However, most confusing, was the inclusion of colloquialisms derived by the corrupted use of occasional French, English, and Italian words. And the enormous variation in dialects added confusion. This made the reading of most names, dates, and locations of capture almost impossible for Bernstein, who was as knowledgeable of Middle Eastern languages as any man alive. It was almost as if the Libyans had a language of their own and were deliberately causing disorder.

The debate began, Bernstein and Younis leaning over the table and waving lists at each other. Neither man could read the other's lists and insisted on using his own language. The argument grew heated.

Bouchett interrupted the harangues with shouts of, *"Monsieurs, Francais, Anglais!"* But his pleas for a compromise language went unheard.

As the Arab and the Israeli shouted and waved documents, Brent began to realize he was witnessing a typical Middle Eastern dispute; almost a ritual. Each man must establish himself as strong and inflexible. If it were not this issue, it would be another. This was to be a long, long session, the tiring American told himself.

Finally, by noon, with the constant intervention of Bouchett, who seemed to possess infinite patience, and Brent Ross, and surprisingly, Major Alai Said Otoba, a compromise was reached. English would be used. It was common to both sides and understood by most of the men present. Brent suspected this was the intent of the debaters from the very beginning. Brent sighed with relief when Bouchett finally suggested the group break for lunch.

Bernstein, Brent, and Elroy ate lunch in the colonel's quarters which were a duplicate of Brent's. They were actually handed a menu and Brent ordered soup, rice, and fish garnished with cucumbers and radishes. He washed it down with hot tea.

Brent decided not to discuss Nadia's visit with his companions. Nothing had happened, it was personal, and he had a strong aversion to discussing his relations with women with anyone—even Yoshi Matsuhara. It was unmanly, weak, and bordered on gossip. Instead, his mind was on the muddle of languages and dialects that had thrown so many obstacles in their way. He addressed Bernstein over the low table. "Is Arabic actually that complicated, or was Younis deliberately trying to cause confusion?"

Bernstein sipped his coffee and answered, "Both."

"He's plenty smart an' he's slicker'n a greased hog." Elroy said.

"True."

"You said *'both,'* Colonel," Brent reminded the Israeli.

"Yes, Brent. Arabic is truly very confusing. Hebrew is fairly consistent, but remember, Arabic is spoken by two hundred million people from Persia to Spain— that's eighty degrees of longitude. Very strong dialects have grown up. For instance, 'How are you?' is *izzayak* in Egypt, *keefak* in Lebanon, *shlownak,* in Kuwait and *shekhbarak* in Libya." He sipped his tea, "Do you know something as basic to Arabs as water is *maya* in Egypt and *maah* in the Gulf?"

"This is going to be tough," Brent said.

"Agreed." The Israeli looked at Brent's meal and chuckled. "Still back in Tokyo, Brent?"

Brent nodded. "I guess after ten years my tastes have changed."

Bernstein glanced at his watch, "It's 1900 hours there now."

"Yes," Brent agreed. And then nostalgically, "Admiral Fujita's probably poring over his maps and Yoshi's probably picking up Tomoko, right about now."

"Life was much simpler back on *Yonaga*, wasn't it?"

A touch of a smile toyed with the corners of Brent's lips. "I never thought of it that way, but I guess you're right." He drank some tea. "I must admit I'm beginning to believe I wasn't cut out to be a negotiator."

"You're a man of action."

"Thanks, Colonel." He poked at a piece of very rare fish.

"Cain't get much action sittin' on your butt," Elroy offered.

Brent and Bernstein laughed. "True. True," Bernstein said. "But remember, more can be accomplished by patient men sitting on their butts than all the planes and bombs on earth."

"Amen!" Elroy said.

"Right on, Colonel," Brent said.

Bernstein turned back to Brent, "You miss them? You miss *Yonaga*."

"Of course. I've served with that crew for almost a decade. The admiral's the greatest tactician, the most talented man I have ever met, and Yoshi's my best friend, Colonel. You know that."

"Does Yoshi always arrange his schedule to spend Sunday night with Tomoko?"

"Always, Colonel."

Bernstein said. "I miss him, too. A great man, and Tomoko Ozumori is a beautiful person—vivacious, full of life."

Brent smiled. "He's with her every possible mo-

245

ment."

"I can understand that. Do you think they'll marry?"

Brent nodded. "Someday. I think so."

"You'll be best man."

"And you can be ring bearer, Colonel." They laughed.

Eleven

Air Group Commander Yoshi Matsuhara was not laughing when he arrived at Tomoko Ozumori's house. However, he was smiling inwardly with happy anticipation. Driven by burly young Chief Watertender Eichi Nakahashi, the Toyota Lexus LS 400 pulled to the curb at precisely 1800 hours, one hour earlier than Brent's prediction.

Twenty-year-old Seaman Guard Raitei Arima sat in the rear seat with a 7.7-millimeter Arisaka, Type 99 rifle between his knees. Arima was shorter than Nakahashi, but as wide as a door, and could handle the heavy 4.19-kilogram Arisaka as casually as a drum major twirling a baton. Dressed and equipped as all seaman guards, Arima wore leggings and an armband identifying him as "Shore Patrol" in both English and Japanese. Ammunition pouches were attached to his duty belt, where a short vicious baton, knife, and handcuffs also hung.

Yoshi always smiled when he watched the young man walk. With long thick arms and short stubby legs, his hands swung as low as his knees. In fact, some of his fellow seaman guards referred to him as "the gorilla," but never within earshot. Admiral Fujita had insisted on the posting of *Yonaga*'s own guard over the woman a day earlier than anticipated. Raitei Arima would be a formidable one, indeed.

247

Although Tomoko had not answered her phone that afternoon, Yoshi found no reason to be apprehensive. The train she had expected to take from Ashikaga arrived at 1400. She may have missed it or could have been forced to take a later train because of the crush of travelers. After all, you took your life in your hands every time you tried to force your way on board a commuter train.

Yoshi and Chief Nakahashi both exited the Lexus together. They had passed a police car parked around the corner at the end of the block. Both officers had been drinking tea, chatting, and laughing. Yoshi did not see how they could have kept Tomoko's house under observation from their position. For one thing, a small commercial building blocked their view. And in addition, they seemed totally uninterested in their assignment.

While Seaman Guard Raitei Arima took a position on the walk with his rifle slung over his shoulder, Yoshi told the chief to wait as he approached the house. There was a strong odor of decay. The chief waved at one of the fields that surrounded the house. "An animal died, Commander. Became fragrant fast in this heat."

Yoshi nodded and walked to the door. The smell was stronger. He knocked. No answer. He knocked again. Louder. Nothing. The chief, who was leaning against a door of the Lexus, shifted uneasily and began to follow Yoshi who was walking hurriedly around the house. Arima, too, started to move toward the house. Something was amiss. "Wait, sir!" The flier ignored the chief.

Then Yoshi saw it. A neat circle cut from one of the windows in the rear of the house. A professional tool, sharp and diamond-hard, had been used. The window was wide open. Placing his hands on the sill, he jumped, muscled up and squirmed through the opening. He was in the kitchen and the smell of death was strong. He could hear footsteps outside in the yard and his men talking to each other.

Yoshi pulled his Otsu from his shoulder holster and approached the swinging doors to the dining room. He pushed through into one of the foulest stenches that had ever assaulted his nostrils. Thick and heavy, it coated his sinuses, mouth, throat, lungs. He nearly gagged. As he walked across the room, the stink became overpowering and there was the humming sound of swarms of excited insects. Slowly, in a crouch, breathing hard, pistol ready, he moved to the entry to the main room.

Now he knew. He was sure. Whispering, "No! No," he entered the main room. There he saw her—or it, because what he saw was a ghastly mockery of his beloved Tomoko.

Nude, she was hanging from a wire a half-meter from the floor. The pressure of the wire on the back of her head had turned it down, so that she appeared to be staring at him with bulging eyes, mottled blue-red by burst capillaries. Looped several times, the wire had dug deeply into her neck, tearing flesh, leaving a collar of dried blood that had oozed and coagulated on her neck and shoulders. Her neck had stretched, like the bloody stem of a dead gazelle. Blue-purple splotches covered her entire body.

Hurling himself to the floor like a supplicant invoking a deity, Yoshi pounded his fists on the wood so hard his wrists ached. "No! No! No!" he screamed. "Not my Tomoko!"

He groveled, rubbing his face into the tatami mat as if self-flagellation could bring some relief from the horror, the anguish.

He heard the chief's voice behind him, "Sir. Please,

sir. We must call the police. The phone is dead." Immediately, Chief Nakahashi regretted the use of the word 'dead'.

"The police!" Yoshi screamed. "By holy Amaterasu, I will kill the swine who did this!" He waved his pistol wildly, "And I will kill those filthy, lazy dogs at the corner who let it happen. They should have smelled her!"

Leaping to his feet, he ran turned toward the door. He never made it. The young chief brought him down with a tackle. Then Arima was on him, too. Manhandling a officer was unprecedented, but this was an unprecedented moment. Neither enlisted man hesitated. In fact, the chief would have knocked the commander out, if necessary.

The pair rolled him over and Arima sat on his chest, pinning his arms to the floor with his knees. Under ordinary circumstances, the powerful fighter pilot would have had a good chance to free himself, bested both young men; at least punished them both severely. But not this evening. Suddenly, the pilot felt chills, like a man with dengue, and shook uncontrollably—his teeth even chattered. Shock had deprived him of rational thought, the ability to control himself.

Firmly, Chief Nakahashi pulled the pistol from Yoshi's grip and pocketed it. Arima dragged the commander to his feet while Nakahashi jerked Yoshi's arms behind him and snapped Arima's handcuffs on his wrists. The flyer screamed, spat, cursed, raved, frothed at the mouth like the lunatic he had become. Grimly, Arima and Nakahashi each grabbed an arm and dragged Commander Yoshi Matsuhara through the door. He keened like a wounded animal all the way to the car.

Harry "High Wire" Goodenough had succeeded.

"Her neck was hyperextended, fracturing it, Admiral. This was the primary cause of death, although she had been severely beaten. Also, the coroner's report placed time of death as sometime late Thursday evening, early Friday morning," Chief Hospital Orderly Eiichi Horikoshi said from a chair facing Admiral Fujita's desk.

"Was it slow?" Admiral Fujita asked.

Horikoshi shook his nearly bald head. A medical genius who had served Admiral Fujita since 1940, he spoke as casually as a man discussing a sporting event, "No, Admiral. Fortunately, it was fast. You see, the hyperextension fractured her neck, paralyzing her respiratory and cardiovascular centers. Death came very quickly."

"But at the end of a wire, it could not have been very pleasant."

"She had a few bad moments, sir."

"There was more?"

The hospital orderly tucked his thin, withered lips under the welter of wrinkles surrounding his mouth, "Yes, sir. She had been raped and sodomized. He may have used a foreign object. She was torn, had bled where he entered her. Even her cervix . . ."

"Sacred Buddha," Fujita exploded. "That devil, Harry Goodenough."

A rare show of emotion crossed Horikoshi's face. "Not even the devil could tolerate this fiend, Admiral."

"And Yoshi Matsuhara?"

"The horror Yoshi-san saw would have moved even the great Buddha of Todaiji to hysteria."

"Cracked stone."

"Yes, sir. But he is a strong man. When they brought him into the sick bay he appeared to be a raving madman."

"I know."

"I tried to sedate him, Admiral, but he refused. He could think of nothing but revenge. Screamed it to the gods and Buddha."

"I thought you gave him a sedative."

"No, sir. As I said, he refused. Refused a bed and would only sit in my office. Lieutenant Commander Nobomitsu Atsumi was at his side immediately."

The old admiral nodded. "I remember. I saw him."

"Your visit had a very powerful calming effect on Yoshi and so did Atsumi's. He respects you both and has been taking commands from you for over a half-century."

"He is back. I could see reason returning in his eyes."

"True. Very quickly."

"He is a samurai, accustomed to great blows and great losses, Eiichi-san. I expected no less of him, and more important, he expected no less of himself."

"He is truly an astonishing man, sir. As you know, medicine is not an exact science. It is much easier to repair a broken arm than a broken mind."

"Very true, but Yoshi's mind is made of armor plate." Fujita patted the leather-bound copy of the *Hagakure* on his desk. "The book tells us, " 'Seven times down, eight times up and the only worthy death is in battle, facing your enemy.' Yoshi-san lives by this book."

The old orderly rubbed his chin. "So very true, sir, and I think military discipline has played a big part in his ability to regain control of himself. Your appearance and Atsumi at his side were very powerful influences."

"There is more, Eiichi-san."

"Yes, Admiral. His hunger for revenge knows no

252

bounds. At this moment it may be the single thread that gives his life purpose, perhaps, even keeps him in the realm of sanity."

"He is in his cabin."

"Correct, sir, with Commander Atsumi. They are studying reports on our new pilots."

"Good. Good. Back to work. The best thing for him." The old admiral rubbed his tiny chin and began to tug on the single white hair. "According to Ephraim Schneerson and Admiral Whitehead, this murder was undoubtedly committed by Harry Goodenough—the beating, the rape, the wire—even the way the glass was cut. Schneerson said he uses the same tool when he makes an entry in that fashion."

"It should leave readable traces like the markings on a bullet."

The old admiral nodded and smiled. "Yes, Eiichi-san. Arrogance to the point of carelessness. Or maybe it is conceit and he wants us to know he did it. Admiral Whitehead calls it his 'M.O.'—'Method of Operation.' He is very consistent. The Tokyo police, Mossad, and NIC are working on the glass and tracing the wire at this moment."

The hospital orderly shrugged in a gesture of helplessness. "But Admiral, by now Goodenough must be out of the country."

"I know. Schneerson has already informed me that Mossad informants reported Goodenough in North Korea as early as Saturday."

"Then by now, he could be anywhere in the world."

"Probably the Middle East." And then bitterly, "Gone back to Kadafi to collect his million-dollar fee."

"Swine! Swine!" Horikoshi spat. "Then, the scales will never be balanced."

The old admiral smiled. "We will find a way, Eiichi-

253

san. A samurai always does."

The old orderly smiled, but he was not convinced.

There was a knock. Horikoshi opened the door. A clean, shaven, military appearing Commander Yoshi Matsuhara was standing in the doorway.

The admiral dismissed the hospital orderly and the pilot entered, coming to attention in front of the admiral's desk. Fujita waved Matsuhara to a chair. Yoshi sat rigidly, cap on his lap, face stern, eyes cold and glistening like brown marbles. "I was not a samurai last night, Admiral. I forgot the code of Bushido. Acted like an old woman—a hysterical old woman. I am a disgrace to you and this command."

The old man hunched forward. "Not true, Yoshisan. You are one of my most valued aides, the best air group commander in the world."

"I have shot down nearly fifty enemy aircraft, killed perhaps a hundred men, two with my bare hands. I prided myself on my strength as the samurai warrior. But last night I was a blubbering weakling. Betrayed you, my command, myself."

The old man struck the desk with a tiny gnarled knot of a fist. "Nonsense! Not true, Commander. Last night you were human. You saw death in its foulest form. No warrior, not even a samurai, could be prepared for what you saw." The black eyes focused on flyers' eyes with the intensity of sunlight through a lens. "You are human, have human feelings and human reactions. Do not condemn yourself for that." The old man fell silent for a moment and then asked, "You are not contemplating *seppuku?*"

"I should, sir. But there is too much revenge to be savored to think of suicide."

"And *seppuku* is what the enemy wants."

"Obviously, sir." Bitterness drenched his words, "And it is not just Tomoko Ozumori. There have been so many. The butchery of Captain Colin Willard-Smith in his parachute still cries out for vengeance, too."

The old admiral beat the desk with two fingers like crooked twigs. "Kenneth Rosencrance and now Harry Goodenough."

"Yes."

"We spend our lives chasing demons."

"Yes, Admiral. That is why we exist."

"The fates tell us you may meet Rosencrance up there." He pointed skyward. "But you know your chances of ever finding vengeance against Goodenough are very slim. Why, I understand, he is a master of disguise, languages, the perfect assassin with no pity in his soul."

"I know about that, Admiral."

"You lost your family in Curtis LeMay's great fire raid on Tokyo in nineteen-forty-five." The pilot nodded. "And Kimio Urshazawa in Ueno Park in an ambush." Another nod. "And now, Tomoko Ozumori."

"And, sir, you lost your family to the *Enola Gay* at Hiroshima."

"True. We have all taken great personal losses, great blows when you add all our dead comrades of the past decade to family, friends." He scratched an earlobe reflectively. "And yet, we honor our duty, continue to engage our enemies."

Yoshi nodded at the *Hagakure* and quoted it: " 'Dying without reaching one's aim is to die a dog's death.' "

The old sailor smiled. "True Yoshi-san, and it teaches, 'If a man's spirit weakens, he becomes the same as a woman and his world has ended.' " He tapped the book. "This, I know, could never happen to Commander Yoshi Matsuhara."

"True, sir."

255

Fujita pinched his tiny nose. "Are you *shinigurai,* Yoshi-san?"

"Crazy to die, sir?" The pilot shrugged. "Perhaps; I will know when we engage the enemy."

"Do not throw your life away. *Yonaga* needs you. Free men everywhere need you." The old man took a deep breath and it was obvious a distasteful subject had entered his mind. "Yoshi-san, Lieutenant Kunishi Kajikawa is one of our best fighter pilots, an excellent squadron commander."

"True, sir."

"Let him assume some of your duties."

"You are grounding me? Let Harry Goodenough succeed where Rosencrance and all of his killers have failed?"

"No! No! No! We have already been over this ground. Let Kajikawa take over the bombers, you keep the fighters."

"Respectfully, sir. I feel I can discharge my duties as Air Group Commander at my usual level of efficiency."

"You assured me once you would remove yourself if you felt your age caused a drop of efficiency that could imperil your men."

"Yes, sir."

"Do not let your hunger for vengeance impair your judgment. Anyone can die. That is easy. Serving well, discharging one's duty when it weighs like Fuji-san and bends a man's back like a wet reed, that is the true ordeal, the true test of a man's strength."

Leaning forward, Yoshi placed a hand on the *Hagakure*. "My word on the book. My word on my ancestors. My word as a servant of the Emperor, I pledge to ground myself if I feel I cannot lead with maximum effectiveness."

The old man sighed, "Very well, Yoshi-san." He

rubbed his temple as if he were trying to free a new thought. "Yoshi-san, you are a follower of Zen?'

Yoshi expected a drift into religion, especially Buddhism. The old man was testing him, weighing him, probing in his usual abstruse, oblique manner. Yoshi knew that before he left, Admiral Fujita would know more about his state of mind than a battalion of psychiatrists. He answered simply, "All good samurai follow Zen. It fits our destiny better than any other religion."

"True, but I heard you turned away from the great patriarch, Bodhidharma."

The pilot was not surprised. Nothing escaped the old man's eyes or the eyes and ears of his informants. The old man knew so much, Yoshi had even searched his cabin for hidden microphones. Found nothing. "For a time, perhaps," Yoshi answered. "But, last night, Commander Atsumi and I spent hours meditating."

"That is the only road to enlightenment." The old admiral drummed the desk. "A man who has knowledge but lacks true wisdom is a blind man with a lantern. He can find nothing."

Yoshi smiled for the first time. "Bodhidharma's Zen is pure, free of nonsensical ceremonies, scriptures, useless trappings." He nodded to himself. "I feel I should return."

"Good." The old man was in a realm he loved almost as much as waging war. The penetrating eyes narrowed and he dampened the thin line of his crinkled lips, "We all know that enlightenment can only be reached through intuition and meditation upon it. And remember, Yoshi-san, a man must witness his stream of awareness with an balanced attentiveness, a detachment." The pilot nodded agreement. Fujita pressed on, "In so doing, he can see his own experience as a set of impersonal processes which comprise the sense of self. What most men do not comprehend is that understanding can go no further than the human mind will tolerate. Westerners try to break this barrier by dividing reality into 'subjects' and 'objects' which, of course, is far too simplistic for us."

Caught up in the admiral's mood, Yoshi brightened. He knew he was being manipulated, but enjoyed the topic which was one of his favorites, too. "Yes, sir. These things are obvious in our Christian allies. It is difficult for them to comprehend our idea of no 'self,' that a person has no ongoing identity." He chuckled. "After all, this is a direct challenge to their preoccupation with the 'ego'—the core of their psychology, their view of life." He leaned forward, hands on knees, "How can anyone believe that one's view of the world is unaffected by where one stands?"

"You've been reading Einstein."

The pilot smiled pensively. "I thought we were talking about Zen, Admiral."

"Maybe Einstein was a follower. He did find enlightenment through intuition."

"Do you think he knew it, Admiral?"

"Perhaps. But it made no difference."

"Very true, sir."

The old man glanced at a bulkhead-mounted brass clock. "I have called a meeting for 0900 tomorrow morning in Flag Plot. I want you there."

"I was planning on being with my training squadrons at Tsuchiura."

"I know. But this meeting is too important. It is for the entire staff." The old military authority crept back into the voice, "I will expect you."

"Aye, aye, sir."

Twelve

The staff meeting was convened the next morning. Although Flag Plot was the largest compartment in "Flag Country," it was crowded by the fourteen officers who sat around the long walnut table.

Commander Yoshi Matsuhara was flanked by Lieutenant Commander Nobomitsu Atsumi and the escort commander, Captain John "Slugger" Fite. A big white bear of a man with a raucous laugh, Fite was a veteran of World War II and was as vicious as he was jovial, killing enemy survivors in the water with unabashed glee. His son had been tortured to death in Syria, and his hatred for Arabs knew no bounds. To him, the scales would never be balanced.

Although Tomoko's dangling, putrefying body was burned into Yoshi Matsuhara's soul like afterimages that refused to fade and her stench still layered his throat, his demeanor was as businesslike and professional as ever. He actually appeared calm. Every man in the room was concerned about the air group commander. As a flier and leader, he had their confidence. As a friend, their respect, even love, the close attachment only men who fight and challenge death together can have for each other. Camaraderie is far too weak a word to describe this bonding like straps of steel.

The room was as quiet as a mausoleum, the usual friendly buzzing and casual banter missing. In fact, it was much like a wake. Most of the men were intimately acquainted with death in its most violent forms, had seen it up close, in great abundance and dismembering fury. Yet, the gruesome slaughter of Tomoko Ozumori struck them all to the heart like a hot poker. It had been a foul and disgusting killing of a helpless woman. It violated the code of Bushido. This a samurai could neither tolerate nor understand.

Their hearts went out to Yoshi, but overt signs of sympathy, even concern, were out of the question. Such behavior would be embarrassing and degrading to the flier. Instead, the concern was shown in a glance, tone of voice, in a gesture.

"Gentlemen," Admiral Fujita said, motioning toward Ephraim Sneerson. "I have received a message from Colonel Bernstein transmitted in plain language. He claims the negotiations are proceeding, but that language barriers present a formidable problem, far more serious than he anticipated. He feels it will require more than a week just to translate names and identify Arab prisoners. There has been very little problem identifying our men."

Lieutenant Sahei Tsuda, the soft-spoken young dive bomber commander, said, "Admiral, we are to continue with the negotiations after," he glanced at Yoshi, "after the incident of the past weekend? How can we trust men like these who murder while they speak of peace?"

"They are Arabs. Trust, integrity are unknown to them, duplicity pandemic." Fujita hunched forward,

"But I pledged to the Emperor that we would continue with negotiations — in Tripoli with the Bernstein team and Geneva with our special envoys Nishio Kanji and Mori Tokumitsu." He looked down the table at Yoshi and his pragmatic side broke through, "We cannot allow a single incident, as loathsome and repugnant as it may be, to alter our plans, influence our strategy. This is precisely what the enemy wishes." He made a sweeping gesture, "And remember, we are planning a surprise of our own. The longer our negotiators continue bargaining, the better our chances of success."

Admiral Whitehead spoke up. Obviously, he was still opposed to Fujita's plan to strike into the Mediterranean, "As I have already informed you, Admiral, the Arabs are quite aware battleship *New Jersey* is not on her way to the scrap yard. They know she will join our forces." Sneerson added his confirming nod.

"I know," Fujita said. "But our intentions are still unknown to them." Whitehead fell silent. He had already argued the point many times without success.

Ephraim Sneerson said, "According to Mossad, the Arabs expect us to either sortie into the Atlantic to reinforce our garrison in the Canary Islands or make an amphibious assault on the Mariana Islands."

"Have you leaked the rumor that we are preparing to mount an assault on the Mariana Islands?"

"Yes, sir," Sneerson said. "The information has been leaked to known double agents. In fact, Mister Amberg even allowed a double agent to see invoices detailing the loading of special short-range bombardment ammunition on *New Jersey* and similar ordnance for our destroyers.

"Good, Mr. Sneerson and Mr. Amberg, well done." Fujita turned to his executive officer, Captain Mitake Arai. "You have intensified the training of our amphibious forces?"

"Yes, sir. The six modern LSTs from the Self Defense Force and eight old assault transports and cargo ships we bought from the Americans are continuing practice landings daily near Hiroshima. We are certain many curious eyes have been watching."

"You have maintained a facade of secrecy?"

"Yes, sir. The landing beaches are off limits and the crews have been restricted."

Frail, old Chief Engineer Lieutenant Tatsuya Yoshida asked, "Our men—the prisoners at Al Aziziyab. Any report, sir?"

"Only what the International Red Cross has told us. They are still alive."

"Respectfully, that isn't much," said Paul Treynor, the captain of the carrier *Bennington*.

"True, but that is all we have." The old man struggled to his feet and walked stiffly to a chart of the Middle East. It was time to detail the entire plan to the staff, reveal the latest intelligence, reiterate strategic and tactical imperatives, seek opinions, answer questions. He stabbed the chart with a pointer. "All of you know our primary objective." He thumped the chart and spat, "Rabta!" There were angry rumbles. He glanced at Sneerson and the American CIA agent, Elliot Amberg, who sat quietly at the far end. "Kadafi will have his twenty-kiloton atomic bomb in less than three months." Anger roared through the room. Raised hands quieted them. The pointer tapped, "And here he is making his mustard and nerve gas and here he has in operation a fast breeder reactor." He nodded at Sneerson and Amberg. Amberg turned off the lights and Sneerson flicked the switch on a projector. Immediately, a picture was flashed on a white screen at the far end of the room.

Yoshi leaned forward. This was new. Tomoko was

banished for a moment. The picture showed a complex of buildings covering an area of perhaps ten square kilometers. Some were square, others rectangular, and one was round with a large rectangular building attached. Huge cables led to an enormous switching station nearby. Resolution was unbelievably clear. Even vehicles and men could be seen. Fujita stabbed his pointer at the projection, the long thin stick and his arm leaving black shadows on the screen as he moved. There were notes in Hebrew and English on the photograph. "Taken from a high-flying Israeli Lockheed P-38," Fujita explained.

The pointer moved from building to building. The raspy voice intoned a cantillate of outrage: "Poison gas works, storage, maintenance, barracks." He paused. "And our primary target, an atomic reactor."

"The tall round building," Nogi said. "That is the reactor?"

"Yes. It is about four stories high and is very vulnerable."

"Why, sir?"

"Because it was built by Russians."

Fujita gestured to Sneerson who explained, "It is a duplicate of the Chernobyl reactor, a fast breeder with no containment building. It uses a graphite moderator, which is a large block of graphite that slows down neutrons. Each fuel rod is in its own tube with a constant flow of water circulating to keep the whole mass cool. If the water is shut off, or the flow interrupted, as was the case at Chernobyl, the fuel rods will heat up. The graphite will ignite when the flow of water is restarted. The core would burn, disintegrate. It is a clumsy, vulnerable system—requires very close monitoring."

"Sir," young Lieutenant Sahei Tsuda said, "if we bomb it there could be severe radioactive fallout, U-

235, U-238, plutonium, strontium, cesium." He shrugged and pounded his knuckles together. "And other elements. Why, in Russia, over two million people in Byelorussia were dosed with fallout alone. The cloud drifted over Scandinavia, affected millions more. Dispersed into the earth's atmosphere. A meltdown could . . ."

It was a revolting subject, especially to Japanese, and Fujita shook his head in frustration, interrupting, "I know, Lieutenant Tsuda. None of us want this! In the name of Amaterasu, this is an abomination that could turn the stomachs of the gods." The small intense eyes roamed the distressed faces. "But the enemy gives us no choice. The complex is refining uranium, enriching it to the fissionable isotope U-235. Calutrons take an enormous amount of power, and the reactor is the principal source."

Lieutenant Nogi shifted his weight uneasily, voicing a question which was on every man's mind, "Is there an optimum point to target—a way our bombers can destroy this monster without causing a huge cloud of radioactivity—the possibility of a meltdown?"

Whitehead, obviously, agitated, spoke before Fujita could answer. "If we blow this reactor, spray radioactivity into the atmosphere, the whole world will turn against us, regardless of our motives. I can guarantee you American public opinion will be outraged." There was the sound of many disquieted voices.

Fujita raised his hands, looked at Whitehead, and continued, "We can take it out without causing that kind of catastrophe, Admiral Whitehead." He stabbed the pointer at a huge switching yard, at two large buildings near the reactor and showed his own depth of knowledge, "We'll bomb this switching complex and here the auxiliary generators they use when power is lost to power the safety network—leave the

264

core untouched. Without a place to transmit their power and with their auxiliary power lost, they would be forced to shut down. Anyway, the plant should be shut down when our raid arrives."

"Why?"

"Because they cannot take the chance of having the core in operation during a raid."

Schneerson said, "They will always shut down when there is a threat. They can't take any chances."

Whitehead persisted, "To take out those buildings so close to the reactor will take surgical, precision bombing. And think of the concussion!"

For the first time, Fujita relaxed and nodded. "Our dive bombers can do it. We have the finest dive bombers and pilots in the world and they will use one-hundred-kilogram bombs. Our targets are soft."

Tsuda beamed at the compliment and shouted, *"Banzai!* My eagles can do it!"

Schneerson waved a hand, and said, "The reactor is built to withstand a Force Five earthquake. Strongly resistant to horizontal motion. This should work. Even a hit on the reactor building with a hundred-kilogram bomb may not damage the core."

Whitehead drummed on the table, nodded, and pointed to the obvious, "But the reactor can be put back into operation."

Fujita gestured at Schneerson. The Israeli said, "True, but it will be off line for at least eighteen months."

Fujita added, "And Kadafi will be sent a message he will never forget!"

"Banzai!"

Whitehead thumped the table with both fists. "Risky, very risky, but it can be done if we have the most skillful and disciplined fliers on earth."

"We do," Fujita said, pride filling his voice.

More shouts of, *"Banzai!"* and the tension began to drain off.

Lieutenant Nogi revived some of the stress, "Sir, we know carriers *Magid* and *Al Marj*—the converted Spanish *Reina de Iberico*—are in the Mediterranean and, according to news reports, they will be joined by carrier *Baku* and cruisers *Dzerzhinsky* and *Zhdanov*. There are over two hundred fighters based at Al Kararim, Mistatah, Zuwarah and Tripoli." He stabbed a finger at the chart. "Respectfully, sir, these must be neutralized before we even think of attacking Rabta."

The old man leaned on the table. He was tiring. "More precisely, over two hundred fifty fighters, Lieutenant." Everyone was surprised when the old man dropped the subject of fighters. Nogi bit his lip while Fujita shifted his eyes to Rear Admiral Byron Whitehead. "You have the specifications on these new ships?"

"Yes, sir," the American said, rising.

Fujita signaled Amberg. The CIA agent turned on the lights and turned off the projector.

Whitehead looked at some documents. "First, they will dock at Tripoli tomorrow. Carrier *Baku* is a sister to *Kiev* and *Minsk*. *Minsk* was renamed *Daffah* and we sank her off Gibraltar."

"Banzai!"

Whitehead waited for the shouts to fade and continued, *"Magid* is in mint condition with well-trained air groups." He shuffled some papers. "Both *Magid* and *Baku* are thirty-seven-thousand-ton ships with nine-hundred-foot flight decks, which have been rebuilt to rectangular configuration. NIC figures they can operate sixty to seventy aircraft each. But don't be surprised if that is a conservative figure.

"But Admiral," Lieutenant Sahei Tsuda said,

"*Baku* could not have her air groups adequately trained. We all know it takes months of hard work and practice to train efficient groups."

Fujita interrupted. "True, Lieutenant. We anticipate the Arabs will hold her out of action." He returned to Whitehead, "The cruisers?"

"*Dzerzhinsky* and *Zhdanov* are big, formidable, actually of World War Two design." He glanced at his documents, "Sixteen thousand tons, length six hundred eighty-nine feet, beam seventy-two feet, speed thirty-two." While the officers scribbled notes, he went into detail, describing geared turbines, 110,000-shaft horsepower, the enormous AA firepower of their twelve 100-millimeter rapid-fire dual purpose guns, thirty-two thirty-seven-millimeter automatic weapons, the sixteen thirty-millimeter machine guns; air search, surface search, even navigation radars; the 3.9 to 4.9 armor belts and the 4.9 facings on the turrets. He looked up into a mass of very sober faces. "And, keep in mind, they both mount twelve six-inch guns and I can assure you, their AA will be augmented with new twenty-millimeter and forty-millimeter batteries."

Tsuda and Nogi both looked at Yoshi Matsuhara. The air group commander just stared down at his pad, which was as empty as his expression. His mind was somewhere else, engulfed by a nightmare.

Grave looks were exchanged. Captain John Fite spoke up. "Fire control radar?" Everyone knew the escort commander was anticipating torpedo runs—the ultimate horror of the destroyer skipper.

Whitehead said, "Removed in accordance with the agreement reached eight years ago at Geneva." Fite nodded, but the set of his jaw was hard.

Fujita said, "These ships would not dare challenge *New Jersey*."

Lieutenant Taneo Nogi added with bravado which was not quite convincing, "Or our air groups, Admiral."

"True. And all of you know we will have two squadrons of the new Grumman FX-1,000 based at Gibraltar."

Lieutenant Tsuda said, "Respectfully, sir, they can give us cover when we sortie into the Med, but, not all the way to Rabta and our air groups will be engaged by enemy land based aircraft. And our battle group can operate only about one hundred fighters. If you subtract forty for CAP, that leaves only about sixty for other operations."

"Yes, Lieutenant. I am quite aware of the logistics of this operation," the admiral said with a tinge of acid. "The Israeli land, sea and air forces will attack."

Obviously the bomber commanders were worried and Nogi joined in, "Israeli fighters cannot reach Rabta, sir." And then he dared, "And give my B-5Ns protection."

The old man thumped the table with the pointer and stared at Yoshi. The air group commander stared back. They were the only two who knew of the acquisition of the bases on Sicily and Yoshi knew it would remain so. "You are correct," Fujita said matter-of-factly.

Nogi said, "We will be massacred."

"You can resign."

The young man gulped his frustration back down. "No, sir. I do not wish that."

"Then no more defeatist talk. It is unsamurai."

"Yes, sir."

Fujita gestured to the executive officer, Captain Mitake Arai. Arai stood and said, "This is the third time we have made this run." He moved to a chart of the world and picked up a pointer. "As all of you know, threading our way through Indonesia, crossing the Indian Ocean and entering the Red Sea is out of the question. Therefore, we must take the long route, a run of over twenty-four thousand miles to our objective." He traced a line, "We will sail southeast, pick up *New Jersey* here, off Tarawa, double Cape Horn, enter the South Atlantic here, head northeast, pass the Falklands and Canary Islands, and then enter the Mediterranean. A forty-four-day run at twenty-four knots." More nervous looks.

Captain Fite said with surprise in his voice, "Twenty-four knots! Why, we'll burn fuel like water out a broken hydrant. And that's a helluva strain on our machinery."

Arai glanced at Fujita, who nodded almost imperceptibly. Arai continued, "True, Captain Fite. But we must not give the enemy any more time than necessary, and at that speed enemy submarines would have trouble tracking us. Remember, they have at least eight old diesel-electric *Whiskey*-class subs." He struck the chart in the southeast Pacific. "Once we are spotted headed southeast for Cape Horn, he will expect us in the Atlantic for certain." He thrust the pointer at five different spots, "We will burn fuel lavishly, you are correct. Tankers will refuel us off Tarawa, off Chile, the Falklands, Canaries, and again just before we make the Straits of Gibraltar."

Fite nodded, but he wore a troubled look, crumpled like yesterday's newspaper.

"Very good," Fujita said. Arai sat down. Fujita eyed his officers silently. A master psychologist, he would let his men stew in their apprehensions for a moment and then open new, but routine subjects. "This is Monday; we will get underway for the Mediterranean on Wednesday. As Captain Arai has already pointed out, the less time we give the enemy to prepare, the better." There was a buzz and the men glanced at each other. Most of the looks were uneasy. Fatalism thickened the air. "Engineering," Fujita said to Chief Engineer Lieutenant Tatsuya Yoshida, "is your department ready?"

The old engineer struggled to his feet. There was pride in his voice, "Boilers four and nine are back on line. Fuel tanks topped off. My department is ready to give you thirty-three knots!"

The antique scribe, Commander Hakuseki Katsube, who had been uncharacteristically silent for the entire meeting, suddenly came to life to everyone's despair. *"Banzai!"* he sprayed almost the length of the table. He had obviously forgotten his dentures and the men closest to him dabbed at their faces with handkerchiefs.

The ship was ready for sea, and every man in the room knew it. But military imperatives and rigid protocol demanded a reaffirmation in a strict ceremonial form. The executive officer, Captain Mitake Arai, reported on the training and condition of the crew; Rear Admiral Whitehead reported electronic communications and ESM units ready; Lieutenant Commander Nobomitsu Atsumi reported new barrels on all machine guns, and magazines filled; Commander Yoshi Matsuhara reported all air groups ready; *Bennington* was reported ready by Captain Treynor; Captain John Fite reported twelve *Fletchers* and the British destroyer *Haida* ready for sea and that the captain of *Haida,* Commander Clive Coglan, had recovered sufficiently from his wounds to take command. This brought another wet *"Banzai!"* from Katsube.

"Good. Well done," Fujita finally said. "We will get underway at 0500 Wednesday." He turned to Yoshi with an afterthought. "We will take on your air groups here." He rose, stabbed the chart at a point

270

east of Honshu. "The usual place."

"Aye, aye, sir."

The old man clapped twice and faced a small shrine on the bulkhead opposite him. He began to speak, and immediately Lieutenant Taneo Nogi stiffened. Fujita was actually reciting the lieutenant's great grandfather's — General Nogi's — death poem which had been written in 1912 just before the general's *seppuku* during Emperor Meiji's funeral. "My sovereign, abandoning this fleeting life, has ascended among the gods; with my heart full of gratitude, I desire to follow him."

The room was filled with shouts of *"Banzai!"* and *"Tenno heiko banzai!"* Lieutenant Nogi beamed.

Yoshi remained silent. He wished the admiral had closed the meeting in another way.

The old man seemed to sense his thoughts, adding, "And remember, a great philosopher once said, 'I shall never act differently, even if I have to die for it many times.' "

Yoshi heard Whitehead say in wonder, "Why, he's quoting Socrates. I'll be goddamned."

"You are dismissed," Fujita said. The men rose, bowed.

As Yoshi stepped into the corridor, he stopped in midstride. She was there. Hanging. Eyes staring. Flies. White rice. The stink choked him. He held his breath. Suddenly, he felt Atsumi's hand on his arm.

"This way, Yoshi-san. This way." He tugged on the pilot's arm and the apparition vanished.

Side by side the two officers walked down the passageway. Atsumi said, "The funeral is tomorrow?"

"Yes. Her son, Ryo, has made all the arrangements."

"You will go, Yoshi-san?"

271

"If duty permits."

"Where?"

"At the Sensoji Temple in Asakusa."

"The Gods of Wind and Thunder dwell there, Yoshi-san."

"True. And we will take them to the enemy, Nobomitsu-san."

"If duty permits, I will attend the services with you." Atsumi gestured to his cabin door. "Come in. I have a bottle of saké that should be opened."

Yoshi nodded and the two officers entered the cabin.

Thirteen

When the battle group stood out, dawn was flooding the eastern horizon, rouging high cirrus with vermilion and orange while bleeding bloodred on low-hanging clouds. Acting navigator Lieutenant Commander Nobomitsu Atsumi hunched over the small chart table on the flag bridge while Quartermaster First Class Hio Rokokura relayed bearings on the fast fading Boso Hanto Peninsula and the oncoming islands of o Shima, To Shima, and Miyake Jima. Atsumi had piloted Tokyo Canyon so many times that he felt he could sortie with his eyes closed. But the rigorous routine was followed, bearings constantly verified by radar.

After passing the sea buoy, Atsumi relayed the last position to Admiral Fujita, who stood at the front of the bridge between the talker, Seaman Naoyuki, and a bank of voice tubes. Atsumi heard the old man shout to Naoyuki: "To the flag bridge, at the dip, make the hoist, 'Left to one-eight-zero, speed twenty-four.' " The talker spoke into his headset. Fujita continued barking commands, "Add 'Execute to follow,' and repeat the command to all vessels on bridge-to-bridge."

Atsumi left the chart table and took a position between Admiral Fujita and Rear Admiral Whitehead.

He could hear bunting flapping in the force-three wind. Quartermaster Rokokura reported, "All ships answer, sir."

"Very well. Two block!" The flags and pennants snugged up to the yardarm.

"All hoists two-blocked, sir."

"Execute!"

As the flags and pennants whipped down, Fujita shouted down a tube, "Left standard rudder. Steady up on one-eight-zero, speed twenty-four!" Turning with precision that would have made a corps de ballet envious, the two carriers and thirteen escorts held their standard steaming formation of a wedge of five destroyers escorting each carrier; one directly ahead, two off the bows and two off the beams. Two more *Fletchers* ranged two miles ahead of the battle group while *Haida* trailed.

"Steady on one-eight-zero, speed twenty-four, one hundred twenty-eight revolutions."

"Very well." Fujita shouted at the four lookouts, "Keep a weather eye out for periscopes. The Arabs always keep a patrol out here. They can snoop and shoot and sometimes their Allah smiles. Those Russian 533 torpedoes pack a powerful Semtex warhead."

The four young seamen continued their search with renewed enthusiasm.

It was almost noon when they left Mikura Jima to starboard and changed course to one-three-zero. Then radar reported large formations of aircraft approaching from the north.

Always cautious, Fujita said into Naoyuki's ear, "ESM, I want a report on IFF?"

"ESM reports friendlies, sir."

Soon the roar of engines could be heard and dozens of low-flying specks could be seen on the horizon. The commands, "Prepare to receive aircraft! Plane handling detail to the flight deck! The smoking lamp is out on all weather decks and hangar deck!" echoed through the ship and Admiral Fujita brought the force into the wind. Handlers and emergency personnel in red, green, and white overalls scurried across the deck to their stations. Holding two large yellow paddles, the control officer mounted his platform just astern of the island. Pennant Two—a white ellipse on a blue background—was hoisted and the fearsome steel mesh barrier cranked up amidships. A pair of destroyers took up lifeguard positions astern of both carriers. *Yonaga* was ready.

Majestically, the big dive bombers and the torpedo bombers swept around the ships. High above the fighters circled. They would land last. Atsumi smiled as he studied the eclectic force. The influx of pilots from all over the world had brought with it a huge array of aircraft.

Yonaga's bomb groups still consisted of Aichi D-3A dive bombers and the old reliable Nakajima B-5N torpedo bomber. However, two Englishmen, two Americans, a German, a Russian, and a Pole flew seven of the bombers. The collection of high orbiting fighters was as disparate as the bombers were consistent. The majority were still the Mitsubishi A-6M2 Zero. However, led by Commander Steve Elkins, twelve American Grumman F-6F Hellcats swept over in their elements of two like blue killer angels, their great new 3,100 horsepower Pratt and Whitney engines roaring, superchargers whining. Elkins had been timed in level flight at 470 knots. Not even *Bennington*'s F-4Us could match that speed. And six needle-nosed Supermarine Seafire F-47s swept in graceful orbits. All were piloted by Englishmen. Two, flown by Flying Officer Claude Hooperman and Pilot Officer Elwyn York, clung to the elevators of Yoshi Matsuhara's red, green, and white fighter. Yoshi had often said the pair were the best wingmen on earth. "I am still alive," he had said once to a group of senior officers in the wardroom. "That is the best proof."

Yoshi Matsuhara's hybrid fighter appeared clumsy, almost as if it defied the laws of aerodynamics to remain airborne. A long, oversized cowling housed its brute of an engine, the awesome Sakae 43 *Taifu* (Typhoon), which was nothing more than a reworked Wright-Cyclone R-3350 engine. Designed to power the old Boeing B-29 Superfortress, Atsumi felt the R-3350 had no business in the nose of an A-6M2 which was originally designed for a 950-horsepower Sakae power plant. But Yoshi had insisted, completely rebuilding the fighter from tail hook to engine mounts. Even new wing spars had been installed, a big self-sealing fuel tank and armor plate positioned behind the cockpit to counterbalance the monster in the nose.

Performance was shocking. The fighter could stand on its tail and climb like a rocket, once exceeded 500 knots in level flight before the propeller tips approached the speed of sound and buffeting forced Yoshi to throttle back. It could turn with a hummingbird, and knock a man senseless in dive pull-outs that also approached the velocity of sound. Matsuhara had been very, very careful in testing the aircraft. It could kill you as easily and quickly as it could kill your enemies.

All of *Yonaga's* aircraft wore the same blue stripe around the fuselage, indicating *Koku Kantai* (First Air Fleet). A large "Y" on the vertical tail fin identified *Yonaga*, followed by a three digit number to show the type of mission and the individual aircraft.

Atsumi moved his glasses to *Bennington*. Her air groups included all American aircraft. Fighters were evenly divided between Vought F-4U Corsairs and two new squadrons of Grumman F-8F Bearcats. All wore the *Koku Kantai* blue stripe on the fuselage, but were marked with a large "B" on the tail to indicate *Bennington*. Atsumi could see the eager smile on Fujita's face as the old man put his binoculars on a squadron of the American Bearcats.

The Japanese were awed by the new F-8F. The enemy had nothing in his air force that could match it. Powered by the 3,300 horsepower Pratt & Whitney R-2800-B, it was a very compact fighter. In fact, it was actually smaller than the Zero with four feet less wingspan and a fuselage that was two feet shorter. It weighed a ton less than the F-6F. Despite its typical stubby beer bottle "Grumman" look, it was a beautiful little plane with graceful lines, tear drop canopy, and high tail fin. As lethal as it was graceful, it killed with its four wing-mounted cannon. And it was highly maneuverable and almost as fast in level flight as Yoshi Matsuhara's Zero. As durable as it was speedy, the Japanese were lucky the little fighter arrived too late to see service in the Greater East Asia War. However, it had given a good account of itself in Korea, Indo-China, Vietnam, and Thailand, continuing in service until 1966. It was an incredible aircraft. Atsumi chuckled with satisfaction.

Nobomitsu glassed *Bennington*'s bombers. A varied assortment of aircraft had been blended into the carrier's bomber groups. There were the old reliable Douglas SBD Dauntless, but now, eight powerful Curtiss SB2C Helldivers had been added. But most promising and lethal was the addition of six Douglas A-1B Skyraiders. Atsumi knew that if everything else failed, this was the bomber that Fujita hoped to punch through to Rabta. It, too, had seen service in Korea, Indochina, and Vietnam.

Rear Admiral Whitehead had repeatedly pointed out the aircraft's specifications. Powered by an upgraded Wright R-3350 engine, it was a sturdy bomber capable of carrying four tons of bombs or torpedoes at 350 miles an hour. However, because of sophisticated installations of ECM and radar equipment, the pilot and radar operator sat side by side. This Fujita and Matsuhara had found unacceptable. The Skyraider would be cold meat for the enemy's fast new fighters; especially the new, modified Messerschmitt 109. McDonnell-Douglas designed a new canopy, placing the radar man behind the pilot where he could man a twin fifty-caliber power turret and still maintain his radar watch. The aircraft still carried enough sophisticated electronics to make night bombing runs. In fact, all A-1Bs were equipped with a searchlight attached beneath the fuselage.

Switching his glasses from one new American aircraft to another brought reassurance and bolstered Atsumi's confidence. All men who war wish for the fastest, deadliest, most powerful to fight beside him. However, there was an old lingering ache dating back half a century to the Greater East Asia War. All of the warplanes — the Hellcat, Helldiver, Skyraider, Bearcat, Corsair — were developed by the Americans during the war while Japanese research, development, and new production lagged tragically behind. When Nobomitsu looked at the old Aichis with their ludicrous fixed landing gear, the antiquated Nakajimas with the long three-man "greenhouse" canopy, he realized how completely Japan had been out-thought, out-designed, and out-produced. Fujita had told him long ago that his boyhood friend and fabled father of Japan's Imperial Navy, Admiral Isoroku Yamamoto, had said before the Pearl Harbor attack, "We can never defeat this giant. I can run wild for perhaps eighteen months, but that is all." How true. How true.

Nobomitsu was distracted as the first Nakajima screeched aboard. A good landing, the pilot caught the first wire. Quickly, the barrier was dropped and the aircraft towed and pushed to the forward elevator. Then bomber after bomber slammed down on the deck followed by the fighters. One fighter with a defective tailhook ground-looped into the barrier, where it was bent and crushed like a toy plane made of wet cardboard. Quickly, white-clad men equipped with new American foam sprayed the wreck and Chief Hospital Orderly Eiichi Horikoshi and four of his men rushed up with a stretcher and carried the pilot's limp form to the sick bay. Fujita cursed and pounded the wind screen. "Casualty report!" he shouted at Talker Naoyuki. "Get that trash off my deck!" Within minutes, the wreck was pushed over the side.

Then Flying Officer Hooperman and Pilot Officer York drifted in with their sleek Seafires. Both caught their wires with panache and confidence. Finally, Air Group commander Yoshi Matsuhara roared aboard. Because he was nose-heavy, Yoshi landed at a higher speed than the other fighters, nose slightly elevated. Notwithstanding, he came aboard gracefully like a hawk settling on his roost. Pulled down hard by the cable and bouncing, he still managed a perfect three-point landing. Atsumi relaxed. At least when landing, Yoshi's mind was on his work, not on Tomoko.

Quickly, Admiral Fujita shouted orders and the battle group came about onto its base course of one-three-zero. "Standard sea watch, Condition Two of readiness, the starboard section has the watch!" he shouted. There was the sound of thousands of boots pounding decks as men rushed through the veins and arteries of the leviathan.

279

Nobomitsu glanced at the admiral. Putting to sea usually put Fujita into a jovial mood. But not this day. Instead he was quite somber, his mind on Brent Ross, Irving Bernstein, and Elwyn York. Rear Admiral Whitehead was of the same mind. He said to Fujita, "Sir, the enemy is aware we are at sea."

"True, Admiral Whitehead. A hundred thousand eyes saw us stand out."

Nobomitsu Atsumi joined the exchange, "The enemy knows."

"Of course."

"Our negotiators are in danger."

The old man bit his sliver of a lip. "Very great danger." Gripping the windscreen with both hands, he stared off into the haze drifting like legions of phantoms over the endless sea. His voice was low, husky, "Free men have always been forced to build their temples on mountains of corpses, on an ocean of tears and on the death cries of men without number."

Rear Admiral Whitehead dropped his glasses to his waist and stared at Fujita. Deeply moved, the American said, "A great philosopher once said, 'No man is an island and any man's death diminishes me, because I am involved in mankind; therefore never send to know for whom the bell tolls, it tolls for thee.'"

The old Japanese eyed the American from the corner of his eye. "A great truth, Admiral Whitehead, and as eternal as the sea slipping beneath our keel."

The old man lifted his glasses and stared off into the far distance.

Fourteen

Bernstein had been far too conservative in his estimate. Two weeks passed and all of the Arab prisoners had not yet been properly identified. Because the Arabs refused to allow observers into their prisoner of war camps, Bernstein would not permit interviews of prisoners held by the allies. These obstacles seemed senseless to Brent, but he was fast learning the infuriating techniques of Middle East bargaining. Bullheaded obduracy on both sides seemed to be the order of the day.

The language barrier was brutal. Translating from Hebrew to Arabic and from Arabic to Hebrew and finally into English was maddening in its complexities. Hours were spent arguing over the identity of a single Arab prisoner. And every other Arab seemed to be given the name of "Abdullah," "Mohammed," or "Ibrahaim" in a variety of spellings. Sometimes a man would carry two of the names and occasionally all three. There were squabbles over units, obscure villages of birth, and the sloppy records kept by the Arabs invariably added to the confusion.

Brent spent long days watching as prisoners' names were laboriously translated and written in English by the secretaries Merhdad Amini and Naguib Mahfouz and the interpreter, Haj Walid Khaled. At the same time, Brent, Bernstein, and Elroy toiled through the long lists of Arab prisoners, translating phonetically, listing alphabetically while trying to group by rank or rating, unit and place of capture. Coffee was consumed by the gallon. Because Bernstein's list was much longer than Younis', Younis often sent Merhdad Amini to help the Israeli translate. Merhdad seemed knowledgeable, efficient and very pleasant. He always sat close to Brent. He smelled of perfume. Brent edged away every time the young man leaned close. The American began to have very strong suspicions about Younis and his two young secretaries.

It was even difficult to count the number of prisoners held. Recent fighting had added to the totals and a few had died. Now, the Israelis held nearly 4,000 prisoners-of-war. The Arabs admitted they had captured 342 Israelis and only 25 American airmen. Five other airmen, three Japanese, an Englishman, and a Pole were in their camps. Brent felt this was a blatant lie, that there were many more, but there was no way to refute the claim. The only hard, reliable number was the 42 prisoners held by Admiral Fujita.

And the arguments over a ratio of exchange became bitter. The Arabs argued for ten-to-one, Bernstein countered with five-to-one and no more. It was as if both sides had thrown up roadblocks and would not budge. Brent twisted in his chair with frustration. Elroy drummed the table.

Then Younis injected a new element. The Arabs seemed to value two prisoners held by the Japanese more than any others. The first was the incompetent Frenchman, Commander Henri DuCarme, who had commanded destroyer *Abu Bakr*. Brent had sunk the *Gearing* Class destroyer northeast of Okinawa with the old British destroyer *Haida*. The second was the aged dive bomber pilot Major Horst Fritschmann, who had been shot down by Commander Yoshi Matsuhara in the same engagement. Brent could not understand why anyone could want DuCarme. Perhaps, it was to punish him. The debate consumed one entire afternoon.

The next morning a solemn Bernstein called Brent and Elroy to his cabin and told them of Tomoko Ozumori's death. The news had been relayed from Mossad headquarters in Tel Aviv for "information only" because of the woman's close connection to Commander Yoshi Matsuhara. Only a minor item, no details were given outside of the fact the victim had been raped and murdered.

Fury gripped the three men. Brent pounded the table, cursed, thinking of the beautiful Tomoko who had been so kind, so gracious, showing genuine affection for him. He had loved her; it was impossible not to. And the loss to Yoshi must be devastating, like losing his arm, his soul, his reason for existing.

"It's possible," Bernstein said. "Get at Yoshi by killing Tomoko."

"Bloodthirsty skunks," Elroy said.

"Savages," Brent added.

"We can't let it affect us," Bernstein cautioned. "The Arabs are probably responsible or maybe *Rengo Sekigun* or it could've been a chance thing — a random killing by a lunatic." He shook his head. "We can't be sure." He looked at his two companions. "One thing's certain, we must carry on with our mission. One killing amongst thousands cannot disrupt us."

"Of course."

"Agreed."

However, still seething, the trio walked to the conference room.

The argument over Commander Henri DuCarme and Major Horst Fritschmann resumed as soon as the Israeli delegation was seated. But the news of Tomoko's brutal murder had put a capstone on Bernstein's wrath and he reversed the prisoner exchange ratio, insisting vehemently that five American survivors of the B-25 raid on Rabta—Colonel Latimer Stewart, Captain Ronald Sparling, Lieutenant Jerome Hennessy, Lieutenant George Woodford and Lieutenant Terry Dunne—be released in exchange for DuCarme and Fritschmann. Sheik Younis refused flatly, turning his table too, proposing quid pro quo for these valued prisoners. Bernstein was on the edge and Brent knew it. His intransigence showed it. Brent, too, was spoiling for a fight. The heat grew, Bernstein finally shouting, "Out of the question!"

At that moment the first explosion occurred, with an Arab, not Bernstein. Major Alai Said Otoba erupted, "Go fuck a dead camel, *Juden!*"

A rush of blood turned the Israeli's face crimson. Bounding to his feet, he shouted, "Right after you douche the scorpions out of your mother's cunt, Arab dog!"

Brent, Elroy, Otoba, the secretaries Merhdad Amini and Naguib Mahfouz, interpreter Haj Walid Khaled all vaulted out of their chairs. Four alarmed guards stepped forward. Brent's mind was filled with Tomoko, Yoshi. He wanted to vent his rage on someone. It was a charged moment, filled with the potential for blood, broken bones, chipped teeth, and, perhaps, cadavers.

Quickly, Emil Bouchett acted, *"Messieurs, messieurs, s'il vous plait.* We can make no progress this way."

More guards entered the room, AK-47s levelled.

Bouchett was joined by Sheik Younis, "Gentlemen," he soothed with an oily voice. "Control your-selves. Please find your seats."

"Please! Please," he and Bouchett had insisted, motioning with their palms down. Slowly, the negotiators sank back into their chairs. The guards relaxed, but a background of angry words could still be heard.

At that moment, Brent almost singlehandedly torpedoed the entire conference. In what was to appear to be a conciliatory gesture, the dainty secretary, Merhdad Amini, sat beside Brent. "Control yourself, Commander," the young man had whispered through full rosy lips while the babble of the other men filled the room. His voice was whiny like a pestering mosquito. And then he dared to almost touch Brent's cheek with his lips, "I can come to your quarters tonight and we can have a private, ah—intimate conversation." Brent's mind was still confused with thoughts of Tomoko and Yoshi and he said nothing. Maybe the mosquito would squeak away.

Encouraged by the American's silence, Amini offered, "All night long, if I please you." Brent felt a hand on his leg and stiffened. Then the hand crept up.

Under ordinary circumstances, Brent would have knocked the hand away and ordered Amini to leave. But not this day. The pent-up rage burst the dam. Roaring like a wounded bull, he punched an open palm into the frail young man's hollow chest like a battering ram, knocking him out of his chair, sending him sliding across the floor like a rag doll thrown by an angry child. The chair clattered across the floor after him.

On his feet and glaring down at the cowering secretary, Brent shouted, "Keep your goddamned hands off of me, you lousy fag!" Leaning over the helpless little man, he raised a massive fist. Amini screamed, the high-pitched cry of a terrified girl, and a circle of guards closed in. However, Bernstein and Elroy grabbed Brent and pulled him back into his chair.

More bedlam. Every Arab was on his feet again, yelling, gesticulating. Finally, Bouchett, Younis and Bernstein managed to quell the disorder and the glaring, red-faced Amini returned to his place next to Younis. As Brent cooled and he managed to force Tomoko from his mind, he became convinced he had just been tested by more than Merhdad Amini. He was sure Younis, and perhaps others, were involved; probably even Kadafi. They were sly, conniving, Byzantine in their intrigues. Amini never came close to the American again.

The negotiations resumed, slow, hesitant, and dispirited. It was no good and Brent knew it. But they must continue, must try. He yearned for *Yonaga* and his old companions.

Finally, to his surprise, a minor agreement was reached. After much persuasion by Bouchett, Brent and Elroy, Bernstein grudgingly conceded a swap for DuCarme and Fritschmann. The pair would be traded for Colonel Latimer Stewart and Captain Ronald Sparling—quid pro quo. Because DuCarme and Fritschmann were held in the naval prison at Yokosuka, they would be flown to North Korea at precisely the same time the two American prisoners were flown to Israel. Later, it was deemed safer and more convenient to fly Stewart and Sparling to Gibraltar. Bernstein immediately sent a message in plain language to Mossad headquarters in Tel Aviv detailing the agreement. There the information was rebroadcast to Fujita's forces. Tel Aviv reported an acknowledgment. However, this was not true. The battle group was approaching the southern tip of South America and radio silence was strictly enforced. The report of an acknowledgment was made in an attempt to mislead the Arabs. No one knew how much they knew.

Near the end of the third week Brent met the big blond man. Stepping out of his quarters, he almost ran headlong into him. With long silver hair and pasty white complexion, the man was very big; a little taller than Brent and nearly as heavy. His face was rough and pitted as if he had suffered from a severe case of the pox when a youth. "Sorry, old boy," the big man said in a crisp English accent. And then, smiling. "Bloody clumsy of me." A strong aroma of garlic rode on his breath.

Brent stared at him for a moment—tight denims, black leather jacket, gloves, boots. He seemed completely out of place, as if he had just parked his Harley Davidson and was looking for the nearest beer hall. "My apologies," Brent said cordially. "I was careless."

The man looked him up and down. "By Jove, you've got to be Commander Brent Ross, 'the American samurai.' Right, old man? Heard you were about." Heavy lids hooded the man's probing blue eyes. There was something ominous buried under that affable exterior.

Brent chuckled. "That's what the media call me." He stared steadily at the stranger. "And you."

"Just call me Harry."

"Harry? That's it?"

"Yes, Harry. That's good enough." The man threw his head back and rocked with laughter. Brent wondered. He saw nothing funny. Finally, the man controlled himself and said, "A private thing, sorry old man."

Brent was intrigued by man's eyes. They were icy cold, like the rimes of ice that collect on a ship's rigging in polar latitudes. He was on guard, goaded by an inexplicable premonition. Only a glim portent, a hunch, the instincts of a man who had practiced war for his entire adult life. He asked casually, "Are you here for the negotiations, Harry?"

The big man shook his head. "Negative. I have a debt to collect and then I've got to get cracking." He waved, "To the east — a bit of work."

Brent was puzzled. He felt he was being taunted, but the man's courtly manners dampened the suspicion. "For England? Prime Minister John Major? The Foreign Office?"

The Englishman chuckled. "You might say that, but unofficial." He glanced at his watch. "Got to buzz off, old chap. See you again soon, I hope, Commander."

The pair shook hands and parted.

The negotiations dragged on for another week before the Arabs were convinced they had a reasonably accurate accounting of the prisoners held by the Israelis and the Japanese. A small amount of progress was made when DuCarme and Fritschmann were flown to Pyongyang while at precisely the same time Colonel Stewart and Captain Ronald Sparling were flown to Gibraltar. Bernstein disliked the arrangement, but he was convinced that the concession had to be made for the sake of progress. The reporters were ecstatic with the news. At last they had something to report. The world's media were filled with optimistic editorials and talking heads filled television tubes with praise for the negotiators.

Brent shook his head. Actually, very little progress had been made. The major stumbling block now was the ratio of exchange. The Arabs continued to insist on at least a ten-to-one exchange in their favor. Bernstein refused flatly. He had made one concession, he would not make another. "Five-to-one," he persisted as he had from the very beginning. The negotiations stumbled on and frustration grew. Fatigue showed on every face.

During these interminable weeks, Brent had seen very little of Colonel Moammar Kadafi, the Spaniard, Saavedra Miguel de Medina-Sidona, the Moroccan, Mana Zaki Alaqi, and the Turk, Hadja Khalfah Pasha. The Englishman, Harry, had vanished as mysteriously as he had appeared. Brent gave him no more thought. And the reporters remained cloistered, confined to the conference room where they played cards, cursed, groused, and waited impatiently for their official handouts.

There had been no more formal, extravagant dinners. Most of the negotiators ate breakfast and lunch in their quarters, but took their dinner in the dining room, ordering from the menu. Usually a small orchestra played, and occasionally a girl danced for the men. On several occasions Nadia slinked across the floor, always with her eyes on Brent, always closing on him with her thrusting hips. On these occasions, Bernstein and Rubin giggled and Brent felt his face warm and his food became hard to swallow. For some unexplained reason, she had never returned to his quarters. He had expected her the night after her first and only visit, and as he watched her dance, he felt hollow pangs of disappointment. She must have satisfied the old woman, Hanan, and for safety's sake avoided the American's quarters.

Then, one night after a particularly tempestuous dance, the knock came. He had just showered and had picked up the lists of American prisoners when he heard the shy tapping. Slipping into a robe, he opened the door. Nadia was standing in the small alcove. She had that timorous, expectant smile on her face. "May I come in, Effendi?"

She was fiercely attractive in her skimpy costume, but a warning bell sounded in the back of the American's mind. "Is it necessary? I'm very tired and I have work to do."

"For just a moment, please."

"Hanan?"

"Yes. The old woman."

He waved her in and she sat on some pillows, dropping her bag on the floor beside her.

"Obviously, Hanan was satisfied with your last visit."

"Yes, Commander."

"Now, on your second visit, she expects you to sleep with me."

The girl sighed. "Much is expected of me."

"Too much. You said baksheesh would work with the old woman."

"Yes. She has accepted it before."

He walked into his bedroom, rummaged in his nightstand under an incense pot, and returned with one hundred dollars. "Will this do?"

Smiling, the girl accepted the money and stuffed it into her bag. "It should, Effendi." She brightened, "Let me give you a massage, Effendi?"

"It's not necessary." He waved at her bag. "You have enough to satisfy Hanan. You may leave."

"Too soon, Effendi. The guards saw me come in. I should remain long enough to provide a service."

"A massage?"

"Yes. It would relax you, Commander."

Brent sighed and sank back. Weeks of tension had caused his neck to ache and the muscles of his back seemed to be permanently bunched and knotted. The idea of a massage was appealing. "Just my back."

The girl broke into a broad grin. "Oh, yes, Effendi. Just your back. You will sleep much better."

Brent nodded and walked into the bedroom. This time he had no reservations about dropping his robe and stretching out on the bed. However, Nadia did not immediately begin the massage. Instead, saying, "Incense," she stuffed two jeweled containers with what appeared to be shredded dried leaves, placed one on each nightstand and lighted them. At once thick lines of smoke twirled to the ceiling, then turned down and enveloped the bed. The odor was strong, somewhat harsh, yet sweet. It was very pleasant.

"Frankincense," she said, answering his unvoiced question.

"So much, Nadia? The whole room is full of it. And it's strong."

"Breathe deeply, Effendi. It will help relax you." She sat next to him and he could hear her opening her bottles. And now everything began to seem so pleasant, and he became impatient for her hands.

They came, soft yet strong, slippery, moving in small circles. The delightful smoke billowed and the hands moved lower. He inhaled deeply and the aroma seemed to glaze his mind. Suddenly, everything about him was silk and satin and the girl's touch was incredible. She seemed to have much greater finesse, or was it his mood?

The hands followed the same route as the first night, roaming like tiny oily animals with minds of their own. And this time, when she pushed on his hip, he rolled over without objecting. He wondered why. She had agreed, only his back. He seemed nearly powerless.

The smoke thickened, enshrouded and gripped inexorably with vaporous tentacles. But the tentacles were beautiful, almost tranquilizing. He was entering a dreamlike mirage where the walls of his room, the furniture were magnificent paintings, the girl a paradigm spawned by his fantasies. Frankincense was amazing. Or was it frankincense? It was very strong. Did it have a drug in it? Hashish? He had never smelled hashish and didn't know, or, at that moment, really care. He stopped wondering as the girl moved closer and he could feel her breath on his cheek.

Now she was rubbing and licking his neck. "No!" he said. He grabbed her hair. She ignored him, moved lower and his hands slipped from her head as if his muscles had been melted by the growing sexual heat.

The maddening tongue continued downward and this time her hands found him and his arousal was so strong the caress of her fingertips pained him. He had never been so helpless, so completely in the power of another.

She fondled him, "Ah, you are a big man, a great man, and it is all for Nadia."

Suddenly, she left him and he almost groaned with frustration. Rising on her knees, she shed her bra and hip band, stared down at him. She was rubbing herself, lathering herself with oils. He watched, fascinated as her hands moved over her breasts, stomach, hips, thighs, everywhere. She stared back. Then, never taking her eyes from his, she slid over him and mounted him. As her body dropped down and the hot center of her slid over him like heated oil, her lips pulled back into a grimace of pure bliss, crying out a long, "Aaa-laah!"

Then she moved her hips, slowly at first, great silky breasts swaying with the movements. She knew what she was doing, measuring her movements, slowing him, controlling him. She threw her head back, and arched her back so far he could no longer see her head, her breasts jutting straight up at the ceiling like identical peaks, hair brushing his ankles. Now the drive of her hips duplicated the erotic movements she had used in her dance. Then, slowly, she came erect again, always moving, running her hands over his chest, his stomach, gripping his buttocks, pulling and easing rhythmically.

His eyes were riveted on her; the contorting face, swaying hair like a silken curtain, swollen red-tipped breasts, the hard muscles of her stomach like cords. A golden goddess of love. He had never experienced anything like this.

His breath was hard to find. He felt perspiration beginning like small rivulets all over his face, chest and torso. He reached up. Caressed her breasts. Then she leaned forward so that he could grip them more firmly, kissed him, running her hands through his hair, muttering soft Arabic words of love in his ear.

Her control of herself and him defied belief. But slowly, apparently overcome by her own sensations, the deliberate leisurely movements of her hips quickened, became short, jerky. She began to sigh, then moan with each downward drive. Suddenly, throwing her head back, she screamed at the ceiling and shuddered, digging her fingers into his buttocks and pulling herself down with amazing strength. He felt himself release with an enormous burst of sensation that brought a shout to his lips. She collapsed on top of him, muttering, "Effendi, my marvelous Effendi." They kissed each other fiercely.

Then he could hear her breath in his ear and he could only sigh back and gulp down more of the frankincense. He expected the girl to roll from him, but, instead she remained prostrate on him, breathing hard, sighing with each breath.

Stretching her legs full-length down his, she did not allow him to slip out of her and at the same time she

293

took his hands in hers and stretched out his arms. A cross on a cross. "You are a great man, Effendi," she said through her gasps. "I will stay the night. You left much of you within me for Hanan to find. Much."

"I'm glad, Nadia."

"You have more, Effendi, much more."

"Yes. Much more."

"I will claim it before the night is out."

She rolled from him, but snuggled close, draping an arm around him. She was limp, sagging in her relaxation like a willow after a heavy rain.

The smoke seemed to be thinning and his breath came back and with it some disturbing thoughts. Rolling from Nadia to his back, his mind began to run kaleidoscopically like a VCR on fast forward. Was it the smoke? Strange. He was tired and he should sleep. But instead disturbing thoughts began to push aside the euphoria of sexual gratification.

Had he done something wrong? Perhaps, betrayed his colleagues? Had he betrayed Ruth, too? Why was she on his mind? He twisted, turned, muttered to himself. He was on what might be the most important mission of his career and, yet, he had started a liaison with a belly dancer in the "tent" of colonel Moammar Kadafi. Stupid. He sensed trouble could explode in his face.

Suddenly, he saw Admiral Fujita, Yoshi Matsuhara. God, he missed them. Why were they on his mind now? Maybe, it was Tomoko's death that troubled him. She had never been out of his thoughts. And Ruth lingered through it all, smiling with adoration in her eyes. Did he need her and his old comrades that much? What was happening to him? What were they all doing at this moment? Maybe, Ruth had a new lover already. Besides her passion, she was a realistic young woman. And the admiral—planning his next battle, no doubt. And Yoshi must be mourning Tomoko. Poor Yoshi. Too much tragedy for one man. And he might be *shinigurai*. How horrible.

Nadia stirred. Ran a hand down his chest and abdomen and found her prize. Then the lips returned to his chest and the licking began. The head moved lower and the specters vanished.

The next morning Brent knew something unusual was brewing when he entered the conference room. All of the reporters were present, seated at their long table, recorders ready, expectant looks on their faces. Kingsbury waved and smiled. Brent returned the salute.

The Arabs seemed especially agitated. Staring at Bernstein balefully, Major Alai Said Otoba began by announcing, "While you have been negotiating with us, with men of good faith, a battle group left Japan and is already headed north in the Atlantic." He threw a wounded look the reporters' way and then named *Yonaga, Bennington, New Jersey,* gave the number of escorts as thirteen and the position of the group as southwest of the Cape Verde Islands. "In addition, you have been allowed the use of the fighter strip at Gibraltar and two squadrons of the new American fighter, the Grumman FX-1000, are now based there along with three squadrons of Spitfires." He threw up his hands, gesticulating his helplessness and frustration. And then sarcastically, "Is Admiral Fujita bringing these warships on a goodwill tour, *Yahud?*"

Colonel Irving Bernstein rose and met sarcasm with sarcasm, "My, what a stirring performance. In the cinema you would be given an award for such talented acting."

"That is enough!" the major roared.

"No! Not enough!" The colonel threw a glance at the engrossed reporters. "I'm sure the Russian carrier *Baku*, Spanish carrier *Reina de Ibérico*, cruisers *Dzerzhinsky* and *Zhdanov* are in Tripoli preparing for a romantic Mediterranean pleasure cruise along with carrier *Magid* and cruiser *Babur.*"

The Arab officer waved dramatically. "We must protect ourselves from Zionist oppressors."

"I know, you poor oppressed people. After all, there are only two hundred million of you attacked by four million Jewish savages."

Before Otoba could retort, Moammar Kadafi swept into the room. He was followed by the Spaniard Saavedra Miguel de Medina-Sidona, the Moroccan, Mana Zaki Alaqi, and the Turk, Hadja Khalfah Pasha. After returning the welcoming gestures and greetings from the Arabs and reporters, the new arrivals seated themselves. Bernstein, Brent Ross, and Elroy Rubin only nodded.

Everyone was settled when Brent came upright as if someone had connected a high voltage line to his chair. Dressed in a long, shapeless black gown, Nadia entered, escorted by two guards. Although her eyes were downcast, she stole a sheepish glance Brent's way. There was fear in her eyes. Brent felt his stomach lose its bottom, and the emptiness bordered on nausea. Bernstein and Rubin both glanced at Brent, and several of the Arabs looked across the table and snickered. The secretary, Merhdad Amini, seemed especially amused, openly sneering at the American.

Following a silent cue from Kadafi, Sheik Iman Younis took the floor while the guards herded the girl to a place behind him. There she stood, wringing her hands and looking around fearfully. The reporters hunched forward, the other men stared. The air was charged like the space between two passing clouds with opposite polarity. Lightning was about to crack and everyone knew it. Brent cursed himself, he knew what was coming.

Younis waved grandly, "There has been a betrayal of my master's tent — of his boundless hospitality."

The Arabs groaned and looked at each other in horror. The Moroccan, Spaniard, and Turk appeared confused.

Younis stabbed a finger at Brent, "The American has seduced one of our virgin dancers."

"Virgin!" Brent shouted incredulously. "You're out of your goddamned mind."

Younis ignored him and the Arabs chorused, "No! No!" Hands were wrung, angry words grumbled.

"Yes. Ruthlessly, Commander Brent Ross took her most prized possession from her. Asked her for a massage, but instead he forced himself upon her."

There were groans and several Arabs pounded the table. Merhdad Amini actually sobbed into his hands.

Brent leaped to his feet. "Utter nonsense. The girl came to my room, drugged me, came on to me, took advantage . . ." Drowned out by laughter, he realized how utterly ludicrous his explanation sounded. Unfortunately, the truth sometimes sounds foolish. He was experiencing one of these moments.

Younis nodded at Major Otoba who took over like an assistant district attorney prosecuting the foulest of criminals, "It is simple," Otoba said smugly, "let the violated girl tell her story."

Nadia spoke to her hands which she was wringing before her. "It is true, the commander insisted I come to his quarters."

"You have been there before?"

"Yes. The first night of the conference. He asked me to give him a massage."

"And did you?"

"Yes."

"That was all?"

She bit her lip. "No. He made advances."

"Lies!" Brent screamed. Bernstein pulled him down. "Let her finish," the Israeli cautioned.

Otoba continued with the questioning, "You would not return because of his advances?"

"Yes, Effendi."

"Then why did you go to his quarters last night?"

"He offered me a hundred dollars." She reached into her bag and pulled out a fistful of money. She held it over her head for all to see. More groans.

"For sex?"

The girl looked up, agony twisting her face. "Oh, no, Effendi, I swear on the Five Pillars of Faith, I am — I mean, I was a virgin. The hundred dollars was for a massage. He burned something in two *min elim* that filled the room with smoke — made me too weak to resist."

"Hashish?"

"I know not what hashish smells like."

"Why did you take the chance. You knew he had evil designs on you?"

"True, Effendi." She looked around, tears staining her cheeks. "But I am just a poor Egyptian girl from Cairo and my parents lost everything in the earthquake. I was only trying to help my poor father, mother, brother, two sisters, all so young . . ."

"Crazy. Foolish lies," Brent burst out. "Ask Hanan."

"Hanan?" Otoba asked, puzzled. "Who is Hanan?"

"The old woman," Brent retorted. "Ask Nadia about Hanan."

Nadia shook her head. "I know nothing of a

298

Hanan. Who is this Hanan?" She stared around, brown eyes wide, confused and guileless.

The Arabs stared at Brent as if they were looking at a crazy man. Otoba turned to Younis who shook his head, then Kadafi smiled and gave a negative gesture. "No one here has ever heard of your Hanan," he said.

Now Brent realized how completely stupid he had been. A fool. A dupe of a simple plot based on the oldest intrigue on earth. A sexual trap and he had fallen headlong into it. He cursed his overactive libido. It had happened before: in 1987 when Kathryn Suzuki used her sex to lure him into a Sabbah assassination plot on the north shore of Oahu; in 1989 his hands were all over Dale McIntyre while assassins lurked in the shadows of the French restaurant of Tokyo's Imperial Hotel. His feverish preoccupation with Dale had led to the death of the loyal, brave guard, Watertender First Class Azuma Kurosu, and nearly claimed Dale's and his own. Now, again, his rampaging lust had played to the same scenario for the third time.

True, he had been drugged. He knew that, now. But, still, in the final analysis, he could only condemn himself. In his mind he couldn't control himself, pure and simple. The whole delegation would be discredited, made to look foolish before the entire world. Those leering reporters would see to that. Only the wise Robert Kingsbury was shaking his head. He had a very sad look on his face. Brent felt Bernstein's hand on one shoulder and Elroy's on the other. They, too, were behind him, trying to control him. Perhaps they did not understand, but they knew him too well to believe he would willfully endanger the mission, put their lives at risk.

Otoba said, "May I suggest, Commander Ross, you have polluted your mind with so many drugs and satanic thoughts, you have been overwhelmed by your own private devils."

Brent tried to rise, but Bernstein and Elroy pulled him back. Bernstein stood. "Fascinating little drama," the Israeli said. "But how can you be so blatant with your lies."

"Lies?"

"Yes, lies." He pointed at Otoba and then Younis. "You claim Commander Ross overwhelmed this," his voice suddenly dropped octaves, dripped with sarcasm, "virgin — with hashish."

"That is correct. You heard her," Otoba said, playing to the reporters. "May the Prophet burn me on the day of fire if every word is not true."

"Virgin!" Bernstein mocked. "Well, get ready for a little heat on that day of fire because she'd give the whole profession of prostitution a bad name."

"Enough, *Yahud!*"

"No! Not enough, you pile of camel dung."

There were shouts of anger and Otoba's eyes bulged as if pressure were pumping up inside his skull and would explode at any moment. Bernstein raced on, "You body-searched us the very first day." Now it was Bernstein's turn to play to the reporters, "And believe me, gentlemen, they didn't miss a single orifice." He turned back to Otoba, "So, just where did Commander Brent Ross conceal this evil drug? Behind his eyeballs?"

Obviously rattled and infuriated by the insult, Otoba waved his hands angrily and fired back, "I know not where you infidel devils find your evil." A gaffe. He had chosen the wrong words. The reporters hunched forward as a man at the insulting charge. Even the Russian, Vladimir Rostovsky, seemed offended.

Otoba began again, "Just where the hashish was

300

concealed is academic. The only important thing is that Commander Ross had it and used it for his own carnal purposes."

"Nonsense!" Bernstein retorted with the confidence of a man who had spent a lifetime entangled in Middle-Eastern intrigues. "You played the oldest game in the world with Commander Ross." He waved at Brent, "You heard his side, Nadia came to him, she was not coerced, no one put a gun in her back." He looked at the girl, who was studying the intricate patterns of the Maksoud rug under her feet and then moved his eyes to the reporters, "I challenge you, the representatives of our honored Fourth Estate, to investigate her claims — her destitute family suffering in the wreckage of their home in Cairo. The father, the mother, the pathetic little brother, sisters."

Kingsbury spoke out, "Right you are, Colonel Bernstein. If the young lady will give me the details our United Commonwealth News Service would be happy to give it a go." He stared at Nadia expectantly. "And, by Jove, we can get cracking on that straight away — give you a report on their condition, the whole bit, parents and nippers. Wouldn't that be jolly good?" Brent detected a touch of irony in the voice. He suspected the Englishman did not believe a word of the girl's story.

The girl stole a look at Otoba, then Younis and finally Kadafi.

"What's wrong, young lady?" Bernstein asked, acid dripping from each word. "Forget your own address? Speak up!"

Nadia's voice was so soft, it was barely discernible, "There has been so much destruction — they would be hard to find."

"Oh, no problem," Kingsbury declared. "We'll find them, the whole lot."

301

Bernstein's laugh was sharp like the edge of a killing blade. He scoffed, "My, my, Nadia, the little flower — ah, the deflowered flower, you must be deeply concerned."

"What do you mean?"

"Why didn't you rush home to search for them, to be with them, your parent, little brother and sisters?"

"Enough!" Kadafi shouted, finally entering the debate. Obviously Otoba was losing credibility and the dictator had to call a halt before all was lost. Kadafi's eyes moved from Bernstein to Elroy to Brent. "You have raped my hospitality while your battle group makes a treacherous approach. It is all a plot to distract the free Muslims of the world." He gestured at Nadia, "And one of our most virtuous has been foully violated."

"That's a goddamned lie," Brent shouted.

A gasp of horror filled the room. No one talked to "The Leader" with those words, with that attitude.

"Stand!" Kadafi demanded.

"Screw you!"

The dictator gestured and six guards pulled Brent, Bernstein and Elroy from their chairs and held them erect.

"You must be punished," Kadafi said. His small eyes narrow like a rodent's. "I could put you to death for this, Commander Ross."

"Leave my colleagues out of this. I am the accused in this web of lies."

"I ain't gunna cut an' run," Elroy said. "I'm with Commander Ross."

"And I, too," Bernstein said.

"My, how gallant, how chivalrous," the dictator jeered. A great thunderclap of laughter boomed through the room. His raised hands restored order. Suddenly, his face was softened by a quick change in

302

mood. He said magnanimously, "To show how Muslims act mercifully in the eyes of Allah, I declare all three of you persona non grata."

There were shouts of, *"La iläha illa-l-Läh!"* and *"Muhammadum rasulu-l-Läh!"*

Brent could not believe his ears. He expected harsh treatment, even death. The three-inch pipe up the rectum, filled with diseased rats had even come to mind. But persona non grata meant "unwelcome." It was a very mild punishment, indeed. Kadafi must be performing for the reporters, trying to present the face of the humanitarian, the benevolent leader.

Bernstein, too, was taken aback. "You wish us to leave?"

"Yes."

"Immediately?'

"Of course." Kadafi conferred with the interpreter, Haj Walid Khaled, and returned to the Israeli delegation. "You will be flown to Gibraltar. The arrangements have been made." A sardonic sneer twisted his face. "After all, your English friends should welcome you."

"Why Gibraltar?"

"It would be easier and safer. I have given my word you would be returned safely and agreed that one of my aircraft will return you." He waved, "The air space to the east is dangerous. Your forces started an offensive near Beersheba just an hour ago."

There were angry cries and the table was pounded by incensed Arab fists.

Still playing the great humanitarian, Kadafi stared at the reporters and smiled. "If any of you gentlemen care to leave, there is room on the transport for you. However, you may remain, if you wish."

Kadafi was definitely trying to curry favor with the media. Brent was convinced that if the reporters had

303

not been in the room, there was an excellent chance they would have been slaughtered.

The dictator continued, "Of course, our gallant troops are throwing back the attack on all fronts." Cheers. "And may I suggest, if Admiral Fujita is foolish enough to challenge me, to try to force the Mediterranean, it would be a simple matter for you to join him. In that way, we can kill all of you together, honorably in battle." His stare was as hard as gunmetal. "A fate that is far too good for all of you."

"Allah akbar!"

Brent clenched his fists on the table and felt beads of perspiration begin to form on his brow. He longed to punch the dictator senseless, scream out his wrath. Bernstein tugged on his sleeve and he managed to hold his tongue.

Casually, Bernstein asked, "We'd be happy to return the favor. When do we leave?"

"Go pack. The plane is waiting."

Emil Bouchett finally spoke out. "But *Messieurs, les negociations?*"

Kadafi shook his head. "They are over. I can only deal with honorable men."

One insult too many. Brent could not swallow it. "Now look here . . ." he finally erupted. Bernstein stopped him and pulled him toward the door.

Muttering to himself and flanked by his guards, the big American left the room.

Fifteen

From the air, Brent could see all of the famous fortress of Gibraltar. Although it was very early, the sun was bright and the air clear as polished crystal. He had seen "the rock" many times from the sea, but this was the first time he had flown in. The big Libyan Lockheed Constellation, wearing the identical white paint with green crosses of the Israeli DC-6 that had taken the party to Tripoli, made a wide sweeping turn to line up on the tiny strip that jutted out into the bay formed by three long moles.

"About two hundred yards wide and maybe two thousand yards long," Robert Kingsbury said, staring at the runway through his window.

"Looks like a matchstick. Shoot, we've got corrals for dogies bigger'n that back home."

Bernstein craned his neck. "Are those FX-1,000s still with us?" he asked.

Brent jerked his finger to the rear. "One's off our starboard elevator and the other must be to port."

"Right," the Canadian, Sidney Grant, shouted from across the isle. "He's there. I wish he'd go home." There was nervous laughter.

The Grumman FX-1,000 was one of the most vicious fighters Brent had ever seen. Small, like the Bearcat, it housed an enormous 4,400 horsepower Pratt and Whitney double Wasp engine. With four-blade propellers that were at least thirteen feet long, it was gull-winged like the F4U Corsair. There the resemblance ended. With a small bubble canopy, its narrow fuselage tapered into a raised tail with slender horizontal and vertical planes. Its armament was awesome. In addition to four twenty-millimeter cannons in its wings, another cannon of at least thirty-millimeter jutted from its propeller hub. Crutches for bombs and auxiliary tanks were visible under its wings and fuselage.

"How in hell do they cushion the recoil of that big cannon?" someone had asked when the pair of fighters had first shot past, making at least 400 miles an hour.

"Sure 'nuff cain't figger that one," Elroy had said. "Must o' come up with sumpin' new." And then he showed his knowledge as a fighter pilot, "I figger it must be a new hydraulic system. An' look at that wing. It's narrow, like the Davis wing on the old B-24 Liberator." He scratched his head. "Fast, but the wing loading must be sumpin' else."

"What do you mean?"

"Fast, but maybe it cain't turn with the older fighters."

Now the big transport was letting down. Brent could see the flaps drop giving the plane a nose-down attitude, and he could feel the landing gear thump down. Then the engines speeded and whined as the propellers were rotated to fine pitch.

Brent could see all of the fabled peninsula: the huge rock which stood almost 1,400 feet high with a nearly perpendicular north face; east side gashed with tremendous precipices; south almost as formidable as

306

the north; and the west side not quite as rugged as the others, sloping to the sea. A small town was visible on the west side at the foot of a short, narrow isthmus connecting the rock to the Spanish mainland.

"Gibraltar," one of the reporters muttered as if he were studying a myth come to life.

Bernstein said, "Ironically, the name is derived from Arabic."

Arabic?"

The Israeli nodded. "Yes. 'Gibraltar' is derived from the Arabic *gebel al Tariq,* which to them meant, 'Rock of Tariq.' Tariq ibn-Ziyad landed there in the eighth century when he lead the first Muslim invasion of Spain."

"I'll be darned," Elroy said.

"We're landing in the middle of a lot of history," Brent said.

"A lot," Bernstein agreed. "And in a lot of water, too."

Looking out the window, it seemed the plane was indeed settling into the Mediterranean. However, at the last instant, when everyone expected a big splash, the end of the runway flashed under. The big transport plopped down so hard Brent expected the tires to explode. Luckily, they did not.

The landing was rough, the Arab pilot galloping down the runway, finally bringing the big plane to a screeching halt in front of the small terminal.

"Allah akbar!" several of the reporters shouted through their nervous laughter.

Waving at the cockpit, Elroy yelled, "That suck-egg mule couldn't bust a pussycat. I seen mavericks with a brandin' iron up their ass that didn't buck like this."

Quickly, the frightened and relieved passengers disembarked and a crisp British colonel with a waxed mustache and attitude that belonged in the Khyber

307

pass a century ago, singled out Bernstein and his party and pulled them aside. The reporters were led to the lounge of the terminal. A young lieutenant approached the colonel shyly and stood behind him.

"I say, Colonel Bernstein, Commander Ross, and Lieutenant Rubin. Right?"

"Right you are."

"Colonel Sean Townsend here." His palm-out salute was so rigid that his hand quivered. The trio returned the salute. The colonel gestured to the young lieutenant, "My aide, Lieutenant Wesley Watkins." More salutes. "This way, gentlemen." He gestured at a khaki-colored Land Rover. "Got a bottle of scotch waiting."

"Best news I've heard in months," Brent said.

The men laughed.

Seated with Bernstein, Elroy, and the two British officers at a table in a conference room in the terminal's VIP section, Brent relaxed as the first delightful charcoal-flavored swallow of Haig & Haig coursed down. "We're SIU—Special intelligence Unit," Townsend said.

"SIU?"

The colonel explained that he and Watkins were regular army—"Sandhurst, and all that rot"—but had been detached to the Special Intelligence Unit which had been created specifically to track the Arab-Israeli-Japanese hostilities and to aid the allies whenever possible. "After all, we lost three carriers to the bloody blighters," the major said with his first show of emotion. "And the two squadrons of the new American fighter, the FX-1,000, will be a big help."

"Your own fighter strength?"

"Three squadrons of Spits. New, more powerful

Rolls Royce Merlins, but only a third of the range of the FX-1,000 and not nearly as fast. Nothing is." He gulped down his drink and Watkins refilled all of the glasses. "We'll need them all when Admiral Fujita's battle group steams through the straits."

Stunned, Brent looked at Bernstein. Bernstein said, "How can you know? Maybe, he's bringing reinforcements to the Canary Islands."

The Englishman shook his head. "Then why battleship *New Jersey*? And we have unimpeachable intelligence that an all-out attack will be made on the Arab works at Rabta. You know they are very close to producing an atomic bomb."

"Yes, I know."

"It's a challenge, old boy. Throw down the gauntlet and dare your enemy to pick it up—meet me in the lists, lance to lance." Townsend glanced at Brent. "The way of the samurai, right Commander?" He did not wait for an answer, "You've got to be 'the American samurai'!"

Brent nodded. He was tired of being reminded of the sobriquet and it showed, "Right. I'm in the tabloids right along with Fergie and Princess Di."

The Englishman's smile vanished and he twisted the ends of his mustache. "Didn't mean to offend, old man."

"No offense," Brent answered. A month-old copy of the *Manchester Guardian* on the table with a scattering of equally outdated magazines caught his eye. A column head read, BRITISH ASSASSIN SUSPECTED IN TOKYO MURDER. The heading wrenched his guts. He said to Townsend, "That article—" He gestured at the paper. "Does SIU know anything about the murder of a Tomoko Ozumori? She was murdered almost two months ago in Tokyo."

The Englishman nodded grimly. "Yes, indeed. Undoubtedly, it was done by Harry 'High Wire' Good-enough."

" 'Garlic Mouth'," Bernstein said.

"Right you are." He described the horrible circum-stances of the rape and butchery.

Revulsion soured in Brent's throat and he could only mutter, "Good God, no!" Bernstein and Elroy looked pale and unnerved.

Through the pain a light glimmered in the far dark recesses of Brent's memory. *Garlic! Good enough or Goodenough! Near crazed laughter.* Synapses con-nected and merged and a horrible suspicion broke from his subconscious. The scotch suddenly burned his stomach. "Big guy, blond, dressed in a black jacket, denims, boots, stinks of garlic."

"That's the bloody blighter to a 'T.' But how did you know, Commander?"

"I met the son-of-a-bitch in Libya."

"No!" Bernstein gasped.

Brent explained the encounter in the hall and the object of Goodenough's visit. "I'm sure he was wait-ing for me—had fun with me." He rapped the table so hard with his big knuckles the glasses jumped. "And he said he had business in the East."

"In the East?" Bernstein repeated, confused.

Suddenly, it all came clear. "Oh, no," Brent ex-claimed. Everyone stared at him. "He's after Ruth."

"Why?"

"Don't you see, Colonel. He's killed Yoshi's woman—got to him by murdering her."

"But you've only known Ruth Moskowitz for a very short time. How could they consider her 'your woman'?"

"You said the Arab mind defied logic."

"True," the colonel conceded resignedly.

"And she is Mossad."

310

The colonel nodded. "Then, she would be a prime kill."

"Warn her! Alert Mossad, Colonel."

Bernstein nodded and looked at Colonel Townsend. "I'll send a message."

The British colonel waved at a door. "The WT, ah, wireless transmitter, is in the next room. Do you need computer assistance for encoding your signal?"

"No. I'll send the message in plain language. I want the Arabs to pick it up. If Brent's right, they might just call him off if his objective is Ruth Moskowitz, or other personnel, for that matter." The major handed Bernstein a pad and the Israeli quickly scribbled a short message. Townsend handed the sheet to Watkins, who rushed into the wireless room.

Brent tossed off the last of his drink and shook his head. "That's not good enough. I've got to return to Israel."

"Sorry, old man," Townsend countered. "But I've got specific orders for you—for the whole lot of you from Admiral Fujita."

"What?"

"You're to be flown aboard *Yonaga*."

"*Yonaga*?" the three men chorused. "When?"

"In the morning and I'll brief you now."

"How?"

Colonel Townsend laughed. "If I told you, you wouldn't believe me." He rose. "Come along, please, and I'll show you."

Following the lead of the Englishman, the men gulped down the last of their drinks and rose. Brent's mind was filled with Ruth. Strange creatures seemed to be tangled in a battle in his stomach and the Haig & Haig curdled and crept up into his throat. She was in danger. He was sure of that. "Oh, Ruth. Please be

311

careful," he said to himself. He followed Bernstein through the door.

Sarah Aranson answered the knock while Ruth prettied herself in the bathroom. Because the bathroom was at the far end of the hall, Sarah could just hear a faint voice on Ruth's radio. She always listened to the local news station while she did her hair and applied just a touch of makeup.

When she opened the door, Sarah saw a tall man with disheveled black hair and olive skin which did not quite fit the blue eyes, intense yet shadowy under thick dark brows. The blue maintenance crew overalls were stretched by his broad shoulders and wide chest. "Maxim Hotel" was stitched across his back, "Freddie" on the front above the left breast pocket. Big biceps bulged under his short sleeves. Strangely, with the assortment of tools hanging from his belt, Sarah saw a coil of wire, not electrical cord but sturdy layered bailing wire.

He spoke in near perfect Hebrew, but an inflection of broadened "ah" sounds indicated British antecedents. Sarah was not surprised. Jews from all over the world with a hundred dialects were to be found in Israel.

"Sorry, madam," he said politely. "We have an electrical malfunction."

"Oh, that's it. The phone went dead a few minutes ago."

"I know, madam." He pointed upward. "And four apartments on the sixth have lost all power." And then with a disarming smile, "May I come in? Just take a minute." She waved him in.

Carrying his toolbox, the maintenance man stepped into the room. When he walked past her, she smelled garlic. She closed the door.

"The phone and the circuit breakers are in the kitchen. The phone's on that counter and the circuit breakers are next to the refrigerator," she said. "If that's what you want."

He nodded and she turned away to return to the sofa where she had been sipping coffee and reading a stack of reports. However, a noise behind her made her turn back. He was only a few steps behind her. An alarm buzzed in her brain and she said sharply, "I told you the kitchen."

The laugh was wild, almost maniacal. "I'm going to break some circuits, but they won't be in the kitchen, they're between your legs." He stepped toward her, face hardened by malevolence.

Shocked into speechlessness, she was suddenly staring into the fierce pitiless eyes of a stalking lion, a fierce bird of prey, a cobra poised to strike, and fear, a cold heavy thing like oil in her guts, sent a million icy prickles up her spine and the back of her neck.

He leaped, big hands extended and clamped a heavy hand over her mouth just as she began to scream. "Never had any kosher pussy," he giggled. "Must be smashing. You take such pride in all your meat."

She punched him in the ribs, but it was like striking iron plate. She brought her knee up into his crotch, but he was ready for her, twisting away and pushing her back toward the sofa.

She tried to bite his hand. Failed. Twisted, brought an elbow up sharply into his ribs and this time she hurt him.

"Bitch!" he cried. "Don't try your amateur karate on me. Then a leg behind his knee threw him off balance and they both fell heavily, crashing down on the table, splintering it and rolling onto the floor.

With almost twice Sarah's weight and with enormous strength, this was precisely what he wanted. Forcing her onto her back, he pushed himself between her legs. With a forearm across her throat which cut off her breath and threatened to crush her trachea, he spread her legs and clawed at her panties, ripping them off. She felt herself weakening and something unbelievably large was driving into her. Again, she tried to cry out, but the pressure on her throat was so hard she began to lose consciousness, brain bursting with bright colors and fluttering lights. Her face turned blue and the horror faded, everything faded.

At that moment, the hard sole and sharp heel of a shoe caught him on the side of the head. Lightning flashed across his retinas. Another kick to the back of his head sent him sprawling off his victim. However, the fine, superbly conditioned athlete quickly shook off the rippling lights and he came smoothly to his feet like a panther, claws bared. Ruth Moskowitz was facing him.

He looked at Ruth and then at Sarah who was still on her back, apparently unconscious. "Two of you! Two Ruth Moskowitzes." He grinned. "That makes it twice as good. I'll just fuck you both." He patted the coil of wire, "And then make you nice necklaces and hang you by them."

Ruth felt fear, an emotion that was almost a stranger to her. Raw waves of panic rose up out of some dark place in her soul, and she fought to control them. A killer. Rape and murder. In a steady voice, she warned, "Don't you think someone has heard all this noise?"

He jerked a thumb once to each side, "Service room and elevator shaft on that side and that kike, on the other side is out of town. I checked the computer before I came up." Again the uncontrolled laughter.

314

"Oh, we'll have a real party, we three. A *ménage à trois* you never dreamed of."

Ruth knew she faced a madman. There had been too much noise. It had banged through the bathroom door even over the sound of her radio. Any other killer would have fled, perhaps to wait for another day, another place. Certainly, someone, above them, below them, in the hall, had heard the noise. As he stepped toward her, hands extended, palms flat in the spear-hand mode, Sarah rolled to her side and moaned. He ignored Sarah and concentrated on Ruth.

Pressing the inside of her index fingers with the tip of her thumb, Ruth balled both hands into vicious one-knuckle fists. Under no circumstances could she allow him to come to grips with her. She must keep him at bay; at a distance. That was the only way she could defend herself. It would be very difficult in the small room.

She could read his expression. It was all there for her to see. Obviously, he expected this slight girl to be an easy mark. He moved against her with too much confidence, too casually. She watched his feet. His weight shifted to his right foot and she correctly guessed a strike to her midsection. Deftly, she moved to the left and struck out with her fist, catching him in the throat. At the same time, she whirled and brought a foot around viciously in a reverse roundhouse kick. She was aiming for his crotch, but her heel caught him on the abdomen instead. It was like kicking a cinder-block wall.

She never completed her turn. Although the blow to the throat had hurt him, he caught her foot with one hand, then grabbed with both, spun her around and threw her across the room like a child throwing away an unwanted Teddy bear. Crashing into the tele-

315

vision set, she fell to the floor in its debris, shards of broken glass cutting her arms and cheek. Instantly, the room was a carousel and the lights dimmed.

Moving toward her, he was gasping, rubbing his throat. Suddenly, he pulled off his wig and long blond hair tumbled free and she could see pasty white skin outlining his hairline. He lapsed into strangely accented English idiom, "Gunna give you a bullockin'. Both of you bloody Jewesses — get some of that kosher pussy. Ain't had a cunt since that Jap. And she was good. Liked it. Hated to chop her."

Groggily, Ruth stood. Again, she balled her fists. "Bloody tough little baggage," he smirked through his heavy breathing, still showing the effects of the punch to the throat. "You're good with your karate, makes it more interesting."

She jumped to the side to avoid his charge, and caught him straight on in the ribs with a one-knuckle fist. Something cracked and she heard him cry out, "Goddamned Soho slut!" She ran toward the door but he brought her down. She rolled. Clawed at his face, trying for his eyes. He twisted and she raked his cheek with her long nails, leaving bloody tracks and torn flesh.

Clearly, he had not expected this. A slender girl who was a tiger; claws, fangs and all. He screamed out like a wounded corrida bull. Slapped her across the face, wrestled her arms to the floor and trapped them with his knees, pushing himself between her legs. He had both hands free. More slaps. The right, the left, palms, knuckles. Her vision broke up into flashing lights and black patches, teeth clashed together, ripped her cheeks and she tasted blood. Blackness was enveloping her and she felt her panties ripped off. "Now, I'm gunna give it to you — both of you like you . . ."

He never finished his sentence. Gripping a heavy brass lamp, Sarah came up silently behind him, swung it with all her power, catching him behind his ear. There was the cracking sound of a branch snapping in a silent forest and he spun from Ruth onto his back, nearly unconscious.

Seeing her bloody, battered niece, Sarah felt fear displaced by hatred, rage possessing her like a ravening beast. Blood. She wanted his blood. Another blow from the lamp crushed his nose and he cried out in pain. Again she hit him, shattering the supra-orbital margin of the frontal bone of his skull and blood drenched his eye and tatters of skin and flesh hung down over his face like a curtain. Ruth staggered to her feet.

Now Ruth was on him, too, punching him in the midsection while Sarah continued to smash the heavy brass lamp into his face. Blood spurted from his nose, teeth flew, his lips split open and ran red. Ruth ran to the kitchen, opened a drawer, and rummaged frantically for her butcher knife.

He rolled, twisted, knocked the lamp from Sarah's hands. Found his feet. Sarah stared at him with amazement. He was indestructible. He swiped at the blood on his face and began to advance. Was he human? A backward swing knocked Sarah against the wall and she slid to the floor. He moved in for the kill. But with one eye filling with congealing blood and obstructed by a flap of skin, he never saw Ruth rushing in from the side with a butcher knife.

Ruth drove the knife into his midsection, upward, with all her strength. At first she felt some resistance to the blade, but the point punched through the layered, tough muscles and slashed into the soft interior, cutting through intestines and ripping out the bottom of his stomach. She did not withdraw the blade. In-

317

stead, she pressed hard on the handle, working the knife, hot blood spurting over her hand and forearm. Strangely, she felt no fear, no horror, instead she was gripped by a deep atavistic surge of elation nearly sexual in its intensity. She shrieked triumphantly in his face, spraying spittle.

Staring at her, eyes glazed with disbelief, he screamed, an incoherent cry without form or meaning. Slowly, he sank to the floor into his own blood, which was already puddling. His head lolled from side to side and he vomited gore, limbs jerking in spontaneous, nerveless movements.

Squatting beside him, Ruth reached into his fly, pulled his flaccid penis out and held it like a dead snake. Wild giggles shook her body. She felt drunk, a loss of reason, logic, ability to control or even feel emotions. She tittered uncontrollably, teetering on the edge of lunacy. How could there be any humor in this situation? But it all seemed so funny now. She pulled the organ up to full length, "Proud of this thing?" she goaded. "Doesn't look like much, soft as mush. Couldn't do a thing for the horniest teenager."

He tried to sit up but could only raise his head slightly. His eyes rolled like loose marbles. He coughed more blood and his arms and legs continued to jerk and tremble.

Sarah reeled to her feet and stood behind Ruth. "Give the *shmuck* some of his own Arab justice, Ruth," she exhorted.

"Thieves have their hands cut off, rapists have their . . ."

"That's right, Ruth, cut it off."

"Hmmm," Ruth pondered like a housewife inspecting a piece of meat in the local market, "I think you've made a worthy suggestion, Aunt Sarah, and he hasn't even been circumcised." She raised the knife and stared into his eyes. There was terror there. "I'll take care of that for you, after all, you are in Israel. I'll be your *sandek*." Grasping the glans, she stretched his organ full length.

"Aaah! Aaah, no!" he bubbled through the detritus filling his mouth and throat.

At that moment three security men burst through the door. "Stop, Miss, stop!" one of them shouted.

"No!" The knife flashed down, cut through its target like a cleaver through sausage. Blood flew in a crimson haze and shot over Ruth's face, arms and blouse. She dropped the severed member just as strong hands grasped her shoulders and pulled her away. "You'll kill him!" one of the security men screamed.

"No! No," she cried hysterically. "I haven't killed him enough — can never kill him enough!"

The two women hugged each other like a pair of drunks on a street corner and sobbed uncontrollably.

Sixteen

Brent felt the icy wind on his face and his body trembled with the vibrations of the Pegasus XXX radial engine that powered the antique Fairey Swordfish. Colonel Sean Townsend had not mislead them. They were indeed surprised. He still had trouble believing that he was actually flying in this ancient warplane that came into service in 1936. They were only making 100 knots.

Brent trembled with more than just the vibrations. It was very cold at 12,000 feet. He shifted his shoulders against the restraints and grasped his arms, trying to shake off the effects of the cold which penetrated like frozen daggers despite a wool-lined jacket and flying suit, sheepskin gauntlets lined with stockinette fleece and a Type C wired naval helmet with goggles. And his face irritated him, the oxygen mask sticking to his flesh and causing a thin layer of perspiration to form and cloy with his persistent stubble. Brent cursed his tough beard and wished he had shaved twice and much closer.

"All we've got, old chaps," Townsend had said that morning as a rating drove Brent, Colonel Bernstein, and Elroy Rubin to the flight line. "Behold, the

'Stringbag,' " Townsend had chortled as the Land Rover screeched to a halt in front of two of the biplanes.

"Why these old crates?" Bernstein asked.

"Only aircraft we have with an arrester hook."

"Where in the world did you find them?"

"The Fleet Air Arm at Yeovilton had them both in their museum. Kept them in boffo shape, spit and polish and all that — tip-top flying condition."

"Cain't believe this, Elroy drawled.

"Did their bit and more, you know," Townsend said pridefully. "Scouted for *Warspite,* off Narvik, put a fish up Bismark's arse, sank one 'Eytie' battleship at Taranto and damaged two others. Served throughout the whole bloody dustup."

Standing before the aircraft were two pilots as archaic as their machines. Townsend explained that both had served with 836 squadron, which was the last operational Swordfish unit. In fact, Brent's pilot had been the last commanding officer of 836 Squadron. He was retired Commander Bertram Hollister. The second pilot was Lieutenant Harvey Proctor.

Hollister was all business, but sometimes a droll sense of humor crept through. "You, sir, Commander Ross, will fly in the telegraphist, air gunner's cockpit — man our devastating Lewis gun."

"That's WW One," Brent had said. "Point-three-oh-three caliber, ninety round magazine."

"Right you are, Commander Ross. But it's a ninety-six-round magazine. Be sure to shoot down any of Kadafi's ME-109s foolish enough to venture into range."

The Englishmen all laughed. Brent saw no humor in the remark.

"And you, Colonel Bernstein," Hollister continued. "You can enjoy the spacious luxury of my observer's cockpit. And please, gentlemen," he jibed, tongue firmly in cheek, "please note all of our cockpits are air-conditioned with the freshest of sea breezes." Again only the Englishmen laughed.

"How will you know where to rendezvous with *Yonaga?*" Bernstein asked.

Townsend answered, "We had a signal from Admiral Fujita an hour ago and I just picked it up from the WT. You will rendezvous with fighters and be led to the battle group."

Brent sighed. "The whole world must know where they are."

Townsend nodded and grimness hardened his face. "Actually, they're somewhere off the Canaries."

"Secret transmission?"

"No CNN reported it, this morning."

"CNN?" Brent repeated in shock.

"Yes. They were actually trying to track the battle group with a DC-3. The CAP drove them off with warning shots."

"Good Lord."

The strumming of wires, the thump of the propeller, roar of exhaust brought Brent's mind back to the present. He looked at the wing tips only twenty-two feet away. There was nothing between him and oblivion except a fragile metal airframe, a pair of fabric-covered wings, tortured wires, straining struts, and an old 750-horsepower engine. Glancing up at the wide center section of the top wing, his heart took a jump as if it were trying to clog his throat. The fabric on the wing was actually bellying up into the suction above the airfoil, the vacuum that pulled the machine into the sky. A rip in this fabric and they were all dead men.

He looked around at the limitless dimensions around him. He was insignificant, a meddling insect that could be stamped out at the whim of the elements, a crack in a strut, tear in the fabric, a stuck valve in the engine. He was a trespasser, a transient speck that could vanish in a blink like lint on the wind.

He shook his head to purge the morbid thoughts, pounded his ears. They ached and his sinuses felt like they had been blown up by a tire pump. He looked at the other "Stringbag" flying just a hundred feet off their starboard side. He waved. Elroy, sitting in the gunner's cockpit, waved back. The wave was stiff and Brent knew the Texan was freezing, too. He looked overhead at their escort. Just 1,000 feet above, six Grumman FX-1000s cruised, weaving and turning to maintain station over the two slow biplanes.

At that moment the first pair of Grumman F8F Bearcats swept past. Dropping out of the thin overcast, they shot by with such velocity, they appeared more like projectiles fired out of a gun than winged aircraft. They hurtled down at a speed that was at least four times that of the Swordfish. Brent heard voices squawking on the fighter frequency and the FX-1000s turned back. Within seconds, two Bearcats flew far ahead, two to each side and four more astern and very high. Staring at the lethal little plane, Brent cheered and waved. He could not hear the others, but every man in the antique biplanes was waving. They were almost home.

Then he saw them, two *Fletchers* knifing through the sea, leaving boiling white wakes. The whole battle group must be close behind. Then he caught sight of the great carrier, and then, a mile astern, *Bennington*. A few minutes later, he saw on the far horizon, the squat, lethal hull of the *New Jersey* with her nine sixteen-inch guns trained fore and aft. Escorts were neatly spaced around all three capital ships. The massed power brought a feeling of confidence and the knowledge he was almost home a rush of anticipation.

As he watched, *Yonaga* and her escorts turned simultaneously into the wind. With perfect synchronization, it was as if one mind, one hand, was on the helm of every vessel. And literally one was: the mind of Admiral Hiroshi Fujita. Pennant Two flapped at *Yonaga*'s yardarm. She was ready to receive aircraft. Losing altitude, Hollister passed her on her starboard side turned ahead of the carrier and then flew past her port side. Crewmen were waving and pointing. Brent was sure most of them were laughing.

Finally, the turn astern of the carrier and Hollister began his approach. Brent could see the landing control officer, yellow paddles extended, bending from side to side, leaning, working the Swordfish down. Brent prayed the old pilot had one more good landing in him. Finally, the paddles were crossed at the officer's knees and Hollister cut the throttle. With the three-bladed propeller just ticking over, the biplane fluttered and washed about in the breeze like a glider. To counter drift, Hollister opened the throttle a couple notches, the Pegasus roared, and the "Stringbag" seemed to swoop down onto the deck like a drunken hawk. The horrified control officer waved his paddles frantically and then pointed them both toward the bow. Hollister ignored the "wave off" and pulled the throttle all the way back, almost killing the engine. Brent closed his eyes and crossed himself.

First he felt the divided-axle landing gear pound onto the deck so hard he thought he was going to go through the bucket seat. A bounce and then a silent shout of joy as the arrester hook grabbed a cable and the old plane was jerked down to a bouncing a halt. Brent opened his eyes as he was flung forward against his restraints by his own momentum. "Thank God," he breathed to himself. And the wings were still on. "Remarkable!"

Immediately, Hollister switched off the idling engine and Brent could hear the old Pegasus hissing and ticking as it cooled. The breeze wafted the exhaust back, and the stink of burned petrol and oil filled the cockpit. Almost instantly, handlers and a small vehicle were pushing and pulling the aircraft forward while other handlers climbed up on the Swordfish. While Brent pulled off his clumsy gauntlets, a young rating in a head to toe yellow suit reached in and disconnected his oxygen and radio leads. "Welcome home, Commander Ross," he said as he unsnapped the single lock that released Brent's seat belt and shoulder harness.

Sighing with relief, Brent said, "It's good to be back in one piece." The rating laughed.

Brent hoisted himself out of the cockpit.

Commander Yoshi Matsuhara was waiting on the deck as Brent jumped down from the wing. Clutching Brent like a father finding his long-lost son, he said, "Your back, Brent-san. Thank the gods. Amaterasu has been kind."

Slapping Yoshi on the back, Brent said, "Lord it's good to see you, old friend."

The two men separated and Bernstein grabbed Yoshi's hand. *"Shalom,"* the Israeli said, grinning with unabashed affection.

"Shalom aleichem," the Japanese laughed back.

"I'll make a Jew of you, yet, Commander," Bernstein quipped.

"Right after you show me your *Yamato damashii* by beating me in a bout of kendo, you old *shlepper.*"

"Will a sound drubbing in chess do, *schlemiel?*"

Everyone laughed and then hurried toward the island as Lieutenant Harvey Proctor galloped his

Swordfish down the deck. Before the last cable pulled the bomber to a complete halt, Lieutenant Elroy Rubin leaped from the aircraft and ran to the island. "Whew. Near busted my butt in that gallopin' goose. Shoot, I done rode longhorns that weren't that ornery." He saluted Yoshi who saluted back.

With the salute, Yoshi became all business. "Admiral Fujita is waiting for you."

They hurried into the island and headed forward to the elevator. Yoshi said, "You heard about Tomoko, Brent-san?" The joy of reunion vanished.

"Yes. Horrible. I'm sorry."

"Did you hear the latest newscast?"

"Civilian?"

"Yes."

Brent shook his head negatively. "We've been flying for the last six hours."

"Harry Goodenough made an attempt on a Mossad agent named Ruth Moskowitz."

Brent stopped in his tracks. Irving and Elroy gathered close.

"Oh, no. Good God, no. We were afraid of that."

"You know her, Brent-san?"

"Yes."

"They fought him off. They are bruised and battered but all right. He's in critical condition—not expected to live."

"They? Who?"

"An old friend of yours, Brent-san, Sarah Aranson—Sarah Aranson and Ruth Moskowitz nearly killed him."

"Sarah Aranson?"

"Yes, Brent. According to the report, Sarah is Ruth's aunt."

"Oh, my God!"

Yoshi provided no more information. Late for a

326

meeting with his air group commanders, he hurried below to the gallery deck.

Walking through the island and acknowledging the salutes and welcoming remarks of crewmen, Brent's mind was whirling with thoughts of Ruth and Sarah. Now he understood the strong resemblance. Sarah always looked youthful, probably almost like Ruth's twin, if she still held her years. All the way up to Flag Country in the elevator and while walking in the passageways, the thoughts of the two women filled his mind. Did they compare notes on him? Of course they did. Oh, God, they must have had some good laughs. But they were unharmed. Fought off a professional assassin and almost killed him. They were tough, knew their karate and judo. Petite, slight women, both of them, but well-trained and superbly conditioned.

His thoughts were interrupted when they halted at the admiral's door. A brief knock and the door was opened by a seaman guard.

Admiral Fujita was seated behind his desk. While the three officers bowed and seated themselves in front of the desk, the old man's eyes studied silently. He gestured and the seaman guard stepped out into the passageway. Then Brent caught the Admiral's eyes probing his. He wondered what thoughts were working through that labyrinthine mind. He had seen the spark of emotion when the admiral first saw him.

For ten long years they had fought side by side, forging a bond of steel, tempered in the crucible of battle. Yet, Brent had fallen into a trap in Kadafi's "tent," been the dupe who had been conveniently blamed for the collapse of the talks. At least, that was how the Arabs painted the picture. Did Fujita buy it? And what difference did it make? Everyone knew both sides had been preparing for battle while the talks droned on, both in Libya and Geneva. Yet, he had been in a position of trust and could be court martialed for his behavior, dismissed, sent home in disgrace. Bond or no bond, Fujita would do it if it were the correct military decision.

"Colonel Bernstein," Fujita began, "I would like an oral report now and a written report later on your negotiations"—he looked at Brent—"and ancillary events you experienced in Libya." Brent twisted uncomfortably.

Bernstein gave a complete description of the talks, Arab intransigence, Kadafi's irrational behavior, the almost insurmountable language barriers, lavish entertainment and clumsily contrived treachery directed at Brent Ross.

"Treachery?"

"Yes, Admiral. Commander Ross was drugged and led into a seduction by one of Kadafi's dancers."

"I am quite aware—the whole world is aware. The media pounced on the story." He turned to Brent, "You were drugged?"

"I won't make excuses, Sir."

"I know, Commander, but please tell your story as you experienced it."

"She used hashish—burned it. I didn't know what it was, I have never smelled it before."

"You paid her."

"A hundred dollars. It was supposed to be a bribe to get her to leave—out of my room without an incident."

The old man sighed. "Colonel Bernstein, are you convinced that Commander Ross was tricked?"

"Most definitely, sir. I knew the girl, saw her approach—she was nothing but a trollop, trained for her nefarious task." He hunched forward, "It's an old Middle East trick to disparage an enemy—have him violate the hospitality of your tent." He pulled on his tiny spade of a beard, "Keep in mind, Admiral, she had visited Brent on the first night and he had remained aloof to her. She had to drug him to make her seduction."

"Right on, Colonel," Elroy added.

"Very well," Fujita said. "I knew you would not jeopardize the mission willfully, Commander Ross." He tapped the desk. "The book is closed."

"Thank you, sir." Brent's tight muscles eased and he sagged back.

Fujita said, "Contrary to what you may think, your mission was not a complete failure. Colonel Latimer Stewart and Captain Ronald Sparling are back in the United States. Commander Henri DuCarme and Major Horst Fritschmann were released to North Korea and returned to Libya."

"DuCarme was a total incompetent, sir," Brent said. He handled *Abu Bakr* like a complete idiot. He should've sunk *Haida*."

"That is why Kadafi wanted him."

"Sir."

"According to intelligence, DuCarme was executed in a most ingenious fashion." There was the silence of creeping fog and the men stared straight ahead. "It was their delightful pipe up the rectum treatment with rats added for amusement. It takes a long time."

"My God," Elroy said.

"Sadists," Bernstein cried out.

"But not unexpected."

"Correct, Admiral," Bernstein said. "They can no longer surprise with their savagery."

The old man nodded. "All of you, a job well done."

"Well done?"

"Yes, you gained time for us."

"Sir," Brent said. "Even CNN knows your inten-

329

tions and the Arabs may be savages, but they're not fools."

"Our battle group is headed for the Med, Admiral," Bernstein said. "Correct?"

"That is correct."

"The works at Rabta—nerve and mustard gas, the atomic bomb."

"They will have a twenty-kiloton bomb within a few weeks or less, Colonel Bernstein."

"It could all be a ruse, a scheme to lure us in within range of their land-based aircraft, Admiral," Brent suggested.

"I have considered that," the admiral answered. He shrugged his bony shoulders. "Intelligence tells us differently. The bomb is a real menace. We can take no chances. We must attack even if the whole thing is a fraud."

Elroy said, "Admiral, they's got more fighters than the hair on a hound dog's hind leg. Our bombers cain't bust their way through."

The old man smiled. "We have Sicily."

"Sicily!" the three men chorused.

Fujita explained how the Italian government, with the intervention of the Pope, had allowed the Israeli Air Force to use three fighter strips on the island. "And," he concluded, "they will base at least four squadrons of the latest version of the North American P-51 Mustang on the island. They can give us cover and with their enormous range, even escort our bombers to Rabta."

"The enemy carriers and cruisers?"

"We will engage them. The cruisers, *Dzerzhinsky* and *Zhdanov*, cannot outgun *New Jersey*." The tiny fingers clashed and finger tips drummed. "And remember, their air groups for their new Russian carrier, *Baku*, will not be completely trained. I suspect they will pull their surface forces back and plan to stop us with land-based air power."

Brent said, "But we can still find ourselves engaging both carrier based and land-based aircraft."

"Yes. I welcome the challenge." Fujita's rheumy eyes moved from man to man. "Bushido teaches the samurai to always attack, seek out his enemy and destroy him in one final, decisive battle." The eyes continued their restless movements. He smiled. "I know what you are thinking." He did not wait for a response. "You think we can be falling into our enemy's trap, that we can be destroyed." The silence was heavy, like weights on the backs of all the men. "True, but remember"—he patted the *Hagakure*—"the book teaches us, 'One should not hesitate, but make his decision in the space of seven breaths, and if there is a choice of living or dying, it is better to die facing one's enemy.' "

At that moment, one of the phones rang. Leaning forward, Brent picked it up and handed it to Admiral Fujita. The old man listened for a moment and the placed the instrument in its cradle. He said in a calm voice, "The *New Jersey* has just been torpedoed."

Seventeen

From the flag bridge, Brent could see a huge black pall hanging over *New Jersey*. Brent Ross, Rear Admiral Whitehead, and Lieutenant Commander Nobomitsu Atsumi all flanked Admiral Fujita and stared through their glasses. Fujita brought the entire force into a wide wheeling turn, pivoting on the battleship as a hub.

Repeatedly, Fujita had tried frantically to contact the captain of *New Jersey*. He tried again: "Bridge to bridge. To Captain McManus. Damage report!" Fujita shouted at the talker, Seaman Naoyuki.

"Nothing yet, sir."

"Sacred Buddha! We cannot remain here."

Brent stared through his glasses at three destroyers charging at flank speed off *New Jersey*'s port bow, water frothing at their bows like sun-maddened dogs. They seemed to have the scent. Great columns of water shot skyward as 600-pound depth charges ripped the ocean. Fighters of the CAP swooped and dived. One actually fired a burst into the sea to the port side and ahead of one of the destroyers.

"He has him," Whitehead said. "They can see him from the sky. An eye in the sky is the best sonar."

Two of the destroyers moved in at flank speed,

crossing, firing K-guns and dropping charges. The third, too, cleaved the point of attack, dropping charges as fast as they could be rolled and fired. Then Brent saw it. Heaved from the sea by two great explosions, a black-hulled *Whiskey* broke the surface and wallowed in a welter of mist and roiling seas. High pressure air blew spray in sheets from her vents.

"She's blowing her tanks!" Brent shouted.

"She's done for," Whitehead said. "Must be taking water."

Fujita shouted at Naoyuki, "To DD-1. No prisoners."

The talker spoke into his mouthpiece.

Brent watched as crewmen scurried from the dying submarine. Casually, a destroyer machine gunned the men off her decks and in the water. There was no pity in Brent, instead, he felt a deep sense of satisfaction, a twisted kind of fulfillment. He licked his lips and smiled.

He shifted his glasses to the battleship. One torpedo should not cause severe damage to an armored, belted and compartmented ship of the *Iowa* class. But the new semtex-tipped 533 torpedo packed a terrific wallop.

Fujita spoke softly into Brent's ear. Instead of admitting his eyes were failing, he said, "You have the best eyes on the ship, Brent-san, is she listing?"

"No, sir, they must be counterflooding. She's drawing a little more water forward, but she is underway at a reduced speed."

"Give me an estimate."

"Maybe twelve knots."

The old man stared through his glasses and nodded.

Naoyuki's voice galvanized everyone. "Damage report from Captain McManus. A preliminary damage control survey reports a torpedo hit between frames forty-seven and sixty at a depth of about seventeen feet on the port side. A hole about twenty-four feet long by ten feet high has been opened. At the point of impact, the antitorpedo bulkheads and their transverse stiffeners broke or have been damaged. Have taken water in the pump and dynamo rooms with minor flooding in Boiler Room Two. Have banked the fires. Am proceeding at reduced speed while damage repaired. Request permission to put in Gibraltar."

Fujita pounded the windscreen. "In the name of Amaterasu, what have the gods inflicted upon us?"

Whitehead said grimly, "Perhaps we should wait, sir. At least let *New Jersey* jury-rig repairs."

The old man shook his head. "We will proceed." He waved. "Our power is in our eagles. Let the devil send all his hordes, we will kill them all."

The lookouts, Atsumi, all shouted *"Banzai!"* Brent added his.

Fujita said to Naoyuki, "To Captain McManus, permission granted. Will proceed without you. I will leave two destroyers to escort you. Good luck!"

While Naoyuki spoke into his mouthpiece, the old man leaned over the voice tubes and brought the entire force back to its base course—a course that would take them to the center of the Straits of Gibraltar.

Staring into his glasses over the stern, Brent could see the wounded battleship steaming slowly with her two escorts. He felt a deep sadness, an empty feeling of loss as when a close friend dies. And they would miss those big sixteen-inch guns.

334

* * *

The day they entered the Straits of Gibraltar was dreary and portentous. The sky was solid gray, as if it had been sloshed with dirty laundry water. Only a glowing gray-white ring overhead hinted at the presence of the sun.

"*Ark Royal* was lost here, Admiral Fujita," Whitehead had warned when the force approached in the early morning.

Fujita's encyclopedic mind went to work: "Torpedoed by U-81 in November of 1941. *Ark Royal*'s damage control was appalling. She sank thirteen hours later and she had two tugs from Gibraltar to help her. Her captain should have been court-martialed."

Fujita increased speed to twenty-eight knots and with a dozen FX-1000s added to the CAP, the force swept into the Mediterranean. Brent felt a fateful clutch of predestiny, somber foreboding. He had known it many times. The feeling of powerlessness to control his own fate that all men suffer before battle had returned. True, he was anxious to meet the enemy, to kill him, annihilate him, but, he, too, could be obliterated. The decisions propelling him into mortal danger had been made long ago by many men in all parts of the world. He was a pawn, nothing more than a sacrifice in a global chess game of life and death. Thousands would die in the next few days, without choice, without benefit of their own decisions. It was a turn of the wheel, the flip of a card, a crap game. He had stepped to the table many times. Would he roll a seven this time?

His thoughts were interrupted when a staff meeting was called in Flag Plot.

* * *

Pointer in hand, Fujita stood before a map of the Mediterranean while Commander Brent Ross, Commander Yoshi Matsuhara, Rear Admiral Whitehead, CIA agent Elliot Amberg, Lieutenant Commander Nobomitsu Atsumi, and Colonel Irving Bernstein, with Ephraim Sneerson at his side, stared intently. Lieutenant Sahei Tsuda, the dive bomber commander, and Lieutenant Taneo Nogi, the torpedo bomber commander, also hunched over the table. However, the Executive Officer, Captain Mitake Arai, had the deck and was not present. With the enemy so near, the admiral would not trust the ship to a junior officer.

Fujita traced a line through the Mediterranean to a point southeast of Malta. "Our launch point. We should be there in about fifty-four hours." He glanced at Tsuda and Nogi. "We will launch twenty-seven Aichi D-3As and twenty-seven Nakajima B-5Ns. That will leave us with twenty-five Aichis and twenty-three Nakajimas in the event we engage enemy surface ships."

"The enemy fleet, sir?" Lieutenant Tsuda asked.

Fujita gestured toward Schneerson. The Israeli said, "They have vanished from the eastern Mediterranean. But there are reports three enemy carriers, two cruisers and escorts are here"—he stabbed the chart—"north of Crete in the Sea of Crete steaming on an easterly heading—opening the range."

Nogi said, "Your Mossad operatives spotted them?"

Schneerson shook his head, "No, CNN."

Atsumi suddenly exclaimed, "Sacred Buddha, war is becoming the best show on television."

336

Whitehead chuckled sardonically, "Can boost ratings—that's for sure."

Staring at the chart, Brent Ross was troubled. He entered the discussion. "That's an ideal position. They're over five hundred miles from Israel and about the same distance from our launch point." He threw a hard look at Nogi. "And they can change course at any time."

Whitehead observed, "They have three options—attack us or make a dash for the Suez Canal or head for the Bosporus and the Black Sea."

"True," Fujita acknowledged. "In any event, no matter how they commit themselves, our reconnaissance or Israeli aircraft will search for them. Their only safe haven would be the Black Sea. But not even a motor launch could transit the Dardanelles without being sighted."

Whitehead was skeptical, "This move by the Arab fleet could be an old Apache trick to lure the calvary In."

"Apache? Cavalry?" both Tsuda and Nogi said, looking at each other in confusion. The other Japanese, too, seemed puzzled.

"Yes," the American rear admiral said. "Let your enemy think you're retreating, tempt him to move recklessly, and then ambush him." And then before thinking, "It worked at Midway."

There were coughs from the Japanese, strained looks, and Whitehead suddenly examined his hands awkwardly. His gaffe had opened an old wound. His face glowed red.

Picking up Whitehead's thinking, Brent cut through the silence with an emphatic statement, "They'll attack us, sir."

"You are convinced, Commander."

"They'd have nothing to lose, Admiral Fujita." He gestured at the chart, and Fujita nodded acquiescence. Brent walked to the chart and used his finger as a pointer. "If I were the enemy commander I would steam toward us until I cleared the western tip of Crete. That would put him four hundred miles east of our carriers. And then launch everything he's got."

"We'll sink them all," Nogi said smugly.

Fujita picked up the thread of Brent's concern. "No. I believe Commander Ross is right. There is a good chance the enemy battle group will reverse course and steam east under forced draft out of range. Our bombers could never catch him."

"Don't you see," Whitehead said, regaining composure. "His air groups can land in Libya. They don't have to return to their carriers."

Nogi pounded his head. "How stupid. It's so obvious." He looked up. "That means he could throw as much as one hundred fifty carrier-based planes at us."

Brent said, "Very few fighters, if any."

"Why?"

"The threat of Israeli attack. He must maintain a strong CAP."

"Good thinking, Admiral Whitehead and Commander Ross," Fujita said. He thumped the chart thoughtfully while Brent returned to his chair. He made his decision, "We'll send every bomber that can fly to Rabta and keep our strong CAP. If for any reason our returning eagles cannot land on *Yonaga* or *Bennington*, they can proceed to Sicily." He glanced at Matsuhara, Tsuda, and Nogi. "Include that option in your point option data." The flyers chorused, "Aye, aye, sir."

Katsubé suddenly blurted, *"Banzai!"* Everyone ignored him.

Brent was upset. Why had Fujita not anticipated this enemy tactic? His age was showing. He was tired. Unable to even stand erect. And why had the other Japanese followed his thinking so rigidly, without question, a single challenge? It was bushido, the inflexible law that dictated blind obedience, the abandonment of personal volition. It has been shown throughout Japanese military history. Suicidal *"Banzai"* attacks. The kamikazes. *Seppuku* in the face of defeat.

Bernstein's voice broke through his depression with encouraging news. "Remember, the Israeli Army will launch offensives all along the Ben Gurion Line tomorrow."

"Yes," Fujita said. And then looking around at the faces of his staff, "This should keep the enemy occupied—divert most of his air power."

"Sir, I will lead my eagles in their attack on Rabta," Nogi said.

"Correct. All works in the complex except the reactor."

"My ordnance, sir? After all, my aircraft are torpedo bombers."

"What would you recommend, Lieutenant Nogi?"

"Four two hundred-fifty-kilogram bombs," Nogi said, slipping back into metrics. He glanced at the Americans, "That is, four five hundred-fifty-pound bombs."

"Better than torpedoes," Whitehead quipped. "Can't sink that place."

There was a tension relieving chuckle.

Fujita looked at Yoshi and continued, "Commander Matsuhara, you will escort the bombers to their target. We will keep Commander Steve Elkins' twelve F-6F Hellcats for CAP. You will take six Seafires and twenty-nine Zeros as escorts."

"Only twelve, sir?" Whitehead said. "With the enemy threat?" Fujita waved him off impatiently.

"*Bennington,* sir?" Yoshi asked.

Fujita looked at Whitehead. "Captain Treynor will keep all twenty-four of his F-8F Bearcats for CAP." Whitehead nodded and Fujita thumped the chart four times. "Captain Treynor will attack with all of his bomber strength, twenty-four TBFs, twenty-four SBDs, and eight SB-2Cs. They will be escorted by his two squadrons of F-4Us. Their assignment will be to mop up at the Arab bases at Tripoli, Al Kararim, Mistatah, and Zuwarah."

"Mop up?"

"Yes, ten hours before we launch, Israeli fighters and bombers based on Sicily will attack all enemy airfields."

This time Katsube's *"Banzai!"* was joined by those of the other Japanese and Brent's. Optimism swept through the room like a spring breeze.

"Bombers?" Brent Ross asked looking at Schneerson. "I thought you only had fighters based there."

Fujita gave the floor to Schneerson. The young Mossad agent said, "Top secret until now, Commander. We have sent most of our mediums and heavies to Sicily—stripped ourselves. That's why we haven't been able to maintain an effective reconnaissance over the eastern Med." He glanced at some notes. "The bomber force includes two squadrons of North American B-25s—twenty-four Mitchells in all. Three Boeing B-17 Flying Fortresses, two Consolidated B-24 Liberators and twelve Douglas A-26

Invaders. Three squadrons of our new, souped-up P-51s will escort them."

There was backslapping, and spirits soared higher than they had been since the loss of *New Jersey*.

Brent interrupted the celebration, *"Bennington's* Douglas A1-B Skyraiders. They are our most powerful bomber, have our best radar. How do you plan to use them, Admiral Fujita?"

The old man leaned on the table. He was obviously tiring. What he revealed was news to everyone. "Yes, they have highly sophisticated radar equipment — can find their targets in complete darkness. We will utilize this advantage. I will send them in at night."

"Before our strike or after?"

"Before our strike and after the Israeli attack. We will launch them while four hundred miles at sea. This will give them a seven-hundred-mile run-in. The Arabs will expect us to launch at dawn, south of Malta, at about two hundred miles, which was our launch point in 1986. The Skyraiders will fly at a hundred feet or less to avoid radar. This long-range launch, low-level attack at night should take the enemy completely by surprise. They will concentrate on Rabta's radar, AA, and all targets except the reactor. I have been assured they will see the four story reactor building very clearly on their radar screens. And, the Arabs might just think we will be content with just the Israeli and Skyraider strikes."

"The Arabs' night fighting capability?"

This time Fujita nodded at Bernstein. The Israeli said, "The Israeli Air Force has never mounted a serious night raid on the enemy. As far as we know, his night fighting capabilities are limited, but, of course you know the entire complex is ringed with heavy AA emplacements—all calibers from mobile twenty-three-millimeter multiple mounts up to one-hundred-twenty-two-millimeter quick-firing cannons." The men nodded soberly. "And the Russians have supplied their best radar, the P-10 and Knife Rest B. However, the Skyraiders should catch him unaware and the Israeli Air Force attack should help disrupt his entire air defense network, too."

"Good. Good."

Whitehead's mind dwelled on another problem. Thoughtfully, he said to Admiral Fujita, "Do you plan to take the Skyraiders back aboard at night—illuminate *Bennington*?"

"Negative, Admiral Whitehead. They will be launched at 0100 and return after dawn at about 0600."

Whitehead shook his head and showed his experience as a carrier man. "Treynor could be caught trying to launch and receive aircraft at the same time."

"True," Fujita admitted. "However, the Skyraider has an enormous range. They can orbit our battle group or fly to Sicily if we cannot take them aboard." Whitehead nodded.

"Any more questions?" Fujita asked.

"*New Jersey?*" Tsuda asked.

Fujita sighed. "She is under repair at Gibraltar, now. Captain McManus will get underway as soon as the hull is patched."

Whitehead said grimly, "She's out of this operation."

"I am afraid you are correct, Admiral," Fujita said. He turned to the shrine and clapped twice. Everyone stood. Atsumi supported Katsube.

Fujita invoked Buddha's first sermon. "May the

342

Wheel of the Law turn our way. Let us find the middle path and find our way past hedonism and nihilism to asceticism and the Four Noble Truths. Only in this way can our karmas become pure, and only the pure of heart can prevail in the perils to come." He fell silent for a moment, raised his head to the heavens, and called upon Shinto: "Oh Izanagi and Izanami who created our sacred islands and begat the sun goddess Amaterasu-O-Mi-Kami, the moon goddess Tsuki-Yomi and storm god, Susano, be at our sides in the strife to come. Bless our arms and help us prevail in the name of your progeny and our Emperor Akihito."

"Banzai!" and, *"Tenno heiko bansai!"* filled the room.

Bernstein raised his hands. "Admiral Fujita, I would like to speak for the Jews and gentiles in this room."

"Of course."

The Israeli opened a book of psalms. He read from the twenty-fifth psalm: "Unto thee, Oh Lord, do I lift up my soul. Oh my God, in thee do I trust, let me not be ashamed, let not my enemies triumph over me. Yea, none that wait on thee will be put to shame; let those be put to shame who deal treacherously without cause. Show me oh Lord, thy ways, teach me thy paths . . ." He looked up and added, "And let me destroy thy enemies!"

Cheers and more shouts of *"Banzai!"*

Fujita quieted the men and turned to Yoshi Matsuhara and said, "Commander some of your haiku. You are our best poet."

"Thank you, Admiral," Yoshi said modestly. The pilot mulled self-consciously for a moment, tucked his lips under and said, "I have bared my sword, let

343

it not be sheathed, until it drinks the blood of my enemy."

The men roared their approval for a full minute. Then Fujita quieted them. Face cracked by a rare smile, the old sailor said, "This meeting is closed. Return to your duties."

The men filed from the room.

Eighteen

The blaring command, "Pilots man your planes!" sent Commander Yoshi Matsuhara running across the flight deck. It was a lumbering run; parachute slung under his backside like a cushion, helmet, goggles, and clipboard in hand, sword bouncing at his side and hitting his leg, inflatable life jacket snug around his waist. He was hot: flying suit, "belt of a thousand stitches," with icons sewed in for good luck tight around his waist; two pairs of wool socks and fleece-lined flying boots. Finally, with the help of a rigger, he heaved himself up onto a wing, found the stirrup and made a big swing of legs to get into the cockpit. A few curses and jerky movements of his rear end settled the parachute into the bucket seat, and then his crew chief, Shoishi Ota, adjusted his safety harness and snapped the lock closed. Yoshi pulled down hard on his helmet while Ota connected oxygen and radio leads. Pulling his gloves on, Yoshi glanced at the instrument panel. All was ready. He nodded at Ota and the crewchief dropped down to the deck and moved ahead of the aircraft and to starboard, eyes fixed on his pilot.

Yoshi followed a routine that had helped keep

him alive for over a half-century. After assuring himself the canopy was locked open in take off position, he pushed down on the brake, likewise assuring himself it was locked. In short jerky movements he moved the control column forward and backward and side to side, turning his head while pushing the rudder stirrups, watching the ailerons, rudder, and elevators respond. He dropped the flaps and retracted them. The controls were tight, responsive. It was time to unleash the 3,200-horsepower brute under his cowling.

He leaned forward and switched on his magnetos. The flow of current brought the instruments to life and his left hand moved to the throttle and mixture control quadrant, pushing the throttle slightly ahead, the mixture control all the way to full rich. The turn of a corrugated knob set the Curtiss constant-speed electric propeller on fine pitch. Satisfied, he nodded at Ota, who was standing well clear of the propeller. Yoshi circled a finger over his head, and Ota responded with the same signal.

The commander punched the fuel booster and starter. Instantly, there was the whine of the energizer, and the big eighteen cylinder Sakae 43 *Taifu* began to fire with a barrage of bangs, gasping sputters, and coughs that shook the airframe and caused the wings to rock from side to side. The four-blade propeller jerked spasmodically with the stubborn engine until a sudden salvo sent it whirling in a blur. Within a minute, the faltering stopped as both banks of cylinders began firing, ripping open the peace of the morning with disciplined savagery.

346

He glanced at his fifteen American instruments which were inherited from the original prototype Wright Cyclone: tachometer reading 1200 rpms, oil temperature 97 degrees, oil pressure 45 pounds, manifold pressure 37 inches of mercury, cylinder head temperature 157. He nodded his approval and glanced to the left and rear at Pilot Officer Elwyn York's Seafire and then to the right at the Seafire of his other wingman, Flying Officer Claude Hooperman. Both Englishmen had preferred to keep RAF rank designations. Yoshi came back to York as the Cockney cranked up his engine.

The conventional way to start a Merlin was to pour a flood of electricity into the engine until its twelve cylinders began to fire. When the first two Seafires came aboard, Yoshi had seen this done by inserting starting handles on each side and winding furiously, coaxing the engine into life. This was slow, blistering toil that exhausted the strongest crewman. To avoid this tedious, backbreaking labor, specially designed trollies loaded with batteries had been imported from England. They could start the Merlin with a high-powered jolt or two. At that moment a burst of power from accumulation batteries sparked York's Merlin to creaking, wheezing turns. Finally, the Rolls Royce popped, crackled and roared to life, York carefully nursing it into a smooth idle.

Turning his head and using his rearview mirror, Yoshi could see row after row of Seafires and Zeros warming, backfiring black smoke and sending a blue haze over the stern. He took a deep breath and felt an amalgam of satisfaction and apprehension. He had power there, behind him, but the news from the Israeli attack had not been good. There was no word from the Skyraiders which had been swallowed by the night sky six hours earlier.

The Israeli attack had been met by swarms of Messerschmitt Bf 109s, Spitfires, Fock Wolfe 190s, and a few P-51s. Casualties had been heavy. Fourteen Israeli fighters had been lost, 13 B-25s, one B-17, and one B-24. However all of the fields at Tripoli, Al Kararim, Mistatah, and Zuwarah had been bombed and strafed. Damage had been enormous, with hangars wrecked and fuel dumps set afire. A bomb dump at Al Kararim had exploded. The Israelis claimed at least 50 enemy fighters destroyed in the air and, perhaps, another 150 fighters and bombers destroyed on the ground. Apparently, with *Yonaga*'s battle group far out of range at the time of attack, surprise had been almost complete. However, now Yoshi knew there would be no more surprises.

Radio Tripoli had been bleating for two days. "Assassins and the murderers of innocent women and children have been attacking Libya day and night." The broadcasts always eliminated the names of the targets. Then the usual, "All enemy attempts to slaughter the innocent have been thrown back with heavy losses by brave men from all over the world who have gathered to fight oppressive Japanese and American imperialists." And the announcers warned, "An elite 'Jihad Special Attack Corps' has been formed. The men of the 'Special Attack Corps' have pledged to sacrifice their lives to destroy the infidel imperialists."

"Arab kamikazes?" Fujita had said skeptically when the first reports had been copied.

"The Shi'ites can do it," Whitehead had warned. "Suicide attacks killed hundreds of American marines in Beirut and at the American embassy."

"Let them come," Fujita said. "We will help send them to their Muslim paradise."

Inevitably, with each broadcast the announcers closed by telling of bloody repulses of the Israeli attacks along the Ben Gurion Line and gave accurate estimates of the position of Fujita's battle group and promised they would all be sunk. Although Yoshi expected this propaganda, he found it disconcerting. "Special Attack Corps" had an especially menacing implication. The name had been borrowed from the Japanese suicide flyers of the Greater East Asia War, and every man knew it.

Another vexing, far more personal worry, took his mind from Radio Tripoli. It was his bladder that seemed to lose some of its capacity with each passing year. He was always very cautious about his liquid intake before a mission. In fact, he had drunk only a small amount of tea and then forced himself to urinate to the point of pain several times. It was almost inevitable the Zero's elimination tube would freeze at high altitude and he would probably be in the air for seven or eight hours; maybe more. Relieving himself would be impossible without suffering embarrassment when he landed. Learning from the Englishmen, he had only had a slab of dark hard bread for breakfast. Of course he had consumed the traditional samurai pre-battle saké toast and a single chestnut. That was all. Nothing that could blow him up with gas at altitude and cause bubbling distress in the middle of a dogfight.

349

He strained his eyes to the south. Where were the Skyraiders? There had been one garbled signal from the flight leader, Colonel Kent Tynan, that indicated heavy flak, jamming, and difficulty in finding the target. Had they succeeded? Why no word? Then despite a conscious effort to put Tomoko out of his mind, the epic horror crept back, crowding out the mission, everything. Even the smell seemed to fill the cockpit. His beloved reduced to stinking carrion and deliberately left for him to find. It was not just Goodenough. Everyone knew that. It came from the top. It was orders, bought and paid for. He would kill more of them. Gain some measure of revenge for Tomoko. Particularly that creature Rosencrance. The butcher of his wingman Willard-Smith and so many more. It had been rumored Rosencrance's Fourth Fighter Squadron had been transferred from the Marianas to the Middle East. If the gods were kind, they would meet and he would taste the sweet draught of revenge or die in the attempt. Even if he had to ram Rosencrance.

Then a voice crackled in his earphones, "Colonel Tynan reports three of his aircraft shot down, three dropped bombs in target area but results unknown."

Then Yoshi saw them. Two Douglas Skyraiders flying low and slow. Yoshi cursed. Only two, not three. They were approaching the *Bennington*. A flare arced from the second bomber. He reached down to a black baked enamel switch panel and threw Number Four. The carrier wave of the bomber frequency hissed in his ears. He heard Colonel Tynan's voice. "This is Madonna Leader.

350

Madonna Three has a wounded man. Request instructions."

Yoshi clamped his hands over his earphones as *Bennington* responded, "Madonna Leader this is Spark Plug. Madonna Flight proceed to Flapjack."

"Roger. Madonna Leader out." The Skyraiders passed over on a northerly heading that would take them to Sicily.

Yoshi scanned his instruments. At last, engine, cylinder head and oil temperature were up, pressure gauges satisfactory, and he was ready to take off. He gunned the engine and watched the tachometer climb to 2300, engine temperature hold steady, manifold pressure climb. Good! Twenty-three hundred was his take off rpms. He glanced at the bridge where Admiral Fujita, Brent Ross, Colonel Bernstein, and Rear Admiral Whitehead stared down. He waved. They waved back.

He shifted his eyes to the starboard bow where the control officer stood on his platform with his paddles at his side. Yoshi saluted him. The officer saluted back and pointed both paddles toward the bow where the steam vent was streaming a ribbon of vapor directly down the center of the deck. Thumbs up to Ota and the chocks were pulled and the handlers released his wings.

Yoshi punched the throttle ahead and released the brake and shouted, "Tomoko, this is for you!"

The fighter leaped like a caged bird fleeing to freedom and clawed its way into the air.

The sky was a beautiful soft blue, like the finest velvet, and the view from 25,000 feet was stupendous. Yoshi could see over 200 miles: to the west a corner of Tunisia, to the east the Gulf of Sidra, and below the greenish belt of the Libyan coast-line, while behind the Mediterranean lay like expensive blue-green wrapping paper caught by the sun in glittering ribbons of light. He could even detect the curvature of the earth.

He had no time to admire beauty. Ahead lay the monotonous brown-gray of the vast Libyan Desert, the enemy, and death. There was smoke in the distance, climbing at least 12,000 feet in the air. Rabta. The Skyraiders had done a better job than he had suspected. Then he noticed a yellowish tinge to the smoke. Mustard gas. They had hit the gas works.

He checked the rows of dials in front of him, searching for trouble. Rate-of-climb indicator, air-speed indicator, artificial horizon, all normal. Fuel pressure, oil pressure, oil temperature, RPM boost gauge, cylinder head temperature precisely where they belonged. Fuel gauges, magnetic compass, turn-and-bank indicator were working perfectly. Fuel mixture on lean and propeller pitch coarse. Finally, his eyes fell on the thermometer. He shivered.

It was very cold outside; the American thermometer showing 60 degrees below zero. The sun warmed Yoshi's face and shoulders, but the lower half of his body was in shadows, the cold biting cruelly. He tightened his scarf and adjusted the small cockpit heater which kept his right foot warm while his left foot numbed with the cold. He turned his head in the timeless ritual of the fighter pilot; his neck and back ached. He blamed the discomfort on the cold, never on aging muscles.

352

Brown-black puffs distracted him. Flak had picked them up the moment they crossed into Libyan airspace, scattering black blobs across the sky as if someone had shaken a loaded paint brush at the sky. Each burst spawned two more as the gunners volley fired, doubling and redoubling until the sky was blotched with malignant black patches, mottled with white puffs, veined with red green and yellow. Luckily, the bursts were wide and erratic, the gunners having trouble with the high-flying fighters. But the bombers 10,000 feet below were not as fortunate. The air boiled with destruction. Yoshi saw an Aichi touch a splotch and blow up, a flicker of incandescence that pulverized an aircraft and two men in the time it took to draw a breath. Another D3A was hit, and it turned slowly and headed back for the sea trailing petrol.

Yoshi thumbed the cover off his firing button and switched on his microphone. "Edo Flight, this is Edo Leader. Arm your guns." A hail of acknowledgments filled his earphones as he threw a switch and a red light burned on his panel. Then another switch brought his reflector sight to life, a 100-centimeter pink reticle glowing on transparent plastic just inside the bulletproof glass screen. They were only minutes from the target. Where were the enemy fighters? He turned his head in a continuous movement like a spectator at a furious tennis match. But saw nothing but empty sky marred only to the southwest, where a moving junkyard of grubby clouds swirled with inner energy which made even the gaps look somehow stained and dark. Could there be fighters there? It could be a dangerous place to fly. A desert storm might be brewing.

York's voice: "This is Edo Two. Me cock's up. Them buggers is about."

Hooperman's voice. "How can you tell, old boy. That divining rod's no bigger than a bit of cooked noodle and wouldn't know the difference between a bordello and a nursery."

"Radio discipline!" Matsuhara shouted. And then his peripheral vision caught them. Dozens of black specks on the western horizon, streaking out of the brewing storm where they should not have been. Now, it had become a perfect place for an ambush. Yoshi cursed. He should have expected it, expected the unexpected.

They were diving, making a run on the Aichis and Nakajimas. Had *Bennington's* raid been a failure? It was up to *Bennington's* air groups to take out what remained of the enemy strips at Tripoli, Al Kararim, Mistatah and Zuwarah. From 25,000 feet he had seen three of the bases and they appeared to be in ruins with no aircraft in operation. After all, they had been pounded by the heavy Israeli raid the day before. There must be another strip, perhaps more that intelligence had not uncovered. It made no difference. Dozens of black Messerschmitt Bf-109s were racing in at full throttle. They must engage those 109s. That was the only reality. He cursed himself again.

Yoshi switched on his microphone. "Edo Flight, this Edo Leader. Enemy fighters at two o'clock low. Edo Yellow give top cover, all other sections attack! Follow my lead. Hold your sections until first pass, then individual combat."

While the section leaders answered with "Edo

Blue," "Edo Yellow," "Edo Green," Yoshi turned his propeller to fine pitch, punched his throttle ahead, enriched his mixture, kicked right rudder, and rolled toward the ME-109s that were hurtling in like black darts.

Streaking downward, two stage, two speed supercharger screaming, Yoshi felt his tea and brown bread regurgitate like vinegar. There were at least forty enemy fighters, probably more. And he saw three black P-51s and two Spitfires in the enemy sections—the usual "finger four," four planes flying in pairs—the Arabs had used for years. No Focke Wolfe 190s were to be seen and the red Messerschmitt of Kenneth Rosencrance was nowhere in sight. Maybe the Fourth Fighter Squadron was still in the Western Pacific. Yoshi pounded the padded combing and cursed, cursed the absence of Rosencrance, cursed his own late interception.

The lead elements of the enemy fighters tore into the Aichis and Nakajimas. One Nakajima shed a wing and cartwheeled across the sky like a drunken acrobat, shedding wreckage like torn clothing. Another, hit in a bomb, exploded in its millisecond of glory, taking its executioner with it. An Aichi staggered off, reeling and twisting as if the pilot had drunk too much saké before taking off.

A dozen enemy planes turned toward the Japanese fighters raining down on them. Certainly, they must have seen the menace above. Should have expected it. But they had ignored Yoshi's squadrons. There must be more of the Arab aircraft above. They would be the responsibility of Lieutenant Keizo Kazutaka and his Yellow Section of nine Zeros.

355

A ME-109 jockeying for his killing angle behind a desperately jinking Nakajima grew in his sights. Yoshi concentrated on the enemy plane. The Arab pilot was so determined to kill the bomber that he committed the fighter pilot's cardinal sin of flying straight and level for perhaps a dozen seconds. He sat perfectly centered in the pink reticle of Yoshi's sight. Throttling back to reduce the vibrations, the enemy magnified easily and beautifully as if Yoshi had been working a microscope. He pulled up the nose gently and made the image drop. A touch of the stick and he moved the pip ahead for a one-half-length deflection. The wings reached the sight bars. "Now!" He pushed the red button.

Flames spouted from his wings and cowling as two twenty-millimeter cannons and two 7.7 machine guns raved to life. A raging blaze of gunfire, red winged with yellow, so brilliant he blinked and his eyes watered. Bullet streams flickered and slashed across the Messerschmitt.

It was only a two-second burst, but every round struck home. A shell blew off the cowling, others ripped open the forward fuel tank and drenched the cockpit. Then the 109 blew up, high-octane fuel mixed with oxygen making a furnace heat that incinerated the pilot, boiling him in his own body fluids before he could even open his canopy.

"*Banzai* Tomoko!" Yoshi shouted, pulling the control column back into his stomach. He must regain altitude. Dogfights devoured altitude. The man with altitude was usually the winner.

Now the sky was madhouse of twisting, firing, burning planes. The fighter frequency was filled with triumphant whoops, warning shouts, cries of fear. Yoshi heard an Englishman, Flying Officer Todd Wheeler, cry out, "I'm hit!"

"Bail out Todd!"

"I've bought it."

Trailing flame and black smoke a Seafire bored into the desert at 450 miles an hour. There was a gigantic blast. No parachute.

Rubin's voice: "Yahoo! Scratch one stinkin' skonk!" A Messerschmitt, tail blasted to tatters, spun and twisted like a seared moth crazed by a candle and then tumbled out of sight far below.

"Behind you Matsushima! Two of them."

"See them. Give me some help."

York's voice, "I'll bugger the bastard, Matsu!"

Yoshi saw a Seafire send a long burst into a black Spitfire. Trailing a white mist of glycol, the British-made fighter dove out of the scrap and raced downward and to the east. York did not pursue. Instead he stormed back into the scrap.

Yoshi had pulled up above the fight. Fully occupied with the Japanese fighters, the enemy left the bombers unmolested. The Aichis and Nakajima squadrons had been reduced by about ten aircraft, but the remainder bored on. The smoking Rabta complex was close ahead. He whooped with joy. The reactor building appeared intact; however, many of the large buildings around it were burning or showed bomb damage. The Skyraiders had done a much better job than he had expected.

Then Lieutenant Keizo Kazutaka's voice galvanized him. "Enemy fighters, eleven o'clock high," came through his earphones.

Yoshi looked up into the glare. His eyes widened and he shouted out a strange guttural sound cast with joy, anxiety, and hate. Twelve Messerschmitts led by a red machine with a tiger-striped 109 flying as wingman. The butcher Colonel Kenneth Rosencrance and his picked killers the Fourth Fighter Squadron. And his effeminate, murdering companion, Lieutenant Rudolph "Tiger Shark" Stoltz was hard on his rudder. Between them, they had accounted for over sixty allied planes. Yoshi owed them a debt; owed them for Tomoko, for Willard-Smith. He punched the great engine into overboost, and with a roar like an enraged lion, the incredible power plant pulled him in a near vertical climb.

He repeated his pledge: "Tomoko, this is for you!"

Nineteen

"Radar reports a large flight of aircraft ap-. proaching from 095, range 130 miles, flying low, Admiral," Seaman Naoyuki reported. "IFF reports aircraft unidentified."

"Sacred Buddha," Fujita said. Then, turning to Brent and Rear Admiral Whitehead, he added, "You were right. Must be the enemy's carrier air groups." Then to Naoyuki, "That is Scout Three's sector. I want a report."

"Scout Three does not answer."

"They've taken him out," Whitehead said.

"We have fifty minutes," Fujita said. Then a barrage of orders: "Stand by to launch all fighters. All AA batteries stand by. Send the order to *Bennington*. Escorts assume AA stations."

The *Fletchers* on *Yonaga*'s beams moved in close, helmeted AA crews at their guns.

Brent glanced down at the deck. The engines of six of Elkins' Hellcats were kicking over and beginning to warm. Soon, they would join their six airborne companions. *Bennington,* too, was preparing to launch all of her remaining fighters.

Quickly, the great ships came into the wind and

the aircraft raced into the sky. Soon, there were twenty-four F-8Fs and twelve F-6Fs, orbiting.

Brent tightened the chin strap of his helmet, and adjusted his life preserver. Everyone stared through his glasses to the east. The fighters circled at reduced speed. Conserving fuel. Waiting. It was dangerous to commit the fighters too soon. The Japanese had done this at Midway to American torpedo bombers and it cost them four carriers to dive bombers. Brent knew Fujita had this lesson in mind.

Suddenly, on the far eastern horizon, Brent saw flashes. Through his glasses, he could make out the upper works of one of the outlying *Fletchers*. Flame and brown smoke was leaping from her five-inch guns. Naoyuki said, "Julia One reports at least fifty enemy bombers closing at low altitude. Engaging."

"Julia One. That's DD-1, Captain Fite," Bernstein said.

Fujita barked orders: "Alert CAP. *Bennington* is to keep one squadron of Bearcats over the carriers. Our F-6Fs and a squadron of *Bennington's* Bearcats are to intercept approaching raid. Expedite! Engage! Engage! All AA batteries stand by! To *Bennington,* maneuver independently, am going to flank speed."

Naoyuki spoke into his mouthpiece, listened for a moment and said, *"Bennington* acknowledges, sir."

"Very well. All ahead flank!"

Immediately, Brent could feel the tempo of the great engines seven decks below pick and *Yonaga* surged ahead. His mind was not on the engines. He watched as the enemy planes approached like a

360

plague of locusts — torpedo bombers low on the water, dive bombers at about 7,000 feet. Then he saw the fighters. He caught his breath. Swarms of high-flying crosses with needle noses and squared off wingtips. ME-109s.

"Enemy fighters, Admiral," he reported quietly. "At least twenty-five, high."

"Sacred Buddha!"

Four of the *Fletchers* began firing. The machine-loaded five-inch, thirty-eight caliber guns fired so quickly, the ships appeared to be burning like pine forests, smearing the sky around the enemy with black bursts.

Elkins led his twelve fighters in a big sweeping turn to the north and pounced on the torpedo bombers like a lion digging his claws into the back of an antelope. On his first pass, four of the enemy planes were shot down.

Then twelve Bearcats, ignoring their destroyers' fire, met the diving enemy fighters in a head-on interception, the shrinking sky between them becoming a moving embroidery of tracer and incendiary and cannon shells. The heavy cannons of the F-8Fs told immediately. A 109 blew up, another had its fuselage ripped off just back of the cockpit, both pieces, rolling, pitching, tumbling and disintegrating. Another lost a wing at its root and came apart like a plastic toy that had been badly assembled.

A blinding blast pierced Brent's eyes like a glimpse of the sun at high noon as a Messerschmitt and a Bearcat met hub-to-hub. Thousands of pieces no larger than torn newspapers were flung over square miles of ocean. Another Bearcat, oil tank shot through, streamed black smoke as if it were unrolling a dirty endless bandage. Rolling gracefully, the pilot bailed out and drifted toward the sea under his white canopy.

Elkins had taken a terrible toll of the enemy bombers. Only twenty-five to thirty were left. But they bored on toward the carriers. Now Brent could make them out in detail. Junkers JU-87 Stukas forming their single line in preparation for their dives. Then he noticed two of the dive bombers were the American built Curtiss SB2C Helldiver—the same plane that had dive-bombed him at *Bren-ah-Hahd*. And the torpedo bombers were a mixed bag and all American built: North American Texan trainers powered up with new engines, maybe four Grumman TBFs, and a single twin-engine Cessna.

"Starboard battery stand by to open fire!" Fujita shouted. "Local control!"

The sixteen cannons of the starboard battery would endanger both enemy and friend alike. But everyone knew Fujita had no choice. "Commence! Commence! Rapid fire."

Brent automatically clamped his hands over his ears as the sixteen guns fired as one. He was in the middle of a thunderstorm, an erupting volcano. Tongues of flames eight feet long leaped from the muzzles, and the bridge was engulfed with smoke and the smell of cordite was stifling. Immediately, the sky was splotched with more exploding shells. More bombers dropped into the sea. Brent counted only nine F-6Fs and maybe twenty of the enemy fighters had broken through the Bearcat screen and were streaking into the F-6Fs. The Hellcats were forced to turn to meet the new threat.

Then, the twelve Bearcats held in reserve and nine of the surviving Bearcats that had made the interception of the enemy fighters, pounced into the burning, exploding chaos, and the entire horizon became a churning, flaming madhouse. There was no organization, no ordered pairs, no control. It was every man for himself as if they had all entered the bowels of hell and nothing ruled except a killing frenzy. Planes spun, exploded, crashed, burned. The slaughter would have sickened the devil himself.

Some of the bombers were surviving, pressing in. "Secondary battery, commence! Commence!"

The twenty-five-millimeter triple mounts roared out a hail of fire, the staccato drumfire like a hundred demented drummers pounding their instruments with all their power. Blizzards of tracers struck the torpedo bombers and four more crashed in towers of water and debris. But some would get through. Some always did. Brent steeled himself. He had been under Arab air attack many times. But never had he seen suicidal tenacity like this.

Whitehead had the same thoughts. "They're coming in like kamikazes!" he screamed over the bedlam. The word 'kamikaze' shocked everyone. There were looks of consternation, fear, resignation.

"Must be Shi'ites!" Bernstein yelled.

Brent caught his breath. Shi'ites! The most fanatical Muslim sect. Those responsible for the suicidal car bombing of the marine barracks at Beirut that killed over 250 American marines. And the irony struck him, a Japanese carrier under kamikaze attack. Ludicrous but utterly unfunny.

Brent looked up. There were four Stukas and one SB2C left. The first Stuka winged over into its dive. "Right full rudder!" Fujita screamed. "And hold it!"

The old German plane hurtled down, dive brakes down, big black bomb looming large beneath its fuselage. Dozens of twenty-five-millimeter guns fired at it and a Bearcat jigged in from the side. A burst of cannon fire shot off the Junkers' spatted wheels, and then the radiator was blown off. Veering sharply to the left, the bomber streaked into the ocean, raising a great tower of water and wreckage. However, the second bomber, the Curtiss SB2C, was hard behind his dead leader. Another Bearcat tried an interception, but was struck by some of *Yonaga's* AA and limped away.

The big plane plunged down. Brent stared up, mesmerized. Two thousand feet. He should drop his bombs. No bombs. Instead the Helldiver angled toward the center of the carrier's flight deck.

"He's going to ram!" Whitehead shouted. "Okinawa again!"

Everyone ducked. Brent looked up just in time to see the Helldiver's starboard wing hit by a twenty-five-millimeter shell. The dive brake was blown off and the aileron flapped loose, held on by only one hinge and its tab control linkage. Brent whooped with joy as the big bomber sheered off to the port side. There was a blast. Water shot as high as the bridge and cool mist rained down. Everyone stood, thanking a variety of gods.

Now an AT-6 was close aboard to starboard. But he was having trouble lining up for his torpedo run on the twisting carrier. Instead of releasing his torpedo, he flew through the storming tracers and rammed *Yonaga's* starboard side.

There was a blast at the starboard quarter, and a fire ball followed by black smoke roiled skyward. Gasoline, but no jarring blast of high explosives.

Fujita screamed, "The fool. His torpedo did not arm." And then to Naoyuki: "I want a damage report."

Naoyuki's response was almost immediate, "Damage Control reports no damage, sir. He hit the armor belt."

"Very well."

There were only two more Texans in the air and a pair of dive bombers. All four attacked the carrier simultaneously. This was the most terrifying moment of Brent Ross' life. Madmen, determined to kill him at the cost of their own lives, were rushing at him at hundreds of miles an hour from four different directions. He straightened his back, squared his jaw. No one would ever know of the fear he felt, tearing his guts as if he had eaten a mouthful of frozen glass.

"Left full rudder!" Fujita screamed, taking the carrier out of its circle to the right and reversing the maneuver. It was precisely the right tactic. Both dive bombers tried to ram. One, with a dead pilot, plummeted into the sea and exploded off the starboard bow. However, the second streaked down directly on Brent's head. This man would not miss. He seemed to be coming right down the barrels of the twenty-five-millimeter guns in the foretop and on platforms welded to the funnel. One shell hit his tail, punching a hole in his rudder, jamming his elevators. Then, at the last second, he swerved, flattened his dive until he was almost belly-down, struck the bow, bounced off spiraling, with his nose down tail high as if his aerodynamics had been reversed, streaming wreckage, and actually ricocheted a hundred feet before exploding. Cheers, and more gods were celebrated.

Brent turned his attention to the Texans. Both dropped their torpedoes at the same time.

"Right full rudder!"

One torpedo passed ahead, but the other bubbled a white trail into *Yonaga's* starboard side. Brent grabbed the admiral's shoulders and braced himself. The semtex warhead sent a shiver through the whole ship like a gladiator who had taken a sharp blade. A tower of water at least two hundred feet high shot into the sky, held still for moments as if it had frozen, and then collapsed back down into the sea in a welter of spray and mist. Smoking, the Texan passed over the deck not more than twenty feet high, did a graceful half roll and slid down into the sea, belly up like a dead fish. Within seconds, it had vanished in the ship's wake.

Cursing, Fujita shouted down the voice tubes and at Naoyuki at the same time: "All ahead slow, steady on zero-three-zero, damage report!" He looked around and spoke to Brent, "Enemy bombers."

"Gone! Destroyed! Gone," Brent repeated as if he were trying to convince himself the danger was over. He pointed to the southern horizon. A few planes were visible fleeing over the horizon pursued by AA from the *Fletchers*. But no bombers were in sight.

"Bombers?"

"Every one of them was destroyed, Admiral Fujita," Brent said.

Bernstein said, "By all that's holy, they did try to ram."

"Kamikazes," Fujita said with awe in his voice. "Sacred Buddha."

Naoyuki said, "Damage report from Captain Arai—Torpedo hit between frames eighty-six and ninety-two at a depth of twenty feet, just below the third deck. The blister was blown open, frame eighty-nine was pushed inward about a foot. An eight-inch fuel oil filler line was fractured and a stiffener penetrated the two armored bulkhead between frames eighty-eight and ninety below the first platform. Storerooms three-oh-three and three-oh-five have been flooded. No further damage. Three dead and four wounded."

"Watertight integrity?"

"Secure except for the two damaged storerooms."

"Speed—I need more revs."

"Suggest speed not to exceed sixteen knots until all bulkheads in the area can be checked and shored if needed."

"Very well." Fujita leaned over the voice tubes. "Give me revs for sixteen knots."

"Sixteen knots, sir." The engines picked up and a voice reported, "Sixteen knots, eighty-three revs, sir."

"Very well."

Everyone had been too busy with the enemy attack to track *Bennington*. But a lookout called, "*Bennington* is burning, Admiral."

Shifting his glasses, Brent brought the carrier into focus. Smoke was billowing forward, but no explosions or the furnace-yellow bursts of flame that could spell disaster. "She took one forward, sir," Brent said.

Naoyuki said, "Spark Plug reports a plane crashed into her bow. His bomb did not explode, but we have a fire on the flight deck and another one forward in the hangar deck. Twenty-four known dead, twelve wounded, four missing. Fire almost under control."

"Can you receive aircraft?"

"Affirmative." Fujita gave Naoyuki the details of *Yonaga*'s damage and concluded, "I can receive aircraft." Naoyuki relayed the information on ship-to-ship.

"We're very lucky," Whitehead said.

"God was watching and working," Bernstein added.

Fujita nodded. "We had the right deities on our side this day, gentlemen."

"Amen. Amen."

Brent looked up. Sixteen Bearcats and seven Hellcats were circling. A flare arced from a Grumman. "Stand by to receive aircraft!" Fujita shouted.

Slowly, the carrier turned into the wind.

Powered by the new Daimler Benz 3,100 horsepower Valkyrie, the Messerschmitts of Colonel Kenneth Rosencrance's Fourth Fighter Squadron plunged at tremendous speed into Lieutenant Keizo Kazutaka's covering Yellow Section. The nine Zeros had just made their turn and began their head-on interception when both Rosencrance and Stoltz opened fire on Kazutaka, who was leading.

Caught by converging bullets and cannon shells, the Zero had no chance. Kazutaka had just punched his firing button when tracers flickered past, some from the tiger shark fighter in his sights and others from the red ME to his left. He blinked, feeling the vibrations of his gunfire and hearing the meaty thud, thud of cannon fire. More tracers swept past, and then twenty-millimeter shells whizzed along the fuselage, smashed through

368

his tail, punched scores of holes in his instrument panel, scattering glass and shattered wood in his face, gouging deep holes in his flesh like a hundred daggers. Before he could scream, a single round hit him, blowing most of his chest, lungs and stomach all over the cockpit.

The flurry of shells battered the engine, ripped opened the oil header tank and bashed through the reserved petrol tank behind it. Fuel gushed and mixed with Kazutaka's blood before it ignited. Lieutenant Keizo Kazutaka never felt the blast-furnace heat that immolated him.

Hanging on his propeller in a near vertical climb Yoshi Matsuhara screamed with anguish. Kazutaka's Zero was belching yellow-orange flame and making a long, brilliant streamer as thin and bright as a guidon's pennant. Then a wing folded up, broke away and the Zero was just a piece of falling junk. And two more of Yellow Section had been shot down in The Fourth Fighter Squadron's first pass. However, one of the 109s had taken a dozen hits and twirled into a strange descent like an autumn leaf tumbling and oscillating from side to side in gusting wind.

Looking up at his rearview mirror, Yoshi caught a glimpse of glistening disks and airfoils behind. He jerked his head around. Hooperman and York were back off his rudders. Without command they had disengaged below and joined their leader in meeting the new menace above. Yoshi felt a clutch of emotion; there was loyalty and sacrifice in the stoic Englishman and the undisciplined Cockney. They would follow him through the nine rings of hell, and, indeed, that was precisely what they were doing when they challenged the Fourth Fighter

369

Squadron.

Rosencrance turned abruptly and headed for Rabta, leaving the disorganized survivors of Yellow Section in his wake. The bombers. They were the biggest menace. And they were easy meat.

Yoshi gave the stick an almighty shove to the left, kicked rudder and rolled into an interception course. Fourth Fighter squadron was now ahead of him and below to the south. At full military power, the tachometer pushed the red line at 2,850 and the cylinder head temperature began to climb. Heating. The damned engine was always heating. The water-methanol injection gave an added boost but did not cause the needles to even flicker. Yoshi grunted and gripped the control column yoke tighter.

York's voice: "Edo Leader, this is Edo Two. Your bare arse is showing. You'll get buggered faster'n a fag in Soho."

Hooperman's voice with unbelievable aplomb: "I say, Edo Leader, this is Edo One, slow her a bit, old boy. You're pulling ahead too far. Leave some of those rascals for us."

Yoshi's airspeed indicator showed 480 knots and the airframe was vibrating furiously. If he pulled out of his dive at this speed, he would black out in spite of the new American pressure suit he was wearing. He could be cold meat for any ME passing by. He eased the throttle and watched the needle drop.

Hooperman: "That's better."

Now Rosencrance had plunged into the bombers. His eleven fighters had been joined by at least six from the fight above. It was like a shooting gallery, the fighters first diving through the slow bombers and then pulling up and catching them from below.

370

At least ten Aichis and Nakajimas were burning, spinning, crashing into the desert. But Nogi and Tsuda still bore on, leading their men to their targets. Rabta was very close and already Tsuda's dive bombers had dropped their dive brakes and coarsened the pitch of their propellers. There were swarms of bombers left. The enemy could never shoot them all down.

Then Yoshi, his wingmen, and the remnants of Yellow Section plunged into the melee. Yoshi sent a squirt into the belly of an ME banking toward a Nakajima. Shot through the buttocks and genitals, the enemy pilot screamed all the way to his grave just inside the first security fence of the complex.

Hooperman scored: "Got the bloody swine." A Messerschmitt smoked toward the ground.

York's voice: "There they go!"

One after another at least twenty Aichis dropped off into dives and plunged down on the reactor. At the same time, Nogi's Nakajimas began their horizontal runs on the remaining buildings. AA was strangely quiet. Either the enemy gunners were afraid of hitting their own aircraft, or most of the enemy emplacements had been put out of action. The dive bombers struck with amazing accuracy. Not one bomb struck the tall, domed reactor building. Instead, explosions ripped the switching station, knocked down transmission towers, and blew several nearby building to bits. Not one spark had come from the downed lines. As Schneerson had predicted, the enemy had shut down the reactor.

Black, brown, yellow and white smoke covered everything. The bombing had gone exactly to plan, but the price had been high and was growing. Maddened enemy fighters hounded the bombers as

371

the big slow planes turned toward the sea. More Nakajimas and Aichis crashed into the hard baked soil. But the Japanese fighters wove through the maelstrom, firing, taking their toll.

Suddenly, the enemy fighters broke off and clawed for altitude. Perhaps, they realized that the fight for Rabta was useless. The facility had been demolished and it was senseless to waste more precious fighter pilots in a lost cause.

Yoshi looked around. The surviving bombers with eighteen or nineteen Zeros and a lone Seafire were making for the sea. He grunted satisfaction and began to turn with them. Then he noticed the "Tiger Shark" Messerschmitt was trailing a white mist and had dropped below and far behind the other five survivors of the Fourth Fighter Squadron. A glance at his fuel gauges assured him he had over half his fuel still left. Shouting *"Banzai,"* he reversed his turn and headed for the wounded enemy.

Rosencrance, followed by the remaining four members of his squadron, wheeled into a sharp turn toward Stoltz. But he was late; too late for such a veteran, experienced pilot. Eight aircraft converged on the space occupied by one. Yoshi already had his killing angle on Stoltz and Hooperman and York were flaring out slowly to give support. The geometry of all the converging vectors spelled collision and every pilot knew this. But no one altered course.

Yoshi skinned his lips back until his gums showed as the pip of his gunsight centered on the canopy of Stoltz's garish fighter. A thousand yards. Too long. Tracers whipped by. There were thuds and holes appeared miraculously in his starboard wing. Then he felt more than saw the two Seafires roll to the left and open fire on the attacking 109s. The tracers stopped.

Five hundred yards. Too long. The guns were harmonized for three hundred. A good pilot, Stoltz banked hard to the right. But his damaged engine could only give him about 250 knots. He rolled desperately, but only managed to expose his belly instead of his canopy. His squared-off wingtips touched the sight bars.

Yoshi eased the throttle two notches. Firing at near zero deflection and at short range, he could not miss. He pressed the button. Bullets and shells rampaged the length of the enemy's fuselage. The right elevator frame flew off, the retractable tailwheel was blown free, and more coolant sprayed as a shell exploded in the radiator assembly.

Frantically, Stoltz looped over into a dive and dropped out of the pink reticle. But Yoshi threw everything to the left and then down, rolling with his enemy and bringing the belly of the stricken Messerschmitt back into his sights. Four shells hit the fighter directly back of the engine, blowing the right main wheel completely free, dropping the left wheel which flopped from side to side, and hashing the radiator and oil cooler assemblies to junk. Then it was either pull back on the stick or ram.

Banking away, Matsuhara could see the Daimler Benz belching black puffs of smoke as if Stoltz were trying to signal someone. The enemy pilot was finished and he knew it. Rolling the dying fighter gently to the left, he dropped out of the cockpit. The drag chute popped open and then the main canopy blossomed. Stoltz's black-clad figure began to descend, oscillating slowly beneath the white umbrella.

Yoshi looked for his wingmen. He wanted to kill Stoltz in his chute. An eye for an eye for Willard-Smith and a modicum of revenge for Tomoko. But to the south and below, Hooperman and York were locked in a desperate battle with Rosencrance and three of his pilots. The fourth 109 was smoking and headed for a landing in the desert.

York's voice: "I'm 'it. The old windmill's bought it."

Yoshi bashed the throttle with his palm and turned toward the fight. Rosencrance was jockeying for a killing angle on York, who had slowed and dropped as his damaged engine backfired gasps of blue-black smoke. Hooperman had looped above and was diving down on the Messerschmitts. But he could never break through the three black fighters between him and York.

Yoshi's airspeed indicator showed 490 knots and the engine was heating. He shook his head. Brought his spinner to the red 109. Eight hundred yards and full deflection. An impossible shot, but he had no choice. He aimed five lengths ahead and high for bullet drop and pressed the button at exactly the same time Rosencrance pressed his. The renegade American's tracers plunged into empty space as the Seafire with its low wing loading whipped into a tight roll.

Yoshi saw his tracers arc and drop all around the red fighter. Suddenly, a yellow fire mote sparkled on the hood and another blinked just back of the cockpit. Yoshi shouted with joy. A miracle.

Startled at such an incredible shot, Rosencrance rolled away into the ME's favorite escape maneuver, the dive. And his four pilots followed him. They had enough. Quickly, Yoshi and Hooperman took positions above the damaged Seafire.

Yoshi's mind was not on Stoltz, Rosencrance, or his vengeance. Only the doughty, brave comrade who limped along on the verge of crashing. He would lose more than a wingman, he would lose a priceless friend, a bright mind and a sense of humor that was a joy to all that knew Pilot Officer Elwyn York. If York could nurse the Seafire along, he would shepherd him home or die in the attempt. And he knew Hooperman felt the same way.

"Can you make it?" Yoshi asked.

"Took one in the gut. Bloody engine's firin' on nine or ten instead of twelve. Oil temp and coolant way up. Maybe the ol' 'ore will 'old together at twelve hundred rpms."

Hooperman's voice: "Try, old boy. A hundred trollops in the East End would starve without you."

"If I make it, I'm gunna kick your arse, your nibs."

"Tally ho, old boy. The pleasure's mine. Meet you in the lists."

"Lists, mists, shits! I'll kick your bloody arse from one end o' the flight deck to the other."

"If you can land that junk, be my guest."

Slowly the three fighters headed for the coast.

Twenty

From the flag bridge Brent had watched as returning bombers and fighters straggled in for more than an hour. Vainly he searched the southern skies for signs of Yoshi Matsuhara's red, green, and white Zero. When last seen pilots had reported Yoshi, Hooperman, and York were attacking the Fourth Fighter Squadron. A foolish move, indeed, but not unexpected. They were probably all dead. Maybe, they had all become *shiniguari*. Rushed to their deaths. Brent had never fallen into such a deep abyss of despair.

Another concern gnawed at him, pulled him further down. After twelve hours on the bridge, Fujita had sagged and would have fallen to the deck if Brent had not caught him. The burden of years and the terrible strain of innumerable battles had taken their toll. Gently, two seaman guards had helped the old man to his bunk. As the ancient sailor left the bridge he did not forget his duty. Turning, he said, "You have the deck, Admiral Whitehead. Steam course two-nine-zero, speed twenty until Damage Control reports all bulkheads secure. Continue recovering aircraft and send me reports of damage inflicted on the enemy and our own casualties. Commander Ross will remain as your JOD." Only then did he leave the bridge.

Brent reflected on the irony in the change of command. An American rear admiral in command of a Japanese carrier he would have gladly sunk fifty years earlier with an American commander as his Junior Officer of the Deck. What a strange world, history turning on itself with all the reason and rationale of a whirlpool. But his mood was too dark to find humor in anything. He shifted his glasses to *Bennington*.

Bennington was in good shape. Her bow showed the harsh yellow-brown scars of the fire, but her battle efficiency had not been impaired. She had taken aboard her surviving aircraft and kept a CAP patrol of six Bearcats in the sky. *Yonaga*, too, showed little effect from the torpedo hit. Captain Arai's damage control party had shored up the weakened bulkheads and pumped out Boiler Room Two. The two flooded compartments would remain flooded until they could put into dry-dock. However, the damage had not even required counterflooding, only the shifting of some fuel from starboard to port tanks. And Arai had approved an increase in speed to twenty knots.

Brent had almost given up hope for Yoshi and the Englishmen when word flashed up from radar: "Three aircraft. Low. Approaching from the southeast at slow speed."

Brent's heart soared. Yoshi, Hooperman, York. But it could be the enemy. He had shown a shocking willingness to die and Whitehead shouted at a fatigued Naoyuki, "Alert the CAP! AA crews stand by!" Then, before the American rear admiral could order Admiral Fujita informed, radar reported the golden news, "IFF reports friendlies!"

"Very well." Brent knew Whitehead could take no

chances. "One section of CAP intercept and verify," he ordered. Elkins vectored three of his Hellcats on a reciprocal course, heading directly for the approaching aircraft which were still not visible from the bridge.

Brent narrowed his eyes and peered through his glasses, turned the focusing knob gently and studied the horizon. Then he saw them. The flashy Zero with the oversize engine and two Seafires. His heart soared like a gull taking a thermal. Joy. Pure unmitigated joy. But one Seafire was in trouble, flying below his companions and trailing smoke in small puffs. Then Brent saw the markings on the tail. It was Pilot Officer Elwyn York. Brent reported the sighting just as two foretop lookouts made the same report.

Whitehead's voice: "Two block Pennant Two and stand by to receive aircraft." Because they were headed directly into a force three wind, it was not necessary to change course. Whitehead threw a switch and the fighter frequency hissed through the bridge speaker. "Can you land that Seafire, Pilot Officer York?" the American rear admiral asked.

York's typically sacrilegious retort shocked and brought titters as his landing gear unfolded, "Right up your arse, guv'nur!" Whitehead jerked rigidly upright and his eyes widened.

Yoshi's voice: "Discipline, York!"

"Buggeration, Edo Leader. I can land this ol' 'ore on the queen's lap an' give Princess Di and Fergie a bloody good jig-a-jig, too."

"Is your landing gear locked?"

"I've got the bloody green light."

"Permission to land," Whitehead said, not able to suppress a grin.

The damaged Seafire approached the stern. York appeared too high and Brent saw the landing officer begin to wave him off. Everyone stiffened with concern. But the Cockney knew his aircraft, knew the damaged Seafire at its slow speed would drop, and had compensated. Just before he crossed the stern, the fighter plunged down as if someone had punched holes in its wings. Then a burst of its sputtering engine, flaming backfires, puffs of black smoke and the fighter lunged ahead as it fell heavily to the deck, bounced, caught the second wire, rolled and finally was pulled to a smoking stop, engine dead.

White-clad fire fighters, handlers, and York's ground crew raced to the fighter and swarmed over the aircraft. Within seconds, the engine had been smothered with foam and the pilot pulled from the cockpit. Then it struck Brent. York was terribly weak. The show of bravado had been part of the Cockney's impregnable shield of machismo. However, as the pilot walked to the island, he pushed off the helping hands and assumed his usual swagger. Then he leaned against a gun tub and watched Hooperman and then Matsuhara land.

When Yoshi leaped from his Zero, Hooperman and York rushed to him. Then, the trio formed a circle, locked arms and danced like farmers at an old-fashioned American square dance. Brent laughed so hard, he felt dampness streaking down his cheeks. Whitehead, too, was laughing while he gave orders to haul down the pennant and secure the aircraft.

Then, the entire crew saw a strange ceremony that would forever perplex their view of the Englishmen. Hooperman kneeled down on the deck, bent over on his elbows and exposed his backside. York stepped close and kicked Hooperman so hard he sprawled across the deck on his face. Then Hooperman stood and grabbed York's hand. Then arm-in-arm with Yoshi, the trio left the flight deck.

Brent was wiping his nose when Naoyuki said, "Commander Ross. Report to Admiral Fujita's cabin immediately, Sir."

When Brent entered the admiral's cabin, the old man was seated behind his desk, alone. His creased and wrinkled face was drawn and unusually sallow. One hand was on the *Hagakure* and the other was on the desk, a bent elbow appearing to help hold the old man erect. He looked like a corpse that had refused to give up the ghost. Fujita waved the young American to a chair. At that moment there was a polite knock and Yoshi Matsuhara entered.

Still in his flight suit, he smelled of engine oil and his goggles were outlined on his face by oil fumes and grime like a raccoon. "You sent for me, sir?"

"Yes." Fujita pointed to a chair.

Brent was on his feet. His dear friend was alive, unhurt, strong, still the greatest fighter pilot on earth. Without hesitation the two men embraced and patted each other on the back. "Well done! Well done!" they shouted at each other.

Smiling, Fujita said, "Please, gentlemen, you can celebrate later. We still have a war to fight." The two men seated themselves.

The old sailor patted some documents on his desk and Brent realized he had not spent all of his time in his bunk. "According to preliminary reports, our bombers carried out their mission with precision.

All targets were destroyed and the reactor was not damaged," Fujita said.

"Correct, sir," Yoshi said. "That is what I saw from my cockpit." He shrugged, "Of course, I only caught glimpses, but I was over the target. Tsuda and Nogi should be congratulated."

"They are both dead."

"Definite?"

"Verified. Both died like samurai, in the best tradition of bushido." The admiral recited a preliminary report of casualties. They were heavy, but not crippling. Over forty of *Yonaga's* bombers had been shot down and twenty-one fighters lost. But the destroyers were still plucking pilots and aircrews from the sea. The admiral continued, "Radio Tripoli reports their 'pharmaceutical' works at Rabta have taken serious damage but the enemy was routed."

"Of course," Yoshi said. And then the pilot asked, "You were attacked. I saw damage to *Bennington* — her bow."

"Yes. A kamikaze."

"Kamikaze?"

"Yes, Yoshi-san. Ironical, is it not?" And then the admiral described the torpedo damage to *Yonaga* which was not visible from the air.

"The enemy surface forces?" Yoshi asked. "You must have engaged them."

"They sent their air groups and then steamed out of range."

"Then he still has three carriers and two cruisers."

"Correct."

"A powerful force."

Brent entered the exchange. "We still have work to do — sink that battle group, retake the Marianas."

The old man nodded. "True, Brent-san. We will

return to Japan, rebuild our air groups, and attack again." He showed sudden, uncommon emotion, "And again and again until our enemies are annihilated."

"It never ends," Yoshi said. "There is always evil to be fought by good men."

Fujita nodded his wise old head and the stoic oriental returned. "Perhaps it is more than that, Yoshi-san."

"What do you mean, sir?"

"Perhaps, it is the nature of man himself that keeps us at work."

Brent was fascinated by the implications of Fujita's last words and the emotion of the moment brought an old poem he loved back. He said, "A wise American named Henry Wadsworth Longfellow once wrote, 'There is a reaper, whose name is Death, And with his sickle keen, He reaps the bearded grains at a breath, And the flowers that grow between.'"

"Wise, indeed," Yoshi said. "We reaped our grain, but lost our flowers."

"The Yasakuni Shrine is crowded with the spirits of our heroes," Fujita added. He patted the *Haga-kure*. "But remember, the wisdom of the book tells there is no better demise for the samurai than to die with his sword wet with the blood of his enemy." Tilting his head back, he slitted his eyes and said, "Duty weighs heavy, but death is as light as the down of a swan." He looked long at the two men who were so precious to him. "You are dismissed, gentlemen."

The two officers stood, bowed, and left.